THE DAMASCUS
CHRONICLES

Written by
Dominic R. Daniels

ISBN: 0692292411
ISBN 13: 9780692292419

Dedicated to

Phil Daniels
Mary Daniels
Sandra Dee Murg
Mary Anne Delehanty

PART ONE: THE DEADLY DAME

1

HIT GONE WRONG

The city streetlights began to light up the desert night sky with colors of reds, pinks, purples and blues, putting on a show of grand splendor. Past the bright yellow-colored light bulbs, signs that glittered and flashed erratically, past the sounds of rattling coins falling from the multitude of slot machines in the casinos that the crowds passed through day and night, the laughter of happy drunks that filled the air of the ever vibrant, ever vice-filled, good ole Las Vegas. A new time in a new age, the city had become a massive metropolis in a new era, the year 2020. Up on the rooftops in the west district of Sin City, a shadowy figure came out of the corners, leaping from one rooftop to the next with ease. Landing on the roof of an old yet refurbished penthouse, he looked down through the thin sheets of glass of the skylight. Below in the eclectic dimly-lit study, he could see a group of men. One was dressed in a rich Italian suit, surrounded by an array of bodyguards dressed in black suits. The other two were wearing regular clothes. The two men faced by their boss. Standing, as if before a judge waiting for their final sentence. Franco Scarfo sat angry at his desk while taking in his thoughts about his two employee's most recent screw up.

"I don't give a fuck that we lost 500 grand on the transfer coming from the downtown bank, I don't care about the pressure coming down on us from the fucking cops, what I give a damn about, boys, is how you two fucking screw-ups let 20 million dollars of my money in merchandise get boosted on the truck last night," yelled Franco. Franco, about 42 years old, was a natural bad ass. Built strong like an ox, he was very good looking and had a strong sex appeal with the ladies. A powerful underboss to the Scarfo crime family. Ruthless and deadly. The kind of guy that no one would dare mess with. He was god. What he said was law. If he wanted to you dead. You're dead!

"Boss it wasn't our fault!!!," said Pete squirming. A young punk and creep. One of Franco's hired muscle.

"Bullshit!" exploded Franco with fiery rage, getting up pushing over his desk on the floor with smashing his crystal lamp on the floor. Franco pushed the barrel of his gun to one of the thug's heads as he knelt, groveling on the ground.

"Boss! I swear to Christ it wasn't our fault," screamed Pete.

"Don't lie to me, you little piece of shit!" interrupted Franco, clenching his finger slightly, almost pulling the trigger.

"Honest! Oh God!!! Please don't kill me!!!!," Pete begged. "Morey and I were driving the truck down to the warehouse when of all of a sudden some fucking mysterious black car pulls up to us, shoots out our tires. I get hit by broken glass in the face, then I lose control, the truck turns over, down we go and the next thing you know we're both out cold and I find myself in a gutter in the alley," wailed Pete.

"You really expect me to believe that," Franco retorted.

"It's true Boss, Pete's not lying," whined Morey. Morey was a spineless, sack of shit coward. A lower level thug and runner with Pete Rangoon. Both of them, losers with no balls to match. A race horse with its nuts cut off could stampede resiliently better than them on any given day.

"Where were you when this happened?" yelled Franco.

Morey moaned, "I fell out of the truck into a ditch..."

Kaboom! The skylight exploded as glass shards flew to the floor. "AHH!" screamed the men, dropping to the floor. Smoke bombs fell from above.

"What the fuck is going on!" Morey cried. A shadowy figure dropped through the skylight on a rope, and the men began to shoot at him. Guns blazing, they shot into the settling smoke, hitting nothing. The shadowy figure darted to a corner and pulled out a pistol and Uzi, killing most of Franco's men, swiping his gunfire from side to side swiftly like a bat flying out of hell. Dressed in a black leather trench coat and black leather pants, his hair was dark as the night and long like a god of rock and roll. He face was hard and chiseled. Yet beautiful and hypnotic like a fallen angel with gleaming eyes, whispering into the night. With a tough as nails expression and smirking smile across his face. Masked by dark sun glasses. Blasting away, enjoying the thrill of the slaughter. The men fired back taking cover behind the couches and liquor cabinets. Vases and expensive suede couches and liquor table stocked with expensive cognac and spirits in the meeting lounge were shot to pieces with glass bottles exploding from the machine gun fire as the figure ducked and shot back. He rushed from the corner to behind the circular bar near the side of a staircase that lead into a small upper side room where the vault was located. The dark figure pulled a grenade from his inner coat, pulling the pin out with his teeth and hurled the grenade into the mix, distracting his targets to escape. A large glass window was at the end of the upper stair case, to crash through.

"Shit!!!!" Pete yelled. The grenade exploded, blowing a hole in the floor killing many of the henchmen with bodies and gore flung all over. The carpets soaked in scarlet blood and death. The figure made his way out from behind the bar, rushing up through the stairs when all of a sudden a gorgeous woman in a black biker leather suit jacket and pants ran into him. Her was black as darkness. Her eyes intoxicating. Her skin soft and pure with lips red as a rose. She was carrying stolen jewels and cash from the opened safe. The two of them fell to ground as they collided, causing the shadowy figure's sun glasses to fall off and revealing his face. Franco and his men confronted the two intruders in the hall and went in straight for the kill.

"My money! Kill them!" yelled Franco.

"Don't just stand there, help me!" yelled the girl at her fellow attacker. He just smiled. The mysterious figure and the girl fired at Franco and his men, wounding Franco in the shoulder, and in the exchange of crossfire the girl was hit.

"OOOHAAh!" she screamed in pain.

"Hold on!" the mysterious figure commanded, picking her up and jumping out of a nearby window. Franco climbed over the corpse of one of his men as he ran to the window.

"You cocksuckers! You're dead! I'll find you!!!" Franco screamed, firing his pistols at the rooftops as he watched the assailants flee.

2

DAMASCUS' PAD

The mysterious figure jumped from rooftop to rooftop still carrying the trembling girl.

"Nice shooting back there wise ass, you could have gotten us both killed," said the girl through gritted teeth.

"It didn't help that you got in the way! What were you thinking, being there?" retorted the man.

"I was trying to rob the safe, no thanks to you. Still … you saved my life," the girl whispered softly, looking into his eyes, and then she kissed him quickly.

"What was that for?"

"Just to repay the favor. I like a man that has balls," said the girl.

"You're something, lady! You're also hurt," replied the man.

"It's just a scratch, I'm fine."

"You're bleeding, come on," said the man.

"No hospitals please. The police have been looking for me." The girl winced in pain.

"I know a place where you will be safe."

"Wait, how do I know I can trust you?" asked the girl.

"I just saved your life, didn't I?" replied the man in a low voice. "Don't worry, I won't hurt you. Here, put this handkerchief on the bleeding for now and grab on tight. It's a long way down to the ground," said the man confidently. He lowered himself and the girl on a grappling hook to the street in the alley.

"Come on, let's get out of here, the bacon boys will be here any minute," said the girl.

"No problem," replied the man coolly, knocking over a stacked bunch of cardboard boxes that had been concealing a strange motorcycle. "Hop on."

The two sped away quickly, threading their way through the alleys.

"Nice bike."

"Thanks," replied the man. "So tell me what's your name?"

"Serena Bellmont," said the girl.

"Sounds sexy," replied the man.

"You're sweet!" replied Serena.

"The name is Damascus," replied the man.

"What kind of name is that?" Serena replied.

"You can call me Michael," replied Damascus.

"Where are we going?" asked Serena.

"My place. You'll be safe there; the neighborhood is so dangerous not even the cops would think of going there," replied Michael.

"Thanks, I feel safe already!" said Serena.

Michael chuckled softly as they headed down through the dimly-lit alleys to his pad. Michael drove the bike to an underground garage deep below an old abandoned three level theater/apartment building at Otis Way, a neighborhood that had long seen better days. The wind blew a warm breeze into the dusty summer night; Michael opened the front door with his key and the two headed up the old wooden stairs, creaking as they went. The lock of door released as Michael turned another key.

They entered a richly furnished apartment, red silk curtains shot through with golden brocade, mahogany wood tables and fine oak chairs, a black suede couch, and a stylized glass coffee table. On the end tables were Italian murano glass lamps with fine brass trim. A silver chandelier illuminated the room with light and a charming fireplace was faced with rich red brick. The walls of the apartment were draped in antique Lebanese tapestries alongside beautiful paintings with the flare of Tunisia. A red stained glass hookah stood in the center of the room next to a fine mahogany wood humidor. A small, elegant bar stocked with expensive liquor and fine European wine stood against one of the walls.

"Interesting vintage. You have fine taste I see," said an astonished Serena. "I have to admit I'm quite impressed, I expected it to be...different."

"I get by well. It helps to compensate for living in a bad neighborhood filled with crackheads and drug dealers," replied Michael. "Here, come into the bathroom, I'll patch that up quick."

Serena followed her host to the bathroom to dress her wound. "You know, I'm actually surprised that you didn't freak out back there, when you saw me kill those guys at the penthouse," Michael mused.

"Spilled blood doesn't bother me. I grew up seeing soldiers killed every day as a child. That's what you get when you're put to work as a child solider in a socialist country."

"You're kidding!" Michael was astounded.

"No that was home; bloodshed, vodka, and week-old cabbage and potatoes for dinner. Looking up into the sky after sunset seeing the stars above, it's just another day in the killing fields." Serena lit up a cigarette and exhaled a thick puff of smoke.

"A hell of a life," said Michael.

"It's life," agreed Serena.

"Here you go, better now?" asked Michael, as he finished cleaning and bandaging her wound.

"Yes, thank you."

"You can lay low here for a while until the heat blows over. I think you'll find yourself to be comfortable here. The bedroom is across the hall," said Michael as the two walked back into the living room.

"That's very kind of you," said Serena, "and surprising for someone who just killed twelve mobsters back there."

"Just cleaning up the streets, I call it. Besides, scumbags like that deserved what they got," said Michael.

"Trigger happy, huh?" giggled Serena.

"You could call it that."

"So let me guess – you're a cleaner," said Serena.

"On occasion," Michael replied, as he removed a bottle of wine from the bar cabinet.

"Red wine, my dear, or white?"

"Red, please."

Michael poured her a glass and his guest reclined on his posh couch, sipping her wine. "Speaking of which, you didn't do too bad yourself back at Scarfo's penthouse. Where did you learn to shoot like that? questioned Michael.

"My father was a skilled sniper in the KGB. He taught me everything. Also, my mother was a radio operator who taught me how to decode messages. Sometimes I would sit next to her when she tapped out on the telegraph. She was killed when I was eleven in a fire fight in Moscow," replied Serena sadly.

"I'm sorry," said Michael.

"When I came to America I chose to do something less noticeable …" continued Serena.

"Thus choosing the way of the professional thief," interrupted Michael.

"I take what I want, when I want, where I want, and it pays better too," responded Serena with a smile. "What about you, what's your story?"

"Just an average citizen providing the citizens of this scum-filled town with an unnecessary public service. Why do you care?" snapped Michael.

"Just wondering that's all."

"Why?" Michael persisted.

"Because I'm curious, and you are more than you seem to be," replied Serena, eyeing a picture frame sitting next to the lamp. She picked it up and asked, "Who is this?"

"That's my sister, Katrina. She's dead,"

"I'm sorry, I didn't mean to upset you."

"It's okay, I guess I'm still trying to move on," Michael replied.

"What happened to her?" asked Serena.

"Forget about it!" said Michael. "It's getting late, why don't you get some sleep, you could use it to rest that arm of yours. I'm catching some shuteye." He crashed on the suede couch.

"All right, goodnight," replied Serena, to Michael as she went into the bedroom for the night.

A couple of hours went by and the old antique clock on the fireplace mantle struck two am. Michael began to toss and turn in his sleep. He woke up and was surprised to find Serena lying next to him, looking at him with her beautiful green eyes.

"AHHH!" "What don't do that!" said Michael, half asleep.

Serena just giggled. "Sorry. I couldn't sleep and I felt lonely, so I hope you didn't mind me being next to you. You sleep so beautifully," said Serena.

"Just don't do that again. You scared the hell out of me, damn," Michael replied.

Serena climbed on top of him, and slowly lowered her lovely head to his, kissing him passionately with her scarlet lips. She unbuttoned his shirt and pants, and feeling her hot breath steaming on his neck and the sweet perfumed scent of her jet-black long hair, he unzipped her bra. They made love, kissing passionately, each moment passing in mutual ecstasy and lust.

The golden rays of the early morning sun began to shine through the curtains and onto the two lovers asleep in each other's arms. Serena woke and dressed quickly, for she knew that she must escape the rays of the sun from touching her vampiric skin. She vanished from the room, but not before leaving her new lover a note that she would return to him.

3

THE NIGHTMARE BEGINS AGAIN

A strange vortex of blues, reds, and greens surrealistically pulled Michael in, floating and falling through a strange portal of the past. The day became night, and he found himself in a home with European flare; black marble tile floors, white marble pillars that stretched down an endless hall that was lined with a burgundy carpet trimmed in gold. As Michael approached a great marble door, he saw a ghoulish sight. The white walls began to bleed streams of blood and the twisted statues on the wall seemed to come alive. They looked at Michael with their eyes glaring a hideous green, while some stuck out their tongues with a serpentine look. A woman screamed in terror and the room filled with the sounds of gunshots blasting through the thick trails of smoke released by the emptying gun barrels, the shell casings falling to the ground in slow motion. An old man appeared, wearing a fine suit of aristocratic appeal and European cut, a boa constrictor crawling up his hand that quickly turned into a pipe. A sinister seal tattooed on his right hand appeared in a twisted veil of darkness. The old man started to speak, but silence was all that Michael heard as the dark figure disappeared. The monolithic doors opened, revealing a man clothed in a deep navy suit, his eyes covered by a white mask, his hair golden blonde like the morning sunrise. He held a pistol aimed at a lovely woman dressed in an aquamarine dress. Her right side gushed blood as the man in blue fired three shots, blowing bullet holes through his innocent victim. Her blood spurted out on the white wooden walls of the old study and she fell to the ground dead, her blue eyes open and her body limp. Michael looked up at the killer's left hand to see a gold ring that bore a strange insignia. Then, he felt the flash of a ghastly red, the hot light of terror.

"Katrina!!!" Michael screamed as he woke up in deep horror, disorientated and perspiring heavily, rivers of sweat running down his forehead. "Katrina," he whispered softly. Shaken and disturbed, Michael walked into the bathroom, staring into the sink and mirror while splashing water on his face to cool the fire that had been burning his blood with fear. Lighting a cigarette, he sat down on the edge of the bathtub and gazed out at the nighttime metropolis of Sin City. He took a long drag and let the smoke flow out as he released his thoughts. Coming out of the bathroom, Michael got dressed, putting on his black leather jacket, black silk tie, red dress shirt, and black suit pants with belt. He pulled on a pair of black leather boots. His mind raced with thoughts of the last 24 hours. "Yeah, it's been a hell of a day."

4

A PUNK AND A JUNKY

Michael noticed the note that Serena left him on the coffee table. He smiled a little after reading it, then headed out the front door. He checked his cell phone, noticing a message to meet Jackie at Marty's Lounge down on 26th street. Lighting up another cigarette with an old pack of matches he had in his pocket, Michael strolled down the street, the sirens of police cars rolling mingling with the sounds of the happy drunks walking along the dark boulevard. The street corners were decorated with lovely girls, the local denizens of 26th street showing off their nightly for-sale flesh to easy customers. On the other side of the street was an open alley where street people warmed themselves over trashcan fires.

A few local street punks stepped in Michael's way. One of the big ones wore a red spiked Mohawk and was dressed in black jeans and a chain covered T-shirt. He started getting cocky. "Hey, buddy! This is our street."

"I don't see your name on it, pal," replied Michael gruffly.

"Hey Joey, this guy's looking for trouble," said one of the other punks.

"I think we should give it to him," said another punk, laughing at Michael.

"Get him!" yelled the big punk.

Michael cross-kicked the big one, knocking him down hard and breaking his two front teeth. A skinny punk wrapped his chain around Michael's neck but Michael reversed the attack, throwing the guy down and breaking his right leg. "Fuck!" squealed the skinny punk in pain.

"Okay smart guy! Die!" screamed the big punk.

Michael whipped out his switchblade and back flipped behind his big opponent, holding the razor-sharp blade next to his throat. "Back off creep! Or I slit your throat!"

"Okay, okay man! We were just joking, don't need to get serious," whined the big punk.

"Come around here again bothering innocent people, and if I see you guys, I'll rip out your guts and make you swallow your own spleen. Now get out of here!" raged Michael.

"No problem man, we're going!" they all said, backing away slowly.

Michael released his grip from his captive; the street punks took off running up the street like little cowards. "Damn punks!" Michael said to himself. He brushed off his jacket and continued on to Marty's Lounge. He stepped through the door and at the back of the dark, candle-lit bar, seated in a red booth, was a young man in his mid twenties, dressed in a black sports coat and tan pants, with slick black hair and light brown eyes. He signaled Michael to come over to the booth. "Hey Mikey!" called the young man happily.

"Jackie! How's my little kid brother been doing?" Michael asked as the two hugged.

Jackie Santerini was the inside guy, the wise ass, the hot headed kid with a love for shooting first and asking questions later, the guy that would make you laugh then kill you laughing, the trickster at heart. "I'm good, man," replied Jackie. "What kept you?"

"I had to deal with a few pricks that came my way," replied Michael.

"That's my brother, always looking for a fight!" said Jackie.

"Better to finish a fight when someone else starts one!" Michael said in return.

"What are we standing up for, please sit down. Hey Marty!" Jackie called over to the bartender, who was cleaning a glass. "One screwdriver and a dry vodka martini, secret agent style, for my friend here!"

"Yeah sure!" said Marty in return as he quickly mixed the drinks.

"Here you go boys, take it easy tonight, okay?" said the pretty waitress as she handed over their drinks.

"Thanks honey," said Michael, grinning slightly as he slipped her a five-dollar bill.

"So tell me, what happened to you, you were supposed take care of that thing with Franco Scarfo?" Jackie was serious.

"I got most of his guys, didn't I? Besides someone interfered," said Michael.

"Who was it? DEA? Feds?"

"No one, just some nobody being at the wrong place at the wrong time."

"That's not good," said Jackie, concerned.

"But don't worry, the problem has been neutralized," said Michael.

"Good, glad to hear you took care of it. Anyway, Don Felice wants you, Anthony, and me to pay a little visit to one of Franco's guys uptown."

"Who is it?" Michael asked.

"A little weasel I like to call a true pussy. The guy is practically scared of his own shadow."

"Let me guess, Pete Rangoon. He's a chump, a junky. What do you possibly think you can get out of that loser?"

"There have been rumors floating around that Giorgio Scarfo has gotten some new heavy associates. We confiscated looted money three nights ago," said Jackie, being careful to speak. His suspicions about bugs in a room made him uneasy at times.

"You think Rangoon was in on the heist with the guys who jacked us?" asked Michael.

"Does a bear shit in the woods?"

"Yeah!" said Michael, getting the drift. "You know our job was a lot easier back when the Costa and Moretti Brothers were running things."

"That's because there was no shit going down like today. Back then it was just smoke and blow, come and go. The business wasn't as messy as it is now. Today it's a whole new story. Why are we bringing up this old shit?" Jackie was annoyed.

"I just miss the old days sometimes," said Michael wistfully.

"I miss them sometimes too." Jackie smiled.

"Anyway, why would this new thing bother the Don? Godfather Scarfo is always finding new people," said Michael.

"These aren't the usual muscle the godfather uses. He's using people in high places and the word is that they're corrupt Feds, politicians, maybe higher, I don't know," said Jackie.

"Do you think Rangoon will know anything?"

"If he doesn't, I think we might be able to get him to tell us someone who might. Besides, the important thing is getting that fucking money back."

"Okay, let's go!" said Michael. They rose and hurried out of the bar.

5

A THRILL TO THE KILL

Racing down the urban streets in Jackie's blazing red firestorm sports car, Jackie and Michael picked up Anthony Santerini at the Scarlet Lady Gentleman's Club, which Anthony owned. Anthony Santerini was the baddest motherfucker of all in Vegas. He owned all the strip clubs in town, had tabs on every hooker who worked his streets, and had the tongues of the pimps that shook down his girls cut off before their very eyes. He crushed their heads with his own hands, which caused him to also be known as "Crusher". One thing was for sure, never fuck with Anthony Santerini.

Approaching the long doors of the car came a big, haughty well-built man in his mid-forties, with a rough face that bore a few scars from the many bar fights he had been in. He had a nice clean thick head of black hair and wore a silver ring on his left pinky and a shining set of brass knuckles on his right hand. He was dressed in a black suede jacket, a brown and black silk shirt, black suit pants, a rich brown leather belt, and slick black dress shoes. "Hey Assholes! How are you two?" laughed Anthony.

"Get the fuck in here, wise guy," laughed Jackie.

"Sorry boys, I couldn't resist. So tell me, where is our little friend tonight?"

"Sal gave me a call. Rangoon is at Nick's Pool Hall Bar in the Red Light district," replied Michael.

"How the hell can you believe anything that tightwad prick ever says!" Anthony exclaimed.

"Hey, don't disrespect Sally. I know he's a greedy bastard and a miser, but when it comes to taking care of business or making money, you know his word's as good as gold," said Michael.

"My ass!"

"All right! Shut the shit up! I'm trying to drive here," yelled Jackie, annoyed as he sped through the city streets.

"Enough you guys, we're here," Michael cautioned.

The car pulled in quietly to the rundown parking lot at the rear of Nick's Bar.

"Now remember, were just going talk, nothing more, nothing less. Got it?" said Michael firmly.

"Got it," replied Jackie and Anthony.

The trio got out of the car and stepped briskly to the back entrance of Nick's and entered the shabby bar. Thick cigar smoke filled the dilapidated cesspool's air and the rotted wooden floorboards emitted the smell of moldy mothballs. Michael gave the greasy bartender a hard look. The bartender pointed his index finger to the basement door. Down here was best place to find any junky; the basements of such shit hole back alley bars were notorious for harboring drug dens, and this one was in particular the perfect spot to find a two-timing loser like Pete Rangoon.

Down the stairs the trio moved, to the den where the hookers and drug addicts found heaven, an absolute bliss reached by indulging in crack, heroin, and cocaine. Michael spotted the slimy, grungy guy, about 28 years old, in the back corner, snorting away among the wasted dopers. His hair was long and greasy, his clothes featured an assortment of mysterious stains, and his jeans were dirty with splits all over the legs. On his feet was a pair of old sneakers with holes in them.

"Rangoon!" called Michael.

"Hey baby, look. It's Mr. Rock Star!" laughed a hooker sitting next to Rangoon, as she snorted blow.

"Shut the hell up, whore!" said Anthony, pushing her to the floor.

"Stupid guinea!" yelled the whore, struggling to stand.

"Get outta here, bitch!" yelled Anthony, smacking her across the face. The hooker ran off frightened.

"Snnnah! Who the shit are you supposed to be hot shot, Ha! Ha! Ha!" laughed a very wasted Rangoon.

"Okay cokehead, I want some answers, and I want them now!" yelled Michael, angrily picking up Rangoon and pressing him hard against the badly chipped brick wall.

"Fuck you!" mocked Rangoon. Michael threw Rangoon across the small room, where he landed on a small wooden table, breaking it in two and knocking over a glass candleholder, which shattered on the floor.

"Oh shit! Call the cops!" screamed the dopers in the room, running away from the action.

"I got nothing to say to you!" Rangoon spat angrily.

"Anthony, break his arms in two!" Jackie commanded firmly.

"With pleasure," Anthony grabbed Rangoon from the side and locked him tight in a deep grip, immobilizing him. Slowing Anthony began to pull Rangoon's right arm back, the sound of the bones in his arm cracking as Rangoon screamed in agony.

"Pete, don't fuck with me, you know your boss doesn't give a fuck about what happens to you. Now who the hell made the drop on the big job!" yelled Michael.

"What?" asked Rangoon.

"Don't play cute with me," raged Michael, bashing in Rangoon's head and breaking his nose.

"I don't know man!" yelled Rangoon as blood flowed from his broken nose.

"Anthony!" signaled Michael. Anthony tightened his grip on Rangoon's arm. Rangoon again screamed in pain.

"Who?" yelled Michael.

"It was Steiner! Fucking Morey Steiner!!" screamed Rangoon.

"Next! Who the hell is Godfather Scarfo's new muscle?"

"What?" said a dazed Rangoon.

"Who are Scarfo's new people?" Michael yelled in Rangoon's face.

"I don't know!" screamed Rangoon, barely able to withstand the intense pain. "AHHH!!!!!!!!" cried Rangoon as his right arm snapped, dangling broken like a chicken with its head cut off.

"Where is he?" Raising his gun under Rangoon's neck, Michael cocked the trigger.

"Forget it D! He knows nothing. Let's go," said Anthony.

"The Deuce Motel!" said Rangoon, wriggling in pain.

"You say anything about this and you're dead, you fucking junky!" Jackie kicked Rangoon in the balls.

Michael, Jackie, and Anthony left Rangoon squirming in pain on the dirty floor of the drug den. Back in the car, frustration built between the three men.

"Do you really believe that bullshit back there?" asked Jackie.

"Not a damn bit," replied Anthony.

"Morey couldn't have been able to fully organize a job like that, he's too much of an idiot to be that clever. No, this heist was pulled off by some higher up guys. I can feel it," said Michael.

"The question now, is who and where does this lead to Scarfo's secret connections?" Anthony mused.

"There's only one way to find out. Let's go pay a visit to Morey," said Michael.

"Hold it, the deadbeat will recognize us from the last time we shook him down. Remember, he owed Joey Boseta ten G's from the race book," said Jackie.

"Yeah, he's right. Mike you'd better take care of this schmuck. He doesn't know you," suggested Anthony.

"Drop me off near Brooks Street; I have to pick up some things," said Michael.

"Yeah, sure," said Jackie.

6

CODE OF SILENCE

Michael headed up the stairs of the abandoned storage yard on Brooks Street. He unlocked an old safe that was hidden in the corner of a rooftop loft. In the distance behind him on the upper roof of an adjoining building a mysterious figure was spying on him. Michael grabbed his equipment from the safe and jumped onto the fire escape. He was headed to The Deuce Motel. The mysterious figure followed stealthily behind him.

Hotwiring an old beat up car on the street, Michael sped off to locate his quarry. Pain preyed on his mind; he could not get his nightmare from the previous night out of his head, his sister murdered by the masked face son of a bitch pulling the trigger. "Who are you, asshole?" said Michael to himself, still hearing his sister's screams from the dream.

Michael climbed out of the car and once inside the rundown motel he headed upstairs, to room 23, where he saw through the room's entrance window Morey sleeping. Morey was a middle-aged man and a slob to boot; the room was old and looked worn down. Pulling out a pick, Michael opened up the door discreetly, and as he let himself into the room he noticed it was empty. The bathroom door was closed, so Michael lay in wait behind the thick green curtains that hid the windows.

Morey emerged from the bathroom and began to pour himself a drink from a bottle on the nightstand and Michael came behind him, grabbing him and shoving a pistol to the side of his captive's head. Morey was stunned.

"Tell me exactly what I want to know and you might just live," said Michael sternly.

"Just don't kill me, please," begged Morey.

"Who did Scarfo use to organize the heist that let my client's capital get taken?" interrogated Michael.

"You know I can't tell you that, if I do they'll kill me."

"If you don't tell me, you're dead right now where you stand," said Michael angrily, pushing the gun hard into Morey's temple.

Morey was gripped with fear. "I just know I saw a guy with blonde hair wearing a blue suit and a white mask speaking to the boss. Besides, what does it matter, a few days later someone else hit our organization and made off with it," stammered Morey.

"What!" Lighting struck Michael's spine. "Give me a damn name!"

"I don't know!" screamed Morey.

"Don't push me! Tell me now, or you get a bullet." Michael cocked the trigger.

Morey elbowed Michael in the stomach hard, causing Michael to drop his gun; Morey then grabbed a steak knife from the dinette set on the table and lunged at Michael, slashing his coat. Michael kicked the knife out of Morey's hand and Morey fell to the floor. He crawled to grab Michael's gun where it lay. Just as he was about to aim, Michael pulled out his other pistol and shot Morey in the chest. In a furious rage, Michael continued to fire, pumping bullets into Morey's legs, paralyzing him, as Morey screamed in agony. "You asshole!"

"Shut up you little bitch, you kiss your mamma with that mouth?" Michael mocked.

"Go fuck yourself," cried Morey, wriggling like a rat in a trap. Michael kicked Morey in his side.

"Damn prick! You got blood on my three-hundred dollar slacks!" yelled Michael, wiping the blood off with a strange smile. Just as he was about to kill Morey, holding his pistol steady, the sounds of police sirens roared in the distance. "Shit," grumbled Michael, knowing it was time to go.

Suddenly, he looked at the window and saw a figure there. It was Serena, but not the one he knew. Her skin was white and her fangs were displayed in a mocking grin, ready for a bite.

"You!" Michael said in shock. She jumped into the room and grabbed Morey, who was somehow still alive and began feeding his off blood, sinking her teeth greedily into his neck.

"Hello baby," said Serena, showing her fangs as blood covered her red lips.

"What the hell!" Michael jumped out of the window, landing on a parked car below. He jumped off the car, but in a flash Serena was standing in front of him.

"Miss me?" she leered.

"What are you?" asked Michael, shocked by her bloody fangs. He squeezed off a shot at the devious she-devil. She drew near to him and easily dodged the bullets. Michael raised his gun in fear, clicking the empty gun. No bullets left. Serena pounced behind him, knocking the gun out of his hand.

"What! No kiss this time?" said Serena, wrapping her arms around Michael. She sunk her fangs into his throat as she picked him up and flew both of them to a rooftop. She released her fangs.

"You're nearly dead, yeah lover, you got about a minute to live, tell me, tell me do you still want vengeance, I can give it to you, I can give you all your heart's desires," Serena whispered.

"Yes," gasped Michael, barely alive. Serena flew herself and Michael back to his apartment, where she laid him on the bed. Michael was very pale.

"Drink Michael, drink my blood and live forever!" Serena slit into her chest over Michael's lips, and grabbing her waist, Michael drank. He drank with an insatiable thirst.

"Enough!" She pulled away. Pain shot through Michael's body, his veins turning blue as the color in his face faded away, his heart pulsing a million beats at once, his eyes dilating. Everything was distorted; his vision was blurred and the room swerved, he felt drunk from Serena's blood burning like venom through his veins as he yelled in pain. His life flashed before his eyes as he died in her arms. "I know what you crave most inside your soul. I saw that hunger inside you the first time I looked into your eyes, and so I shall give it to you, your bloodlust," said Serena. Her eyes glowed red.

7

REBIRTH

As the moon began to rise, Michael woke disorientated and afraid, his head throbbing. He could barely remember what had happened the night before, but he was back home and in bed. Serena sat up beside him, naked. The bluish moonlight shimmered on her elegant pale skin.

"What happened?" said Michael in a panic.

"Are you all right? You passed out so I brought you back here," answered Serena softly, wrapping her arms around his chest and kissing his neck gently.

"No, I feel cold; my chest feels numb. What's going on, what happened?" said Michael. Looking in the mirror he saw his eyes were now blue, his fingernails were sharp and long like claws, and his skin was pale.

"Don't worry; it happens to us all in the beginning," said Serena. Looking in the mirror, Michael noticed two small holes in his throat, and touching them gently, he felt the deepness of the bite.

"What the hell did you do to me?" Michael rubbed his eyes, looking in the mirror over his dresser.

"I just gave you what you have always wanted, now enjoy it!"

"I did not want this!" yelled Michael in anger.

Serena zipped in front of him. "Yes you did, you wanted; you craved it, like how I craved you."

"What happened? I can't remember," asked Michael in fear and confusion.

"You're changing. Let's just say – understand I have given you something so very few people are given."

"Oh yes, and what the hell is that?"

"A gift," said Serena.

"Gift, what gift?" asked Michael, confused.

"Immortality," replied Serena with a cruel grin.

"What! You must think I'm crazy! Why didn't you just kill me? Why, why this!"

"Because, I saw the pain that haunts you. You want revenge for the death of your sister, that's why you go out night after night doing what you do," said Serena.

"How do you know who I really am or what my feelings are? What if I'm just another cold-blooded killer?"

"I know you have a humble heart; I felt that in you when we made love that night, even though you have chosen to do what you do. I care about you, and maybe I'm a little selfish too."

"You know nothing about me. You're just a thief," retorted Michael.

"I'm not just a thief, I'm the best," said Serena. "Also, you saved my life that's why I couldn't kill you."

"There's also another reason, isn't there? Isn't there!" Michael exclaimed.

"Yes," Serena paused, looking deep into his eyes. "I think I've fallen for you."

"So what do you want from me, I'm surprised, shocked but surprised," Michael said.

"Do you want me to lie to you, or do you want the truth?" said Serena bluntly.

"No, just I thought it would take some time, you know, normal relationships don't blossom this fast and not in this way, especially with me being turned into a vampire!"

"Don't be too alarmed. I know it seems strange at first, but in many ways you'll be stronger and faster than you were before, and you'll be immune from sickness, and possess great powers."

"It hurts like hell," said Michael, feeling his muscles tighten.

"The pain will cease in a few hours. You're body is slowly dying, but don't worry because we never grow old," said Serena.

"You mean I'm dead, is that what you're telling me?" retorted Michael.

"Undead actually. Get used to it."

"What do mean undead? Get used to it?"

"Do you believe in the supernatural?" asked Serena.

"You mean vampires, werewolves, monsters, all that jazz? You mean they really exist?" Michael was now curious.

"Yes, but not like it's played out to be. Imagine; just imagine if you will, living a life with without the suffering of most human beings, no longer a slave to the expectations of mankind's society. You are now higher up on the food chain, a work of art, darling," said Serena.

"This is so unreal, but, I feel good," said Michael as a rush of energy surged through his body.

"After all, you wish to fill the bittersweet craving of revenge, come on, you know you do. I could see that you in your eyes when you were looking at the picture of your sister. I could sense that she was wronged in some way. All a guy like yourself has to ask is, what do you have to lose? Nothing really."

Michael split in two a heavy wooden table in the corner with his fist, his face grinning with delight over this power he now possessed. "You have a point, maybe this could work out after all."

"You see, your powers are already beginning to take form," said Serena.

"I like it." Michael smiled wickedly.

"Why shouldn't you?" Serena pushed him onto the bed, slowly kissing him passionately on the lips.

"You're damn good," said Michael, responding to her.

"You're not bad yourself," Serena replied. They kissed deeply. The chimes on the clock struck two am as Michael fell asleep in Serena's arms.

The next night Michael woke with a thirst he had never known. The streets of Sin City called to him.

PART TWO: THE DARK GIFT

8

"LET THE HUNT BEGIN"

The night was warm and inviting. A new world was waiting for Michael. He hadn't known what love was until he gave himself to Serena and she gave herself to him.

He was very hungry and needed to go out and feed, so the two lovers hit the streets. The scent of blood was everywhere; ordinary mortals passed it by. Michael's senses were sharp and he was surprised to feel an odd presence from a stranger walking past them.

"Don't worry, our kind is everywhere. It's a curse for any of us to harm our own," said Serena.

"You felt him too?" asked Michael.

"No, but I could tell. The dark gifts we each possess can differ. Understand this though – one gift each of us possesses is the natural ability to detect our own kind by scent. There are many different types of our kind. For example, look at that whore and man on the corner. Her scent tells me she is a succubus vampire, and she will drain her lover tonight while sleeping with him, draining all of his pranic and sexual energy. Then she will kill him."

Michael saw the man fall under the charms of the succubus's lust right then, as she kissed him. Michael could see the victim's life force slowly draining as they walked into a shady hotel. "Amazing," he said, intrigued with this new breed of beings.

"Anyway, you've seen me feeding on your blood and now you need to feed your hunger. I know the perfect place," said Serena.

"Without blood or life force energy, we die, it's simple as that," stated Serena.

"Where are we going?" asked Michael.

"Hunting."

Serena jumped onto the rooftop and Michael followed. Leaping from rooftop to rooftop he could see the psychedelic colors of vice glistening from the strip, his heart racing with strange excitement. Somehow, he was beginning to enjoy this new calling.

"Let's have some fun first. Tell me, do you like to dance?" asked Serena.

"Shall we?" replied Michael. Serena slithered into position while Michael slid into battle mode, the two circling around each other gracefully as if they were in a choreographed dance.

"I should warn you, I don't mind hitting girls."

"All the more fun. Let's see what you got, hot shot," replied Serena.

"Rah!" they both yelled as they clashed. Extending their claws they began to fight, dodging each other's attacks swiftly. Serena flew around Michael, knocking him down.

"Hey, no fair! Want to play rough, huh?"

"I'm still waiting," said Serena playfully.

Michael jumped from one rooftop to the next, charging at Serena. She appeared in front him, trying to knock him down a second time, but she failed miserably as Michael kicked her, knocking her down to the ground. Getting up quickly she leaped off the rooftop, landing atop the bullet train that was moving on the rooftop bridges beneath them.

"Not bad, little girl!" said Michael, dropping down to join her on the top of the moving train. "But it's time to conclude this."

Serena flipped forward in an attempt to knock Michael off balance. Ducking, he grabbed her arm and swung her down hard on the steel roof of the train. "Damn, you're good," said Serena catching her breath.

"Aha, I'm not as much of a weakling as you thought, you little tom girl," laughed Michael.

"Shut up," Serena lightly giggled. "You're good, but not good enough." She flipped him on the train's roof so that she was lying on top. They kissed.

After helping him up, they jumped off the moving train onto the lower rooftop above an alley on Aspen Street. Serena's ears rang; the call and taste of blood was near. "Hold up," said Serena. She could hear something below.

9

ALLEY ASSAULT

Michael looked down and saw a group of drug dealers in the dark moon-lit alley. One of them was in the process of raping a girl who looked about 16, while the others were beating up her brother. "Give us the money you owe us you little brat!" yelled a tall one, flashing a gun in the kid's face.

"I couldn't make the delivery on time, please don't!" screamed the young man.

"Too bad, you little shit!" said a fat one, bashing the kid the ground.

"You know the deal: you deliver the goods, we get our money and you get a taste. You fuck us over, we fuck you over," said the shortest one.

"How about I cut that dress off your pretty little sister there!" The fat one grabbed the young girl and dragged her screaming to a far corner in the shadows.

"No, please don't! She's just a kid, don't!" The young man begged for mercy.

"Boom!" A pistol fired, killing the young man. His brains splattered on the wall and the little girl screaming at seeing her brother murdered.

Serena floated down silently behind the dealers and lunged from the shadows, grabbing the short one from behind and slitting his throat with her claws. She sunk her fangs into his jugular as the blood gushed out, his life drained.

"Shit!" yelled the tall one, firing his gun at Serena, who easily dodged the shots. Michael grabbed the punk, lifting him up and grabbing the gun and crushing it. He ripped the flesh off the punk's face with his claws and then fed off him, draining his life force.

"What the hell?" screamed the fat one as Michael jumped in front of him. "Stay back you freaks, or I'll kill her, I swear!" The fat one put his knife against the girl's throat.

"Coward!" yelled Michael in rage. Michael zipped his pistol out, fired, and hit the target all in one move; the bullet went straight through the bastard's head, a clean shot. The fat prick released the girl as he fell to the ground dead.

Screaming hysterically and crying, the little girl ran to Michael, hugging him fiercely as if to release the trauma she had just been through.

"Oh! Thank you!" cried the girl.

"I'm not going to hurt you, kid," said Michael.

Looking over Michael's shoulder as she hugged him she saw the corpse of her brother lying dead in the alley, a pool of blood surrounding his head.

"Ricky!!!! Oh, God!" "Help!" screamed the little girl, she ran to her dead brother and clenched his body to her tightly; she could not let him go. The sounds of sirens ran from up the street.

"There's nothing you can do for her, come on we have to go now!" said Serena.

"No, we can't just leave her here," said Michael. The sound of the sirens became louder. "Here, take this kid." Michael handed her a card with Saint Mark's Abbey Church on it.

"What?"

"Go to Father Paul, and stay there until the police call you. Tell him an old friend of his sent you. He'll know, now go, you'll be safe there from the streets," instructed Michael.

"Thanks," cried the girl.

"We have to go now!" yelled Serena. The two of them disappeared in the shadows, flying back to his place.

Back at the downtown police station a priest was speaking with an officer who stood next to the young girl.

"Thank you for bringing her in Father, we'll take it from here." The officer shook the priest's hand and the priest left the room.

"What did you see honey?" asked the officer.

"The man in black, he saved me," said the girl.

"Who?" The officer asked. The girl could not say anymore; shock had caused her to black out. "Get a medic in here now!" yelled the officer.

10

"HUMANITY RESIDES WITHIN"

Michael and Serena ran into the Michael's pad, breathless and irritated with each other's actions.

"You stupid idiot! You could have gotten us both killed!" yelled Serena in anger.

"I couldn't let that prick kill that girl, Serena, I couldn't," protested Michael.

"Pathetic!" Serena spat.

"What the hell is that supposed to mean!"

"I said you're pathetic."

"You're a real heartless bitch!" retorted Michael.

"What!" Serena yelled. "We are the shadows, the hidden; vampires do not interact in mortal affairs, do you understand? Never! Even what we witnessed tonight," yelled Serena.

"Even when an innocent teenage girl is being raped?" said Michael.

"Yes, even in that case, we must not have contact with humans. Doing so could result in us being hunted or killed. Those are the rules for our survival; we are immortal but not invincible."

"I refuse to follow some ancient code. My life is mine to rule and mine alone," said Michael.

"You're mine. I gave you your life." Serena pushed Michael in frustration. "Without me you would be dead!"

"And I saved yours, or do you forget that without me you'd be riddled with 38 caliber bullets back at Scarfo's penthouse," yelled Michael, grabbing her arm with anger, though he dropped her arm as he looked at her. Tears sprang to Serena's eyes and she dropped to the floor crying. Michael left the apartment, slamming the door behind him; he sped off on his motorcycle, cruising to relieve his stress.

Four hours later he came home, feeling guilty for confronting Serena. The apartment was quiet and dark; however, a light flickered from the living room where a small fire burned in the fireplace. Serena was on the couch curled up in a blanket, half asleep with a few books and a glass of red wine on the table in front of her.

"She couldn't handle it," Michael said to himself before walking in. He quietly walked over to her on the couch, leaned over and kissed her softly on the forehead. Serena stirred slightly, happy to see that he came home, unlike all the others that had left her. "Hey," she said softly, "I'm sorry."

"It's okay," said Michael.

"No, you're right, it was good to save that girl's life. I forgot what it's like to care about others; I forgot what it's like to be human."

"Serena, I know that we're expected to be hidden from the world, but please understand, even if we are no longer of this world, we can learn from the mistakes we make. Just because we are what we are does not mean that humanity is removed from us. It's still in each of us." Michael gently stroked her hair.

"Do you really believe that? But we take lives."

"It doesn't matter, for all the evil that is in any person, a fragment of good survives too."

Serena kissed him. Michael went over to make himself a rum and cola at the bar to try to relax; as he sat down on the couch,

Serena wrapped her arms around Michael's waist, hugging him in guilt.

"Thanks," she said.

"It's okay," Michael repeated. They kissed passionately and fell asleep on the couch together.

11

"THE PSYCHIC GIFT"

All of a sudden sharp, piercing pains hit Michael. His muscles became so tense that his veins turned dark blue. His eyes changed to pure white and his ears rang with urgent screams. He saw a vision; he was looking at a man in his thirties, tied up on a chair in what seemed to be an old, abandoned factory. The man, in his late thirties, had brown hair, brown eyes, was dressed in a derby brown hat, brown coat, tan pants, and black shoes, his face bruised and bloody from being beaten.

Serena woke in shock. "Michael! Michael!" she screamed, horrified at the sight of her lover having what seemed to be an epileptic fit. In a flash it was over. Michael lay motionless on the floor and then came out of his trance. He was breathing harshly and perspiring heavily.

"I saw him," Michael panted.

"Him, who's him?" asked Serena nervously.

"Fredricks," yelled Michael.

"Who?"

At that same moment the telephone rang and Michael answered eagerly. A young man spoke on the other end of the line in panic, "Hello, hello, Michael!" yelled the young man.

"Tommy, is that you man? What's wrong!"

"Mike, thank God," said Tommy.

"What the hell is going on?" said Michael.

"Mike, they got Danny!"

"Who has him?"

"Two of Frank Scarfo's guys, I spotted them around the corner of the shop, they grabbed Danny," babbled Tommy.

"Did you get the license plate number?" asked Michael.

"Yeah, why?"

"I can trace it to them. Quick, give me the plate number."

"110568. Get to them quick, they're going to kill him!" Tommy screeched.

"I'm on it!" yelled Michael as he hung up the phone.

12

"RESCUE"

"**D**anny you dumb knucklehead!" Michael said to himself in the car with Serena.

"Who's Danny?" Serena asked.

"An old friend of the family and mine, damn you! Danny, Damn it! He's always getting himself into shit! What the hell are you looking at, what's with the face?" Michael glanced at Serena.

"You! I have never seen the gift react that fast to a fledgling," said Serena.

"What?" Michael asked.

"The dark gift that we possess – normally it takes many years for a fledgling to develop their abilities. Many die after changing. Their human bodies can't withstand the transformation of being turned," explained a surprised Serena.

"You mean to tell me that I could have been fertilizer and you kept this from me all this time?"

"Well you came through, didn't you," protested Serena.

"Thanks!" Michael retorted. He hit the tracking device on the dashboard as they sped off into the night.

The scanner began to ring with a pinging sounded as they closed in on their quarry.

"We got a signal," Serena said. Michael stopped the car in front of Scarfo's meat packing plant. Another car was already parked in the shadows. The back gate was locked tight; so was the whole facility, which was built like a fortress. Michael hit the high beams, and with tires screaming he rammed the car through the gate, crashing right through the main wooden door of the factory. As they sprang out of the car they saw a tall lanky man and a short pudgy man holding Danny Fredricks over a giant meat grinder, the blades spinning fast and sharp.

"Okay pig, where's the money?" demanded the short, pudgy man.

"It's in my coat," yelled Fredricks.

"Get it!"

"What is this? This is 10 grand. Where's the other 20, you chiseler!" yelled the tall man.

"Aw Al, come on! Would I screw my partners over?" Fredricks asked.

"Yes!" both of them yelled.

"Hey Al, let's see if this pig can fly!" said the short man, and Al replied, "Let's, Sonny!"

"I don't think so, assholes!" Michael leapt onto the platform.

"Waste them!" Sonny yelled, as they opened fire. Michael dropkicked Sonny, knocking him down. In a whirlwind Al grabbed Serena, locking her in his grip. Serena neatly broke his wrist by twisting it backwards.

"AHHHAAHA!" screeched Al. Slipping to the ground he dropped his machine gun, which fell to the floor. Firing as it landed, the bullets cut through the chains that held Danny from being sliced into lunchmeat.

"No!" Danny screamed as the chains broke. Plummeting downward, Serena reached Danny in a graceful acrobatic dive, pushing him away from the grinder blades before the chains fell apart into the activated machine, smashing it to pieces. Sparks flew onto the ground near some old rusted half opened barrels of fuel that was used to run the machines. Some of the barrels had leaks in them as small puddles of fuel began to catch fire.

Scarfo's two goons ran out of the place with all the others, just before the whole factory blew.

Michael, Danny and Serena hijacked Al's car; Scarfo's thugs gave chase, firing at them. After ditching the car, they fled to the bullet subway station, Fredricks thanked his two rescuers with a little present: five thousand dollars in cash and a shipping list that had important dates on them.

"You're still doing cons, you greedy son of a bitch!" Michael exclaimed.

"Come on Mike, a guy has to eat," said Danny.

"Yeah, and I have to bail your ass out of shit every time you mess with the wrong people," Michael replied.

"Sorry," said Danny.

"Ah piss on it, man it's nothing." Michael winked at him.

"Thanks for your help. Someday I may be able to repay you for being a good friend. Keep in touch; we'll do lunch."

Michael nodded. "Yeah right." He smiled as Fredricks boarded one of the departing trains.

13

"THE STAKEOUT"

"**D**o you think he'll be okay?" Serena asked.

"Fredricks is okay. Now let's look at that list," replied Michael.

Serena pulled the shipping list out of her pocket and inspected it carefully. "There are listings of dates and times here for cargo shipment pickups," she said.

"Let me see that."

"Here." Serena passed him the list.

"Whatever Scarfo's men wanted from Fredricks was more than just cash. This list also contains all the merchandise they plan to move out, as well as the manifest that comes with it. If this information was released to the press, Scarfo could take a major hit to his operation. Danny really hit a big one this time. It's no wonder they wanted to kill him," Michael mused. "They've got a shipment moving out tonight."

"What are we waiting for?" Serena asked.

"Let's go," said Michael.

"Where to?"

"The industrial district."

They boarded the express train and zipped to the other side of town. From within the old abandoned Bards Bureau Storage

Warehouse came angry voices. Below the rafters that were covered in beds of dust and decay, a crowd of men grumbled and bellowed with distaste for one another's business practices.

"The deal was for 20 million, Garcia, not 30!" Franco yelled to a muscular Spanish man with a twisted black mustache, rugged beard, and knife scars on his face. The Spaniard was dressed in a black leather jacket, army fatigues and wore a machine gun pistol on his belt. His eyes burned like those of Satan himself.

"That was the deal, but you changed it when you dicked me over with only half!" Garcia spat.

"Sonny, kill this fucking wetback," yelled Franco as both sets of men drew their guns on each other.

"Go ahead, Dago, whop, asshole! Shoot!" Garcia challenged.

"You greasy, bean eating son of a bitch!" yelled Franco.

"By the way, there's a remote-controlled bomb linked to inside one of the crates. Pull the trigger and this place goes boom!" mocked Garcia.

"You're bluffing," Franco fired back, holding his pistol half cocked.

"Am I? Hey! Antonio!" Garcia yelled to one of his thugs. The thug removed a remote detonator out from his jacket pocket.

Franco called off his mens guns. "Tell you what, Franco, I'll give you the guns back if you cut me a percentage on the take from the dope you got coming into town."

Garcia coolly replied, "Forget it!"

"You got no choice; I'm your only way to get the stuff in and out of the states safely."

"Give me a guarantee."

Garcia tossed Franco a packet of files containing important information.

"You fucking snake!" said Franco as he skimmed through the files.

"Oh yes, we know everything about you Scarfo. Our government is especially looking to protect its image and would go to pieces if what goes on with your country and mine, including this little venture, was released to the public."

"He has it all – on the organization, shipments, hit lists, Swiss bank accounts, and prison records," said Sonny.

"Think of it this way, gringo – you do business our way, you protect your ass, we protect ours, and we each get a cut," said Garcia coolly.

"Filthy bastard," grunted Franco reluctantly.

Suddenly, a clinking sound came from the catwalk above, as a broken pipe fell.

"What was that?" said Al.

"Look up there!" yelled Garcia.

"It's them, those two freaks from the plant!" screamed Sonny.

"Kill them!" ordered Franco.

"Duck!" warned Serena, grabbing Michael from the rafter. They both hit the floor as shots landed against the side of the railing.

"Thanks!" said Michael.

As the couple returned fire, bullets flew through the air; goons below fell to the ground and live ammo spurted everywhere. Blood gushed from bodies being shot to pieces, heads exploded, and limbs were torn off. Garcia extracted a grenade launcher from one of the crates and fired it over his head.

"Look out!" Michael yelled. The explosion from the grenade destroyed the left side of the railing, throwing Michael and Serena against some crates and breaking them into splinters. The noise of gunfire stopped, and as the smoke and debris of the dust settled, Franco and Garcia's men moved in carefully to inspect the aftermath.

Suddenly, Michael emerged from the broken crates with Serena behind him, his fangs bared in anger and his eyes burning blue with hate. He noticed another man standing next to Franco. The man's face was covered in a white mask and he was dressed in a blue suit, identical to the vision Michael has seen in his nightmare.

"YOU!" Michael roared in anger as he recklessly lunged to attack. Sonny fired his pistol, wounding Michael and Serena in the chest. Serena kept him from getting killed as she slammed a smoke grenade against the ground. The grenade caused a thick cloud of gas to fill the air, and as all of the men coughed and sputtered in the gloom, Serena and Michael vanished without a trace.

"Where the hell did they go?" yelled Sonny.

"I don't know but I want them dead!" Franco yelled at Sonny and Al. "Garcia, you have a deal. Gather as many men and weapons as you can, find those two, kill them, and bring me their heads on a platter!"

"Would you prefer their eyes ripped out or their noses cut off?" agreed Garcia.

"Franco, I saw that guy at the penthouse three nights ago," said Sonny.

"So it was the same guy. I thought so." Franco nodded. "They must not interfere again with this operation. Find them."

14

Serena opened the door to the rooftop loft in the old theater where Michael lived. Blood was flowing from her body, and with Michael still bleeding from his chest, the two fell to the ground over the threshold.

"I can't feel anything," moaned Serena.

"Just hang on baby, I've got you," said Michael, holding up Serena on his right shoulder.

"It hurts," said Serena. Michael pulled out the two bullets from his chest with blood on his hand. Serena pulled out the two bullets from her chest as she winced in pain.

"Stay here, I'll find you blood," said Michael gritting his teeth bearing the pain. Glancing out the window he saw a tabby cat on the fire escape, and using his telekinetic gift he was able to command the furry beast to come into the apartment. Michael slit the cat's throat with his switchblade, giving the creature to Serena. She tore into the cat's flesh, feeding aggressively. Her wounds healed quickly and her eyes returned to their natural color. Michael healed faster, for his injuries were less severe than Serena's. Michael saw a rat run out of a little hole from the base board of the wall.

"Disgusting," said Serena.

"It's just a rat," said Michael, and grabbing it, he looked into the rodent's little black eyes; Michael's own eyes glowed yellow as he drained his victim's energy. Dropping the corpse of the pest, Michael was healed. At that moment both were restored.

"Are you all right?" asked Michael.

"Thanks, I'm fine now," said Serena, feeling relieved from the pain. "That was too close."

"At least we're in one piece."

"Cool." Serena's breathing was a little heavy.

"After all, I can't let you die on me now can I, love?" said Michael.

"Do you mean it?" said Serena looking into Michael's eyes with curiosity.

"Why the hell not? We were a pretty good team back there," smiled Michael.

"Thanks."

"I've found more than just a girlfriend, I've found a partner."

"Are you serious?" questioned Serena.

"Why not? As deadly as we are together and as compatible, we make the perfect team. Besides, I admire a woman who knows how to kick ass." A wicked grin spread across Michael's face.

Serena gave him a grin of satisfaction. "I have a little present for you." She handed him a high-powered rifle and laser canon gun.

"Where did you get this?" Michael asked.

"I managed to confiscate a carrying case of guns from the warehouse just before we vanished," said Serena.

"I have to hand it to you sweets, it looks like we have us a whole new ball game. The Don will be pleased with these toys," Michael chuckled.

"Come on. It's time to sleep. We need the rest; we'll figure something out tomorrow night." They walked downstairs to the bedroom, undressed and dove underneath the cool covers of the bed and slept.

PART THREE:
THE PAST COMES BACK

15

"RECOVERING THE GOODS"

Michael woke from his deep slumber about an hour after sunset. Serena was already up. Michael caught the scent of blood coming from her and he knew that she had gone to feed before he woke. "I guess you're not too hungry this evening," he said.

"How did you know?" asked Serena.

"I just could tell, I felt it."

"Show off. Oh well, how did you sleep?"

"Comfortably," replied Michael, as he stretched and got out of bed.

"How about some breakfast? My treat," she offered.

"Sure, but just some coffee, I'm not that hungry for anyone tonight," Michael answered. He dressed quickly, pulling on a sports coat and jeans, along with black leather shoes. The two headed out down to Jack's Coffee Shop.

"So tell me," Michael asked as he sipped his coffee, "how did you get the gift?"

"I was born with this condition. It wasn't until I was 20 when the symptoms began to awaken, the thirst, depression, and the insomnia. There was even times while I slept that I felt my spirit leave my body, then flow back in," said Serena.

"How did you handle it?" asked Michael.

"I cried a lot. People often ridiculed me in college because of my pale skin; they thought I was a freak. When I came to America after leaving the KGB, where I was an assistant to my uncle, I went to school at night, studying botany and medicine. I became an outcast."

"Horrible," said Michael.

"I only had one friend, he was such a sweet man," said Serena.

"Tell me about him." Michael was intrigued.

"His name was Joshua. He and I were very close friends in college until graduation. We both dreamed of being doctors. He knew that I was different and yet he treated me so kindly and lovingly. I remember how he always kissed me tenderly. Our loft used to be so cozy and he would bring me fresh-cut lilies and white roses every day; they filled the air with sweetness. Whenever we made love he took my breath away. It was the happiest time in my life.

As we approached graduation we both thought of getting married, having children. We would talk about it often, sometimes jokingly."

"Did he ever know about, you know ... the gift?" Michael asked curiously.

"He didn't know, but I think he wouldn't have cared anyway, he loved me too much to care," said Serena. "Then, one evening as we were walking home together through the park we were approached by a man in a dark coat. It was so dark that night; I couldn't see the guy well. The guy pulled out a gun and stuck it to Joshua's head. Joshua gave him his money, and after that, the bastard killed him anyway. The man ran away in the darkness. I chased him, but he had disappeared into the night. I ran back and held Joshua in my arms crying and screaming, but no one could help him, not even me. He died seconds after he was shot.

After that, I lost my compassion for people. Before then I never fed on them, but after Joshua's death I didn't care. I went back into the KGB and have never been the same since. That was 80 years ago."

"I'm sorry," Michael said.

"It's all right. I guess we all have demons from the past that haunt us in life," said Serena.

"Do you still miss him?"

"Sometimes I do, but I'm happy being with you."

"Why did you choose me?" Michael asked with curiosity.

"Because I see myself in you. We are the same in some ways, and also eternity is a long time to be all alone."

"I'm curious how long you've been this way?"

"Let's just say I've lived for a long time," she replied. "How old are you, by the way?"

"I'm now thirty," said Michael. "There's one thing I'm wondering about. Where do we come from? You know, I still don't understand it all."

"You will in time," said Serena.

"When?"

"In time," said Serena. "The truth is, I used to ask myself the same question about vampires, what I am, how the whole thing started, our history. I have heard different myths and legends that our kind is descended from ancient Egypt, Rome, Asia, and the Slavic regions. I've read different ancient texts, talked to different old ones, always finding nothing, who knows?"

"So you know nothing," replied Michael.

"One thing that I have learned is this. We are what we are and maybe it is best to leave some things alone. Just accept what we are and live with it," said Serena.

"I wonder how a supreme being could let something like us exist," said Michael, as he twirled the lucky dog tags he wore around his neck.

"Wondering can be a dangerous thing, love; wondering can drive a vampire to insanity," said Serena seriously.

"But aren't you a bit curious? Don't you ask yourself, why, why!" protested Michael.

"Trust me, searching only makes the torment stronger. Besides, if a divine creator did make us, then what would be the point of looking for answers?" said Serena, annoyed.

"Do you believe in God?"

"I don't know if there is one, but I'm open to the idea that there is. What about you?"

"I used to believe there was; now I don't know. I question every-thing now," said Michael.

"I feel the same," Serena nodded.

"You know it's kind of funny." Michael smiled slightly.

"What is?" Serena looked with her lovely eyes into Michael's.

"I used to love reading vampire and mythological stories when I was a kid. I actually wanted to be a monster make-up artist in the movie business. Now I'm one of them, a monster, that is." Michael chuckled.

"Ironic isn't it?" smiled Serena.

"What do you think about the feeding?" wondered Michael.

"Nothing much. I know it may bother you now, but you'll get used to it."

"Still, those punks deserved it," said Michael with no regrets.

"The hunger is power," replied Serena.

"Yeah, but what about things that can harm us?"

"Sunlight can weaken us, fire can kill us, decapitation can defi-nitely kill us, and holy water and crosses don't do anything, that's just in the movies."

"What about impalement?"

"That can also kill us. Regular wounds in general can't harm us," said Serena.

"Good to know," said Michael. "Just thinking, what do you like to do for fun, I mean what are your passions, besides this nightlife?"

"Well, I love to dance and when I was a little girl I took ballet lessons. I dreamed of being a famous dancer for operas and plays, but that was long ago," said Serena. "What about you?"

"I like playing my electric guitar and reading books," said Michael.

"Really, me too!" exclaimed Serena, smiling. "So tell me, what made you come out here to Vegas?"

"I think you already know; you seem to know my thoughts," said Michael.

"I can't always read people's thoughts, much less know everything about them. Tell me," she pressed.

"Two years ago, I was on a mission in Turkey working for the CIA's central (ADGS) operation anti-drug and gun smuggling unit, associated with INTERPOL. My sister Katrina and I were assigned to monitor, detect, capture, and arrest the main warlord that was in charge of an organization. My sister went undercover working for the Prime Minister, Turish Strossinburg, as his personal liaison. She knew the language, customs, and traditions, as our uncle had lived there for seven years. We suspected that Strossinburg was our target, considering every criminal act that he and his cabinet had committed since his appointment to office in 2010. Also, before that he was one of Turkey's highest-ranking military generals. He was involved in assassination hits, corruption of military power, blackmail, money laundering, biochemical weapons development – the list went on forever. The only problem was to find proof. For a while everything seemed to be going wrong, and then one day we found evidence from a hacker, documents that could convict and sentence him, with the help of the United Nations. It was the discovery of secret documents on biochemical weapons to be sold to a buyer. On the day we infiltrated his headquarters, we found a twenty-eight year old woman covered with blood laying dead in his study."

"Katrina?" asked Serena.

"Yes," said Michael. "I remember seeing the evil bastard grinning just before he shot her. I didn't see the guy's face; it was hidden under a white mask. I wasn't in time to be able to stop him. Just before he jumped out of the window, a bomb went off. The blast engulfed the whole room in fire and blew me out of a sixth story window. I landed in a tree below. After being sent back to the states I could not remember anything: who I was, where I was, or even my own name. I was in a coma for three months. After I woke up, I could barely move. My jaw was smashed in, my legs were broken and my body was severely burned. I was in bad shape, hooked up to feeding tubes and respirators. Days turned into weeks and weeks turned into months. After about a year in the hospital, my memory began to come back. The same nightmare has haunted me night after night, even now. Somehow in all that hell, I learned that there was a God and that his name was Felice Santerini. The family learned about my experience from Jackie. We grew up together and were very close as kids in New York. Until the accident happened, I had no dealings with his crew. The deal was they would save my life with the best doctors and medicine that money could buy. In return, I would work for them exclusively. I also learned from an old friend in the unit that my sister's killer was in Vegas through various reports from Strossinburg's dirty little network. He came to Las Vegas to get away from the media reports of Turkey's list of suspected terrorists. However, no one in the United States could trace any leads to prove who he really was. So how could I refuse? I've been trying to find that rat bastard ever since. Then just last night at the warehouse, I spotted the man that killed my sister."

"Scarfo and your mystery killer seem to be working together," said Serena.

"It seems that way. And by the look of it all, this killer has some political connections in high places. I recognized the ring he was wearing; it's the same one I've seen in my nightmares. Franco Scarfo is in league with some very powerful organizations; all I need to do is to find out who they are and take them down," said Michael.

"I want to help you," Serena said.

"No, this is getting dangerous. I need you to stay hidden in the trenches," said Michael.

"I can look after myself!" Serena exclaimed. "Besides, I can be your eyes and ears. Remember, a thief in the night is like a shadow," she continued before Michael could open his mouth to contradict her.

"All right then, have it your way," Michael replied coolly. His cell phone rang.

"Michael! Michael!" yelled a gruff man's voice through the phone.

"Yeah?" responded Michael.

"It's me, Sal!"

"Salvatore, what's wrong?"

"We got us a situation here!"

"What happened?"

"We're losing our protection money to Frank Scarfo's guys on the eastside. Take those son's of bitches out!" yelled Sal.

"Sal, cool it, are you sure it's Scarfo's guys?"

"Do I sound like I'm kidding? Get your motherfucking ass down to Sidney's and get back that money. When you got it, bring the cash to Paulie down at the Turquoise Terrace Tower; he'll deliver the money to Riffman."

"Who's this Riffman?" asked Michael, confused as this familiar name passed through his mind.

"Let me worry about that, just get the money!" Sal was pissed off.

"I forgot to mention that this little venture is not our only problem," said Michael.

"What do you mean?" asked Sal impatiently.

"The drop that was made, well, someone else got to it after we obtained it from Scarfo's guys. It happened before we could finish the transfer."

"WHAT!!! FUNGU! Strunzoo Cani!" Sal swore in Italian.

"Relax, Salvatore, I'll get the collection and then we'll worry about recovering the other sum."

"Get that damn money! Call Jackie, now!"

"Damn!" yelled Michael as he hung up his cell phone. "I've got to go." Michael got up to leave in a hurry, snatching up his coat and dropping a tip on the table.

"What's wrong?" asked Serena.

"Business, don't worry love, I'll be home by two."

"Be careful Michael and take this just in case." Serena handed him a little bottle of blood for food. She kissed him good luck as he headed out the door, thanking her with a smile.

16

"MAKING COLLECTION"

Michael took off in his 1963 hell Kat with the pistons blazing; he was headed down to the eastside of Las Vegas' business district. He caught air off a bump in the road, and flipping out his cell phone coolly, said, "Jackie, its Mike. Gather the crew. We got to clean the collectors."

"Got you Mike, grab us on the Strip at the Dingo Hotel and Casino in Old Vegas," said Jackie.

Michael zoomed to the back lot of the Dingo, where Jackie, Anthony, and Sal waited impatiently.

"That damn idiot Paulie! How the hell could he let 500 g's get slipped under his nose like that, fucking ball breaker!" Sal lit a cigarette. Sal was an old timer Dago by heart. Dressed in an Italian suit and pants, he wore two gold rings on his right hand and wore the finest shoes; he had a small crown of grey hair around his forehead and old blue eyes.

"Don't talk that way about Paulie, Sal. He's a made man and a decent one at that," said Anthony. "Besides, if anyone should be calling the kettle black I would say it's your fucking fault."

"Ahh, that's bullshit, you son of a bitch. You think I would screw over the Don and the organization like that?" asked Sal.

"I'm just saying, if the shoe fits, wise ass," said Anthony coolly.

"Fuck you! Just what the hell is that supposed to mean?"

"Listen dickhead, the Don put you in charge of the operation," said Anthony, getting agitated.

"What! Do you think I stole it?" Sal was getting hot under the collar.

"No, but I just found out from one of our contacts on the north side of town last night that you and your crew did get hit by someone after you boosted the cash from Scarfo's delivery truck."

"I admit it, I found out too, an hour ago at the Bouvard Lounge from Joe. How in hell was I supposed to know? I wasn't actually there on the night of the job. When it was going down, I was doing bookie work at the Maddox Casino for Paulie. Ask Mike, he was on the job." Sal shook his head.

"True, but he headed home after he escorted the truck to your guys. I know because I was the lookout at the drop-off point," said Anthony.

"There's no use bitching about it now. Let's just make this collection and we'll figure it out later," said Jackie.

"Should we tell Mike?" asked Anthony.

"hell no! Not now; this is a major embarrassment on my part with my guys fucking up and he's been put through enough shit lately," said Sal, guilty.

Michael called out to his crew and Jackie and the others hopped in. "What the hell are you doing here?" Michael asked Sal.

"Wanted to make sure there would be no problems. Besides, Jackie told me he was short one guy for a job like this," Sal answered.

The crew raced to Sidney's off-track betting club, just as Scarfo's thugs were loading the back of their large delivery truck with bags of stolen protection money. Suddenly, one of the thug's cell phones rang. "Yeah Boss," responded the thug, and a muffled voice spoke over on the phone. "What!" exclaimed the thug in surprise. "Let's get the fuck out of here!"

The loaded truck took off like lighting, just as Michael and the others got to Sidney's.

17

THE CHASE

"What the hell?" Jackie said.

"They must have been tipped off that we were coming," said Sal.

"Hold on boys, let's nail these assholes!" Michael slammed the gas pedal to the floor as they chased the truck on the highway. One thug pulled out an Uzi and the other pulled out an M-16. Both opened fire on the hell Kat; bullets flew as streams of smoke flew out the windows.

"Shit, they're packed!" said Anthony in surprise.

"What the fuck!" Sal screamed.

The quartet pulled out their pistols and returned fire; bullets zinged between both vehicles as they whipped down the road, with Michael swinging in and out of lanes to keep the gas tank from being hit. Bullets nicked Michael's windshield and shots penetrated his left headlight.

"Shit! They're too heavily armed. Mike, head in closer, I'm going to try something," said Jackie.

"Don't be an idiot!" screamed Sal.

"Fuck it!" Michael's eyes twitched as he floored the pedal. Jackie crawled out of the right side window and climbed on top of the car, barely able to keep his footing. He jumped on the lift stand of the truck and shot off the lock opening the back door, then headed inside the back of the truck. Once inside he started grabbing the bags of money two at a time, tossing them to Anthony through the sunroof on Michael's car. To make matters worse, the cops were behind them and were catching up quickly.

"Cops!" yelled Anthony.

Suddenly the little slit driver window opened from where the driver and passenger were siting and a gun popped out of it, firing at the four friends. Jackie fired back at same time four bullets hit him in the chest. Jackie knocked the gun out of the hand of the thug on the passenger side of the truck and shot him in the head as blood spurted in Jackie's face. Jackie then pressed his gun to the thug driving and yelled, "Stop the fucking truck!" As the truck swerved, a small box in the back fell over, revealing an electronic timer linked to a bomb counting down the 15 seconds left until detonation.

"Oh shit!" Jackie screamed as he bailed out of the back of the truck, landing on top of Michael's car. Sal pulled him up by his arms. "BOMB!" yelled Jackie. Michael turned the car onto a ramp off the highway just as the truck exploded into flames. With the cops still on their tails, Jackie feverishly looked through Michael's glove compartment and pulled out a can of tacks, a hammer and cigarette lighter. Jackie dumped the tacks out the window, onto the street. The tires of two of the patrol cars blew, causing the vehicles to flip over and explode, unleashing a domino effect with the other police cars.

Michael continued to speed off into the abandoned industrial district of town, with more patrol cars in pursuit. Tossing a smoke grenade out of the car, he blinded the pursuers. Luckily, he knew they were near a dark alley that had a lift to an old underground subway tunnel. These old subway tunnels were used in 2010 as a shortcut for people coming from California to Nevada, but had been closed due to broken gas mains underneath the tunnel lines. The car stopped on the lift and headed underground, safe from the police.

18

"ERASING THE EVIDENCE"

The engine of the car died as Michael removed the key from the ignition switch. "Everyone all right?" asked Michael, breathing heavy, trying to digest the insanity that he and the others had just underwent. Michael popped open the little bottle that Serena had given him and chugged the blood inside.

"Let me have a shot of that whiskey," said Sal in the back, mistaking it for booze in the dark.

"Sorry, all gone," said Michael.

"I'm fine, thank you," said Jackie sarcastically as he removed the bulletproof vest out from under his shirt.

"Holy mother of God!" said Sal in amazement.

"Always be prepared, like you said bro." Jackie gasped to catch his breath while he smirked at Michael. Michael couldn't help but smile back.

"You okay Sal?" Anthony asked.

"Real fucking beautiful. We just blew up a shitload of the Don's money with half of Vegas' finest on our asses, not to mention blowing up two police cars and now getting a whole bunch of attention on us from the press, and you have the audacity to ask me if I am okay!" Sal was pissed off.

"I wager this is going to be printed on the front page of every paper and be on every news channel," said Anthony, looking worried.

"Hey it's not too bad, look at these." Jackie tossed four bags of cash to Sal.

"I'm impressed. I don't believe it. After all that you still got the money!" said a shocked Sal.

"Well done kid," said Michael.

"C'mon we got to ditch this car," said Sal.

"That's a good idea, but where? We're in an abandoned subway line," said Anthony.

"I know a way out. There's an old intersecting tunnel that leads out to the wash. From there we can drive the car through the wash to the old salvage yard. There's a car crusher we can use to get rid of the car." Michael hit the ignition switch and the car began to sputter, then stalled. Again he turned the ignition switch but still nothing; only after pulling the choke lever did he get the engine running.

"Yes!" Jackie exclaimed happily.

The car sped quietly through tunnel as a thousand thoughts raced through Michael's mind. "Isn't it interesting how those two thugs knew that we were coming to steal the collection?" asked Michael.

"I'd like to know who planted that time bomb in the truck. Another second less and I would have been dead," said Jackie.

"Franco Scarfo probably, that demented psycho would rather sacrifice a small collection to kill any one of this family, the sick fuck," said Michael.

"After all this is done tonight, I suggest we lay low until pressure from the media dies down," Anthony suggested.

"Don't worry about it too much. I'll tell Paulie what happened. He has most of the cops and city politicians in his pocket; they'll put a spin on all this," said Sal.

"That's fine and all but you forget that the police commissioner, Hamilton, she's an honest cop. She won't put up with innocent cops being slain," said Michael.

"Should we put a hit out on her?" asked Anthony.

"No, don't be stupid Anthony. They'll trace that back to us, it would be too obvious," Jackie fired back.

"Like it our not, we're stuck, we just have to go quiet, low profile for a while," said Jackie.

"Fuck!" swore Sal, upset. The car made it to the end of the tunnel and turned towards the wash. They drove out of the subway tunnel and a half hour later at a quarter to ten, the car stopped at the abandoned salvage yard. The place looked like a massive graveyard. The sky was pitch black and the wind was blowing, the dust resembling skulls and dead faces in the night. The broken and smashed cars were piled on top of each other, and some almost resembled crosses, reminding Michael of all the evil done by men in the name of greed and the hunger for power.

"Let's crush this thing and get the hell out of here. This place gives me the creeps," said Anthony.

"Let's," said Michael as they got out of the car with the bags of money.

Jackie pulled the lever on the magnetic crane that hoisted the car up and slowly lowered it into the crusher. Michael looked on sadly as his favorite ride was taken from him.

"Cheer up Mike, it's better the car than us," said Sal, handing Michael a few grand as a consolation. Michael smiled at Sal in thanks.

Jackie called Paulie to send the private company helicopter he owned from the Turquoise Terrace Tower casino. Within 20 minutes the chopper touched down to pick up Michael and the crew. Jackie handed his cell phone just after he had finished speaking with Paulie on the other line, to Michael just as he was about to light a cigarette inside the cockpit. "Michael, the Don wants to see you and the others immediately," Paulie said sternly over the phone.

"Right away," said Michael calmly. The helicopter landed at Paulie's private airstrip, where a car was waiting for the crew. As they climbed into the car, Michael put in a call to Serena, "Yeah it's me, I need a favor."

"Sure, what is it?" she asked.

"Drop off the case of those things you acquired and bring them down to the phone booth on Rose Street. Wait there until I come for them. I'll see you soon," said Michael. Michael asked the driver to turn onto Rose Street and the driver did. Jackie gave Michael a strange look.

"Trust me," Michael said as the car drove up to the phone booth on Rose Street; Michael picked up the case from inside the phone booth. Serena wasn't in sight. "Good girl," whispered Michael to himself as he got back into the car with the black case.

"What's in the case?" asked Sal curiously.

"You'll see when we meet the Don," replied Michael calmly.

19

"THE DON'S DILEMMA"

Back at Turquoise Terrace Tower, old Don Felice Santerini waited. He sat in his favorite chair and the fatigue in his sad blue eyes showed a certain frailty and the many years of leadership to an organization that now seemed to be tearing itself apart in a struggle for survival; gang violence had increased the last few years. The Don was a handsome man even in his old age; his white hair was thick and shone like pure silver, and he had a short grey mustache and always dressed in the richest of suits. Paulie was also present, mulling in his mind how to handle the situation that had just occurred, as he watched the big screen projector play out the shocking news footage of a collection gone wrong.

Paulie Santerini could handle almost anything. A big man with short black hair with gray marks, he was in his fifties. A guy who was always dressed sharp and had the style of a suave movie star, he had it all: charm, charisma, and a proper zeal for business. He ran six of the largest corporate casinos in Las Vegas, owned two night clubs, and was the Don's right-hand man in the import/export business of smuggling shipments in bonds, paying off teamsters, mass producing pharmaceuticals and illegal drugs, and the production of biodegradable fuel for the United States government. He had a cool head on his shoulders in any situation, and was always one step ahead of the game in the smuggling industry, whether it was before a cop, politician, or Interpol agent.

In the middle the grand entranceway, two large turquoise elevators opened. Michael and company proceeded to the main door of the Don's office as two guards on both sides opened the double doors.

"Gentlemen come in," said Paulie, upset yet poised. The crew stepped inside with trepidation at what they were about to hear. They sat down.

"Gentlemen, what happened tonight was a direct failure of this organization's ability to do a simple job," said Paulie.

"Paulie, we had unforeseen issues. However, during the chaos of this extraordinary evening we did recover most of the collection as ordered," Michael started.

"There is no excuse for failure. This makes us look foolish to the Jews and Koreans working in our organization. I will not tolerate this again," said Don Felice, seriously disappointed as he drew his pistol to Jackie's head. Don Felice Santerini, the man who controlled it all. He had taken over after the war between the Costa and Moretti Families ended in bloodshed and after the extermination of most of both families. He was a serious business person all the time; the kingpin of twelve of Vegas' drug manufacturing plants, running three currency corporations and one large adult entertainment production company, and maintaining ties to three corrupt senators in Washington who closely advised the presidential cabinet. Above all other rules was this: never fuck with the man in charge.

Nervously Jackie stood up, sweating as he said, "With respect, Don Santerini, as we were about to obtain the rest of the capital that was stolen from us, I discovered a bomb that was placed in one of the boxes in the moving truck. So naturally to prevent injury or death we left the scene with what we could."

The Don lowered his pistol, putting it back in his shoulder holster. "It is obvious that the Scarfos' are behind this, but I've known Godfather Scarfo since we were young. He has too much honor to allow a hit like this. This is Franco's doing, that animal of a nephew of his," said Don Felice.

"I think I know why," said Michael.

"Should we call a hit?" asked Anthony.

"No, you do that and the media will be all over us; the public will suspect things. We need to keep the organization to appear as legitimate as possible. If not, it could cost us a massive loss in millions of dollars. No one is making a move, not now," said Don Felice clearly.

The buzzer on Paulie's desk rang and the secretary's voice came out over the call box, "A Mr. Riffman to see you Mr. Santerini."

"Very well, send him up," said Don Felice.

A tall, well built young man with brown hair and blue eyes entered the room. He wore eyeglasses and had on a brown suit and a black tie. "Good evening, Mr. Santerini, gentlemen," he nodded to the others. "I have this week's transcripts and receipts as you requested."

"Very well, please transfer these to our offshore accounts," said Don Felice, nodding to Paulie to hand him the 10 manila envelopes that were stuffed with cash. Mr. Riffman sat down at the Don's desk.

"I hope that there was no trouble in this week's business," said Mr. Riffman coolly.

"None at all," replied Don Felice.

"Shouldn't you be going Mr. Riffman? This is private business," said Michael, annoyed as he felt an unsavory feeling about this man.

"Of course. Thank you for your business, gentlemen." Mr. Riffman shook the Don's hand and exited the room briskly. Leaving the building, Mr. Riffman returned to his car, where he activated the miniature earpiece he had planted under the edge of the Don's desk. Back upstairs Michael presented the gun case to the Don. As he opened the latches to the case and the lid popped up, the Don's eyes grew large and he frowned in anger.

"This is why Scarfo tried to kill us," explained Michael sternly.

"Holy Christ!" said the Don, appalled.

"Franco Scarfo is moving high-grade military firepower to win the little war both families have been having for the last 11 years," said Michael.

"Weapons like these could tip the scales in Franco's favor," said Anthony.

"Where did you acquire this?" asked Paulie.

"I went and did a little snooping down at Scarfo's warehouse the other night on a tip made by an anonymous caller. And that's not all I saw when I was there. I also saw a couple of unsavory characters meeting with Franco Scarfo."

"Who? Columbians, Feds?" asked the Don.

"It appears that Franco is doing business with a terrorist political group called "Diablo's de Negro", also known as the Black Devil's Society. I recognized a tattoo on an arms dealer that spoke with Franco. The guy's name is Sergio Garcia, and he is an insane son of a bitch. He'd kill you just for looking at him," said Michael.

"What!" Mr. Riffman exclaimed, listening over his earpiece.

"Are you for sure?" Paulie asked.

"I'm positive. When I was working as an undercover agent for the CIA some years back I was given orders to take out Garcia's militia in Spain. Garcia had his headquarters at an abandoned military base," Michael explained.

"Why didn't you inform us of this immediately after you found these weapons?" the Don asked firmly.

"Because of the heat that's been coming down on the organization lately due to the smack that was stolen from that bank four nights ago, that neither family has been able to fully recover. I heard from Sal that the family has been getting too much coverage from the press," said Michael.

"From this point on, forget about the lost money. That's not important; what is important is finding the rest of the warehouses that are stocked with these weapons and destroying them before any major harm can be done to this family. The second job I have for you and Jackie is eliminating the source of these weapons," said the Don.

"Giving Garcia a dirt nap won't change anything. He has many loyal puppets who'll just replace him if he's taken down," said Michael.

"Well what then?" asked the Don.

"Mike's right, Don Felice. We need to find a better solution to eliminate this problem," said Jackie.

"I don't know boys; if Franco starts hitting parts of town with this shit, he could wipe us out," said Don Felice.

"Better, however, to form a plan than just rush in," said Michael.

"I agree. You've got balls Mike, you just might be made yet. Very well, lay low for now, and we'll find a solution for this problem in a few days," said the Don.

"Agreed," said Michael. The others nodded in approval of this temporary plan.

Mr. Riffman pulled out his earpiece and as he removed his makeup and wig, he put in a call on his cell phone to the big man himself. "Boss it's Phillips. The secret is out."

"The Don is too much of a chicken shit to do anything. He'll rely on his brains in the organization to make decisions for him," said Franco over the phone, lighting up a Cuban cigar at his desk.

"The guy that discovered our weapons works for Santerini. His name is Michael. I'm scanning databases for information on him." Phillips hacked away on his laptop. "It seems that our guy is my former partner, Michael Victor Damascus from the CIA. This guy was in the top Special Forces unit and was decorated with the Congressional Medal of Honor. I had a feeling it was him when he mentioned Sergio Garcia; no one else had any information on that mission in Spain. It was classified information; he and I were assigned to that mission as partners. I just know he's the same man who also tried to kill you at your penthouse and who was at the warehouse the other night with that girl," said Phillips.

"Interesting. This world is full of surprises," said Franco angrily.

"That's not all he's into; it seems through these sources that he has his hands in local business organizations here in town. I'll dig more up on him. What should I do with him and the girl?"

"What we normally do in a situation like this, Sergeant Phillips, is eliminate the problem," said Franco.

"Don't call me that!" Phillips snapped.

"Shut the fuck up and listen to me good, Phillips! For now I want this Damascus alive and healthy if possible. This guy may be more helpful to us alive than dead. After we have what we want from him, then we'll get rid of him. I want you to send a message to Santerini's organization that they will never forget. You know what to do," said Franco.

"What about the girl?"

"Find her and put her out of the way. We don't want any survivors; too much has already been found out," said Franco.

"Understood," said Phillips.

"That's right Phillips, don't forget that!"

"One more thing. I recovered our little collection money from Don Santerini's own hand," said Phillips.

"Good," said Franco as he hung up the phone, chuckling wickedly.

Phillips put a call in on his cell to his special guy. "Duval it's me, call Martinez and hit the Koreans and the Jews and hit them hard. Let's show these fucks that we own this city," Phillips commanded arrogantly. During the past eleven years in which crime and drugs had crept back into Vegas, most mobs had grown wise; combining whatever criminal empire mass fortunes they could from alliances with the global crime syndicates they ran. They then formed their own corporations by buying out most of the original corporate owners. The criminal consortiums also involved powerful politicians, stockbrokers, and secret individuals who had vast fortunes in the trillions. Even the president was in on it. In Vegas it was all about money through violence, bribes, or blackmail. That's why all of Vegas was going to hell.

On the other side of town at the Royal Dragon Palace Casino, a man dressed in casino business attire was working the halls. He was a muscular black guy, wearing a black suit, a tie, with black hair and dark glasses. He looked rough as he walked to the main owner's office, carrying a black attaché case. Stationed at the large office doors were two bodyguards who patted down the man. Seeing he was clean, they let him in to see the big boss, Mr. Yang, the Palace's owner.

"Mr. Duval Jackson! I'm glad to see you again, do you have the item that we agreed upon?" Yang asked eagerly.

"My employer sent two million in product just as agreed," replied Duval, confidently placing the large case on the desk.

"Excellent, I know it's all there. Would you care for a drink?" asked Mr. Yang.

"Yes, whiskey," said Duval.

Yang opened the glass liquor cabinet behind him and uncorked a bottle of whiskey and poured a crystal glass for Duval. Duval opened the case discreetly, placing his hand inside.

"You know, it's a shame that Frank Scarfo is taking a blow in the percentages, but then a loser like that is always falling, foolish man," said Yang as he turned to Duval with the glass in his hand.

"He's not going down, you are!" Duval exclaimed.

"What?" Yang asked, thrown off. Duval pulled his hand through the case as a barrage of silenced shots put holes straight through Yang. The dead Korean lay slouched in his chair with blood oozing out of his chest. Leaving the room, Duval grabbed the case. He landed a fist to the surprised guards, laying them out. Pulling on a pair of white gloves, he dragged them into a closet. Then he used his silenced pistol to kill them both, locking the door behind him. Afterwards, he came out of the closet wearing a realistic mask to disguise his face; he exited the building.

An hour later Yang was discovered dead and the authorities were at the crime scene with an investigation team taking pictures of the brutal murder. News footage rolled on the television; Paulie watched it at home while lounging in his bedroom. He was having a glass of chardonnay when news of the killing hit his screen.

"Tom Wilkins with Channel 8 News reporting here at the Royal Dragon Palace Casino, where exactly 45 minutes ago a murder was committed. The victims are Shim Yang, the owner of the Royal Dragon Palace Casino and his two bodyguards. All three were found gunned down. The killer was not seen and the motive is unknown at this time."

"Son of a bitch!" said Paulie as he put down his drink and got on the phone with the Don. His hands trembled as he dialed on his antique telephone. "Felice, it's me Paulie." Paulie tried to play it cool on the phone.

"What's the matter?" questioned Felice.

"Our partner at the Royal Dragon Palace was just iced," said Paulie.

"I just saw it right this second on the news. Find out who did this and stop them," said Felice, angrily slamming the phone on the receiver. "Mary, Mother of God," Felice uttered as he continued to watch the news.

"We've just received word from police that at the same time of the shooting here at the Royal Dragon Palace, another shooting occurred at Czar's Palace. The victim was CEO David Brookstone, president of Czar's Palace. Each of the murdered men was the prominent owner of a mega casino chain. The question is why? Police have suspect mafia influence, but nothing definite is known at this time." Don Felice shut off the TV as he got on the phone with his contacts.

"Two million to whoever finds me the guy that killed my clients. Bring me his head in one bag and his family's in the other." Don Felice put down the phone; looking out the window he saw his huge empire coming down around him.

20

"AN UNLIKELY SURPRISE"

The clock struck 1:30 am on Michael's grandfather clock; Serena was worried about her lover. After the meeting with Don Felice ended, the crew quietly stepped outside the building, now more concerned about the future of the Santerini family's survival. To make things worse, they couldn't make a move unless the Don said so.

"For now let's just go home and get some rest; this has been one messed up night for us all. We should starting planning a solution tomorrow morning to handle this problem," said Jackie.

"I don't think that's a good idea," said Michael.

"What do you mean Mike, isn't any time as good as the next?" said Sal curiously.

"My mother's sick in the hospital, and I promised I would visit her tomorrow," said Michael. Of course, no one knew that Michael's mother had died a month before of cancer.

"Okay, you visit your mother, and we'll call you in the evening," said Jackie.

"Hey who died and left you boss!" snapped an annoyed Sal.

"Sal, shut the fuck up! With all the shit that you put us through, you're lucky enough the Don didn't let one of us castrate you for your fuckups!" yelled Jackie, pissed off.

"Fuck you! You fatherless half-Irish bastard!"

BAAAAM! Jackie slugged Sal in face and Sal's big fat ass met the concrete pavement in less than a minute. "Never say that again!" Jackie ordered, angry as hell. Sal looked at Jackie as he sat up, wiping the blood from his lip, surprised at what had happened. Jackie helped him up. "Sorry Sal, sorry," Jackie muttered as he hopped into his car, looking nervous and fearful for what he'd just done. Sal was amazed. Jackie sped off.

"What the hell was that all about?" said Anthony, shocked.

"Jackie's dad left him and his mother when he was three. He hates his father, but I think he hates it more because he never had a father; that's why he always looks up to me as a big brother," said Michael.

"My fucking ass! The kid fucking disrespects me like this, a made man!" bitched Sal.

"Sal, shut up. You got what you deserved. See you tomorrow night," said Michael coldly as he walked up the street. About a mile from home it hit him like a whirlwind. His stomach shrank, his eyes burned red and his fangs began to protrude. He threw up the blood that Serena had given him to drink as it did not agree with his system. Michael then realized he had not feed enough and with no criminal victim in sight it was awfully tempting to drain anyone walking down the street of his or her life force. He knew he wasn't a vampire like Serena; he knew that inside his vampiric soul something darker and deadlier called. As he started to run through the streets he began to hear voices: "Take them, kill them, take them." Michael shook these voices out of his mind, then lost his balance and fell on the street. "What's happening to me?" Michael whispered. On a dark corner further up the street he managed to find a pet store that was closed for the night. His hunger was now growing insatiable as he drew closer to the entrance of the pet shop. A professional hit man, Michael knew to never leave evidence of his identity at the scene of any crime, and he picked the lock on the door wearing gloves he always carried in his pocket.

As he entered the pet shop the place was quiet and peaceful with the sound of little grunts and snores that came from the animals in their cages and pens. Michael loved animals and doing this felt awful, but he would rather take the life of an innocent animal than an innocent human. Michael began to focus his vampiric mental energy through the entire shop. To be merciful he put the animals into a deep sleep; this way, it would be painless and quiet. As all the animals were in a catatonic sleep, he drained them of their life as he walked over to each one quietly. When he was finished, the corpses of dogs, cats, birds, and even the fish in their aquariums were left dead white, like statues.

With his stamina fully restored, he switched the lock back in place with his lock pick on the pet shop door and walked the rest of the way home. It was 3:00 am when he silently opened the door to his apartment. Serena ran to him and kissed and hugged him. She looked disappointed and asked him with those eyes of hers "Where have you been?"

Michael, reading her body language, responded; "Baby, it's been a hell of a night." The two undressed and lay down.

"So tell me where you want to go someday to get away," said Michael teasing.

"Paris," spoke Serena softly.

"We will babe, we will someday," assured Michael, whispering into her ear, and with a kiss of affection the two fell asleep.

An hour later the phone on Michael's nightstand rang. Serena raised it to her ear and said, "Hello," half awake.

"It's Paulie, put Michael on pronto!"

Serena handed her lover the phone and lay back down.

"Paulie?" said Michael groggily.

"Yeah, listen up, two of our influential clients at Royal Dragon and Czar's just got whacked!" said Paulie.

"What, when!" asked Michael, awake now. "Did they say who did it?"

"No, the news just said they were taken out clean," replied Paulie.

"Should I take care of it?"

"No, you're needed on solving this other dilemma with Franco's weapons. We got some other guys handling this one; just thought though you might want to know. Stay in touch with me kid," said Paulie as he hung up the phone.

"Shit," said Michael as he sat up in bed.

"What's wrong love?" asked Serena.

"Nothing baby, just some bad news from the office," Michael replied as he kissed her on the forehead and lay back down to sleep.

PART FOUR: "COP'S INTUITION"

21

JUST A HUNCH

The sunrise touched the sleepless city of sin with a shimmering golden shine. It looked to be a pleasant day for the common couple cruising the city highlights.

But downtown, on the corner of the 34th Precinct, death and murder were just another day at the office. Two large feet stepped onto the sidewalk from an unmarked car. The feet belonged to a behemoth of a middle-aged man dressed in greasy, stained brown pants, and a long brown leather coat with slick black shoes. He also wore a fedora and a badge on a shirt so tight that it seemed the buttons would pop off at any minute. This specimen of law enforcement was Lieutenant Frank Watson. He walked over to a murder scene on the corner where the CSI team was bagging the body of a guy with gunshot wounds in his chest and head, and a second body with punctures on the neck and chest. The second body was so pale it looked like it was carved from marble. Frank lit up his morning cigarette with a look of disgust and frustration and approached his partner, who had just arrived on the scene.

"Well look at this, another fine mess to deal with. Just the perfect thing I need to start another day," complained Watson.

"I'd figure after seeing so many bodies like this you were beginning to wear down a little," said his partner.

"Please Jack, don't insult me. Shit, three murders at the Royal Dragon and one at Czar's last night and now this. Sorry piece of shit this town has become," said Watson, pissed.

"So what do we got here Frank?" asked Jack.

"Standard gun shot wounds to the chest and head on this guy here and one that I think you should look at. It looks like to me this guy took a stabbing to the neck and chest. He was probably held at knife point and then robbed and killed," said Watson confidently.

"I don't think so Frank," replied Jack, getting a closer look at the wounds in the body. "I used to work as a coroner in the morgue years ago. I've seen many stab and gun shot wounds before, but this isn't one of those."

"What do you mean?"

"These four punctures look like they came from an ice pick, not a knife; just look at these jagged indentations here on the main artery," said Jack, examining the body. Jack was a tough old Irish cop, he was the yin and Frank was the yang of their duo. Jack wore a grey trench coat and suit pants with black tie and white dress shirt; he was a respectful cop that stood for the law all the time.

"Probably just another way to take out the garbage; another Scarfo family special, I presume," said Frank.

"Well?" said Jack.

"I wouldn't think too much about it. We'll call the boys from forensics to send the meat truck down here, they will take the stiffs to the coroner's office and we'll get a full report after the autopsy."

"Yeah, I guess you're right. Ballistics will match the bullet shells to the casing book they have, and they'll give us the report later," said Jack.

"Anyway, the police commissioner wants to see us later to report in, but first let's head to the funeral. They'll probably have good food for breakfast after the service," said Watson.

"Is all you can think about is your stomach? How can you want to eat anything after seeing that?" The two hopped into Frank's squad car to proceed to Saint Mark's abbey for Fitzgerald and Scalipelli's service.

Inside the church abbey the dull and melancholy sounds of the old brass pipe organ sung a sad hymn as the procession of Las Vegas' finest entered the church, shaking hands and passing out hellos.

Father Paul Sullivan, a handsome middle-aged priest, approached the pulpit to speak a few words.

"Dearly beloved family members and friends, we gather here today on this day to remember and honor the lives of two great officers, Larry Fitzgerald and Joseph Scalipelli. These two officers fought valiantly to save the lives of the people coming home on the interstate a week ago when a shoot-out occurred on the highway that caused them to lose their lives in an accident caused by violence. It is sad for us to lose these two men, men of honor who showed their duty to their community and to their loved ones. Tragedy seems to be a daily occurrence today now that murder has become so common. It is such a sad thing to see that human life has grown cheap in our fair city, a city that was once a family city, now gone down hill. However, through all of this we still stand vigilant in the face of our God who is with us each and every day. Let us pray for these two souls who have left this world to be with our God through his Son our Lord Jesus Christ. Our Father who art in Heaven…."

As Father Paul continued the service, Jack and Frank sat in the back row of the church, talking about the families of the deceased men.

"Damn shame about what happened to those two guys. They were just kids, rookies. They both just got married a few months ago. Their wives must being going out of their minds with grief," said Frank sadly.

"Good lord, we have to do something about this; every day things are getting worse; we lost nine men last week," said Jack.

"Too many guys are taking bribes and not standing up for the ones who are clean."

"The department is going to hell."

An hour had passed and the service came to an end. "Come on; let's go give our condolences to the widows," said Jack, just as Father Paul finished speaking.

Jack and Frank walked up the aisle with the other officers to give their sympathy to the widows. Frank first spoke to Marsha, the widow of Fitzgerald. After hugging her and the other widow, he told them, "Don't cry too hard, we'll get the bastards who did this. Justice will be served, I'll see to it."

The two widows nodded sadly as the family members of both slain officers proceeded to carry the caskets to the graveyard outside. Once the service was over the two officers headed to the station to report to Commissioner Hamilton.

Back at police headquarters, Commissioner Sarah Brooke Hamilton sat in her cluttered office, her desk stacked to the sky with homicide and drug raid reports. The one window in her office was cracked and a dead plant sat on the grimy windowsill. The commissioner was a young and beautiful woman of 33. She had long black curly hair and wore a beige long coat and dress pants; she had beautiful legs, blue eyes, a cute nose, and lovely red lips. Upon the death of her father, the former commissioner, she had been voted into office.

Frustrated and upset, she called in Frank Watson and Jack Harris.

"Harris, Watson get in here."

"Easy Commissioner, down girl," joked Frank.

"Don't patronize me Frank. What do you have on those two corpses from midtown on the Thirty-fourth?" Commissioner Hamilton barked.

"We just got the autopsy report back from the morgue. One of the deceased has been identified as Louis Scarfo, cousin of mob boss Franco Scarfo, and the other is a John Doe; one with gunshot wounds, the other with ice pick and broken bottle wounds to the chest. John Doe's wallet was missing and the carved symbol was carved into the flesh of his back. Nobody can decipher it. It's probably a calling card of the killer or killers, but we just don't know. If this is another mob hit, it's not a typical one."

"That's great; we'll have the evidence department do a cross check reference on the symbol to match it to any criminal tattoos or markings in our files. We should come up with something," said the Commissioner. "Anyway we just got a report from uptown. There were 12 more homicides in a high class apartment, an uptown penthouse owned by one Franco Scarfo and another report of a robbery of half a million dollars from the Las Vegas First National Bank."

"Shit!" Frank whistled.

"Shit is right; whoever killed those twelve was fast and quick, messy but quick. Shards of explosives were found, Uzi Mac 10 shell casings and a whole bunch of dead bodies piled up nicely, not to mention a safe that was cracked open. The thief left a few dollar bills and jewels still laying around."

"Any clue as to the perps?"

"They dusted the bills and jewels for prints, but no luck, just a bit of gasoline residue but not much to go on."

"You want us to check it out?" asked Frank.

"Yes, you might find something," said the Commissioner.

Just as the two detectives were preparing to head out, a strange report came on the TV.

"This is Mike Lee with a bizarre story that might just leave you afraid, very afraid. At the corner of Otis Way and Devonshire, a local pet shop owner faced a horrible discovery at his shop this morning when he found all of his animals dead in the store. Perhaps the oddest part of this story is that the animals all had died in exactly the same way; drained of their blood. Foul play is suspected."

"But no one knows for sure," interjected Frank Watson over the TV.

"And now our main story; a rise in crime and violence on the streets with a string of grizzly murders has plagued the Otis Way area, each victim drained of large amounts of blood, and drug pushers found murdered in alleyways. Even more disturbing is that the police have not been able to solve these crimes, but sources tell us that police homicide divisions have been working around the clock to find clues. We will have more details on these stories and will bring you any new information that surfaces. This is Mike Lee reporting for Channel 8 News. Back to you in the newsroom, Todd."

Upon hearing this, the Commissioner gathered all the men and women in blue to the squad room.

"All right everyone, listen up. We're getting increased reports from our homicide division and narcotics. Both departments will be now be working together to combat the killings and the increase of illegal drugs in the worst parts of town. Now get on it and let's go nail us some bad guys."

After dismissing the officers from the squad room she called over Jack and Frank. "You heard it boys, get down to the Otis Way area and get this case solved. It's making the department look bad."

"You got it, Commissioner baby," smirked Frank.

"Cute. Now go, and don't come back until you bring some evidence. Go kick ass."

Frank and Jack headed out of the station.

22

"CLUE CONNECTING"

Jack and Frank arrived at the Otis Way area in 10 minutes. With forensics on site combing the area for clues, Jack and Frank went to take a look inside the pet shop and Franco Scarfo's penthouse, as it was close by. The first thing they noticed was skid marks on the sidewalk and alleyway, with indentations in some mud of the tracks. Jack took a shot of the scene with his camera while Frank walked up to the door of Franco Scarfo's penthouse, at least, what was left of it.

Sonny Scarfo and his insurance agent were surveying the damage to the building when Frank Watson walked in to scope out the flat. The place looked like it had been blown up, with bullet holes and large burn marks in the wooden floor and tattered curtains cut to pieces from the gunfire. The apartment itself smelled of sulfur. While surveying the room, Frank tried to link the murders to the other victims he had seen earlier that morning.

After the insurance agent left, Sonny noticed that Watson was still in the room upstairs. He was pissed about a fat boy cop snooping around his side of town. "Hello officer fuck face, what do you want here? You got no warrant!"

"I'm making it my business. Look here, asshole." With the warrant in his hand, Frank pushed Sonny against the wall with his big hands, scaring Sonny shitless with a loud crack against the brick wall. "Alright listen, you little fat bald headed mother fucker, I don't want to hear your shit, I don't want to even hear you breathe, all I want to know is who did this!" Watson demanded.

"Why don't you eat a doughnut and get the fuck out of here. It's a federal offense to commit an act of brutality to a man who is unarmed," sneered Sonny.

"I don't follow the rules and neither do you, you fucking gangster."

"Piss off, pig."

"That's it, let's take a trip," said Frank, blowing his lid as he pulled Sonny to the window, halfway holding him out the window six stories from the ground, holding his gun to the back to Sonny's head.

Sonny was petrified. "Hey! Hey! What are you doing!"

"You want to give me some answers now asshole, or do I have send you on a one way ticket to the pavement?"

"Okay! Okay! I'll talk I'll talk! Just don't let me fall," screamed Sonny.

"That's better guinea," said Frank.

"My boss got robbed a few nights ago. We were having a business dinner with some building contractors at 9 pm when some asshole breaks in and shoots up the place," said Sonny.

"Go on," said Watson.

"I didn't get a good look at the guy, I just saw he was dressed in black and had long black hair and a girl was with him, but I didn't see her that well."

Just then Jack walked in and witnessed Frank's method of questioning. "Frank! For God sakes man! What the hell do you think your doing?"

"Just getting a little info from this cockroach here," said Watson.

"Let him down lad! Now! You're out of line."

"Shut up Jack!" yelled Frank.

"Let him go now!" roared Jack. Frank let go Sonny go, not because of Jack's orders, but because he didn't think he could get any further information from Sonny. Frank stormed out, angry for being reprimanded by his superior officer.

"What were you thinking back there?" asked Jack.

"Nothing, I just like doing things my way. The system is too soft with these mob pricks," sulked Frank.

"You know that if any officer saw this they could report you to the DA," said Jack, disappointed at his partner's reckless behavior.

"I'm not afraid of internal affairs," huffed Frank.

"I'm not going to say anything, Frank, but you better get with the program. We're not above the law," Jack lectured.

"Old man, you're getting too soft," said Frank.

"Yeah I know, now come on, let's go," said Jack as they proceeded to leave. Sonny flipped them off out the window.

"Listen Frank, we need to get more information, we don't have enough to connect these murders to the Scarfo mob or the Santerini mob as a hit."

"I agree. We'll comb the area by checking with any business owners who might have the seen the crime at the time it was committed. If we can find them and get them to give us an eyewitness statement, we'll have evidence," said Frank, lighting up a cigarette, then slamming his mini steel lighter shut.

"That's good. We'll check with the owner across the street that runs the All Night Printing Shop. It's open seven days a week. The owner comes in to run the shop himself from 8 pm until 6 am," agreed Jack.

"Any other businesses open at the time that the crime was committed?"

"Gino's Deli," replied Jack.

"What time you got?"

"It's 2 pm right now." Jack looked at his watch. "We'll come back when the printing owner comes in and when the deli opens at 8 pm. Why don't we check back in at the station to see if the boys in forensics found any information on that carving?"

"Let's go; we better get answers quick. The DA is getting plenty pissed that homicide isn't getting the job done," said Frank scratching the back of his neck.

Jack and Frank hauled ass to get back to the station.

"Tell me Jack, why've you chosen to stay on the force all these years?"

"Lad, I can't stand to see the good people in this city being stepped on," Frank gave Jack a look of concern. "I know I'm getting up there Frank."

"I care about you partner. We've been friends for a long time."

"Yes we have. It's been seven years," said Jack. Frank sighed. "Don't think about it lad, we have a job to do. Besides, I think I would hate being stuck behind some desk; you know how I hate paperwork."

Heading to the computer records room with cups of black coffee and a couple of case files, they ran into Doug Dickens, the archives' keeper.

"Hey Douggy boy how's life in this shit hole!" joked Frank.

"It's better than working internal affairs," Doug replied. "Anyway I dug up the file with picture carvings on the John Doe victim like you asked"

"And?" asked Frank.

"And the carving matched a tattoo of one Jesse Rollens. He spent time in and out of the joint for dealing narcotics, petty theft, and vandalism."

"Looks like he was in the wrong place at the wrong time," said Jack.

"We didn't find a wallet on the victim, as stated in the report, but he did have a card in his back pocket and we also found a small speck of cocaine in the same pocket," said Doug, giving the card to Frank.

"Gino's Deli," said Frank, surprised.

"Rollens probably stopped by there before he was killed. He later made a drug deal and was then killed with Louis Scarfo while making the deal. Louis Scarfo was known for a coke addiction and pimping hookers," said Jack.

"Whoever killed them probably grabbed the cocaine and took off," said Frank.

"I think we have enough here. Let's head to Gino's," said Jack.

"Right, thanks Douggy boy, keep up the good work," said Frank.

"Thanks Frank," Doug replied as the two detectives took off. At 8 pm the Gino's Deli was open, smelling of fresh pizza. A small line of customers waited.

"While we're here, lets grab a pie," suggested Frank.

The owner Dino recognized them and was ecstatic to see his two favorite customers. "Buena Sera, Paisanos, Franco, Jackie, how are you guys!" exclaimed Dino happily.

"We're Good Dino," said Frank.

"The usual then?" said Dino.

"The usual, one large pizza pie with pepperoni, mushrooms, and meat balls."

"You got it. Hey Leo, you heard the man," Dino ordered.

"Got you boss, one special coming up," shouted Leo from the kitchen.

"It's good to see some old faces around here, business has been bad lately since the neighborhood's gone downhill," Dino sighed.

"That's too bad," said Jack.

"So tell us Dino, have you seen anything unusual here the last few nights lad, any strange things?" Jack queried.

"No, why?" said Dino, nervously, his smile turning to a frown.

"We're investigating a report of some murders at the penthouse around the corner and we found a stiff that had your restaurant's card in the pocket," said Frank.

"All right you got me," said Dino, talking in a low voice. "The local crime families have had my place on protection. They said if I told anyone what I saw they'd kill my family."

"You have nothing to fear, those dirt bags aren't going to touch your family. We'll put you and your family in the witness protection program, where they won't be able to get to you," Frank assured him.

"You'd do that for me?" asked Dino.

"It's our duty lad," said Jack, sliding him a card with the contact information for the Witness Protection Agency.

"What do you want to know?" asked Dino.

"Do you know a customer by the name of Jesse Rollens?"

"Yeah. What about Jesse? He's a regular of mine, the guy comes in every week on Wednesday."

"He's dead," said Jack.

"What happened?" asked Dino, shocked.

"We believe that three nights ago, on Wednesday, after Rollens came in here he was followed and later murdered. We found his body in the 34th precinct," said Frank.

"I did see someone eying Jesse down on the corner; the guy looked like one tough customer. But he took off when Jesse left," said Dino.

"What did this guy look like?" asked Jack.

"Tall, Italian guy with long black hair and dark glasses in a black suit and tie, white shirt with suspenders and black shoes. He had a beard."

"He had a beard," Frank repeated.

"Know the guy?" asked Jack.

"No, but I seen his car casing the area for about a week around closing time," said Dino.

"What about Pedro Sarde, the owner of that all night print shop?"

"He's seen the same guy too, I think," said Dino.

Jack thanked Dino as he called into his walkie-talkie, contacting headquarters to escort Dino to a safe location.

"Let's go," said Frank forgetting the pizza. The duo walked next door to visit Pedro, who had just opened up his store for the evening.

"Excuse us Mr. Sarde, police." Frank flashed his badge.

"Yes officers, how can I be of service?" asked Pedro.

"Do you know anything about the shooting that took place three nights ago in the vicinity around 9 pm?" asked Frank.

"Yes. I saw a tall man with long hair in black with a black beard and black coat taking off on what looked like a motorcycle or something like it, after I heard gunshots being fired," Pedro offered.

"Did you say he had a black beard?" asked Watson.

"Anything else?" asked Jack.

"I have a video surveillance of the corner, I had it installed after my store was robbed a month ago."

"We like to have a copy of the tape if you please," asked Frank.

"By all means, here take it, maybe it well help in kicking out these scumbags who killed my son when we were robbed. Take it if it keeps us locals safe," said Pedro assertively.

"Thank you for your help, our apologies for your son," said Jack.

The two hardboiled cops raced back to the station with great excitement to see the tape. Commissioner Hamilton was in the computer room checking over narcotics reports when Frank and Jack bolted into the room with the tape.

"Did you two bring back anything?" asked Commissioner Hamilton, stern with her arms crossed.

"Here you go Commissie," said Frank, handing her the tape.

"Good. Doug, play this tape and let's see what we got," ordered Commissioner Hamilton.

"Right away, boss," said Doug as he loaded up the tape. As the tape played they saw their suspect leave the scene of the shooting, speeding off on a bizarre vehicle of sorts.

"What the hell is that?" asked Frank.

"Wait, pause and zoom in here right where the vehicle is speeding off," said Commissioner Hamilton. Doug obeyed and as he zoomed in, the Commissioner asked, "What's that license plate number?"

"O12489-NV Plate," read Doug.

"Get a trace on that plate from the DMV system and find who it's registered to," said Commissioner Hamilton.

"Searching ... damn. It's unregistered," said Doug.

"Probably a phony," offered Frank.

"Who in the world doesn't own a hover bike; these things are everywhere now days," Jack sighed.

"Well, another dead end," said Commissioner Hamilton.

"We did find residue and strange tire impressions on the ground from that vehicle in these photos," said Jack.

"That's not enough to get a fix on this guy. Scan through the tape again."

Looking once again, they managed to get a brief glance at the suspect's face.

"Bingo!" said Frank.

"Cross reference the criminal files to get a match," said Commissioner Hamilton. Doug continued to scan the computer system, crossing footage with other criminal profiles and mugshots from the robbery with the same guy in it.

"I think we've hit pay dirt," said Doug.

"The guy here taking off on the hover bike and the guy robbing the bank truck are the same guy. He has the same facial features and clothes. Look at the right arm of the assailant, a tattoo marking torn from one of the other thieves attacking him before he made his escape with his fellow accomplices. It looks like two teams were competing for the stolen cash or working together," Frank mused.

"Security guards found the abandoned truck in a deserted alley." said Doug.

"Put out a description on the suspect and let's wait. That's all we can do for now," said Commissioner Hamilton.

"Hold on, the computer system is matching the suspect's facial profile to the system, aha, one class A loser by the name of Johnny Anderson, previously released on charges of possession of receiving stolen property, last known address 3458 Desert Palm Drive Hotel," Doug crowed.

"Let's go, he's ours," said Commissioner Hamilton.

23

"YOU GOT THE WRONG GUY"

Blazing as on wings of fire, tires smoking, the trio raced to nail their man with his pants down. In less than seven minutes Harris, Watson, and Hamilton arrived on scene with backup. Frank flashed his badge at the front desk and grabbing the register list, he quickly found Room 105, Anderson.

Commissioner Hamilton signaled and the three went sliding close to the walls of the hotel hallway. The team crept stealthily to the entrance door, on the way hearing blaring sounds coming from the other rooms. Cocking his 357 Magnum, Frank kept his eyes dead on to the door.

As they smashed open the door, Johnny Anderson was lounging on the couch in his underpants and undershirt, one minute watching the tube, the next pinned to the floor with a bunch of guns against his face. He was a young punk, skinny, and not too smart.

"Hey, what's going on!" exclaimed Anderson.

"On your feet killer," ordered Frank, pissed off.

"I didn't do anything!" yelled Anderson.

"You're under arrest for murder in the first degree, you have the right to remain silent, to have an attorney, and a hope in hell that you get life, otherwise its bubba and injection time," said Frank.

"But I didn't do anything," yelled Anderson.

"Save it for the judge lad," Jack slapped the cuffs on the suspect.

Back at the station the officers uncuffed the suspect and put him in a stall to hose him down.

"Spray him," said Commissioner Hamilton. As they hosed the suspect down she noticed something different, something that was out of place. "Wait pal, turn around, let me see your arm," said Commissioner Hamilton. Anderson complied. "Jack, he has no tattoo matching the footage on the tape," she said.

"You sure?" replied Jack.

"Look at his arms."

"Maybe he had it lasered off," said Jack.

"No man, I never had a tattoo! Never killed anyone, I was set up, it's Damascus, he did this!" yelled Anderson.

"Some how I got a hunch he's telling the truth," said Jack.

"Put him in the interrogation office upstairs. Things aren't adding up," said Commissioner Hamilton.

Grabbing Anderson, Frank brought him to the interrogation office and threw the suspect's ass in the chair. "All right, bozo, talk. Who is this Damascus?"

"The guy who would do anything to save his own hide. We both pulled past jobs, he must have..."

CRASH! A bullet shot through the window behind Anderson, blowing a clean hole through his head. Anderson stood still for less than half a second as his brains fell out; Jack and Frank looked on in horror as Anderson fell dead to the floor in a pool of blood. On the rooftop behind the police building, Michael lowered his sniper rifle. Serena was at his side as his lookout.

"Sweet Jesus!" screamed Frank.

"Anderson you could never keep your mouth shut, you snitch. Pity I had to make you," said Michael.

Serena looked surprised at Michael's reaction. "Let me guess, boss's orders?" she asked, lighting up a short baby cigar.

"When the Don asks I deliver. I hate a rat as much as the Don does, especially one that cheated his own crew out of a score," said Michael.

"You knew he would be picked up?" asked Serena.

"Of course, you gave me the dark gift didn't you? Remember, you said "it" is different for each of us. Apparently I can see visions of the past, present, future, and read people's thoughts sometimes," said Michael.

"Let's go now!" Serena urged.

At the same time, back in the interrogation room, Frank and Jack screamed for backup. They saw two shady figures get into a black car and take off two stories below outside the window.

"Shit! Squad Team, get in here now!" yelled Jack. Frank cocked his gun as he and his partner ran to their car down the stairs to engage the attackers.

"Squad car, 65, officers in need of back up, in pursuit of black 1972 sports car with Vegas plates, murder suspects, armed and extremely dangerous, over," yelled Jack over his car intercom.

"Roger that, deadly force has been approved, shoot to kill," Commissioner Hamilton ordered over the police scanner, as they chased Michael and Serena's car.

24

"CHASE AND SHOOT"

Michael and Serena raced through the side streets with the cops hot on their trail. "All right assholes, you're going down," said Frank, blasting through his side window at Michael's car. He hit the left side driver's mirror.

"Shit!" said Michael as he tried to lose them. The siren screamed as chase burned. Jack took out his pistol and shot at Michael's tires in an attempt to disable the car. Serena shot back relentlessly, but she only put dents in Watson's squad car.

"Damn! I can't get a clear shot," she cried.

"Then take the wheel, he's shooting at our tires," yelled Michael. He opened the sunroof and opened fire with his Mac 10 Uzi, bullet shells flying so fast you could smell the sulfur off each shot from the gun barrel. Jack fired back and hit Michael in the left arm.

"AHHH!!!" screamed Michael in agony. Blood and flesh flew off his arm. Taking back the wheel from Serena, she grabbed a smoke grenade off her belt, cocking the tip into her pistol.

"Hold on," she said as she shot the smoke grenade right at Watson's windshield.

"What the hell!" exclaimed Jack as the grenade exploded, blinding the officers with thick gray smoke. They lost control of the squad car and it spun out, hitting a telephone pole broadside. The airbags inflated, saving their lives. "Watson here! Bring backup now," wailed Frank from his seat. Jack was knocked out from the crash.

Fellow police cars were still chasing Michael and his girl; Michael thought fast and called Jackie. "Jackie, it's Mike. Bring the truck, I can't shake these pigs," he yelled into his phone.

"Where the hell are you!"

"Fox Hole Ave."

"Got you. Lure them to the red light district. In the alley there's a small tunnel. I'll meet you there," said Jackie.

"Thank Christ."

It was Jackie's drinking night and he liked to hit up the red light district bars now and then. Jackie hopped into the moving truck he used to unload merchandise and hauled ass to the meeting spot. With the police still on their tail, Serena grabbed a flash grenade from her weapons bag and tossed it on the street, where it landed in a puddle. The water intensified the explosion with a hot burst of light that blinded the cops.

"Good girl," said Michael as he turned off. Jackie's truck was waiting for them as Michael drove his car up onto the ramp and into the empty truck. Jackie hurried out, closed up the back, and headed off into the tunnel. The cops lost them.

Commissioner Hamilton arrived on the scene to make sure the medics were treating the wounded officers. Approaching Jack and Frank where they lay on stretchers, she was filled with anger. "Who did this Frank?" she asked fiercely.

"Damascus..." said Frank as he passed out.

"We'll get him Frank, by God we will get him," said Commissioner Hamilton.

Jackie delivered his cargo to his customs warehouse and unloaded the truck. Michael's wound instantly healed and he backed out the car and parked it. Getting out of the car, Michael and Serena stretched their legs with sighs of relief.

"That was too close, Michael," said Jackie.

"Relax Jackie."

"He's right Michael," Serena agreed.

"So this is Serena. She's tough and beautiful" Jackie declared.

"Thanks. I'll take that as a compliment." Serena smiled.

"No time for chatting now, we got heat on us," said Michael.

"Take it easy. I sent one the boys to bribe the mayor; he controls the cops so they won't be able to do a damn thing," said Jackie.

"That won't mean anything to the police commissioner. You know she'll do things her way," said Michael.

"For now, we should tie up loose ends," said Serena.

"By the way, how did you cover up yourself from the printing shop's camera when it caught you on film on the night of the job?" asked Jackie.

"Simple. I had a contact of mine who worked in the store steal the tape and digitally composite Anderson in for me and then put it back days before the police even got it. We're lucky to have our spies working all over the neighborhoods. Too bad Anderson figured out the set up." Michael shook his head.

"For now, stay at my private apartment complex. We can't afford you getting caught. You are too important to the organization," said Jackie.

"Thanks, here's two grand." Michael handed the money to Jackie.

"No problem," said Jackie.

"Consider it a down payment," replied Michael. The three sped off into the night in Jackie's car.

25

"DECEPTION AND ROBBERY"

In the car Michael's mind was stirring, planning his next move even as they arrived at Jackie's apartment complex.

"Jackie, I can't afford the cops or anyone to find out anything, and I can't just hide like a coward. Either way, the police will find out something," said Michael seriously.

"There's no such thing as a perfect wise guy, I agree," said Jackie.

"All Anderson said was a name," said Serena.

"It doesn't matter. A name can spread like wild fire in the criminal underworld, especially if the police have any secret contacts. I suggest we destroy the evidence and the ones who know about it," said Jackie.

"We do that and the family will have the Feds and God knows who come down on us. Unless it looks like an isolated incident," said Michael.

"An accident?" said Serena.

"Exactly," replied Jackie.

"I don't like killing cops. Those men have families," said Michael, disagreeing.

"It can't be helped. Our sworn duty is to protect the organization and all its valued associates," Jackie said firmly.

"Very well, but we'll do it my way," said Michael as he went into Jackie's study and gathered the police station blueprints that had been hacked from the city hall database on Jackie's computer.

"We'll proceed to the abandoned subway tunnel that rests under the station and break in through the service hatch, cut the power in the station and release a special gas from the tanks that I have in storage at my pad. The gas contains a compound that blanks out memory and causes delusions; we used it in the CIA to confuse enemies on the battlefield. After exposure to the gas occurs, the brain begins to lose memory; false memories will begin to develop in the victims' minds, and in 24 hours when the effects of the gas wear off, the police will have no memory of what happened."

"Ingenious. That will save us from heat," Jackie said.

"And I won't have to deal with bullshit either," said Michael.

"They'll still have the tapes stored in the evidence room," said Serena.

"That I'll leave to you; you're a professional thief, it's what you do best. In return I'll compensate you both with a portion of the payment I receive on my next contract," Michael offered.

"I'll do it then," agreed Jackie. "Serena, you may be useful for the organization, from what Michael has told me about your background. Are you interested?"

"I'm in as long as I'm provided twenty percent," replied Serena.

"You do this one thing right and you're in."

On the other side of town in the main hospital, Commissioner Hamilton looked through the observation window as the doctor finished stitching the cuts and bruises on Frank's face. Jack was in the same room, resting. After finishing, the doctor met with the commissioner in the hall.

"How are they, doctor?" she asked.

"Detective Watson will be here for a few days. He acquired mild trauma to left side of his brain, but his concussion should be healed in a week. He will be able to return to active duty afterwards," said the doctor.

"What about Jack Harris?"

"Unfortunately, Detective Harris will be here for a while. The crash caused five broken ribs. It also raised his blood pressure from all the excitement. He suffered a severe stroke when he arrived at the hospital. He is stable now, but I strongly recommend retirement when he is discharged. If he were to have another attack, he might not make it," said the doctor.

"I'll bring in his papers when Jack is well. Poor old-timer, it's going to break him to pieces," said Commissioner Hamilton.

Back at Jackie's apartment complex, Michael and the others gathered the tools they needed for the job. Putting a large footlocker on Jackie's favorite oak table, Jackie opened it, seeing all the necessary equipment, consisting of chain cutters, acetylene torches, electric drills, security device scramblers, two sets of facemasks, and a few pairs of black gloves. Michael peeked over to take a look.

"Perfect. Let's head to my place; we'll pick up the other stuff there," said Michael. After arriving at Michael's pad, Michael crouched down in the den and opened a small tile on the floor, pulling up a black case filled with gas tank grenades, a set of flare sticks, and a pair of pistols with silencers.

"We used this stuff to brainwash witnesses when doing interrogations. Too bad it got banned," said Michael.

"It doesn't matter, as long as we get the job done," said Jackie.

"Don't worry about pulling pins. I rigged these babies with a timer on each one; we'll set them all off at once by remote control. Take these portable radios." Michael tossed Serena and Jackie each a pistol and some clips. "Just in case. Don't worry, it's not loaded. Serena baby, grab me a few gas masks from the trunk in the closet, would you please." Michael pointed her to the iron closet.

"Here you go," said Serena, handing Michael the gas masks.

"Good, let's go to work," said Jackie as they headed out the door to his van, carrying the equipment. It was 8 pm and the building was being filled with a string of officers arriving for the evening shift; it was business as usual. However, underneath the station in the abandoned subway tunnel, different things were brewing.

Serena and Jackie began to burn through the sealed service hatch while Michael opened the roof service hatch and began crawling through the ventilation systems to set up the bombs. An hour had passed. "How we doing?" asked Michael over his radio.

"We're doing fine baby, we just cut through the main locks," said Serena as she and Jackie pushed up the hatch lid and began to crawl up the ladder that led into the basement.

"Great, give me ten more minutes I'll have all the gas bombs set. Then you cut the power from the basement electric generators and when the place goes dark I'll set off the bombs on the roof," said Michael coolly. Entering the basement electrical room, Jackie pulled out the chain cutters and began to cut through the locks on the generator cages that guarded the main switch.

"All right Mike, we're ready to pull the switch," said Jackie.

"I'm all set up here over," replied Michael over his radio.

"Ready in 5, 4, 3, 2, 1... "GO!" Jackie counted over his radio as he pulled the switch. The entire station went pitch black.

"Hey, what the hell!" yelled Commissioner Hamilton.

"Someone get the lights!" yelled another officer.

"Grooving," said Michael as he detonated the bombs. From room to room flashes of light and gas blew from the ventilation systems, releasing the toxin and knocking out everyone within the rooms. Some officers became unconscious immediately and others suffered delusional fits until the passed out.

"Go! Go! Go!" yelled Michael over his radio. Jackie and Serena put on their gas masks and headed up the basement stairs to the first floor as Michael lowered himself with his mask on, swinging in from the window. The trio met in the squad room; lighting their flare sticks, they headed to the archive room. "Let's find the tapes in the archive vault and get out of here quick," said Jackie.

"Right," said Serena. Jackie took a quick look in the evidence room and saw a score he could not believe. "I see beautiful green and golden delights, magical dope, tonight is the night, yeah!!," sung Jackie, as he stuffed a spare duffel bag he had on him with stacks of confiscated cash, cocaine, and stolen gold jewelry. "hell yeah," sang Jackie.

Michael spotted Jackie and was pissed. "What the hell do you think you're doing? We have a job to do!"

"Just taking a little kickback," said Jackie happily, showing Michael the stolen stash. Michael and Serena smiled and shook their heads in agreement. "Take it," they said in unison. The trio looked down the hall and discovered that the evidence vault was locked down tight, so Serena took out the drill equipment and began to work on the vault. After about 20 minutes she managed to break the locks on the vault. After a quick search Jackie grabbed the tapes labeled "Anderson and Scarfo Penthouse shooting." The sound of sirens could be heard in the distance and they all knew it was time to go. Racing down the stairs to the hatchway in the basement floor, they could hear police entering the building. One cop saw Michael jumping down the hatch and fired, but Michael disappeared in a thick cloud of smoke; a detonated smoke ball. They headed out the back entrance of the abandoned subway and into Jackie's ride. The trio took off speeding with smiles and laughter; it was time to celebrate their success.

"That was way too easy," said Serena, worried.

"Who cares, let's party! There has to be at least 300 grand here with all this loot," said Jackie.

"Let's head to my place and we'll split up the score," said Michael, pulling out a cigarette to smoke. They sped off to Michael's pad.

Back at police headquarters ambulances had picked up the officers who had been exposed to the toxin and brought them to the hospital, including Commissioner Hamilton.

On the upper west side, Franco Scarfo sat in his luxury apartment snorting a hit of cocaine with Phillips as they listened to the news, hearing of the robbery and poisoning at the police station. "Get a load of this. The cops get a bad case of gas and fall down, the commissioner is in some hospital bed and that's good news for us," said Franco, sparking up a cigarette.

"Wonder who could have set it up," replied Phillips.

"Reported to be done by professionals, with over 300,000 dollars worth of stolen goods, drugs, jewels, and cash," said Franco.

"It would good if we could get the guys who pulled off this job."

"Big fucking score indeed."

"Something's is eating me though."

"What?" Franco asked.

"The anti bioterrorist department discovered a residue of the gas that was used on the victims. The gas changes memory in the brain causing delusion and false memories," said Phillips.

"And?" said Franco impatiently.

"FDMI90 was a toxic gas we used in the CIA to torture enemies. From the description it sounds like the same one."

"What's your point?"

"Only CIA on the COBRAKNIGHT mission, and only personnel in the top class within our unit, had access to this toxin," said Phillips.

"Damascus," they both said.

"The son of a bitch didn't know who you were at the warehouse deal. Find him, get close to him, get him into our pocket, then kill him," said Franco.

"No problem. We'll bring him in and say it's a special job or some bullshit, and then when we get what we want we'll clip him," said Phillips.

"Find out what you can from him; just say you got into town for vacation, or something."

"Right."

"Get on it immediately," said Franco sternly.

Back at Michael's pad, Serena, Jackie, and Michael unloaded the stash on the table to check out their spoils.

"We got the tapes, we got the moola, we got the power baby," laughed Jackie. Serena counted the stacks of cash while Michael weighed the coke on a small scale he had pulled out of the kitchen. Hearing the crisp sound of those bills was so sweet.

"Boys, we got us here just in cash 300 grand," said Serena happily.

"On the jewelry, I know a fence who will give us 20 grand," said Jackie. "How much do you think well get for those 5 kilos?"

"After weighing them, another 300 grand," replied Michael confidently.

"A whopping total of 620,000 dollars. It's going to be a good season," said Michael, laughing as he popped open a chilled bottle of expensive champagne and poured it into some glasses.

"Here's to us, salut!" said Jackie as they toasted their success.

They divided up the spoils quickly. "Mikey baby, why don't we all go some place nice tonight to celebrate," giggled Serena.

"Yeah Mike, that sounds like a good idea," said Jackie. Michael pulled out a card of his pocket. At first he thought was a cigarette. The card read, THE BLACK SPIDER CLUB.

"Ladies and gents, find yourself a tux and dress, we're going to my club for a hell of a night," said Michael.

"I didn't know you owned a nightclub," said Serena.

"There are a lot of things you don't know about me, but we'll leave that for later. Come on, the night is young and I'm sure we all want to paint this town red," said Michael.

They all agreed in eager anticipation.

26

"AN UNFORTUNATE MISTAKE"

The night was young and everyone was eager to celebrate. Serena and Michael went and bought the best tuxedo and dress they could find from MAXIMILLON'S Department Store. They met Jackie on the Strip, with the best glitz of night-life in Vegas among the nightclubs, concert theaters, and casinos. Louie, the bouncer, opened the grand, golden oak entrance doors for Michael and his guests, "Good evening Mr. Damascus, we have a hot lineup tonight, boss."

"Hey Louie, keep it real tonight," Michael replied.

"Have a good time ladies and gentlemen, and Mike don't worry, I always keep the assholes out." Louie chomped on his cheap cigar.

"Yeah you do," said Michael with a smile. Tipping Louie with a hundred dollar bill, Michael breathed in peace; the club had never looked so good. The elegance of the place was extravagant; it was like the posh, dim, candle-lit clubs from classic black and white Hollywood movies. The teal blue walls were marble and a three-level dance floor rose above the main stage. Twin stairways led up to the dance floors and the beautiful Italian-tiled bars were stocked with expensive liquors and cigars. Amid the romantic lighting, the place was filled to the brim with Las Vegas's elite. The flashiest New Orleans jazz band in the city was playing. On the main stage stood a hip old black gentlemen dressed in a black silk suit and tie. He cradled a saxophone and was speaking into a microphone; he was the main MC of Michael's club.

"Ah right ladies and gentlemen welcome tonight to the Black Spider, you get ready to get hopping because we're going to get rocking. Please welcome from New Orleans, Louisiana, the show band that always brings down the house, The Mickey Blues Boys, with me as your host, Mickey Blue Robinson. We're going to play for you an old-time favorite. Here's a song called Raven's Love."

Sweetness filled the night air as the band played. Serena stared in awe at the magnificence of the club. "Right out of classic Hollywood, I love it," she said.

The trio sat down to be served. Serena and Jackie were living it up. "Mike, this place is amazing," said Jackie as the waitress poured him a glass of wine.

"Glad you both like it; I just got the place running a few weeks ago after renovations. Good old Mickster on the stage there sold this place to me a while back, and we've been good friends ever since."

"You know a place like this would be perfect for you know what I mean," said Jackie.

"I've been thinking about that." "So how about it?"

"You tell the Don I'm open for any opportunity as long as I get 40 percent of the action," Michael answered.

"Good I'll talk to him." The audience clapped after song ended. A stunning woman with short blonde hair wearing a glittering red dress walked on stage and the spotlight turning on her.

"And now, ladies and gentlemen please welcome the main beauty of the Black Spider, the sassy, sparkling, and saucy dream, Miss Isabelle Webster," Mickey announced as the drums beat rose and the horns bellowed.

"Hello boys, this one is for you, it's called Lovers Tonight," said Isabelle as she began to sing. The guests applauded. The room seemed to go motionless as they listened to her heavenly voice, which could only be described as angelic. Michael put his arm around Serena as they sat close together and kissed.

As the night went on the two embraced on the dance floor, swaying in time with the distant voice of Mickey singing Jazzing on a Sunday. At the end of the night, after everyone had gone home, Michael met with Mickey Blue, introducing him to Serena and Jackie.

"Mickey, another fantastic performance my man," said Michael, impressed.

"Ah Mike, what can I say, going into business with you has been the best thing I've ever done. Ever since the Scarfos' shut down my old club, I never thought I'd be in the night club business again," said Mickey Blue, shaking hands in agreement.

"I'd like you to meet my girl Serena and my best friend Jackie," said Michael.

"A pleasure," said Jackie shaking Mickey Blue's hand.

"May I just give you a kiss for that beautiful sound earlier," said Serena.

"Sure honey, an old guy like me needs a little sugar now and then," Mickey Blue joked as Serena kissed him on the check.

"So tell me Mickey, where is Isabelle? I want to congratulate her on a great job she did tonight," Michael smiled.

"Sure, she's upstairs in her dressing room. She' s ready to call it a night; you better go see her now if you still want to catch her."

Serena gave Michael a look of disapproval, and then smiling said, "Go ahead, I won't be jealous."

Michael went up to Isabelle's dressing room while the others continued to talk downstairs. He knocked on Isabelle's door. "Come in," she called.

"Issy girl, you killed them tonight. You're going to put this club through the roof," said Michael as he came up behind her to rub her back.

"Mikey, ever since we were kids you've always called me that," said Isabelle, teasing.

"I love you like family, what can I say?"

Isabelle sat feeling a little depressed, looking at Michael with sad eyes, "I wish you could love me the way I do you. Who's the new girl, by the way?"

"Her name's Serena, and what's that supposed to mean?" Michael asked, a little uncomfortably.

"Nothing. I just wish you and me could spend some more time together," Isabelle pouted.

"Look Isabelle, you know I've always cared about you like a sister. What we had a long time ago was good, but things are different now."

"I just miss you sometimes, that's all."

"I know, but it's not going to happen. Ever since Katrina died I've looked at you differently; you and she were so much alike, and every time we were alone and I looked into your eyes all I could see was her. Besides, you have Bobby Scarfo. He loves you deeply, you know that," said Michael.

"I know, I love him but not the same way I love you."

"Please try to accept the way things are now," said Michael.

Giving him a little smile, she hugged him and wished him goodnight. Just before leaving, Michael handed her a gift of 2,000 bucks as a bonus for her performance.

After Michael shut the door behind him, Isabelle fell to the floor and began crying with longing for the man she'd once had. Michael felt sadness creep into his gut as he walked downstairs but cheered up upon seeing Serena's smile. After wishing good night to Mickey, they all went home to sleep the night away.

A day later Frank Watson checked out of the hospital early. The doctor approached Frank with a sad look. "I'm sorry Frank, we tried all we could, but Mr. Harris just let go. I guess the impact of the car crash was too much on his system. He died last night. We didn't want to tell you until you were ready to go back on duty," said the doctor.

Frank lost it and stormed out of the hospital in anger. Without thinking, he ran to the parking lot, and began crying. "Bastards! I'm going to find those sons of bitches and I'm going to bust them one way or another," raged Frank, he then called a taxi to go the police station. Upon entering headquarters he saw that the station was a wreck and that investigation teams were looking over the place. "What the hell happened in here Jim?" Frank asked an officer just coming into the room.

"We had a robbery here last night. The strange thing is, nobody who was here last night remembers a thing, not seeing anyone, nothing. I just came in this morning and found the place like this; the other officers and the commissioner who were here last night were taken to the hospital, but were released this morning. They just got back. Physically they weren't harmed, but they don't remember a thing," Officer Jim Maceson repeated.

"You've got to be kidding me. The place looks blown to hell and no one remember zip," barked Frank in surprise.

"I'm sorry to hear about Jack. Joe told me the doctor broke the news to him when he was at the hospital checking up on you guys," said Jim.

"Forget about it. Did the cameras pick up anything?" asked Frank.

"Nothing, unfortunately," said Jim.

"Damn it. Jim I got a hunch who did this, I got to go." Frank took off out the door.

Frank began to check the computer system in his squad car for any businesses registered under the name of Damascus; the only one he found was Damascus and Son, Tailors.

Frank sped off to the tailor shop. Joseph Damascus, the owner of the store, was just finishing tailoring a pair of slacks when Frank barreled in. "Detective Frank Watson, Las Vegas PD."

"Officer, what's wrong?" asked Joseph.

"What's wrong is my partner is dead because of you," yelled Frank in anger, slamming the old man on a table and positioning his oversized factory style sewing machine with a needle coming down so that it would cut up his face.

"I don't know what you're talking about; I've been here all week! Oh sweet Jesus!!" screamed Joseph.

"He's right, let him go, I was with him working the shop," said a young boy, coming up front from the back of the store.

"Peter! Stay out of this son," yelled the old man.

"No! Let my papa go," protested Peter.

Frank freed the old man just before he could be injured. "Then who else by the name of Damascus could it be old coot?" demanded Frank.

"My older son Michael, that low down, mob hustling bum," said Joseph.

"Who?" Frank asked.

"Years ago, my son used to hang around a bunch of thugs, wise guy bums; he never listened to me and he got pinched once for breaking and entering but the police couldn't find enough evidence to get him convicted so they let him go. Afterwards, he joined the armed services with his sister. Two years ago it was reported to us that she was killed on a mission. Our son was said to be missing, and we haven't seen him since." Joseph paused to catch his breath from the all the excitement.

"It has to be him. Some joker mentioned his name and was killed right before my eyes," said Frank.

"I'd bet, if anything, he's probably still alive," said Joseph.

"Got a picture of this guy?"

Peter handed Frank a picture of a man in his late twenties, dressed in army uniform.

"Do you think he would come here to Vegas?" asked Frank.

"I wouldn't doubt it, he and his low life friends used to stay here in town before he left for active duty."

"Thanks. Sorry about the ruffling up," said Frank as he tossed a hundred dollar bill at the old man and took off out the door.

For days Frank searched every shady place he could think of and for days he found nothing. "I'll find you, you son of a bitch and when I do, you're dead," vowed Frank.

But Michael always remembered to cover his tracks and Frank couldn't do anything but bide his time.

Late one night, Michael was called up for a meeting with Don Santerini and Serena stepped out to do some shopping for their home. Michael brought his mentor the Don a very special tribute.

"My boy, you never cease to amaze me," said Don Felice.

"50,000 dollars in tribute, a gift to you Don Felice," said Michael.

"Jackie has told me good things about you and your girl," said Don Felice, smiling.

"It's always a pleasure to work for you." Michael shook his boss's hand.

"I'm proud of how you handled that little unannounced job you pulled the other night," said Don Felice.

"We got rid of the evidence, and the cops don't remember a thing," said Michael.

"I would still be watchful son," cautioned Don Felice.

"What do you mean?" inquired Michael.

"Word from the street is that some hot-headed cop has it in for you. He roughed up some of our disloyal associates."

"What?"

"An unfortunate mistake," sighed Don Felice.

"Do you want me to take care of these rats?" questioned Michael firmly.

"No. They've already been dealt with, but go and put this pugnacious pig out of his misery; he makes the organization look bad. We can't have two-cent coppers walking all over us, can we?"

"But Felice, I can't, he's a cop," said Michael.

"Do it, kill him and put him in a casket," said Don Felice.

"But to whack a cop – the media will be all over us if they find out."

"Don't worry. We've paid most of the media off."

"I still have reservations about this," said Michael.

"Doesn't matter. We can't have this dick meddling around in our business. If you let this guy go, you'll be the one in a body bag, get me?" said Don Felice, frowning.

"Yeah," said Michael.

"Our guys have seen him every night around 9 pm at Sammy's Bar."

"Very well, I'll remove him discreetly," Michael reluctantly agreed.

Meanwhile, in a grimy old apartment bedroom, Duval cleaned his pistols with a thin gun brush, waiting until he got the call. Franco had one of his thugs from the warehouse incident spot Serena and take her picture. A half-hour later, a knock on the door announced the arrival of the photo of Duval's new target. "Pretty piece of ass," said Duval as he inhaled on a joint, blowing the smoke into a cloud and watching as the smoke thinned out in the room. "Too bad this bitch has to go," he said, smiling sickly as he burned a hole through the photograph with his joint and then stamped out the charred photo on the ground. Pushing the clips into his pistol and grabbing his light, long coat he said to himself "Time to die, girly." He slammed the door shut and set out to find his prey.

Duval drove aimlessly around the city looking for his victim until he caught sight of Serena heading home on Otis Way, back from a wine store with a special present for her lover, a bottle of expensive champagne to commemorate their one month anniversary of being together. Duval stepped out of his car, following far behind Serena, but she could smell his human scent. She smiled to herself and slipped into an alleyway and hid in the dark shadows between the dimly lit street lamps.

"What the fuck?" said Duval as he walked closer to the corner and slid against the wall to peek and aim his gun in the alleyway.

He saw nothing in the dark. "Where did she go?" said Duval under his breath.

"Right here, big boy," said Serena as she flashed out from the shadow and grabbed Duval, shredding his face with her claws, looking into his eyes as hers glowed. She put him in a trance, and then kissed him before she gnawed on his neck, draining him of blood until he fell to ground. Weak, Duval pulled out his pistol to shoot, but Serena stomped on his arm, breaking it and his shoulder while pinning him down. She grabbed his gun and shot him in the head. Blood poured out of his skull like the waterspout of a statue, and Duval lay dead to the sidewalk. Serena dragged his bloodstained corpse to a part in the dark alley to let the other vampires in the area feed off his remains.

27

"KILL THE PIG"

Thursday at 9 pm, Frank Watson had just finished his evening shift. He was tired and frustrated, so he decided to head over to Sammy's Bar for a drink. He couldn't get over the fact that finding his suspect now seemed impossible. At 9:30 he was heading out the door of the bar to be picked up by his wife and young son when the sound of gunshots came from the roof. Frank instinctively fell to the ground, cocking his pistol with fear and looking around. Just seconds before Frank's family arrived on the scene, Michael pulled the trigger on his sniper rifle. The bullet went straight through Frank's heart, killing him instantly. The car stopped at the curb and his young son jumped out, running to his daddy and crying, as Frank's wife screamed with shock. Michael's face went white with shock. He dropped the rifle, seeing the young kid and wife screaming while he stood motionless. "What have I done!" said Michael as he jumped from the roof onto his hover bike and headed back to his pad.

Serena was worried as she looked out the window in Michael's pad.

"What have I done!" again said Michael. He began to lose it, breaking down in tears, his mind swarming with the guilt, the voices again tormenting him. "Murderer, so much for your honor, join us in death, angel of death you are, in death you're ours," said the voices in his mind.

"NO! NO!" screamed Michael as he crashed his hover bike into a guardrail, flying over as it exploded on the highway. Michael fell off the overpass.

Serena sensed her lover was in danger and teleported him from the crash, to bring him home safely. Still in shock and grief from his actions, Serena put him in bed to rest.

For two days Michael heard strange sounds and evil laughs throughout the air, as his mind and body pulsed with incredible pain. His eyes began to turn white and he had convulsions, coughing up blood. He felt worthless and he wanted to die.

Grabbing the knife that he always kept in his room, Michael slit one of his wrists. The blood dripped and then disappeared as his wound instantly healed; Serena came into the room and saw what he was doing. "What the hell are you doing, Michael!"

"I want to end this, I can't take seeing their faces anymore, all the people I've killed, I see them, so much blood."

"Michael! Don't you dare do this. I love you! Are you out of your mind?" screamed Serena with fear.

"Maybe," said Michael. Then he stood motionless and it stopped. The pain left him. Michael came back to himself. He felt very weak and desperate to feed.

Serena took him to a part of the city that was perfect for hunting, where a few scumbags would be easy pickings. Two drug dealers were selling crack to a young kid. Michael's insane hunger went wild and he killed them, draining their life force dry, except for the kid, whom he let go, remembering the face of Watson's little boy.

Falling to the ground Michael began to weep at the monster he had truly become. Serena had forgotten the curse that came along with the dark gift. Many vampires became bitter or cruel or insane, or even suicidal.

Back at the crime scene where Watson had been killed, Commissioner Hamilton saw the forensics team studying evidence while the coroner packed up the body in a van. In anger she vowed in her heart, "We won't rest until every one of these mob bastards is taken down."

After consoling Watson's family, the Commissioner called the FBI; when they heard the story the Feds agreed to help.

Once the reporters had finished at the scene, Commissioner Hamilton put a call in on her car radio. "This is Commissioner Hamilton. I want officers sweeping the scene, no one gets in or out."

"Copy that," said the officer on down the line.

"God, who could have done this?" Commissioner Hamilton looked downhearted as she saw the forensics people zip up Watson's corpse in a bag and load it into the van, closing the vehicle doors behind them.

Across town in the dark shadows of a subterranean grotto lit by burning torches, two vampires were looking at the beauty of the city at night through a shimmering pool of water in a fountain, seeing mortals come and go, one of them a beautiful young blonde, another with the dark beauty of the orient.

"You want to be like them, don't you?" said the Asian vampire.

"Who wouldn't? When you live forever life can be quite boring," said Scarlet the blonde one.

The other looked on the murals on the walls, murals that showed the race of the undead, images of men in dark robes slaughtering vampires, one showing a man in a black with long hair dueling with another man.

"You don't believe the one will come to end this war, do you?" said Marianna the Asian, looking at the mural.

"Maybe the prophecy is just a lie, or a dream," replied the blonde one.

Suddenly the Asian vampire fell to the ground shaking violently in a trance, her blue eyes burning white-hot.

"Marianna!" screamed the blonde as she saw her sister enter a deep trance. The Asian vampire experienced a vision of terror, a man in black with long hair dressed in a black coat, fighting a dark figure in a black cloak that bore the face of a red dragon.

The Asian vampire grew silent as the trance left her.

"What did you see?" urged the blonde.

"The chosen one has come. He will be a great warrior, fallen, fallen to be chosen to rise again to grace," said the Asian vampire.

Helping her sister up, the blonde vampire said, "Tell our Lord, he must know this immediately." The two left the chamber. A dark mist flowed out of the shadows and red eyes appeared everywhere. A deep, resigned laughter echoed and then the shadow beings fled through the cracks in the walls.

28

"AN OLD FRIEND"

For days Michael locked himself away in his room as Serena wept. The guilt from all the killings he had committed was too much, from his years in the CIA up to the present. In the back of his mind he could still hear the screams of his victims begging him to let them live. Michael felt worthless. He wanted to die. He had terrifying nightmares of past assassin missions where he saw his victims being killed and tortured brutally; their eyes were plucked out by CIA agents. As the nightmares continued, Michael found himself in a dark plain of caves, where alien creatures full of teeth and fangs flourished made of fish bodies that stunk like rotting garbage. In the underground scum ponds the he saw bubbling lakes of green and blue blood, giant demon leeches that had human faces; these creatures tormented him by tearing his flesh apart and draining him of his blood. He saw himself turn into a hideous slithering beast with three heads. Then, a huge earthquake occurred, causing a chasm to open up; Michael fell into a deep pool of burning oil and fire.

He woke up screaming in terror; a large demonic creature with the body of a man and the head of an anteater sat on top of his chest. He could feel the weight of this thing crushing his insides. Michael's pupils shrunk. He couldn't breathe and he was kept from screaming as this evil aberration stuck its stagnant snout over Michael's face, sucking out his prey's soul.

Michael screamed as he woke up. His face was covered with sweat and his eyes burned with pain. The night terror was so real to him that his arms felt like they had been singed and his body was covered in bruises. He then passed out again and dreamed again about Anna, the vampire who had seen him in a vision.

After waking from those two nightmares he could not get back to sleep. Insomnia plagued Michael for days from the guilt in his mind and he longed for peace. Serena felt his pain. She too felt guilt and remorse for the killings she had committed and wept intensely.

Then, one night as he lay in bed, Michael felt a strange presence in the room. A voice spoke to him, "Come back to God." Then it left. Michael was shocked; he did not understand what was happening. He thought, "Just me being crazy."

Feeling calmer, he decided to go out and get some night air, while he let Serena rest and get some sleep. He headed to a bar he knew, a bar where he and his old army friends would go whenever they were on vacation in Vegas. It was on the strip and was called the Lagoon Lounge. Michael hadn't been there in years.

Sitting down at the bar he ordered a Cosmo martini, trying to make sense of why he had let the Don talk him into killing Watson. He couldn't believe the shit that had hit the fan a few days earlier in the form of his own personal crisis. In his heart though, he still ached for Watson's family. Although he did not mind killing criminals or rival mobsters, Michael hated to kill innocent people. Even as a vampire he had standards.

A man with blonde hair, wearing dark glasses, a black coat and red tie, came into the bar. "Give me a beer," the man addressed the bartender. The man looked over and saw Michael sitting in sorrow. "It's a sad sight to see a man depressed in a dismal place like this," said the man.

Annoyed by the stranger, he raised his head. "What's it to you?"

"Nothing. I just hate to see an old friend feeling down."

"Old friend? I don't even know you," said Michael.

"Sure you do. Don't you recognize me? It's me, Rodney, Rodney Phillips. Remember Unit 1024 CIA?" Rodney removed his glasses.

Michael's face brightened as he remembered. "Rodney! Oh Rodney I can't believe it, it's good to see you," Michael said as he hugged his old friend.

"It's good to see you too. It's been two years," said Phillips. "I thought you were dead after the last mission we were on."

"I was lucky; after I was in the hospital for a year the doctors were able to get me to recover fully."

"I'm sorry about your sister's death. At the bureau they told me what happened."

"What are you doing out here?" asked Michael.

"I've been on a case here for the last few months. We've been trying to locate some terrorists who are in hiding. I've been taking a few days off; the job has been stressful on me. You look pale yourself, are you feeling ill?" asked Phillips.

"I've been a little under the weather lately," Michael admitted.

"Remember how we used to come here before we got started?" Phillips reminisced.

"Yeah I do – this was our favorite hangout," answered Michael.

"What have you been doing here in Vegas?" asked Phillips.

"After I quit the service, I decided to start over in Vegas. My father and younger brother moved out here but I don't see them. Anyway, I couldn't stay in the CIA after seeing Katrina's murder on the Strozzinburg mission."

"So what've you been doing back here all this time?"

"I opened up a night club on some veteran grant money I received from the government."

"You mean that new one on the Strip that just opened a few weeks ago, the Black Spider in Old Vegas?" asked Phillips.

"That's the one."

"Then how come you're back here again at this old hole?"

"I just needed a place to think. Life has been difficult for me. Ever since Katrina died, all I ever do now is find ways to keep myself busy, to not dwell on the pain," said Michael.

"Maybe you could help me catch these terrorist bastards."

"I think I'll pass."

"The bureau will pay you well. You were the best assassin we ever had. Think of it as showing patriotism to your country again, I know you've always valued that."

Michael sat for a minute and thought. "Very well, but I would do this favor for you as an old friend and nothing more. No payment will be necessary. It'll make me feel alive again to nail some scum and save some lives." Michael felt obligated to redeem himself for killing an innocent man.

"Good I'll inform the team that you and I will be working together. Why don't you join me for dinner tonight at Tommy's restaurant? It might cheer you up a bit," offered Phillips.

The two headed off in Phillips car to Tommy's for dinner. Tommy Santerini came over to the two of them. Tommy was a young man of the age of 26, good looking, smart and always well mannered. He was also the head chef of his establishment, where he was always dressed in a culinary uniform and filled with delight. "Bon appetite gentleman, such a fine duo to dine at my humble abode," Tommy joked.

Phillips answered with a grin. "Please don't flatter yourself Tommy, thanks," he said.

"You two have always been good customers in the past, it's on the house tonight, I got beautiful steaks for you both and some ziti," said Tommy.

The duo conversed while being served the ziti with steamed vegetables and fat, juicy T-bone steaks. "How have you been since Katrina died?" asked Michael.

"It's been hard me for as well. She didn't tell you that we were engaged just before the Strozzinburg mission?" said Phillips.

"No, she told me nothing. Anyway, have you found anyone new?" asked Michael.

"No, not since then, what about you?"

"I've been seeing someone new. Her name is Serena, and she's been the best thing that's happened to me. Although I have been having nightmares lately."

"What about Isabelle?"

"We split after Katrina died, things were not going well," replied Michael.

"Too bad, I thought you two made a good couple," said Phillips.

"Things change Rodney."

The two talked long into the night. As Phillips was dropping Michael off on the Strip, he received a call on his phone. He called Michael back over to the car and said "Meet me at the Lagoon Lounge tomorrow at 8 pm. The Director of CIA Affairs just called me. Our mission will begin tomorrow night."

Before Michael arrived home at midnight he vomited up the food he'd eaten for dinner killing a stray dog for its life force. Most human food is poisonous to vampires but he was sorry to get rid of the fine meal he'd eaten with Phillips.

Serena opened the door, hugging and kissing him. "I've been very worried about you ever since what happened a few days ago," said Serena.

"Things are better now. I'm going to make it all right," said Michael.

"But how?" asked a worried Serena.

"I have a job set up tomorrow. An old friend from the bureau needs my help."

"I don't like it. I feel that something bad will happen," said Serena, not liking this plan of action.

"I have to do this baby. If I can help save some innocent lives then I can make up my debt for killing that cop; it will make me feel better, and maybe there'll be no more bad dreams."

"We take lives, like I said before."

"Even though I kill for hire, I would prefer to kill a scumbag than an innocent man. Call it a sense of twisted honor," said Michael.

"You're a vampire now darling, face it – you're a killer," said Serena.

"That doesn't mean that I don't have a choice. I do, and I want to redeem what little of a soul I have left," said Michael.

Serena looked at him sadly and kissed him. "Hold me tight please," she asked.

"What?" Michael asked as she embraced him and placed her head on his heart. Tears began to run down her face.

"I just don't want to lose you Michael. I love you so much, you know that, don't you?" said Serena.

"I know you do, but I have to do this. I promise to be careful." Serena hugged him tightly; they began to kiss and then made love in the dark night.

The call later that night came from Phillips as Michael waited in his pad.

29

Michael arrived at the Lagoon Lounge the next night at 8 pm. In a corner of the room he saw Phillips and a group of ten men talking and he walked over to them in the dimly lit room.

"Damascus, get over here," said the man Michael presumed to be the team leader.

"Welcome to the team. Now enough chit chat, let's get to business; a band of Al-Qaeda terrorist have been spotted at the Montgomery Casino. Undercover personnel spotted five of our suspects last night setting up a bomb in the basement. It seems their intent is to demolish the place after robbing it to fund their terror cells. Our orders are to locate that bomb, dismantle it, and capture or kill these mad men," said Phillips.

"When do we leave?" asked Michael.

"Immediately."

Speeding off in Phillips' cleaning van, the team changed into cleaning uniforms for undercover duty. After being cleared for admittance into the Montgomery's basement, Michael spotted the terrorists on the lower level.

Signaled by Phillips, the team quietly surrounded the terrorists in an attempt to corner them around the large generators and security computer system.

"Now!" yelled the team leader. The men drew their guns on the terrorists.

"Drop the guns, you're under arrest!" Phillips yelled.

The terrorists retaliated by blowing up a small gas propane tank. The explosion killed two of the anti-terrorist team, blowing them to bits.

"Drop them!" yelled Phillips as he and Michael fired, unloading bullets from their M16 machine guns. Two of the terrorist's heads exploded and brains flew all over the concrete floor.

"Long live Jihad!" screamed one of the terrorists as he attempted to become a suicide bomber, pulling a pin off a hand grenade. Michael flipped off the ceiling and kicked the grenade out of the crazed terrorist's hand, causing the grenade to explode in mid-air. Michael knocked out the terrorist; another terrorist was getting ready to shoot Michael in the back with his AK47. Phillips spotted the terrorist about to shoot Michael and shot him in the head, saving Michael's life. The team leader had managed to teargas the escaping terrorists; the team put them in handcuffs and then marched them outside to an armored prison truck.

The media outside the casino reported the story. In the background, Michael turned to Phillips. "Thanks for saving me," said Michael.

"What are old friends for?" said Phillips, "And we won't forget how you helped us out tonight."

"No problem, keep in touch," said Michael as he caught a cab to head home for the night.

30

"SABOTAGE AND DESTRUCTION"

On the way home, Michael felt he had redeemed himself for Watson's death and he was at peace, for now.

Just at that moment, in the Santerini's business district, Sonny Scarfo and Albert Scarfo sat in a gray car holding two detonators; they had rigged the entire block to blow, disregarding the innocent people that were in these buildings. As they flicked the switches, the entire block was blown up, killing all who were in the way of this firestorm. Massive fireballs fell to the ground, side effects of the multiple explosions that had occurred. The two snakes took off, laughing wickedly to report their boss. From his new penthouse rooftop Frank Scarfo looked over to the burning Santerini district; he held a glass of wine in his hand to celebrate his success. "Bye bye Felice, your time has ended old man. This town is mine now," said Franco Scarfo.

Jackie, Sal, Anthony, and Paulie took in the destruction from the Terrace Tower. They were in shock.

"Oh God, those innocent people." Paulie clenched his hands to his mouth.

"Frank Scarfo!" screamed Anthony in rage.

"That fucking murdering cocksucker ordered this hit," said Paulie.

"All those innocent lives, not to mention that we all had family who worked in that district, all dead!" Don Felice swore.

"I say let's kill the fucker right now!" said Jackie in hateful rage.

"It had to be Frank Scarfo. Godfather Giorgio would never allow innocent people to be whacked," said Don Felice angrily. "Call a meeting immediately. Get Michael and Serena here. We all have to resolve this now!"

Paulie called Michael immediately. Michael had just gotten in the door of his apartment when the phone rang. Serena answered. "Yes, it's Serena."

"Serena get Michael on the phone right now, it's Paulie!" yelled Paulie on the other line.

Michael rushed to the phone. "Whoa Paulie what's wrong?" asked Michael, concerned.

"We just took a major hit in our business district!" yelled Paulie.

"What happened?"

"Franco Scarfo just had his boys nuke the place. We had over a hundred people who worked in that district, people with families," Paulie choked out.

"Oh God!" said Michael.

"Get over here now! Both of you!" yelled Paulie, as he slammed the phone down.

Serena and Michael quickly teleported to the Terrace Tower. They ran upstairs fast and barged into the meeting room where the rest of the family was waiting.

"How the hell did you get here so quickly!" said Anthony in surprise.

"You called me on my new pager, don't worry about it," Michael lied.

"What difference does it make, they're here," said Jackie, all fired up.

"All of you sit down look at this. The media is having a frenzy." Paulie turned up the volume on the TV where the news was covering the story.

"The police are just itching to get us; luckily we've paid off a few city officials. A report has gone out that a broken gas line was the cause of the explosion" said Don Felice.

"We can't just let Franco get away with this. He just killed over a hundred people," said Anthony.

"We won't. I just called on Godfather Scarfo to deal with Franco. He'll have him pay us for the damages and the funerals, and he's also giving his guy a going over," said Don Felice. "Besides, despite the issues Godfather Scarfo and I have with each other and our organizations, he still respects me as a former friend from the old days and he knows that it is against the mafia code to kill innocent people, especially women and children.

"You think that will stop Franco?" Michael asked.

"It will, because if not, the Godfather himself will kill Franco," said Don Felice.

"That'll stop Franco," said Anthony sarcastically.

"Godfather Scarfo has ties to many loyal and powerful allies in the government; he can be very persuasive," said Don Felice.

"What do we do, just wait it out?" asked Paulie.

"I don't know," replied a worried Don Felice.

31

"CONFLICT AND RESOLUTION"

Godfather Scarfo sat at the Scarfo mansion in his study. He was furious at his nephew's actions. Godfather Scarfo had ordered his men to beat up Franco and bring him in to talk. Dragged in through the doors by Godfather Scarfo's bodyguards and tossed on the floor, Franco looked first at the Godfather's shoes, keeping his head on the ground and wriggling in fear. His hands were pinned over his head.

"That's enough boys, let him up," said Godfather Scarfo. Raising his head up to look at Godfather Scarfo, Franco said nothing.

"You animal – you're no longer in this family. Get out!" said Godfather Scarfo, enraged.

Franco flinched with fear like a child. "But I was only looking to protect our interests," said Franco fearfully.

"Killing over one hundred innocent people is not the way we do it. You have disgraced this family's name," raged Godfather Scarfo.

"But – " started Franco.

"But nothing! You're no longer my nephew; your father would be turning over in his grave if he could see you now. I'm tired of holding your hand like you're a damn whining baby! Get out of my fucking sight." Godfather Scarfo bashed Franco in the head with his pistol.

Dizzy, Franco raced out of the Godfather's home and into the night to go into hiding.

"Don't come back! If you do you are dead!" screamed Godfather Scarfo as he slammed his front door shut.

32

"THE PLOT"

Franco pushed full throttle on the gas, racing his car to a small hideout he knew. He called Sergio Garcia and Phillips along the way.

"Phillips, Garcia, get your asses to the hideout – we have work to do!" Franco ordered.

"Got you, Franco."

After arriving at the hideout the three schemed inside. "It's time we take this town," said Franco.

"How? The Godfather is well protected," said Phillips.

"We'll sneak in when he's asleep and rig his mansion to blow. I want to kill that old fart myself; I want him to see his death coming and beg for mercy before I kill him," laughed Franco wickedly.

Later that night Franco, Phillips, and Garcia took off with an armed armor truck, carrying enough sticks of TNT to annihilate two city buildings. They were disguised as private bank guards with the errand of making a deposit drop at the mansion. After being admitted with passes, Phillips and Garcia knocked out the guards and unloaded the crates full of TNT.

Franco crept upstairs to the Godfather's bedroom, where he was sleeping, while downstairs Garcia and Phillips rigged the explosives to the boiler room beneath the mansion.

"In 10 minutes this place is history," Garcia chuckled wickedly.

"Come on, let's get to the truck," said Phillips.

As Franco entered the Godfather's bedroom, he saw that Bobby Scarfo was also in the room. Bobby was the Godfather's favorite nephew, a good man and loyal to the end. He was in his forties and quite fearless, dressed to kill in a sharp suit.

"Don't even think about it," said Bobby holding up his Magnum.

"But how!" Franco exploded.

"The Godfather has never trusted you; he had a bug put on you while you were beaten up," said Bobby.

"It doesn't matter, because in five minutes this place will be blown to bits," said Franco. He leaped through the window, landing on top of the perfectly positioned truck. It sped off into the night. Bobby picked up Godfather Scarfo and jumped through the window onto a car that Bobby had signaled with his auto drive key. Using the auto drive Bobby got the car to a safe location as the dynamite destroyed the Godfather's mansion.

"That was too close, my boy," said Godfather Scarfo.

"I have to hide you in a special location," said Bobby.

"No, an old mobster like me is not afraid to die. I'm prepared for hell anyway," said Godfather Scarfo.

"We'll meet with our contact, Mr. Cragwell; he'll be able to help us," Bobby replied. They drove off to Cragwell's office to talk.

Phillips had just arrived at his private office to rest after a job well done when he received a call. "Mr. Scarfo, yes I understand, right away, I'll meet you immediately. Please come in," Phillips spoke into the phone.

He changed into his disguise with a black wig, mustache, and beard. A half-hour later Bobby and the Godfather arrived in front of Phillips' office.

"It's show time," said Phillips under his breath, as Bobby and Godfather Scarfo entered the office. "Ah, gentlemen what can I do for you this evening?" asked Phillips with a Russian accent, shaking Bobby's hand.

"We need to purchase a special property for my uncle here," said Bobby.

"But of course. I believe I have the perfect one set up for your business."

"You do?" said Bobby.

"Please direct your attention to the center of the wooden cube base in the middle of the room." Phillips pushing a button on a remote that had a model pop up from the cube base's lid, showing a miniature of a weapon installation and safe house outside of the Las Vegas area.

"Impressive," said Godfather Scarfo in awe.

"Titanium alloy installation, unbreakable, with weapon caches perfect for pest control and a private safe house underneath the foundation. Our organization provides services to the government and private individuals for defense purposes," Phillips explained.

"How much?" Bobby asked.

"Five million."

"Done," said Godfather Scarfo, handing Phillips a check.

"Here are the keys," Phillips offered.

After the Scarfos had left, Phillips looked at the check with greedy eyes. "Forget Franco. I don't need his help; with this I can retire. But Garcia will come in handy." Phillips smiled wickedly.

In the car, Bobby had a hunch that something wasn't right.

"What's wrong, nephew?" asked Godfather Scarfo.

"Something isn't right. Cragwell figured out too quickly that we were in need of a protective location. I don't trust this guy," said Bobby.

"You're right. Lucky for us, I never use real checks," said Godfather Scarfo.

"I better tell Michael about this," thought Bobby as he drove on to an old warehouse in which he could hide the Godfather. After dropping off the Godfather and calling bodyguards to protect his uncle, Bobby proceeded to Michael's pad.

Back at Michael's pad, Serena, Jackie, Anthony, and Michael were discussing a way to end the war with the Scarfos just as Bobby knocked on the door.

Michael opened the door in surprise. "Bobby what are you doing here?"

Jackie rose in anger as he spotted Bobby. "What the hell is he doing here!"

"I did not come here to argue with you Jackie. This problem is far more serious," said Bobby.

"Cut the crap Jackie. Bobby is a friend of Isabelle and any friend of hers is always a friend of mine. What's wrong Bobby?" asked Michael.

"Franco nearly whacked my uncle and he destroyed the mansion," Bobby Scarfo reported.

"I knew the old man couldn't stop Franco," said Anthony, upset.

"Apparently Franco has been the cause behind this mob war between both our families," said Jackie.

"Things have gotten too dangerous. Franco must have had spies to have been able to get to us both like this," said Michael.

"What do we do now?" asked Serena.

"We all must inform the Don immediately," Jackie decided. They raced off in Bobby's car to the Terrace Tower.

"Just wondering – have you been visited by anyone doing money transfers lately?" Bobby Scarfo asked.

"Yes, we have; every week a guy by the name of Riffman, a Russian, stops by. He's always wearing a gold ring with a crescent hammer. Why do you ask?" said Jackie.

"We too have a Russian working for us as well, in money and defense transfer contracts. The guy's name is Cragwell and he also wears the same kind of ring," said Bobby. On hearing this Michael flashed back in his mind and remembered the ring that Riffman was wearing the night he came in to collect the protection money. "Did he have a scar on his left eye?" asked Michael.

"Yes," Bobby replied.

"That settles it then, it's the same guy. We've been had," said Jackie.

"I bet it was also the same guy we saw with Franco at the warehouse weapons deal," Serena chipped in.

"It must be, but we still don't know who the guy really is," said Michael as they arrived at the Terrace Tower.

In the Don's office Michael and company gathered and laid out the whole story. After hearing this the Don looked quite stern, his hands clenched up to his chin in deep thought. "I have come to a decision and it's one I regret having to make. As of right this moment, we must all go into hiding. Franco Scarfo has been able to gain much information on both our organizations and he has more advanced firepower than us," Don Felice decided.

"You can't mean it?" interrupted Jackie.

"Yes. I hate to say it, but we must all go our separate ways, for now. It is too dangerous; this could bring the Feds down on us, and I'm sure the police commissioner has already contacted them," concluded Don Felice.

"So that's it, we hide like roaches," interjected Michael.

"Yes son, that's what we must do until we can find a way to expose Franco and his operation to the media. If we can find a way to do that, Franco's days will be over," said Don Felice. With looks of sad defeat they all shook hands and departed each other's company.

33

"NEW ALLIES AND FRIENDS"

As Michael and Serena sped off for home, Michael grew fed up with the actions of the Don. "How do you like that? The Don just expects us to hide under a rock until things are all better; it makes me damn sick."

"I suppose he's only trying to protect his family. Didn't you tell me one time that the 'family' is your family?" asked Serena.

"You're right, he's only trying to look out for our welfare," said Michael. "However, that still doesn't fix how we're going to beat Franco at his game." Michael was frustrated and driving fast.

"Well, I think I might know some people who can help us," said Serena confidently.

"Who?"

"The Coven."

"The what?" Michael asked as Serena gave him a wicked smile, her lovely eyebrows arching coyly.

"They might actually need our help, from what I've been told by the other vampires in the city," said Serena.

"How come you didn't tell me about this before?" asked a surprised Michael.

"I forgot to tell you, sorry," said Serena.

"Where is this coven located? I take it that it's somewhere dark and mysterious."

"Baby, you watch too many movies. It's at the newly appointed Vladimir skyscraper downtown, the financial headquarters of the Zoratus Enterprises Corporation. There are actually many covens in the city, but this one is the largest."

"Vlad, for the Impaler, right?"

"Right," said Serena.

"Oh please." Michael was annoyed by the cheesiness of the name, and Serena chuckled as they sped off to the Vladimir skyscraper.

During the last 20 years, Las Vegas had been transformed into looking more like the vast closeness of New York and Los Angeles with its new monstrous skyscrapers and vast bullet train systems. The only thing that has stayed connected to the past was the Strip, even with the gigantic buildings that now towered over the old casinos and resorts. The Strip's nickname was now "Old Vegas".

After parking the car in a nearby lot, Serena and Michael proceeded to the front entrance of the colossal building. The doorman, who was a vampire, recognized the small symbol on Serena's neck, a vampiric seal of the Zoratus family. After being admitted Serena and Michael proceeded to the center of the lobby where a large, transparent, tubular elevator waited for them; they entered and shot up to the two-hundredth floor, where they would meet a force of mystery.

In a large circular office, with blue drapes and walls decorated in medieval art and weapons, sat a man in a blue cloak, a crucifix around his neck. He wore a silk-cuffed shirt, a red tie and the vampiric seal embroidered on the back of his vestments. His hair was long and as white as a glacier and his eyes burned with bluish fire. His face was aged, wrinkles upon wrinkles, along with scars from endless years of battle. A true Italian and crusader of his faith.

The man was speaking with his eldest son, Darius. Darius was a man whose black hair was sharp as spikes; he was dressed in black leather pants and boots, with an Edwardian vest and black tie. He was half Italian and Romanian.

"Father, why do we waste such time on humans? They do not understand us and fear us," Darius asked.

"My son, these times have grown dark for our family's bloodline. Our kind is turning to side with our enemy. They have given up their belief in the promise of the Lord, of which the angel Gabriel spoke to me. We need new human allies to aid us in the Great Test, especially if we want to end the war," replied the old man.

"It has been a waste of time, seven centuries to be exact. We should be looking out forour own interests" replied Darius.

"Son, if you think this is a waste of time, understand this: the Great Test was difficult in my time and so it will be among this generation of our family," said the old man.

"But how long, for how long, father? What of the future of our species; we are being depleted in number by slayers and by society. We should preserve our kind, not find a way to reform it," Darius pressed.

"Until all of Reynard Desbode's forces and the Society have been crushed. It is then that we will be free from our plight," said the old man.

"Shall I go see Marko then?" asked Darius.

"Yes Darius, go report to Marko; he will provide the information you need for your next mission," said the old man.

"Yes father," replied Darius, bowing in respect and left room.

Darius went to report to Marko and his sister Marianna. Julius's oldest daughter. "Foolish boy," said Julius under his breath.

Marko, the chief chemist and robotics engineer of Zoratus Enterprises, was hard at work on his newest creations. Marianna was looking at plant samples making medical serums. Marko was Julius's blood brother. Though ancient as a elder of the Zoratus vampire coven, Marko was an expert and master in technical weapons development with a firm regard to his work.

"How's it going?" asked Darius, putting on his metaphorical mask.

"Fine, I just isolated the enzymes in these plants," said Marianna, mesmerized, her eyes locked into the lens of her microscope.

"What are you going to use it for?" asked Darius, actually a little interested.

"Antitoxins. The last raid we were in was a nasty one," said Marianna.

"Listen, I was wondering Marianna, why do you still want to help out the old man?"

"Because, I love him, he is our father after all."

"Don't give me that. Is it because of love or duty to honor?"

"Why bother me with these petty questions? Shouldn't you be preparing the strike team for the next attack?" said Marianna, annoyed now.

"It's not them I'm worried about; it's me I'm starting to be concerned with. I'm tired of this futility," said Darius.

"We all chose to serve Father because we desire peace with the humans; in redeeming ourselves, we renew the soul," said Marianna loyally. She was a strong and noble warrior to her clan and beautiful, with eastern Asian eyes, long braided black hair, and peach colored pouty lips. She was dressed in a black PVC outfit. First born, of Julius's children. Half Japanese and half Italian.

"I hate you defending that ideology. We should be accepted for what we are, as vampires; we should not bend to the laws and ways of humanity. We live longer, fight stronger, and are a lot a better in bed, thank you," said Darius, annoying his sister with his arrogance.

"Stop your bickering! Both of you are interrupting my thoughts," said Marko.

"What've you been up to?" asked Darius.

"I have been making you a new weapon to use on the Dark Society's new soldiers, so pay attention. Come here and try this out," commanded Marko.

Pulling off his welding mask, he turned off his welding torch and sprayed a coolant on the weapon.

"Well?" asked Darius. Marko rolled up his sleeves, removing a chain machine gun glove from a small stand. "Hold out your arm," instructed Marko.

"What?" Darius asked, concerned.

"Trust me." Marko fit the robotic glove on Darius's left arm. Finding the trigger tips on his fingers, Darius fired away as the machine gun glove shot rounds of thermite that burned through a test metal, melting holes straight through. "What is the compound?" asked Darius.

"Simple thermite bombs. I was able to protect the weapon from melting with a new alloy I've been developing, we got a lot power here in a little package," said Marko.

"You're a genius after all."

"I know, I know. Now prepare the men for the attack."

"Thanks," said Darius as he left to continue training the men in his underground compound. Marko just shook his head at the young vampire. "He does not understand the importance of what we are doing," said Marko.

"He will eventually. We're trying to reestablish the alignment of our spies and the others in what was agreed upon by the elders of the council," said Marianna as she continued to review her reports.

Serena knocked on the main chamber door but the old man had sensed who it was. "Serena my child, come in, come give an old man a hug," the old man smiling.

"Grandfather," said Serena as they hugged.

"It's good to see you," said the old vampire, smiling at his granddaughter. Michael looked at the old man with a feeling of curiosity. He didn't have much understanding of his new vampiric nature.

"A new lover you have, a handsome and fearless one," said the old man sternly.

"Julius Zoratus, I presume," said Michael as he shook the old man's hand.

"My great-granddaughter did well to choose you," said Zoratus.

"Save the formalities and let's get down to business," said Michael.

"He is bold and forward," said Zoratus to Serena.

"We have come in need of assistance," said Michael.

"Alliance must be earned, young man. I know what you desire, there is no need to ask," replied Zoratus.

"What?" Michael felt insulted.

"Our organization is not like the mafia that you ruthlessly kill for," said Zoratus.

"But I thought that all vampires killed ruthlessly to survive," Michael boldly answered back.

"We only take what we need to survive, and we don't kill anymore to feed; these days, a donor can freely give us his or her blood to sustain us, which is why we are in development of new chemical serums to make up the difference," Zoratus explained.

"Serena tells me that you also own all the blood banks and hospitals in the city," said Michael.

"Our corporation does own the blood banks and hospitals. We also use them to trace the infected ones, in order to protect our kind from exploitation by outsiders," said Julius. "Okay then, I'll spare the details on us and let's get to your contact, Jackie Santerini, who you work for, and the Santerini Family."

"How do you know that?" asked Michael.

"Our global organization has many links to key individuals and our contacts in city have told us much about your former background and who you work with," said Julius.

"Get to the point then; what do I have to do to win your trust?"

"Impatience will get you nowhere, young vampire," warned Zoratus.

"Spare me the sermon, please," said Michael.

"Michael," said Serena, upset at her lover's rudeness.

"Forgive me," said Michael quickly.

"You are forgiven. Now let me bring you to the initiation counsel. There is much to discuss," said Zoratus.

They entered a chamber through the bookcase in the grand library, which was stacked to great heights with old books; a mountain of knowledge towered in the large room. Michael was in awe; he had never seen a library this size before.

"Glad you like the library," said Lord Zoratus.

"It's beautiful," replied Michael.

"I'm also glad to see your pompous friend respects knowledge," chuckled Lord Zoratus to Serena.

"Very funny old man," Michael quipped back.

They descended to the corridor below, where an old medieval stone stairwell led to a cloistered room that held a large marble table. Symbols were assigned to each place at the table, the clan symbols, and the main Zoratus coat of arms was set in the center. On the walls lit sconces blazing with blue fire and around the table were navy blue satin chairs. Four vampires were seated, all of different stature, age, and culture. However, two of the chairs were empty. Serena went to sit with the counsel, but Michael stood in the middle of the room, waiting to be introduced. An older vampire wearing glasses and a lab coat turned to Lord Zoratus to speak. It was Marko.

"Brother, who is this poor creature that your great-granddaughter Serena has brought to us? I can smell his scent and he smells like a dog. Send him away. He is not one with this Coven."

"No, let him stay; I sense that he is brave and a warrior," said Marianna.

"Silence!" commanded Lord Zoratus.

"He is here to aid us, and he will be useful in gaining allies for our cause," said Serena.

"How so cousin?" Darius asked from where he was seated in the corner.

"I can help your organization in many ways Darius," said Michael. This amazed them all.

"How does a fledgling so young posses such great mental power?" asked Marianna.

"Go on then, tell us, I'm sure we would love to know," gestured Marko.

"I have many leads within the United States government, the CIA, and have many other associates within the criminal underworld in this city," replied Michael.

"How many of these contacts do you know personally?" asked Scarlet, the half French/Italian vampire. Marianna's younger sister.

"Exactly two hundred," said Michael.

"A meager number. My war cyborgs could beat that number any day," said Marko.

"Be quiet Marko; machines can not understand the enemy's mind. Only flesh and blood can," said Lord Zoratus.

"If it would please your Coven to know, Julius, I know of certain supply lines within the city where your organization can obtain better advanced weapons, at least compared to your robotics division that is yet to be fully tested," said Michael, reading Marko's mind.

"He does have a point. The war cyborgs have not finished testing. I have seen the weapons he speaks of and they would be of great use to us," Serena chimed.

"A few moments, if you please Damascus. Step outside the room so we can make our decision," asked Darius.

Michael nodded his head in respect and left the counsel room to wait outside the door. He still didn't understand what he was doing, what his purpose was, or the point of being immortal. All of these questions flowed through his mind as if in slow motion. Then all of a sudden the large doors opened again and Serena ushered Michael back into the room to hear the counsel's decision.

"It has been decided that you will be welcomed into this coven and its organization based upon your completion of the coven's initiation trials. If you can complete the three special task we request of you, then you will be welcomed in alliance. However, if you fail, by our ancient code you will be killed. Do you agree to this?" asked Lord Zoratus.

"I agree that I will prove to you I am worthy. But first, I have questions of my own," said Michael.

"Questions will be answered later," said Lord Zoratus.

"With due respect, if you please, I wish to know a little about who I am working for, either human or immortal; it makes no difference to me," said Michael fearlessly.

"You will be told in time. Now leave us until you have been contacted for your first trial. In the meantime, my eldest daughter Marianna will keep you informed," said Lord Zoratus.

"How will we keep in contact?"

"Young fledgling, you have much to learn. Each vampire can speak to another through their thoughts. Believe me, you will know when she speaks to you."

Michael nodded and thanked his new contacts. Then after Serena had hugged her great-grandfather goodbye, the two left to head home for the night.

Back in the counsel room, the rest of the coven continued to speak for the briefest of moments. "Do you think that this unsavory young fool can be trusted? Not all of our kind believes in the cause as we do. As you have said before, many of our kind have turned to aid the enemy," countered Marko.

"Desperate times call for desperate measures; our family bloodline is dying. I am dying." Zoratus groaned in pain as his wound that he had received from his archenemy began to open up. "I'm aware of the risk. We must expand the coven's empire if we are ever able to reclaim the one prize we seek the most, which is that our humanity be restored."

"But what of the rest of the clans we are allied with around the world; surely they can help us?" said Marko.

"The clans have their own battles to fight now. Reynard Desbode's followers have destroyed many of our kind," said Scarlet.

"The Dark Society has grown more powerful than we thought. We must continue to gather new allies if we are to defeat their evil forces. I agree with father and Scarlet," said Darius.

They all nodded in agreement. "We must be especially watchful of the triad gangs in the city. Rumors suggest that they have obtained a powerful force. We must discover what this force is, and if it poses any threat to this Coven and organization, we must destroy it," said Marianna.

"Very well. Contact the young fledgling in five days to give him his first trial and we shall see how much courage he has," said Lord Zoratus.

In the meantime, back at Michael's pad, Serena and Michael sat by the fireplace where golden flames burned brightly. The two gazed at the moonlit sky out of their window and dreamed of happier times.

PART FIVE: THE BLACK SPIDER

34

"LITTLE SALLY COMES HOME"

Friday night and the Black Spider Club teemed with people. Mickey Blue and his band were warming up on the main stage as the crowd was being served cocktails. Isabelle was speaking to Michael behind the stage about the songs she would be performing for the evening's festivities.

"Now listen Isabelle, I want you to knock'em dead tonight. You do this, and I'll get you in a music magazine, you can do it honey," said Michael confidently.

"Mikey have I not always delivered? You know I will," said Isabelle.

"Good. Go for it and kick ass."

"Thanks. You're sweet," said Isabelle as she kissed Michael on the cheek and prepared for her number with Mickey Blue.

Michael left the stage to have a drink at the bar as Mickey and Isabelle began to play the night away. The bartender, Ronny, gave Michael a smile as he poured his employer a Chinese Snake Blood special, the special being actual snake's blood. Michael had a strong taste for the ethnic delights of China. "How have you been boss, you look a little tense tonight?"

"I'm just a little tired, that's all Ronny, but don't worry."

"I just don't like seeing you down."

"I'll be fine, just keep pouring the drinks and keep them coming for the customers, I anticipate this night is going to be a killer."

"Not a problem," said Ronny.

"So tell, me what's been going on lately with you and Mickey?" asked Michael.

"Mickey's been doing well. It's too bad you can't be here every night at the club," said Ronny.

"I know he has a soft spot for me in his heart."

"He told me he thinks of you as a son. Too bad the man has never had children."

"Mickey is a good man and a kind one," agreed Michael.

"Oh well. Say listen, how would like to have one of my newest paintings?" asked Ronny.

"Sure," said Michael. Just then the phone rang,

"Good evening, this is the Black Spider Club, this is Ronny. How may I help you?" Michael heard a muffled voice speak over the phone. "Yes he's here, I'll tell him right away," said Ronny as he handed Michael the phone. "It's for you and it's important."

"Thank you," said Michael as he held the phone to his ear to listen. "Hello?"

"Yes, this is Mrs. Jane Mitchell from the Las Vegas Department of protective child services, I have unfortunate news about your young niece Sally Henderson, your deceased sister's daughter," said Mrs. Mitchell.

"Yes, what's wrong, what's happened?" asked Michael, worried.

"Sally has been staying with your father and younger brother. We received word from the police department yesterday that they were killed in a car accident two days ago," said Mrs. Mitchell.

"What!" Michael exclaimed.

"I know that this is a shock to you, but your niece has nowhere to go. We have tried to find relatives that would take her in, but they are all deceased," said Mrs. Mitchell.

"Of course I'll take her in immediately, she's my relative," Michael agreed. "Where is she now?"

"She is with me at the Protective Child Services building," said Mrs. Mitchell.

"I'll be there in 10 minutes. Thank you." Michael hung up the phone, sad to hear such grim news.

"What's wrong?" asked Ronny.

"My father and younger brother were killed in a car wreck. My little niece has no one now but me, fucking a."

"I'm so sorry Mike," said Ronny, giving his boss a sad look.

"Anyway, tell Isabelle and Mickey Blue that they'll be having company in the penthouse upstairs," said Michael calmly.

"Of course boss," said Ronny.

Michael sat down his drink and hurried out the door to pick up Sally. He hopped into a cab. "Where to Mack?" asked the cabbie.

"The Department of Protective Child Services and step on it," said Michael, handing the cab driver a fifty-dollar bill.

"You got it," said the cabbie as he hit the pedal. Staring out the cab window at the endless rows of massive lights, glaring signs, and many casinos, all Michael could think about was his family. He felt terrible about his absence and the neglect of his true family. The two years he had spent in the criminal underworld had consumed his mind and time and he was very worried about Sally. He had not seen her for a long time and was concerned about how she would react to seeing him. He also knew that he would now have to be especially secretive. "She must never know what I am," said Michael to himself. "I will protect her."

Ten minutes later Michael arrived at the Protective Child Services building. In the waiting room he found a little nine year old girl with brown hair in a ponytail, wearing a red sweater and red dress. Sally was Katrina's daughter from a previous marriage. Mrs. Mitchell was comforting her, as she was crying for her grandfather and little cousin. "Now dear, don't cry, your Uncle Michael is here to take you home," said Mrs. Mitchell.

Sally wiped her tears as she saw a tall Italian man in nice suit smile at her. "Uncle Michael," said a shy Sally. The two stood motionless. They had not seen each other for two years. Then they hugged tightly and a tear ran down Michael's right cheek. "I have to take care of you now sweetie, Grandpa and Peter have gone to heaven to be with your mother," Michael explained softly.

"Thank you so much," said Sally with tears running down her face.

"Come now, let's go home," said Michael. He turned to Mrs. Mitchell and asked, "Will she be all right?"

"At this stage it's too early to tell. I'll keep you informed about the legalities. After the paperwork has been processed, the adoption will become legal," said Mrs. Mitchell, handing Michael the documents.

"Okay," Michael agreed, and he and Sally headed out and flagged a cab to take his niece to the guest penthouse he had at his nightclub. It was dark when they arrived at the Black Spider Club; the club had been shut down out of respect for Michael's loss. Ronny had gone home for the night; the only ones watching over the club were Mickey Blue and Isabelle, who lived upstairs in the double guest penthouses. Michael opened the doors of the club and he saw Mickey Blue come down stairs. "Well now, who is this fine and lovely little lady that we have here tonight?" Mickey Blue asked, smiling. He caused Sally to smile a little in return; she was shy at times but not always.

"Sally, Sally Henderson." She hid half her face behind Michael's left shoulder.

"Tell me honey, do you like music?" asked Mickey Blue.

"A little, will you play something for me?" asked Sally.

"Of course missy," said Mickey Blue happily as he whipped out his saxophone from his saxophone case and began to play a sweet soft melody that sounded like robins singing to their young. Sally began to cheer up a little. Her face brightened and she clapped for Mickey Blue when he had finished playing for her. "That was wonderful," said Sally.

"She loves jazz; I can tell," said Mickey Blue.

"Maybe she will want to be a singer someday," said Isabelle, who had come halfway down the stairs while Mickey Blue was playing. Coming down further, she introduced herself to the little girl.

"Hello, you're very beautiful," said Sally, smiling at Isabelle.

"Thank you sweetie. I'm Isabelle and this is Mickey."

"Are you hungry dear? I've been cooking beef stew upstairs," asked Isabelle.

"A little," admitted Sally.

"Are you going to stay with us tonight Michael?" asked Isabelle.

"Yes, I am, but first I'm going to make some calls. Then I'll join you all for dinner upstairs," said Michael. Isabelle and Mickey Blue escorted Sally up the stairs to Isabelle's penthouse for supper while Michael made his calls at the empty bar.

"Hi love, it's me," said Michael over the phone.

"Are you coming home soon, baby?" asked Serena.

"I'm going to be here at the club tonight. My little niece just came into town, and she'll be staying here in Mickey Blue's and Isabelle's care," said Michael.

"What happened? You sound depressed," pressed Serena.

"My father and younger brother died just two days ago. They were killed in a car wreck. Sally had been staying with them after my sister passed away. Now she has no one but me," Michael explained.

"Can she stay with us? I could look after here darling."

"No, she must not know what you or I am, or our business with you know who," said Michael firmly.

"Will you be okay?"

"I'll be fine. I'll be here for a few days until I can complete the adoption paperwork with the city. Then I'll come home to check in on you. Are you all right baby?" asked Michael.

"I'm fine; you go and keep watch over the little one. I'll see you in a few days," said Serena.

"By the way, any word from the Coven?" asked Michael.

"No word from them yet, but expect to hear from them soon. Normally the trials begin shortly after introductions have been made," said Serena.

"Thanks baby, take care, love you."

"Love you too," said Serena. Michael hung up the phone and went up stairs to join the others.

At dinner they sat and talked. "I hope you're all hungry because I have a lot of this tonight," said Isabelle, bringing out the pot of hot beef stew and serving everyone.

"But of course, everyone knows that you're the most wonderful cook in the world," said Mickey Blue as he spread his napkin on his lap, ready to eat.

"Thank you, Mickey. I'm glad that someone appreciates my cooking, unlike some people here." Isabelle winked, teasing Michael.

"Come on Issy, I think your cooking is great," said Michael, blushing. They all laughed and the penthouse began to feel warm and comfortable. As they passed around food, Sally spoke.

"How did this all happen here, I mean this entire big place?" asked Sally.

"Well, your uncle and Mickey here have been friends for a few years and they dreamed of setting up a night club, so here we all are," said Isabelle.

"I came from New Orleans, playing around the states as far back as the 1990s. I opened my own club, The Swallow's Nest, here in Las Vegas, but it closed down due to criminal elements. Many years later, your uncle here gave me the opportunity to start over with him and that's how we got this place going." said Mickey Blue as slurped down a hearty helping of Isabelle's hot stew.

"What about you?" Sally asked Isabelle.

"Your uncle and I grew up as kids together in Brooklyn, New York, before he moved out here to work for the CIA. We were friends and wrote music together," said Isabelle.

"Is that why you sing?" asked Sally.

"Yes, I love to sing. A few years ago when I was out of work as a secretary, your uncle told me about this club. He gave me the opportunity to pursue my singing career here and things have never been the same," said Isabelle, smiling at Michael. Michael couldn't help but smile back.

"So tell me, how would you like to help me on stage sometime singing?" Isabelle asked Sally.

"I would like that very much. When mom was alive she enrolled me when I was six in dance and singing classes," replied Sally.

"Really, what type of dance?" asked Isabelle.

"Swing," replied Sally.

"You might just have a protégé," said Michael and Sally smiled.

They talked for a long time after Sally had been settled in Isabelle's bed. Mickey Blue bade Michael and Isabelle good night as they went downstairs to have a nightcap at the club bar. Michael poured Isabelle and himself each a glass of red wine.

"You know Mikey, Sally reminds me of you when we were little. You were always shy."

"And you were always teasing me," said Michael as they both chuckled.

"You know it'll be nice to have some company around here. Sally might actually entice you to come around more often," said Isabelle.

"You know the people I deal with. I have to keep certain commitments." Michael shook his head.

"Too bad they have to be such shady people."

"That's business. Do you think I enjoy having to do this? I do it out of duty to the people who saved my life. God wasn't there for me but they were," said Michael.

"God has never abandoned you. What's happened to your faith?" questioned Isabelle.

"I don't know."

"He still loves you Michael, and you know I'll always love you too, no matter what you choose to do in life or how you feel about us," said Isabelle.

"Thanks, I appreciate that," said Michael as he hugged Isabelle and kissed her on the forehead.

A little while later, Isabelle went upstairs to bed. Michael sat upstairs in his office to think. For the first time in years, Michael knelt down under the crucifix Isabelle had placed on his wall to pray to God. "God please help me, please help me, old man, help me to understand why I do what I do. I don't know who I am anymore," pleaded Michael.

Finishing his prayer, Michael went out to feed. His vampiric hunger was agitating him and he needed fresh life force energy. He vomited up the food he had eaten earlier in the alley behind the club and went to hunt in the inner city, draining the life forces of several stray animals. About two hours later he returned, crashed on the sofa in his office and fell asleep.

The next morning at police headquarters, Commissioner Hamilton set up raids with the DA to bust crime rings that may have been involved with the murder of Frank Watson. She wanted to nail every crooked creep she could in hopes of finding answers in the death of her best detective.

She finally got her opportunity when a raid took down a drug lab run by Santerini's criminal organization in midtown. The lab was run out of the abandoned Hillman sugar factory and was being used to produce cocaine. One of the smalltime drug runners from the lab named Jimmy Lemont talked after being persuaded by Commissioner Hamilton's officers. Hamilton broke up the beating, as she herself kicked Jimmy Lemont in the stomach, bringing him to his knees on the wooden floor, demanding information. "All right dirt bag, who's been killing cops in my city? And don't play coy with me. I know either your boss Don Santerini or the Scarfos' set it up." Commissioner Hamilton held the guy by the collar and cocked her pistol, which was pushed against Jimmy Lemont's forehead.

"Okay, you got me; it was Damascus, Michael Victor Damascus! The guy and me pull jobs sometimes, just please don't kill me!" screamed Jimmy as a river of sweat poured down his face.

Commissioner Hamilton removed her gun from Jimmy Lemont's head and told the boys in blue, "Get this garbage out of here. And get a warrant boys, we have a little hunting to do."

Fortunately for Michael, he had registered his nightclub name under Mickey Blue's name. Mickey didn't know that Michael had alliances with the mob; he thought that the building was registered in his name as an act of charity.

Suddenly Serena awoke in her room that was darkened by big red drapes. She sensed psychically that Michael was in trouble, so she called him. Michael had gotten up an hour earlier in his darkened office.

"Michael, it's me Serena, you have to get out immediately. The police know it was you who killed that cop. They'll be looking for you," said Serena.

"Don't worry, I'll handle it," said Michael. He took his pistol out of his coat. Everyone else was asleep. Normally, Isabelle and Mickey Blue would sleep during the day, since they had worked the evening before. Suddenly, there was a small knock on the door. Michael hid the gun in his desk drawer, locking it.

Sally was in her pajamas, looking at her uncle as he opened the door. "Sally honey, you should be in bed still. It's early," said Michael.

"Sorry Uncle Michael, I had a bad dream."

"Well, since we're up I might as well cook you breakfast in the club's kitchen." In the back of his mind he wasn't worried about the police, but he knew that he would have to deal with the police commissioner later that night.

In the kitchen, Michael fried up some eggs and bacon for Sally. He also made some black coffee for himself and they sat down to breakfast. "Sally, do you want to do anything tomorrow? It's Saturday," said Michael.

"No, its okay. I just want to sleep, and maybe go to a movie," said Sally.

"We'll go together. In the meantime we have to prepare for you to go back to the school that your mother had you in."

"I miss school, I haven't been there since Grandpa and Peter died."

"I know you miss them a lot. I know they loved you with all their hearts," said Michael.

"Does the pain ever go away for you since my mom died?"

"Ever since your mother's death, life has never been the same for me. I miss her every day, but I try to push on the best I can," said Michael.

"I guess that's what I have to do, push on," said Sally.

"Tell you what, since you're not going to be back in school for a few weeks, how would you like to help out here at the club during the evenings? I'll give you a hefty allowance, 400 dollars a week, if you help out," Michael offered.

"Uncle, you don't have to do that. Mom would never give me that much," said Sally, surprised at her uncle's generosity.

"I'm not your mother, heaven bless her soul, and besides, you're my only niece."

"All right I'll do it," said Sally enthusiastically.

"Good. Now head back to bed for the day because later tonight I'm going to teach you how to work here."

"I love you Uncle Michael," said Sally, hugging him.

"I love you too Sally, now go back up to bed. I'm going to be working you hard, so get some rest."

Sally went back upstairs to sleep. Isabelle and Mickey Blue came down to greet Michael at noon.

"Good afternoon me boy," said Mickey Blue.

"Same here," said Isabelle.

"How did you both sleep?" asked Michael.

"Good." Mickey Blue yawned, dressed in his blue collared shirt and slacks.

"Not bad. I just wish I could get this crick out of my neck," said Isabelle, stretching in her black tank top and blue jeans. "So what's the agenda for today?"

"What else, let's get this place ready for tonight. Listen Mickey, I have a private appointment later tonight. Do you mind watching over the club while I'm out since Sally is staying over?" asked Michael, remembering he had to take care of Commissioner Hamilton's meddling.

"No problem, just tell me what time you'll be back," said Mickey Blue.

"I should be back by midnight."

The whole day the club's blinds remained closed, but the lights were on. The three of them spent all day cleaning up the club while playing jazz music and other tunes off the old record player. In the early evening Sally was up and learning to work the club before it opened at 9 pm. Michael taught Sally how to stock the bar, call for deliveries, file paperwork of the establishment's bills and tax records, and other little jobs. By the end of the day, they were all beat but the work wasn't over.

"I'm so tired," Sally sighed.

"Honey, you haven't seen anything yet, tonight this place is going to be booming," said Isabelle.

"Can I sit up front to hear you sing," asked Sally.

"You sure can sweetie, but I'm off tonight. Let's put you in some formal clothing anyway; after all, this is a high-end club," said Isabelle cheerfully as she brought Sally upstairs to find her something to wear.

"So tell me, do you like blue?" asked Isabelle, showing Sally an exquisite blue dress lavished with golden trim from a trunk on the floor.

"It's beautiful, can I try it on?"

"I had a feeling you would like it. You know, I always wanted to give this dress to my little girl but I never had one. Now I can give it to you."

"Oh, Isabelle, I can't take this, it's worth too much to you."

"Go ahead, I like you a lot."

"Oh thank you, thank you!" said Sally, anxious to try it on.

Back downstairs Michael and Mickey Blue were talking about the night's lineup. "By the way, what band do we have signed on tonight, since you two are off?" Michael asked.

"A blazing one, The Hot Rodders, a new wave-technotronic rock band," replied Mickey Blue.

"Great. A little rock is just what this place needs; it'll help bring in the younger crowd," said Michael.

After the employees began to arrive at the club, Michael bid Isabelle, Mickey and Sally goodnight and headed out to the police commissioner's apartment to wait for her.

Michael knew people all around town; they kept him informed on the home locations of the top people in the city. Michael managed to hop across the rooftops to the commissioner's home and break in by picking the front door lock; the commissioner was, resting in her bedroom. The place was silent. Michael opened the door to the commissioner's bedroom where she was sleeping comfortably. He walked over to the bed; he wouldn't kill her but he would make a point tonight. His fangs began to protrude, his eyes glowed white, the veins in his face began to show slightly, and his claws began to grow on his fingers.

The commissioner was startled awake and saw Michael standing over her. Frightened by the intruder in her home, she grabbed the pistol she slept with under her pillow and aimed it at Michael's face. Michael knocked the pistol out of her hand so fast that the gun fired; the shot broke a nearby mirror.

"What do you want!" screamed Commissioner Hamilton, horrified at this undead sight. Michael jumped on top of her, cupping his hand over her mouth to prevent her from screaming and placed his gun to her forehead. His eyes now began to burn with a hot red fire as he spoke in anger, "Now listen commissioner, I am only going to say this once; don't make a sound or I'll blow your head off." The commissioner nodded in understanding, so Michael removed his hand from his victim's mouth.

"What are you going to do?" asked Commissioner Hamilton in fear.

"Listen to me. Stay the hell away from Michael Damascus and the Santerinis. I am going to be direct. If you so much as bring one scumbag cop into this, I will cut your heart out and eat it on a plate," said Michael.

"You killed Watson, you bastard!" cried Commissioner Hamilton.

"That's right, but I was only following orders. I can't bear the guilt of whacking another good cop so please don't let it be you. If you value your life, close your investigation and I will let you live," said Michael.

"Go ahead, you bastard! If you kill me you'll be proof that this city needs us."

"I'll do more than that if you don't listen. I will turn you into something so horrible you will beg God for death day and night," Michael promised.

"You mean like you," breathed Commissioner Hamilton.

"Yes, you will become like me, a wretched soul," said Michael.

"All right! All right! I'll close the investigation. Please leave. I can't bear it."

In a flash Michael disappeared from the room. Commissioner Hamilton trembled in fear and shock. She couldn't believe her eye's what she had just seen. She called her second in command right then and ordered the case closed. No one asked any questions.

Michael entered the Black Spider at midnight and the Hot Rodders were blasting on stage. Mickey Blue was watching the band while Isabelle had a drink and kept an eye on Sally, who was so tired that she was sleeping in a corner booth. Michael saw her and said "Poor kid, I worked her too hard. She pooped out before enjoying the show."

Isabelle nodded, giving him the hint. Michael carried Sally upstairs to Isabelle's penthouse and tucked her into bed. He kissed her good night on the forehead and shut the door. The night went on with music playing, glasses toasting, and people dancing, filling the air with love and laughter.

35

"DRIVE BY FOR MIKE"

It was Saturday night, a night for Sally and her Uncle Michael to spend together. Sally was just dying to see a new movie called Journey Beyond the Land of Nod at an old movie theater. They came out of the theater at 2 am after the show and decided to head to Bobby Scarfo's Pizzeria on Aubrey Ave.

"That was great, I loved Ethan Webber as BODON in NOD, he is so cute," said Sally.

"Sally you're just a kid, you're too young to be thinking about boys," said Michael.

"I can dream, can't I?" Sally laughed.

Just then a black car crept around the corner. The front window lowered and a man armed with an M16 machine gun appeared. He was wearing dark glasses and had a shaved head. Michael sensed the man pointing the machine gun in his direction and in a split-second he grabbed Sally and turned around. "What the!" screamed Sally as the man in the car fired, shooting Michael in the back multiple times. Michael fell to the ground, covering Sally. The shooter in the car sped off.

Sally pushed her uncle off, screaming in fear that her uncle had been killed, but there wasn't any blood, so she pulled open Michael's jacket to see the bulletproof vest that had protected him.

Michael exclaimed, "Are you all right!" checking her for gun shot wounds.

"Me! You just got shot!" screamed Sally in panic.

"I'm fine. The vest caught the bullets. Let's get home. We're not going out anymore until I figure out who did this!"

Sally was still in shock. "Call the police," she said.

"No cops," said Michael.

"But!"

"I said no cops! Now let's get you home," yelled Michael, flagging down a taxi.

Back at the club, which had just closed for the evening, Sally was still shaken up from the shooting. She ran into the club and went right to Isabelle, hugging her tight. "What's wrong sweetie?" asked Isabelle.

"Uncle Michael was shot!" cried Sally.

"What?" Isabelle said as she went to Michael. He took off his jacket and vest; his back had bruises all over it. "What happened!"

"We were attacked by a guy in a black coupe, I grabbed the kid and took the shots in the back, lucky the vest caught the bullets."

"Call the hospital!" Isabelle ordered.

"No doctors, I'll be fine. I just have some large bruises. For now, keep Sally here; someone is obviously trying to kill me. I don't want her to be endangered again," said Michael.

"Who would want to kill you?" asked Mickey Blue.

"I don't know, but I'm going to find out. For now, all of you stay here, something is very wrong. I don't want any of you to get hurt."

"You can't just think we're going to let you go through this without our help," said Mickey Blue.

"Yes, you will stay out of this! All of you!" roared Michael.

"But what about Sally's needs? We have to take care of her," Isabelle protested.

"I'll give you some money to pay for Sally's expenses. Your safety is my primary concern. I love you all. You're the only family I have left." They all nodded sadly in agreement.

"What are you going to do now?" asked Mickey Blue.

"I know a guy around town who will be able to help me."

"Not Danny Fredricks, that goofball grifter?" asked Mickey Blue in disbelief.

"Yes, Danny will help me, but I have some others too. Now put Sally to bed. It's late and she needs her rest," said Michael.

"But uncle, I want you to be safe too." Sally hugged him tightly.

"Don't worry, I'll be fine. I have a gun and a permit."

Michael took Sally up to Isabelle's room and tucked her in, giving her a medal on a chain and said, "Now listen, you wear this medal around your neck, it's a guardian angel. If you ask your guardian angel to watch over you they will protect you," he told her.

"I will," said Sally. Michael kissed her goodnight and closed the door. They all went to bed.

For the first time in his life, Michael was frightened. He had never known fear before when he was on the battlefield, but the fear of losing his only loved ones now terrified him. All night he was gripped by fear and was so disturbed that he could not sleep until the next night.

36

"HUNTING DOWN THE PREY"

The next night, after waking up from a few hours rest, Michael searched all over town to find information on the guy that had tried to whack him and his niece. He had not foreseen it this time. Apparently the less he fed, the less his vampiric gifts developed. Deprivation of sleep had also weakened him. A vampire must rest to preserve strength, and without rest they lose power quickly.

Michael couldn't find any information, only shaking heads. The last place he thought to check out was a lounge where associates of Scarfo's hung out at times. Down the block he saw a man in a fine suit heading inside. "Rangoon!" said Michael to himself. He recognized the guy. Inside the lounge he found Pete Rangoon having cocktails with Sonny and Albert Scarfo, bragging in Italian about how he had wasted Damascus. Michael sat in the corner having a drink, wearing dark glasses and a black leather fedora. He listened with his vampiric hearing to the scumbags' conversation.

"So I had this one job to deal with this hot shot, the fucker screams for his bitch when I break him down," said Rangoon. Sonny and Albert Scarfo laughed.

"Did the MD take a fall?" said Sonny.

"Yeah, I took care of the guy easy, him and some little brat," boasted Rangoon.

Michael understood what they were saying. He was so mad that he came close to shattering the glass in his hand, his face contorting as he heard Rangoon's words. He saw that the trio was leaving, so he stepped outside into the alley next to the entrance and pretended to have a smoke.

As the others left, Rangoon was getting into his car when Michael grabbed him from behind. "Who the fuck are you!" yelled Rangoon in shock.

"I'm your worst nightmare asshole," said Michael as he held up Rangoon with one hand by his collar. Removing his hat and glasses, Rangoon recognized his attacker's face.

"You!"

Michael's vampiric nature came alive as his eyes began to burn with white light. His fangs appeared and his claws sprang out.

"What the fuck!" Rangoon yelled.

Michael smiled wickedly and teleported with Rangoon to the top of a nearby building that was very high up from the ground. Rangoon was so petrified with fear that he didn't move. Michael looked into his eyes and said "Give my regards to the Devil in hell," and with an evil grin he jabbed his claws into Rangoon's chest, twisting and churning his organs. Rangoon coughed up blood; he couldn't breathe as Michael drained his life. As Rangoon took in his last breath, Michael said "A junky to the end," removing the cocaine Rangoon was carrying from his pocket. Then he threw Rangoon off the ten-story building, watching him fall until he hit the bottom.

The moon was high and Michael looked at his hands that were covered in blood and said, "Now no one will harm my family, justice is done."

All of a sudden he felt a strange presence, as if someone had put a hand on his shoulder, and he heard a voice say, "Why did you do this? Can't you forgive your enemy?" Michael froze, as this was the second time he had encountered this presence. He shook it off and teleported to a public bathroom, and washing the blood off of his face and hands.

Michael again felt guilty for what he had done, but the guilt did not bother him for long. In his mind he felt it was necessary to protect his niece; he loved her so much that he would kill to protect her.

The next afternoon at the club, after the sun had set, Michael received a package in the mail. It was the rest of the adoption paperwork and he opened it, browsing the file with his reading glasses. He then called Mickey Blue and Isabelle into his office to speak with them.

Michael knew it was too dangerous for his niece to be in his care and he brought this to his associates' attention.

"I see you have the adoption paperwork there for Sally. Why've you brought us up here for this?" asked Mickey Blue.

"Is something wrong Mike?" asked Isabelle.

"Yes, there is. I have come to an important decision and I need your opinions."

"Well?" asked Isabelle.

"It's gotten too dangerous for Sally to stay here with me, and I was hoping that," Michael started, but he was interrupted by Sally who had overheard the conversation outside the door. "No! No!" she screamed, running to him and crying. Michael held her in his arms to comfort her and then looked into her eyes. "Sally, I can't let you be harmed. I think that it would be best if I transfer the adoption into Mickey Blue's and Isabelle's names, as your legal guardians."

"I don't want to lose you, not like mom and the others," a tearful Sally pleaded.

"Mike, you want us both to raise her?" asked Mickey Blue.

"Yes. There are certain kinds of people I have to deal with, Mickey. Isabelle will tell you," said Michael.

"Mickey, he works for the mob," said Isabelle softly.

"Mike it can't be true," exclaimed Mickey Blue, shocked.

"Yes it is," said Michael.

"But!" started Sally.

"I want you both to care for Sally; I don't want her to be harmed. Would you both be willing to do this for me, as friends and as my family?"

"Of course we will, but we have nowhere else to stay but here," said Mickey Blue.

"Then that's how it will be, at least for now," said Michael, handing them the documents to sign.

Sally couldn't believe what she was hearing; she ran out of the room in tears.

"Very well. We'll do this, but we still want you to spend time with her here at the club. With the rest of her family's passing she needs someone for support, and you are her uncle, after all," said Isabelle firmly. Mickey nodded in agreement.

"I'll still be around," said Michael. With this the choice was made, the bargain concluded, though the nightmare was just beginning.

37

"A NEW FAMILY"

For the next two days Sally settled in and finally accepted her new family. She was still upset, filled with fear that her uncle did not love her and had cast her aside like a little rag doll. Sally sat in Isabelle's room looking at the picture of her parents and Michael that had been taken a long time ago, when life seemed simpler and free.

Isabelle came into the room and witnessed Sally look sad at a remnant of her past. She sat down next to the little girl and held her, saying, "He still loves you and we love you too."

"You think so?" asked Sally.

"Yes, he does, your uncle just wants to protect you; ever since your mother died he couldn't bear the pain of losing another member of his family, especially just after hearing the news of his father and younger brother's death. It's broken him inside. I saw him crying a day ago. He doesn't want you to see him so weak," said Isabelle.

"Thank you," said Sally, hugging Isabelle.

Isabelle kissed Sally on the forehead to make her feel better. "Say listen, would you like to help me bake a batch of chocolate chip cookies? It might make you feel a little better."

"Sure. Do you mind if I call you mom, you remind me of her a lot?" asked Sally in a soft voice. Isabelle was surprised to hear that she reminded Sally of her mother and she felt touched in her heart.

"Of course you can sweetie," said Isabelle, drying Sally's tears with a hanky. They both went into the kitchen. Isabelle took out the baking pans, while Sally took out the baking book. They made the cookie mix together and after about a half hour they put the treats in the oven. Sally felt happy that she could relate to another person. She had gained a sense of deep connection with Isabelle and Isabelle felt the same.

The smell of the cookies baking brought Mickey Blue into the kitchen licking his lips. He loved sweets and like a child, found the pleasant aroma inviting. Michael also came up to smell what was baking. They all enjoyed the cookies and had coffee along with the treats.

Later, though still in the early evening, Mickey was practicing his saxophone with his band on the main stage, and during a break Sally asked if he could teach her to play the saxophone. Sally had grown quite a liking for the club and the music that Mickey played.

"Why the hell not little lady, come up here and the boys and I will show you how it's done. But first I want to introduce you to the members of our band. On drums is Smokey Joe.

"Hey kiddo," said Smokey.

"On the keyboard here is Ray Decker.

"My pleasure," said Ray.

"On the trombones are the Wall brothers, Jimmy and Reggie."

"Yo Kitten," the two said.

"You'll have to forgive them, they're still in love with the sixties." Mickey Blue chuckled. "And on the guitar last but not least is the axe king, Maxie Reeves."

"Hey little moppet, lets get bopping!" said Maxie.

All night they taught Sally how to play. She took to it quite well; she was a natural. Sally was beginning to be a kid again and she felt loved by all around her. She had a family again, a family in a crazy world and with a strange lifestyle, but a loving family nonetheless.

Michael came into the room, clapping for his niece. He was so very was proud that she had taken to music. It made him feel, for the briefest of moments, like any normal human uncle. A smile of love played across his face.

Later during the night, after Isabelle and Sally had gone to bed and the club had closed, Mickey was still up in the bar having a late night drink with Michael. Mickey poured them each a cold pint of ale as the two talked. "You know Mike, it's been alarming to me; this secret you've kept from me all this time. Why didn't you tell me?"

"Because I didn't want you to worry."

"I love you like a son, Mike. You're like my child. You gave me a second shot in my life and I've never been able to repay your kindness," said Mickey Blue.

"What else could I do? You were down on your luck and such a talented man, so I wanted to help you," said Michael.

"Just please promise me one thing son."

"What's that?"

"Please take care of yourself and Isabelle when I'm gone. She still loves you."

"I know she does, but I can't be with her Mickey, I have given my heart to the woman I'm with now. Isabelle has to deal with this and accept it; it's just that simple," Michael sighed.

"I know. Bobby is crazy about her, but I think she stays with him because she feels guilty about what it would do to him if she left him," said Mickey Blue.

"I think she'll give herself to him fully eventually, but I'm happy to see that Sally has brought her some happiness to fill the gap in her heart."

They talked into the night. After Mickey Blue had gone up to bed, Serena called Michael. She hadn't seen him in many nights and was very worried. Michael picked up the phone as it rang. "Michael, what's happened, what's wrong? I've been worried about you. You never called home."

"I'm sorry love, the last few days have been hectic due to all the adoption paperwork and watching the kid," said Michael.

"You're not telling me the whole truth; I sense that you were in trouble a little while ago," Serena accused.

"I was shot at a night ago, but I took care of the animal who tried to harm Sally and I."

"What!" Serena exclaimed.

"We're all right," Michael assured her.

"Please come home to me baby, I miss you so much," Serena pleaded.

"I'll come home tomorrow night. It'll be just the two of us at the pad, I promise," said Michael.

"You mean it?" asked Serena.

"Come on Serena, you know I mean it." Michael blew her a kiss over the phone.

"Love you."

"I love you too," said Michael as he hung up the phone. He didn't know it, but Isabelle had been eavesdropping on his conversation from the stairway. She was overcome with envy. She felt it was unfair that Michael had left her because of his sister's death only to go and give his heart to a woman he had known for only a few weeks. She came downstairs to talk to Michael. "So you and the little lady have problems?"

"Isabelle, I know where you're taking this. Don't bring past emotions into this."

"Why shouldn't I? You abandon me for some Russian bimbo you hardly know, when I've known you since we were little kids."

"Shut up Isabelle!"

"Oh bullshit! You let your sister's death ruin us. What did I ever do to you to lose what we had!"

"It just wasn't meant to be. Besides, cheating on me did not help," Michael accused.

"It was a mistake!" protested Isabelle.

"It wasn't meant to be," repeated Michael.

"Oh yeah, I'll show you not meant to be!" Isabelle boldly grabbed Michael by the waist and kissed him deeply. Michael was so enraged that he pushed her away.

"You bastard," retorted Isabelle, slapping him across the face for being rejected, her eyes full of tears. Michael was filled with anger, and yet he stopped himself from exploding. He looked at her with pity and walked out of the club, heading home to see Serena.

Michael was the type of man who kept a commitment once he'd made it. He truly did love Serena, and she was the only one now who could understand him for who he really was and accept him.

Isabelle looked out the window as she saw Michael take off in his car, and began to cry, whispering in guilt, "I didn't mean it." She always found it hard to let go of Michael and of the many other men that she had been with in her life.

Back at Michael's apartment, Serena heard a knock on the door. She threw open the door and jumped up on top of Michael, kissing him, so happy to see that he had safely returned home. The two talked for a long time and then retired as the sun came up.

38

"THE INFORMER"

The next evening Michael received a call from Danny Fredricks, who was keeping tabs on both the police and the criminal underworld. "Yeah it's me," Danny said over a pay phone.

"What's going down?" asked Michael.

"New crime syndicate cartel has moved into town. They made a deal with Franco Scarfo's guys."

"Well, who are they?"

"Chinese Triads and the Russian mafia."

"What are they moving? Guns? Drugs?"

"Rumors are nuclear arms devices, but those are just rumors I've heard," Danny cautioned.

"Sounds like you're being not fully up front," said Michael.

"Oh, there's more bad news. The Feds came down hard on the mayor, who has created a new task force that's assigned to arrest any mobster or known affiliate on sight. I think the government is in on this; they're losing profits in arms smuggling. I've heard from others."

"Continue to keep me posted, and thanks," said Michael as he hung up his phone.

About a half-hour later, Michael got a call from Don Felice. "It's me, Felice. Gather your crew, we're having a meeting at the tower. Come now and call the others."

"Understood," Michael replied as he hung up. After Michael finished making calls to the others he met Serena and the two vampires teleported to the Terrace Tower to meet with the Don. The others were already in the Don's office when Michael and Serena entered.

"Gentlemen and the one lady present, Paulie and I have found a way to rid us of Franco Scarfo for good. Instead of just killing the bastard we'll expose him; let the media eat him up for breakfast," started Don Felice.

"How?" Jackie asked.

"We'll steal and deliver to the media Franco Scarfo's shady criminal records from his district record office," said Paulie.

"Good plan, but that place is guarded like Fort Knox," said Sal.

"I can get in there," said Serena.

"She's right, and I can too," said Michael.

"Then both of you are useful in stealth, which none of us have military training in. Very well, you two will go and do it then," agreed Don Felice. They all nodded.

Jackie's cell phone rang and he went into the hallway to take the call. "Who is this?"

"Someone who wants you to know that you have a rat among you," said the man on the other line.

"What, who the hell is this!" said Jackie in anger.

"It's Salvatore Santerini. He's the one who set you up and stole the money you all made on the drop. You'll find the cash in a briefcase at his bookie joint, in marked bills," said Phillips as he hung up the phone with a rotten grin.

"Steal from us Sal, and now it's your time to take a fall," said Phillips.

"Who the hell?" said Jackie.

As the others left, Jackie went alone to give this news to the Don. It was a cardinal sin to kill a made man without the approval of the Don. "Don Felice, I just got a tip from some guy that Salvatore was the one who stole our money. It's apparently being held at his bookie joint in a safe."

"That is preposterous!" said Don Felice in disgust. However, in the back of his mind he felt that Jackie was telling the truth. "Go and collect the money and when I see it before my eyes, you have my blessing to go and whack the thieving prick," said Don Felice.

A little while later Michael heard Marianna communicate with him telepathically. "Michael San, it is Marianna, your first trial now begins. Spy on the Chinese triads and see what they are up to; they're onto something," Marianna ordered.

"I will," replied Michael in his thoughts back to Marianna. His first trial had begun.

PART SIX: THE HIT

39

THE DARK ONE

Michael jacked a motor bike on the street. As he sped off to Chinatown in the eastern part of the flower district, he flew up to the top of a pagoda rooftop and surveyed the street for triads. His vampiric sight was sharp as an eagle's eye in the dark. Looking down at the lantern-covered streets of Chinatown he spotted two triad members taking a group of European men into a large Chinese restaurant. He followed his quarry by teleporting onto the roof of the building the men had gone into, opening a small window, then snuck in and blended into the shadows where no one could see him. He listened to the conversation. He also saw that they were speaking to a man in black robe with an ensign medallion of some kind. "It's time that we comrades and members of the Orient crush the Italians and bring this city to its knees," said a haughty Russian man with a red beard and dark glasses, slamming his fist against the table. This man also wore a pin with the same ensign medallion as the man in the cloak.

"I agree, the Italians have ruined profits for our people with their quarreling. Let's join together in eliminating them," said one of the triad men.

The man in the black cloak began to wickedly mock them. "You fools; you wish to defeat your enemies with toys. I can show you true power and more, if you wish."

"How so?" asked a triad leader. The man in the cloak slid the triad leader on the table a file folder. The triad leader reviewed the documents inside, nodding and showing it to the Russian mobsters.

"You see, gentlemen, the weapons we can supply to you are vast, beyond what you are using now, even more advanced than the new weapon shipments Franco Scarfo is moving through this city," said the man in the black cloak.

"What guarantee do you have for our organizations?" asked one of the Russian gang leaders.

The man in the black cloak threw out a pendant of the symbol of the organization that he worked for.

"So the legend is true," said one of the triad leaders. The man in the black cloak removed his hood. He was a young man with a scar down the right side of his face, with blonde hair and green eyes; he looked both handsome and evil.

"Alazar Desbode," said the men in great surprise.

"The legends are indeed true, my friends. The Dark Society does exist, and the wicked man does prosper. Do not be frightened. I have come to give you power beyond your wildest dreams, and with your contacts you will become a great advantage to our organization. The documents that you have seen here are the latest reports from our research team in bio arms defense, and are deadlier than the black plague and the Ebola virus combined, with enough force to kill millions instantly. Imagine gentlemen, such power beyond your wildest imaginings, firepower that you'll each receive by joining us."

They men were all shocked. "In return, all we ask for is your loyalty and your souls." Alazar Desbode laughed wickedly as he pulled an orb from his pocket. It was glowing with red fire and blood.

"He is insane," one of them muttered.

"No! You will live forever and more," said Alazar Desbode. They all nodded. "Touch the orb and the pact will be made. Once made it can't be broken."

They all touched the orb at once and it erupted with red, hot light that moved into them and pulled out their souls, trapping their souls for all eternity within the orb. They men screamed in pain, then fell to the ground and slowly rose. Part of the agreement was that they would still live but not be fully human.

Michael teleported to Lord Julius Zoratus's chambers to report on what he had seen. He had never witnessed anything so terrifying in all his life, even though he himself was no longer mortal.

"So you say that this man, this Alazar Desbode, took the souls of those men?" asked Lord Zoratus.

"Julius, I saw it with my own eyes. You have to tell me what is going on; what is this Dark Society?" demanded Michael.

"In time," said Zoratus looking out the window at the stars. "For now Michael, you have proven yourself worthy in passing the first trial."

"I hate it that you're hiding something from me," said Michael.

"Young vampire, it is not time; you're not yet ready."

"What is the next trial then?" asked Michael.

"To find the location of these biological weapons and steal us a sample of the technology. My great grand-daughter will help you on this one." "When do I begin?"

"Tomorrow night after sunset. Now leave me," said Lord Zoratus firmly.

After Michael left, Lord Zoratus called the members of the Coven into his office. They all sat as they heard their lord speak. "It's as we have suspected. Reynard Desbode's son is here and is moving in with the different criminal rings in the city. I do not doubt that the Dark Society has grown and that they have been developing new weapons," said Lord Zoratus.

"My lord, how can we fight our enemy against such power? Our technology is constantly competing with theirs," said Scarlet.

"My daughter, you and your sister Marianna must have faith in the gifts and wisdom that God has given us."

"But father, with due respect." Marianna agreed with her younger sister.

"Hush daughter; is it not God who has helped keep us alive all these centuries, and was it not God who gave us the spiritual insight and divine secrets to see into the hearts of this enemy? We must all keep our faith in God, despite what we are. The promise that was made to us will come to pass."

"But how?" Marianna asked.

"When our ancient enemy's evil empire is destroyed, then and only then we will be granted back our humanity and mortality," said Lord Zoratus.

"Until then we must be patient and wait," said Marko, who agreed with his brother.

40

TRAITOR

ichael got a call from Phillips; "Yes," said Michael over his cell.

"Michael! Thank God! It's Rodney. I need your help! They've taken me hostage," said Phillips in a panic.

"Who!" Michael exclaimed.

"The terrorists we caught; one of their cells captured me and they're holding me in the warehouse district but...MMMMM!" muffled Phillips. Michael heard a struggle occurring in the background and the phone went dead. He turned his car around, racing to rescue his old partner in the warehouse district. Michael was able to trace the call from to an abandoned fireworks warehouse. Hopping out of the car he headed to the back of the building. Armed with a 357 magnum pistol, he kicked open the door and looked around the room. The place was dark. Michael felt uneasy. As he crept into the warehouse a dark figure bashed him over the head with a bat, knocking him out.

A light was on in the middle of the room. Michael's hands and feet were tied to a chair. He came to, groggy and seeing only blurred faces until his sight finally came into focus. He groaned, but grew silent as he recognized the man who came out of the shadows to meet him.

"Hello Michael, welcome to the party," Phillips sneered. At last, the master of disguise had revealed his true colors.

"Rodney what's happening?" asked a confused Michael.

"What does it look like, partner? You're out, done, you're dead," said Phillips.

"But why? How could you!" yelled Michael.

"For half a million in cash, how could I refuse, just like I couldn't refuse the offer when I was hired to kill your sister," laughed Phillips.

"You! I swore that I wouldn't die until I found my sister's killer," replied an enraged Michael. "Then it was all a set up?"

"Not exactly; it's true that I still work for the government. However, Franco is a great employer and pays me much better than the government ever could. Besides, I knew you were always a sucker for patriotism and that this was the perfect set up to get you."

"You won't get away with this!"

"Oh yes I will. In exactly one hour I will be out of the city and in the air. Boys, kill this grease ball. See you around partner!" said Phillips mockingly as his men raised their assault rifles to shoot.

Michael began to change, his transformation fueled by his fury, and his vampiric form emerged. His eyes turned glaring red, his fangs appeared, and he broke free from the bindings and levitated the henchmen across the room in a melee, ripping his victims to shreds. Blood splattered everywhere. Stealing a pistol from a henchman he just killed, Michael began to shoot. The henchmen fired back. Some of the bullets hit cases of gunpowder, resulting in huge explosions; the place was beginning to burn. Phillips ducked to hide from the gunshots and screamed in terror as he saw the unholy creature that his former partner had become. In an instant Phillips had activated an auto-pilot chopper, which picked him up and flew him high into the sky and away from the scene of carnage. Michael barely managed to escape as the building exploding behind him. He vanished just as the fire department came to extinguish the flames. Michael managed to teleport to the city and began the search for Franco Scarfo's headquarters.

41

THE PLAN

Phillips was in a state of madness. His mind was overwhelmed with fear as he reported to Franco what had happened.

"What do you take me for a fool, you idiot!" yelled Franco.

"I swear to God what I saw is true, Damascus was about to be clipped and then the guy turned into the devil himself. I tell you I never saw anything so horrible in my whole life," said Phillips in fear.

"Shut up!" yelled Franco. He hit Phillips, who fell to the floor.

"This guy is too dangerous; we better get some insurance to make him back off, starting with his little niece," said Franco, picking up a newspaper and reading about the death of Damascus's family, which he had ordered in retaliation to the Santerini family. "Bring the bastard's brat to us. Word on the street is that he brought a little girl to his club."

"What do you want me to do?" asked Phillips.

"Blow the place, nab the kid, and we'll see just how tough this devil is," said Franco, chuckling insanely.

Back at the Black Spider Club, the night had just ended. Sally was being put to bed when all of a sudden a blast came through her bedroom window and smoke bombs ignited the room with gas. Sally passed out and was kidnapped by Phillips and his thugs. The thugs left behind a time bomb that was set to annihilate the place.

Mickey Blue and Isabelle ran into the front of the club, coughing from the gas and calling for Sally, when all of a sudden Serena appeared out of nowhere and grabbed them, teleporting them to the rooftop across the street as they saw Michael's club blow to bits.

"Sally!" screamed Isabelle. She believed that Sally was killed in the blast.

"Who are you?" Mickey Blue asked Serena.

"What are you?" asked Isabelle.

"I just saved your lives. You can thank me later. Right now Michael needs our help," said Serena.

"But Sally!" said Isabelle.

"Don't fear; I sense she's alive; she has been taken prisoner by Franco Scarfo," said Serena.

"What!" Isabelle exclaimed.

"Michael is a vampire now, darling. So am I. He never told any of you, as he wanted to protect you," said Serena.

"Are you going to kill us?" asked Mickey Blue.

"Now why in hell would I do that? You're his friends; I'm his girl," said Serena.

Isabelle and Mickey Blue were reassured that they wouldn't be harmed, but getting Sally back was more important. Serena gave Michael a call on her radio to tell him of the news. "Michael, It's bad."

"I know they've taken Sally."

"Where are you? The club has been destroyed and the others are here with me."

"I don't know where they've taken her; we have to contact the Coven and Danny, maybe they can help us," said Michael.

"I'll contact Julius and the others," said Serena.

In all this madness Isabelle and Mickey Blue were still confused and afraid, and so Serena brought them to Michael's pad to tell them the whole story. After hearing all they needed, Mickey Blue and Isabelle were in awe. "How can this be?" asked Isabelle.

"It can be; we exist. I ask myself sometimes how, but we do exist. If there is a God, I also wonder why he let us be made," said Serena.

"You do care for Michael?" asked Mickey Blue.

"Of course I do, I love him."

"I'm sorry." Isabelle finally understood the reason why she could no longer be with Michael.

"Sorry for what?" asked Serena.

"Look at me and you will know."

"Oh, I understand," said Serena reading Isabelle's thoughts understanding Isabelles's realization.

"The only thing that Isabelle and I care about now is saving Sally. We love that kid," interjected Mickey Blue.

"My family can help us, along with some of Michael's contacts," Serena offered.

"You mean there are more of you?" asked Isabelle.

"We live among your kind. We are everywhere; some, like my family, serve a higher power, while there are others like myself who have no one."

"Look, I don't give a damn about any of this; we have to find Sally," said Mickey Blue in anger.

"Yes, we will find her, but for now I must take you to a safe haven. Franco Scarfo will probably find this hideout soon. Is there some place you can go to?" asked Serena.

"Yes, I know a place," said Isabelle.

"Then go now, the both of you, and stay out of this. It is too dangerous. You two could get killed if you don't listen to me," said Serena.

"But," protested Mickey Blue.

"Don't worry. I'll keep you posted; take this radio." Serena handed the radio to Mickey Blue.

Mickey and Isabelle left quickly, flagging down a cab to take them to Bobby Scarfo's, while Serena contacted the Coven for help.

42

FIND THE GIRL

Serena knew where Michael was heading, so she raced across the rooftops to Danny Fredricks' apartment to meet him. Meanwhile, across town, Jackie heard the news that the Black Spider Club had been destroyed and was certain that Michael and his friends had been killed. Jackie called the Don and the others to meet.

Just before the meeting, Jackie broke into Salvatore Santerini's office and found a small safe, just like the informer on the phone had described. After Jackie scrambled the security code, he opened the safe to find a briefcase. "My God," he said in shock as he opened the case and saw the stolen money. He hopped out the window and sped off in his car to bring the Don all the evidence that was needed.

All of the crew was gathered in the Don's study, even Salvatore. Jackie told everyone the bad news. "Boys our best man has disappeared, the Black Spider has burnt down, and there has been no word from him or his girl within the last four days."

"Maybe Franco got them," said Salvatore.

"Oh you think? Maybe you have something to do with this!" said Anthony.

"What! You can't think I would kill one of our own!" bellowed Salvatore.

"Yeah!" said Jackie as he tossed the briefcase he'd stolen from Salvatore's office onto the Don's desk.

The pile of money splashed out. "But I…!" screamed Salvatore.

"I've seen enough," said Don Felice, disgusted by such dishonor. Salvatore tried to bolt for the door, but Anthony grabbed him and pinned him to the ground.

"What should we do with him?" asked Jackie. "Get rid of him; he has brought shame upon this family. Take him to Mead," said Don Felice.

Anthony clobbered Salvatore over the head, knocking him unconscious and then he and Jackie wrapped Salvatore up in the Spanish rug that was on the floor and carried him out of the building. They loaded him into the trunk of Anthony's car.

Don Felice looked down from his office and shook his head in sadness, seeing how greed had torn his family apart.

On the drive out to Lake Mead, Anthony and Jackie picked up a set of chains and weights from Anthony's home. When they got close to Lake Mead, they heard a thump from the trunk. "What the hell is that?" said Anthony.

"That mother fucker, he's awake, I told you we should have whacked him first," said Jackie.

Anthony pulled over. Jackie popped open the trunk just as Salvatore kicked Anthony in the face, dropping him to the ground.

"Son of a bitch!" said Jackie, and he punched Salvatore in the gut. Enraged, Anthony grabbed Salvatore by the head and begun to push in his skull in with his large palms.

"Wait! There's another!" screamed Salvatore.

"What did you say? You fat bastard!" yelled Jackie, pointing his pistol at Salvatore's face.

"Riffman! The guy is Riffman!" yelled Salvatore.

"Thanks – now die!" said Anthony as he crushed in Salvatore's skull. After tying the corpse up with the steel chains and weights, they dumped Salvatore's body in the lake. "See you in hell, you double-crossing prick," said Anthony as they hopped into the car, heading back into the city.

Back in town, Serena tried to contact the Coven for help telepathically but she was too weak from not feeding and two weak to teleport to the Coven headquarters so instead she met up with Micheal. The two headed out to meet Danny Fredricks for help. Twenty minutes later the two vampires arrived at Danny's place. Danny was with Tommy Santerini. They had been laying low since the Black Spider had burned down. There was a loud knock on the door and Danny turned in his chair hastily. "Who is it?" "It's Michael and Serena, let us in," Michael called.

Danny opened the door nervously. "I thought you two were dead!" Danny was relieved to see that Michael and Serena were alive.

"Are you going to hold the door open or let us in?" asked Serena.

"Come in," said Danny. Tommy stood up and ran to Michael, hugging him, relieved that he wasn't dead.

"Tommy!" said Michael.

"Michael, thank God you're not dead! We heard that the club blew up and we thought it was Scarfo's doing," said Tommy.

"No it wasn't," said Serena.

"Who then?" asked Tommy.

"My old partner Phillips." Michael shook his head.

"You can't be serious," said Danny.

"He set us up, all of us; he's been working for Franco all this time, and now he's got my niece," said Michael.

"You need my help?" asked Danny.

"Yes," said Michael.

"Let me help too. That creep Franco had his boys Sonny and Al blow up my restaurant. I want some payback," said Tommy.

"No kid, you're not a solider; they'll kill you," said Michael.

"But!" protested Tommy.

"Stay on the streets with the local thugs and grab info; that's how you can be of use to us. Any information you can get us on Scarfo will help."

"You got it," said Tommy as he headed out the door.

"What about me?" asked Danny.

"Can you get access to the police computer systems?" asked Serena.

"Yeah sure, no problem; remember, I still work on the side as a cop. I know all the access codes within the system from the inside out. What do you need?" Danny sat down at his computer and began scanning the police database.

"Access the police reports on every known hide-out they found on the Scarfos; there's a chance that Phillips might go back to one if it's been abandoned," suggested Michael.

"Searching," said Danny as he tapped into the system. "Got a few; one of them is the abandoned airfield, the last known bust was for ecstasy runners. I wouldn't be surprised if your ex-partner had stashed some vehicles there to get out of town, like a small plane or something."

"That's also a perfect place to hold a kidnapped prisoner; it's out in the boonies," said Serena.

"What about the other locations?" asked Michael.

"The customs warehouse is in the Industrial district, and the last one is at the Baltimore Film Studio that closed down two years ago," said Danny.

"Come on, let's go," said Michael. Danny grabbed his coat and gun. They raced in his private squad car to the old airfield hanger.

As they sped off to the hanger, Serena called Darius for help. "Darius, it's me Serena, I need your help; gather Scarlet and Marianna for a hunt."

"What's wrong?" said Darius.

"The fledgling's niece has been taken prisoner. We need assistance in finding the girl," said Serena.

"What does this have to do with me? It's not my problem," said Darius.

"Now listen here, you self-centered jerk, when your father hears that you wouldn't help save an innocent child's life, he will be most displeased. Where is your sense of honor? Or would you prefer that Marianna make a mockery of you?" snapped Serena.

"I'm there, where do I tell the others to look?" asked a subdued Darius.

"Proceed to the abandoned customs warehouse in the industrial district, the other place is at the old Baltimore film studio. Be cautious; these men you are hunting are going to be well armed. Keep in touch on my cell," instructed Serena.

"With my trusty bow, there will be no problem," said Darius confidently as he saw the others come into his study. He signaled to them; they knew that trouble was in the air. Grabbing their weapons, they flew off into the night to hunt for the kidnappers.

Back in the car, Danny had overheard Serena on the phone and was curious about whom she spoken with. "What did you mean when you said fledgling back there, is that some kind of code?"

Michael gave Danny a harsh look. "She means this," said Michael as his face began to contort, in order to show Fredricks his true nature. "What in hell!" Danny screamed in fear and he nearly sideswiped into a pole. Michael grabbed the wheel to prevent them from crashing.

"Danny! We're not going to hurt you," yelled Michael.

"Could someone please tell me what is going on?" screamed Danny.

"What does it look like?" said Serena.

"You're both, you're fucking vampires?" Danny asked, not sure of what he had seen.

"Um, yeah! It's a long story, could we please not kill each other driving now! I'll tell you the whole story," said Michael.

A few minutes into the tale, Danny was flabbergasted. "Wait! Let me get this straight; you're telling me vampires exist and you're working for some global Coven organization besides the mafia, and you want my help! Exactly when the fuck were you going to tell me all of this?"

"Well, we didn't think it would come to this," sighed Serena.

"Fuck it, let's go get your kid, but you're going to owe me big for this one, very fucking big," said Danny.

"Thanks for understanding; you know we wouldn't harm you; you're a friend," said Serena.

"Wrong missy! I'm Michael's friend! I'm only doing this to pay him back for a favor. No matter what the devil he's become, he's still my friend, but I'm going to need a damn strong drink in the morning. Why do I get myself into this kind of shit!" said Danny.

Michael and Serena couldn't help but laugh at Danny's comments. Just then a car approached them from behind and started shooting. "Shit, we've been followed," said Danny.

"Scarfo!" Michael yelled.

"Don't worry I'll handle them," said Serena, noticing the police shotgun and a box of shells tucked under the back seat. Locking and loading the rifle quickly, she smashed open the back window of the car and fired away, unloading shells one by one in blasts of hellfire. The attackers fired back and machine gun bullets pierced parts of the car.

"Oh shit!" screamed Danny as he tried to shake them. Michael grabbed a grenade from his ammo bag. "You got to be kidding me!" said Danny as he saw Michael pull the pin with his teeth and toss the grenade out the car window. It hit the ground, and attacking car was blown straight off the ground and flipped over, exploding in a ball of fire, killing the attackers. "Definitely should have stayed drunk today," said Danny as he increased his speed up to 100 miles per hour.

"Slow down man! There's no one behind us now," said Michael.

"Cool," Danny breathed, slowing down as they approached the old airfield. They parked the car quietly to avoid attention. Michael loaded his Uzi and M-9, and Serena took the shotgun and reloaded the weapon, putting her compact pistol in her left bootleg. Danny took out his 45-caliber weapon and loaded it, hearing the smooth cocking action of the pistol clip. They were ready to go in with a bang.

Inside, the hanger was dark and only moonlight shone through the old thick windows. The place was neglected and filled with dust and swarms of rats. The trio snuck around with guns loaded, pacing slowly around the room. Suddenly a man turned on a light switch. Fifty men stood in the room, from the rafters to the ground, machine guns cocked and ready to shoot. Sally was nowhere in sight. It was a trap. The trio raised their hands in the air.

Phillips' henchmen chained them to large stake poles stuck in the ground. One of Phillips' henchmen wheeled in a massive time bomb that was encased in a metal enclosure and screwed tight into a steel ground mount. One of the men set the timer on the bomb that would soon blow the place to kingdom come.

"Hah, hah, ha, ha," laughed a large man walking out of the shadows. He revealed himself to the captives he had in his power.

"Franco Scarfo, I should have known, you dirty son of a bitch!" said Michael.

"What a lovely group of freaks, a two-timing cop, a foolish thief, and a wannabe hero hit man," mocked Franco Scarfo. He didn't notice that Serena sat quiet with her eyes closed. She was contacting Darius and the others for help.

"Darius come. We are here," said Serena in her mind. Darius heard Serena and sensed their location. He then alerted the others to prepare for the attack. "Scarlet, Marianna, to the abandoned airfield, our cousin is being held there with her fledgling," said Darius.

"We'll be shocking and rocking," said Scarlet eagerly. Scarlet was the youngest of the entire Zoratus coven. A French vampire, she had beautifully long golden hair and the face of an angel; she had piercings in her ears and she was dressed to fight in her Goth leather clothes.

"Let's go," said Marianna seriously, and they teleported to the spot.

Breaking through the windows, the vampires attacked the guards; Franco's men fired on Darius, Scarlet and Marianna, but as the bullets hit the vampires' undead flesh, their wounds healed instantly. Michael was hit in the crossfire in the neck and felt a sharp pain, but no blood appeared.

"What the hell!" Franco screamed as he ducked to hide from the arrows Darius was shooting into the room that were killing many of the guards. Marianna circled her attackers with a series of zips and spins, unsheathing her sword and decapitating her victims with ease, as if slicing through a vat of warm butter. Fountains of blood flowed from her victims. Scarlet jumped from side to side of the hanger, throwing daggers into the attacker's chests, legs, and heads, impaling them quickly.

Michael managed to break free and unchain Serena and Danny. Franco Scarfo ran from the scene and took off in his car; the bomb was set to go off in 30 seconds. The vampires and Danny managed to get through the back door by kicking it down and jumping to the ground for safety, just as the old airplane hanger exploded. In slow motion, burning debris fell to the ground.

After getting back safely to the car, everyone managed to catch their breath, lucky to be alive.

"Are you all right?" asked Darius.

"We're okay. Just some cuts and bruises; are you each okay?" asked Danny.

"We're fine," said Marianna.

"Thank you all for your help," said Michael.

"Not a problem, you're one of us," said Scarlet.

"In the meantime, we had better form a new plan of action. We still haven't found the girl," said Serena.

"We didn't find anyone at the warehouse or the old studio," said Darius.

"I know a hacker who can help us, if we can get to her before Phillips can," said Michael.

"Very well. We will continue to search by air," said Darius. The others agreed as they flew off into the night. Danny was amazed by this new experience; "Holy Shit! Damn!"

The three sped off in Danny's car, into the early hours of the morning, to find Michael's contact.

43

KAT

The trio sped off to the Luna district, the hot dance club area of town. Michael's hacker lived above the Razor Blade Club in a small loft. She was the best there was and could crack through anything.

Heading into the Razor Blade Club, the trio noticed flashing electric razor lights, the pulsing sounds of techno and hard-hitting house music, and a scene filled with all sorts of musical misfits dancing to the exotic beat; joy riders, goths, ravers, punks, dreamers, humans and vampires alike, all in the same depraved mix.

They climbed up the stairs and heard hard rock music playing from Kat's room; she was Michael's hacker.

"Charming place, what a freak show," said Danny, annoyed by the sounds of the music.

"Hey, I resent that remark," said Michael.

"Just kidding," joked Danny.

Michael knocked on Kat's door; she heard him and turned down the music, peering through the porthole. Unlocking her door, she let Michael and his companions in her loft. Kat's pad was filled with technological bliss, computer system after computer system, VR stabilizers, and best of all, a hacker's dream, a multi super mainframe that could access any coding in the world in the twinkling of an eye. "Michael, to what pleasure do I owe this honor? What do you need from me this time? A hydra x virus, a government system crash, or just a little hex key coding?" asked Kat.

"Cute, kid. No, I got a real ringer for you this time. I need to crack into the city's main frame computer system to look up an old friend," said Michael.

"For the man that saved my life, anything. What are friends for? But please give me a challenge, come on," said Kat.

"Nothing fancy, just do it," said Michael.

"All right hottie," teased Kat, hacking into her computer.

"Thanks kid. This is my girl Serena and this is Danny," said Michael.

"Okay, let's see what we can do. Who are we looking for exactly?" asked Kat.

"Ex-government agent records of one Rodney Clarence Phillips, last known place of access any military organizations and places he may try to escape to," said Michael.

"Sounds like you have it in for this guy," Kat commented.

"Yeah, well I think you would too kid. That asshole nearly killed us all," said Danny.

"Damn! Anyway, I'm cross referencing the data with the city's system and the CIA's mainframe," said Kat.

"Nice thing that your dad gave you access to the system," said Michael.

"Say what, how does a teenager get the equipment to access top-secret government information?" asked Serena.

"Simple. I worked with my father and Mike as a data engineer, back when we where in Turkey, and Mike saved my life from the Prime minister's assassins who tried to kill me. After I found out he was alive, we kept in touch and I do him a favor now and then," said Kat.

"What are you, a genius?" asked Danny.

"Yup, 190 IQ will do that for you," said Kat playfully. She typed away, punching codes into her computer. "Bingo! Last known organizations that this guy was linked to," Kat started.

Danny noticed something on the back of Michael's neck. Walking over, he yanked on the needle and pulled it out.

"What the, ow!" yelled Michael.

"What the hell is that, Danny?" asked Serena.

Danny inspected the small needle dart. "Looks like a transmitter, but that would mean?" said Danny.

Suddenly, a helicopter rose up to the open window. Serena sensed danger. She created a whirlwind of energy around them all as the gunner from the chopper opened fire, blasting firebombs through the window. "The force is too strong, I can't hold it," said Serena, resisting the heat. Fire was her weakness. A man in the chopper fired mini-grenades and the room exploded in flames. Michael teleported them away from the burning loft. The people inside the club below screamed in panic as the place collapsed, killing them all.

44

THE ABBEY

In less than a second Michael had transported them all to safety. With no hospital in sight, he stole a truck and drove them to Saint Mark's Cathedral. He had served as an altar boy there on summer retreats, and he remembered that the cathedral had a hospital wing for its monastery. Serena had been badly burned from the fire. Danny was fine, due to Serena's aid. Kat had suffered the most. She had deep cuts from broken glass and was losing lots of blood.

It was four in the morning and rain had begun to pour as a thunderstorm came over the city. Guarding the vast doors of the gothic sanctuary were huge stone gargoyles, guardian angels and crucifixes. Michael pounded on the heavy iron doors, hoping that someone inside would answer. Inside the cathedral many men of God were kneeling in silent prayer as they meditated on Christ, chanting in Latin. One of the monks heard the nose outside and ran to unlock the doors of the church. He was a young handsome man with short brown hair, blue eyes, dressed in a humble robe. Michael fell to the ground with his wounded friends as the doors opened.

"Oh Lord!" said the man.

"Help us," Michael pleaded as he fell to the ground, weak from not feeding.

Michael woke in a strange room, along with Serena and Kat. The young man who had opened the doors of the church sat near Kat. He had bandaged her wounds and brought her food and water. Danny was nowhere in sight. Serena's burns were also bandaged and Michael saw the cup that Serena was drinking from; Michael could smell blood in the cup, blood that was not human. It was pig's blood. Michael also took a drink from Serena's cup, but it tasted horrible. There was something strange about this monk. How could he have known what Serena truly was?

The young monk came over to see Michael as he sat up on his cot. "You and your friends are feeling better."

"Thank you for your help," said Michael.

"Your young female friend is doing better. Father Paul and I managed to stop the bleeding and we have called the nuns to bring her to the hospital wing for a few days. I am Brother Dominus Sullivan." Dominus was a very handsome man, about thirty years old in appearance; he had a short nose and a lean muscular, body.

"Is the priest here?" asked Serena, who had stood up, though she was still weak.

"He will be back here in half an hour. He has gone to say the morning mass," said Dominus.

"Where is my friend Danny?" asked Michael.

"He left to find someone who needed your help," said Dominus.

Michael noticed a strange tattoo on the young monk's right hand. It was the same seal Serena had on her neck. "You're one of us," said Michael in surprise.

"What are you talking about, sir?" asked Brother Dominus.

"The mark on your hand. I've seen it before," said Michael.

"I have to go," said Dominus, and he left to room only to run into Father Paul, who was surprised to see Dominus acting in such a peculiar fashion.

"What is wrong; how are the patients?"

"Father, the man in black knows what I am; I believe he and the girl know," said Dominus.

"It would not be the first time their kind have come. Let me go and see them, son," said Father Paul calmly.

He entered the room with Dominus in silence. Father Paul had unique gifts; he was blessed with prophetic wisdom and the gift of insight. "Well, well, well. If it isn't my old alter boy, Michael Victor Damascus," said Father Paul.

"It's nice to see you too, Father," said Michael.

"I'm surprised. I haven't seen you since the old days in the service. I heard around town that you took up with unsavory people when you came home. Too bad you didn't come back here, where your heart should have been," said Father Paul.

"What do you mean?" asked Michael.

"It's not enough, son, that you became an accessory to the mob, but you endanger these friends of yours with something much worse. Still, I made a promise to the Lord to help all who come here, and I shall," said Father Paul.

"I'm sorry that I left the faith, but what could I do? You know what happened," said Michael.

"You just don't know when to stop, do you?"

"He is with me now; it's my fault," said Serena, regretful for what she had done.

"I could tell that you were not human the moment I saw that mark on your neck, child," said Father Paul.

"How so?" Serena stammered.

"I know your kind when I see them. The young man who has cared for you these last few days is one of them," said Father Paul.

"A vampire?" said Serena.

"He is my son, and a devout man of God no matter what he was born as. He still serves the church that his true father served at one time," said Father Paul.

"What do you mean, his true father?" asked Serena.

"The man who helped the church fight the war that goes unnoticed, against a dark enemy," said Father Paul.

"Reynard Desbode," Serena breathed.

"Yes, him and his dark empire," said Dominus.

"What is this society, what war, who are you, and how did you know that Serena needed to drink?" asked Michael, confused.

"I am one of your kind," explained Dominus.

"But how could an immortal choose this?" asked Serena.

"Let me tell you a story. A long time ago during the first century, after the passing of the first Christian Emperor, Constantine, the persecution of the Church continued as time passed into the Middle Ages and the Christian Crusades. The pope of that time had formed secret military orders of monk warriors to ensure the protection of the Church from persecution and destruction. Those persecutors were Desbode and his legions. Julius Zoratus was in charge of the Church's warriors, named the Sons of Judah. As a military general for the Church, Julius was loyal to God and to Rome for years. Julius and his armies sought to fight against invaders by any means necessary, to protect the Church and the world. During a great battle of epic proportions, larger enemy forces defeated Julius' army, because Rome had failed to provide him with enough men. As Julius saw the horror of his comrades being slaughtered by the enemy, he met his nemesis, the Dark General Reynard Desbode, the founder of the Dark Society. Legend says that Reynard Desbode sold his soul to the Devil to become a fallen angel. His pagan society had one sole purpose: to destroy the Christian God and conquer the world as his own. Gloating in their victory by showing extreme hatred and animosity to their captors, the Dark Society's general placed a terrible curse upon Julius and his men, mocking their Christian loyalty. Julius and his men were transformed into the undead, neither human nor demon. They had a dual nature split between the two, with no hope of being able to go back to being looked upon as servants of God by the Church in Rome. Some say it was a punishment for Julius's vast vanity and pride. Others say it was a spiritual test of his faith.

They were taken as prisoners and made to be slaves in chains, working the copper mines for the Dark Society. There they were forced to dig for crystals and copper to power vast technology and weapons. All of the prisoners witnessed inhumane and indescribable acts of torture; they were forced to watch as their own families were slaughtered, crucified, and burned alive in fire pits." Said Dominus.

Michael had a vision of these atrocities. Men, women, and children being killed by the legions of Reynard Desbode; the fire consuming its victims, leaving a foul stench in the air. He could smell the blood on the desecrated bodies of the dead. The vision stopped suddenly. "I saw it, I just saw it all," exclaimed Michael.

"He has second sight," said Dominus.

"Tell me more," pleaded Michael, he had to know.

"For centuries Julius Zoratus and his new kind were oppressed. Humans viewed our race as monsters, for you see, the curse came with a terrible hunger: the blood thirst. It was so terrible that those who resisted feeding became insane and committed suicide or ended up in killing innocent victims. Thus spread the stories and myths perpetuating the evil nature of vampires. Our kind existed for centuries before Zoratus' defeat, though we don't know all the facts, just what was written down in certain records.

But from that time on humans feared Julius and his kind and sought to destroy them. Ekal was a rogue vampire slayer who took control over the vampires to gain power and influence in league with the Dark Society. Julius formed an uprising for his imprisoned legions to escape. The plan worked in deceiving the Dark Society's smaller order, which they overran and destroyed. Now the fugitives had another problem. Because of what his kind had done while imprisoned, mostly those who went mad and killed innocent people, Rome saw him and his vampire kin as a threat to the Church and gave orders to hunt them down and kill them all. Documents that chronicle this story say that Julius wept as he received the news that the Church had turned against him in fear. He and his kind fled to different parts of the world and went into hiding. As time passed, up to the present day, Covens all around the earth had formed in attempts at survival. Now as you have seen, vampires have integrated into society and blended into the worldwide industries of business, organized crime and even politics, in order to preserve their existence. The Dark Society still exists but is known only as a legend by most people as well as by many vampires. It has grown in number looking for a way to finally conquer the world," said Dominus.

"So that is why Julius hasn't told me his story. He desires to have the vampire Covens that are still loyal to justice stop this menace," said Michael.

"I never did believe the story myself, nor did I believe in God, until now," said Serena.

"Oh yes child, there is a God; he is here with us right now," said Father Paul.

"Dominus, is Julius your biological father?" Serena asked.

"Yes, he is. I left him and the coven when I was a boy."

"How could you abandon your own kind?" asked Serena.

"Father always told us many years ago that as warriors in the Great Test, we would have to kill in order to win, along with keeping our faith and prayer. I could never kill; the guilt always came. After I killed my first enemy during one mission, I could never go on." Dominus hung his head.

"Young Dominus came here to find peace with God. The Holy Lord directed him to me, so I helped him," said Father Paul. "It was ten years ago when he came here."

"I believe that's why you too came here; I believe that God brought you both here for more than the healing of your physical wounds," said Dominus.

"Oh please, save me from the melodrama," snickered Michael.

"Ungrateful coward; then I should have left you to die," frowned Brother Sullivan. Suddenly the darkness overcame Michael. He fell to the ground and began to convulse. His eyes turned a glowing yellow. The demons that he had allowed to enter his heart took over his mind.

"Let him alone priest, his soul is ours by legal right!" said the demons, speaking through Michael as his body levitated in midair and his eyes rolled upward so that only the whites showed.

"In the name of the authority of Jesus Christ, by the blood of the Lamb of God be bound 700 fold and be silent within," commanded Father Paul as he put his hand on Michael's head. The demons screamed and grew silent as Michael's body fell to the floor. As Michael gained control of his mind, his eyes came normal and the darkness left him. He spat up blood on the floor and snapped awake.

"What happened!" Serena screamed in fear.

"What have you two done!" yelled Father Paul.

"I thought I gave him a gift," Serena shook.

"What you have done, child, is worsen the state of his soul. The Lord has shown me what you have done, who he has become, and what you and he must do to be redeemed," said Father Paul.

"What's happening to me?" asked Michael.

"Son, you have let your soul and that of your lover's be cursed. Because of your wickedness and your choices, you have let the Devil's influence enter you. It is as the demons said; by legal right they share a part of you."

"How can he stop it, Father?" asked Dominus.

"He can't stop it, not alone; he must repent of his sins, and forgive the one he hates most. Only Christ can deliver him," said Father Paul.

"I can't! I can't forgive Phillips, not him. He killed my sister!" yelled Michael in anger.

"That is your test son; God has decided it for you. It is your destiny to face. If you do not let go of your hatred of this man, you will continue to let these evil spirits live inside you; it's your choice," said Father Paul.

"What about me?" Serena asked.

"You must repent as well; your bitterness is the seed of your demons. You too must forgive the man who killed your first love.

When you both have forgiven your enemies and have repented, the demons will leave you. Believe in Jesus and you will be delivered. In the meantime, I will pray and fast for you both. However, as a final test, you will only regain your mortality when you have completed your destiny," said Father Paul.

An enraged Michael vanished as he teleported away from the priest. Serena fell to the ground weeping; she had suffered so much and she longed for her humanity again. She prayed to God for forgiveness and forgave the man who had killed her first lover. As she confessed her sins to Father Paul, he cleansed her through Christ. She had taken the first step to being free, now that she had become a believer in the true light and found God.

"Will he be free?" Serena asked Father Paul, thinking of Michael.

"I think there is still good in him, but only God knows. It's up to Michael to decide," said Father Paul. Serena then thanked Father Paul and went home, yet her heart was filled with despair, the pain she had brought upon her lover and herself ate at her conscience like a cancer consuming her very soul.

45

"GOOD NEWS"

Back at his apartment, Michael fell to the ground in deep anger. Kneeling and looking at a picture of his family, he felt helpless and consumed with grief; he also felt guilty because he was denying his faith in God. He felt fear truly in his soul, fear that his maker couldn't forgive him, or maybe that he would never forgive the man who had taken the person that had meant so much to him. "He's dead and that's that," said Michael to himself.

Serena then came into the living room where he was and kneeled down to hug him. "I'm sorry about all of this. I just wanted to be with you; it's my fault," she was filled with remorse.

"No, I chose this life. I have to accept it," said Michael. "Serena, I can't afford to lose another person. We have to find Sally and protect her."

"We will. Something will turn up," said Serena.

"Maybe," said Michael, with a small seed of faith in his heart.

"Are you all right?" asked Serena.

"Fine for now, let's just go," said Michael.

Before they could leave the phone rang and Michael picked up the receiver. "Mike it's me, Danny. Good news. I managed to beat the hell out of a suspect who witnessed the kidnapping. The guy told me that Scarfo took off in his car with the girl, heading to the Tyrell manor," said Danny.

"I know that old place. It's been condemned for years," said Michael.

"Meet me at Rocko's. He'll boost us the gear we'll need," said Danny.

"Thanks," said Michael as he hung up the phone.

"Danny?" asked Serena.

"Yes, let's go." The two took off on a spare motorcycle from Michael's garage and raced to meet Danny at Rocko's shop.

Across the city at the mansion, Franco sat in darkness and deep thought, trying to think of a way to eliminate Michael and his friends. Out of the blue, the phone rang. "Hello, who is this?" said Franco in frustration.

"Someone who wants to help you take care of your problem," said a voice.

"Who is this?"

"Just call me Desbode. I know someone who will be able to rid you of the pest you have. Call this number, 555-6739, tell them that Desbode sent you. They will give you what you need."

"What do you want out of this pal?" asked Franco.

"Don't ask now; you will know later."

On the other side of town, Michael and Serena arrived at Rocko's garage. The large door opened as Michael and Serena rode inside. Rocko pushed the control switch on a computer board, lowering Serena and Michael down on a lift into a vast underground compound smelling of gasoline and oil; the place was filled with an astounding collection of wires, piping, machine generators, flow lights, and tools of every robotic type. It had been abandoned before Michael found it for Rocko, an illegal weapons smuggling plant. "What the hell did you do this time Mike? It's a war zone out there, all this crap on TV. What's going on buddy?"

"Believe me, Rock, you don't want to know. Anyway, I had a little accident with the hover bike. It blew up on the highway." "Just great, that's swell, Mike. It took me eight months alone to design all the specs on that bike; it'll take me another three just to build another. Don't you ever take care of the toys I give you?" said a disappointed Rocko.

"What can I say, it comes with the job," said Michael.

Rocko noticed Serena giving him a friendly smile. Rocko, was a goofy, techie, geek of a guy; wild and reckless, he was filled with charm and a love for inventing. He was 31 and a close friend of Michael's from their days in the service. Rocko was dressed in his usual rocker t shirts and jeans. He had greasy brown hair and brown eyes and he was a short guy, but always pleasant to be around. "Forget it, it's on your tab," said Rocko.

"You know I'm good for it," said Michael.

"Yeah I know. Say buddy, who's this sexy lady with you?" smirked Rocko.

"Serena, hotshot. I'm his girl," said Serena. Rocko saw she had a gun on her side.

"Let me guess. She's your new partner, too."

"Yeah," said Michael.

"Anyway, what do you need from me this time? I got a bunch of new tech goodies I have been working on lately."

"We have an emergency Rock. My niece, Sally, you remember her don't you?"

"Yeah sure I do, what's wrong?"

"She's been kidnapped by Franco Scarfo. The guy blew up my club and nearly killed us the other night."

"Got any word from the street where Scarfo has taken her?" asked Rocko.

"We know they're holding her up at the old Tyrell mansion," said Serena.

"That old place was shut down because it was near a steel plant that was filled with asbestos," said Rocko.

"What are we going to need?" asked Serena. "A better question to ask is how many guys you think are in there," said Rocko.

"Probably about a hundred at most I think. Frank Scarfo has access to military weapons now," said Michael.

"Come with me into the weapons shop. I'll show you the new stuff," said Rocko.

Danny arrived at the shop; Michael saw him on the camera screen and buzzed him inside, and he came down the lift to meet them.

"Now that we're all here kiddies, we can get cracking. Pay attention," said Rocko as he held up a large strange looking rifle. "What we got here is a Covolt 72 tear gas rifle, combined with an automatic shot gun barrel, easy reload that fires seven shots for the shotgun, single reload for the tear gas grenades."

Rocko threw it to Serena, who admired the weapon. "Oh I'm going to have a lot of fun with this," she said.

"Next up we have the newest in laser sight firepower, an MG30 assault rifle, fires 30 armor piercing bullets, and we got here in this slot a section for exploding tip bullets. On the upper slot is a tip to put on a suppressor, good for close range kills," said Rocko, tossing the gun to Michael. "Exquisite!" Michael loaded the gun and fired at a junk heap, seeing it tear apart.

"Very nice Rock," complimented Danny.

"If you like that one, Danny, I have a special designed just for you. Since you're best with pistols, I've created the Cobra 76 based, which is based on the M9. What we have here is a combined automatic pistol and laser sight. It has an eagle eye scope, and fires both poison bullets and M9 bullets with a smooth cocking action." Rocko loaded the gun and handed it to Danny.

"What about jamming?" Danny asked.

"If you don't press the clip in too hard, it shouldn't jam," said Rocko.

"You going to come?" asked Michael.

"Sorry. I was born a lover, not a fighter," Rocko shrugged. Michael gave him a disappointed look. "I'm just kidding dude, of course I'm coming with you guys. But I'm going in with this baby, the AKG 62, a mini rocket launcher. I call this the Angel Rocket," said Rocko laughing like a fool.

"Holy Shit!" said Michael.

"It gets better. Come with me into the vehicle shop. The place is going to be heavily guarded, and I got just thing we're going to need to bust in there."

They all walked into a large room. Rocko flipped on the light, which illuminated a massive object covered by a sheet. Rocko threw off the sheet to uncover an awesome monster vehicle; a powerful tank on wheels.

"What the hell have you been up to? It looks like a damn tank and halftrack combined!" Michael exclaimed.

"You told me you always wanted to be prepared, so I developed the ultimate ground vehicle; behold, the Cerberus 599 XT, an urban assault vehicle, well built with titanium alloy construction, pressure sensitive bullet proof tread tires, dual chain machine guns, mini canons, and also a nice turbo boost drive train that gives this bad girl one hell of a punch," said Rocko.

"Is she fast?" asked Danny.

"Oh yeah, she's fast, and not only that but we have a stealth cloaking radar system inside on the dashboard," said Rocko.

"Let's load up and head out," said Michael.

"It's time to fire it up. Let's go kill some baddies," said Rocko, talking goofy for fun.

"You play too many video games," sighed Michael smiling.

46

GO FOR THE KILL

The quartet rumbled out on high speed through the desolated, battered part of the city, racing out into the long abandoned underground train line, until they emerged from the tunnel onto a dirt road that led to the old mansion. The giant house was a decadent ruin from another time. It had once been the prestigious home of many actors and famous performers during the early days of Las Vegas. Now it was a decaying tomb, rotting in memories of the past.

Searchlights combed the manor, now a make-shift compound patrolled by men in body armor and guns. Guards patrolled the area constantly. Inside the home, the closed doors of the study hid torn drapes, cobwebs, and a broken set of furniture that looked so old that it would crumble into dust if touched. Sally was tied up in ropes and Phillips was keeping a close watch on her as he lit up a cigarette sitting, backward on an old wooden chair.

"When my uncle gets here you're going to be sorry!" sassed Sally vehemently.

"Shut up you little brat!" screamed Phillips, paranoid as he slapped her across the face; he was still terrified of his last encounter with Michael.

Sally didn't flinch; she had learned to be tough from her uncle. "He's coming and he's going to make you all pay!" said Sally.

"Shut up!" yelled Phillips as stood quickly, knocking over the chair he was sitting on. He strode to the old large window that was covered with dust and cracks and peered out to look for the possible horror that was coming to destroy him and his men.

Franco Scarfo opened the doors of the study signaling to Phillips a need speak with him in private. Phillips left his captive alone and went to speak with his boss in the other room.

"Why do you look so worried?" Franco asked.

"You know damn well why I'm worried," said Phillips.

"No worries, you pussy. I've found a solution. Someone needs us and they sent us a gift," said Franco.

"What?"

"Not what; who." Franco snapped his fingers. A dark figure came out of the shadows and into the moonlit room, covered in purple and black silk.

"What the hell is that!" said Phillips in terror. The figure was dressed in ancient clothing, like a ninja, but his left arm was covered with an armor gauntlet that looked as if it were made of skulls. He wore black boots, a razor sharp claw blade on his right hand, and a katana sword around his back. His eyes were pure red and his face was pale and covered in small battle scars. This man looked like a devil from hell.

"Jubel, make us proud," said Franco, placing in the ninja's palm a pouch that contained diamonds. "Your payment in advance; these diamonds are worth one million dollars," said Franco.

Jubel opened the pouch and looked at the contents. "It will be a pleasure, sir. When will the prey arrive?"

"Soon, I hope. When they come, send these assholes on a one-way trip to hell," Franco ordered.

"It shall be done," said Jubel as he bowed and disappeared back into the shadows.

"Who is this guy; who sent him?" asked Phillips.

"We found some new people. They said they needed us, so I took up their offer," said Franco.

"You're sure this guy can be trusted?" asked Phillips.

"Oh yes, he can be trusted," Franco replied.

The hunters were about to become the hunted.

PART SEVEN: TURF AND WAR

47

THE RESCUE

The Cerberus approached the manor at hurricane speed and Rocko put the clutch in high gear to ram the building. "Everyone ready?" he yelled to his comrades.

"Ready!" the others responded. Danny managed the top chain guns from a small spot on the roof, Serena armed the tracking station, and Michael took command of the mini canons.

Two of the guards on the rooftop were looking out into the distance, speaking softly. One of them held out a lighter for his cigarette to be lit; they spoke in Russian. Like a cracked whip came the thundering pitch of the beast stampeding its way towards destruction.

"Get down here now!" screamed one of the guards, signaling his men to rush to the roof with their AK-47s ready to open fire. Searchlights spotted the encroachers just as Rocko's Cerberus assault vehicle hammered its way out of the tunnel. Danny opened chain gunfire to blast through the barricaded area. "Come on babies, go boom!" said Danny impetuously.

Scarfo's men fired back but their guns were useless; their bullets bounced off the impermeable armor of the Cerberus. Michael opened fire with the mini canons, disabling the security systems of the place and cutting off most of the power to the fortress.

Helicopters swung above the Cerberus and men fired bazooka missiles in the Cerberus' path, blasting a pit causing the vehicle to lose its traction and fall in headfirst. The militia cornered the fallen attackers' vehicle. There was a silence like death itself. Prepared for anything, one of the men standing over the heap opened the hatch.

A hand armed with a gun came out of nowhere, sending a bullet through the guard's skull. With pieces of skull and brain flying as the guard fell down dead, Serena opened the side slotted window of the Cerberus, firing away with an Uzi, killing the guards on the left while Danny pummeled the others on the right with his auto shot gun. Bodies were blown to pieces and human parts littered the ground.

The chopper circled the wreckage to form a second attack. Danny aimed his scope to target the pilot, firing a bullet that shattered the cockpit window and caused the pilot to lose control of the copter and spin to the ground. The chopper crashed and exploded on impact. Hopping out of the disabled Cerberus, Michael and company blew open the large wooden entrance doors of the old manor using a C4. They were wearing gas masks. Danny signaled the team as he saw guards approaching from the main stairway. As the guards fired, the quartet dodged the bullets, ducking and finding cover behind old furniture. "Get down, now!" yelled Danny.

Serena loaded her weapon quickly, then sprouted up, firing tear gas grenades around the room. Green gas filled the room and the guards passed out. The crew proceeded up the spiral stairway and through a grand hallway. Guards popped out from the corridors firing at the intruders. "Here comes that mother fucker right now!" yelled Rocko as he fired his mini rocket launcher. The impact shook the manor and obliterated the guards.

When the smoke cleared, all was silent. The pursuers entered a large round room and the large marble doors slammed behind them on their own. A black mist flowed through the room; a purple light glowed in the mist. From out of the shadows and darkness appeared the ninja Jubel.

"What is this!" said Danny.

"Michael I don't like this," said Rocko nervously horrified at such a sight.

"Have at you, weaklings!" said Jubel as he summoned up five shadow creatures out of the dark mist. They were grotesque and evil, a mangled version of death. They had no physical bodies but could on take human forms and their green eyes glared with the dark, godless presence of a nightmare come to life. "Kill them children, bring me their souls." Jubel disappeared into the shadows.

The creatures swarmed, forcing Michael and his friends back to back as they prepared to attack. Their guns did not affect the creatures.

Then, Serena remembered that light could destroy darkness. She took out a flash grenade and tying it to a holy water flask that Father Paul had given her; she pulled the pin and tossed the device in the air, illuminating the room with blessed, brilliant light. The creatures screamed in a macabre manner, burning up and turning into steam, evaporating away.

"They're gone! But how?" asked a stunned Rocko.

"Light overcomes darkness," said Danny.

"Where did you get that thing?" asked Michael.

"The priest gave it to me," replied Serena.

Jubel reappeared. "My name is Jubel, now die!" he cried as he warped around the room on the attack. Michael fired his weapon at Jubel and as the bullets penetrated his body, he fell to the ground and lay motionless. The quartet closed in slowly with caution to confirm the being's death. Jubel's eyes opened and his wounds healed; rims of smoke spewed from the rapidly healing wounds.

"It's not possible – what the hell is that thing!" said Rocko.

As Jubel sprung up to attack, Michael used his psychic gift to create a sonic blast that disrupted Jubel's thoughts, causing him to become slightly distracted. Jubel came out of it quickly and attacked Michael head on, picking him up and throwing him to the other end of the room. Rocko was dismayed to see Michael unleash his vampiric nature as he charged in fury to attack Jubel.

Serena used another flash grenade and the light blinded Jubel, causing him to become unconscious. The quartet fled the scene as the darkened room returned to normal. Running to the end of the second hall, they kicked open the door of the study that Sally was being held captive in, shooting the guards and untying the girl. Sally was in shock. She had never seen her uncle kill anyone, and she was terrified of his vampiric appearance.

"Don't come near me!" screamed Sally in fear.

Michael grabbed Sally, looking in her eyes reassured her, "I'm not going to hurt you, let's go now!"

"What is going on!" said Rocko in shock.

Michael teleported them out of the manor and to the safety of his apartment. There, he fell to the ground exhausted, and passed out.

48

"THE DARK ALLIANCE"

Back at the manor, Franco smashed the large window in his study in rage when Phillips told him that their target had escaped. Jubel appeared in front of Franco. "Idiots! I'm surrounded by damn idiots! That girl was our only insurance to blackmail Damascus and the Santerinis," said Franco.

"No excuses. I will kill them next time," said Jubel.

"I'm going to give you another chance and this time do it right," said an enraged Franco.

Suddenly, Alazar Desbode came forth from the shadows, startling Franco. "What do you want here? Who are you?" asked Franco in fear.

"Don't be afraid, it's me, Alazar Desbode." He removed his cloak that was covering his face."

Your man could not kill them. He's just as incompetent as mine," Franco spat in anger. Alazar Desbode just smiled and pulled out a vial of dark glowing energy and tossed it to Jubel. "Drink this and you will become invulnerable for a short while when you fight. It will only last for 15 minutes at a time. Say the incantation 'Netis Siku Set,' use it well and destroy these accursed fools," instructed Alazar Desbode.

Jubel removed his hood and drank the potion. As he did, his body levitated and a great white-hot light shot through it, throbbing, and he screamed in a terrible rhythm.

"What's happening to him?" asked Franco, as the transformation took place.

"His body and soul are joining with the darkness. Now he will be complete and nothing will stand in his way," Desbode explained. Jubel fell to the ground on his knees and looked up to his masters. His hair was sharp as spikes, his eyes purple, and his pale skin burned in pain as the dark energy ran through his veins, as invigorating as a powerful drug. "Go and destroy them," ordered Desbode. Jubel nodded in obedience and disappeared.

"Now then Scarfo, the agreement we made, it is time you kept it." Desbode turned to Franco.

"What is it that you want from me?"

Alazar Desbode brought the orb out of his pocket and looking at Franco, chuckled wickedly.

A knock on the door surprised Jackie as he sat in his chair reviewing the documents he'd stolen from Franco Scarfo. Anthony was with him. "Who is it?" called Anthony.

"Let me in you wiseasses, it's Michael and Serena!" shouted Michael from outside.

"What!" said Anthony as he ran to open the door.

"Sweet Virgin Mary!" said Anthony. He stood motionless for a second and then hugged Michael with joy. "Thank God you're all alive, we thought you were dead," said Anthony.

"We were just lucky to survive," said Danny.

"Who is this?" asked Jackie.

"Danny Fredricks, a contact of mine. You know Rocko of course, and this is my niece Sally," said Michael.

"What happened? You all look like you've been through hell," said Jackie.

"Scarfo kidnapped Sally. We found her at the Tyrell manor, and we ran into something I can only describe as the most horrible thing anyone has ever seen," said Rocko.

"What?" asked Anthony.

"Franco has some new assassins working for him, some type of organization," said Danny.

"We can handle them," said Jackie proudly.

"This is no ordinary criminal consortium," said Michael.

"Well what then?" Jackie asked.

"Listen, Serena and I are going to show you something, but just know this: we're not going to hurt you," said Michael.

"You're not making sense," said Jackie.

Michael and Serena then changed into their full vampiric forms and then back into their human forms.

"What the hell!" the two mobsters screamed.

"Now pay attention; what we have to say is very important," said Serena. Michael and Serena laid it all out: the vampires, the Dark Society, the ongoing war.

"You have got to be kidding. This is crazy; you expect us to believe a whacked-out story like this?" asked Jackie incredulously.

"How the fuck can you say that after what we just saw, man! Seeing is believing!" said Anthony.

"Okay, so what if you're right, how do we stop this Dark Society that's made a deal with Franco Scarfo?" said Jackie.

"We have to find a way first. Franco has a new killer working for him, a ninja he calls Jubel. If we're going to at least attempt to take him down, and whatever this new threat is, we're going to need help, and we're going to need to form a truce with Godfather Scarfo. He and his contacts outside the crime families might be able to give us some help, in addition to the people in this Coven that Serena and I know," said Michael.

"The Don is never going to believe this," said Jackie.

"He has to, otherwise we're all going to be dead meat," said Danny.

Jackie called Bobby Scarfo to inform him that Michael and his friends had survived and wanted to have a meeting with both families to discuss Franco Scarfo's treachery. Sally was still afraid of seeing her uncle in his new form, so he took her into the hallway to talk. Kneeling down to her height and looking into her little black eyes he said softly "No matter what I have become, I will always love you."

Seeing that he would not harm her, she hugged him and asked what had happened to him. He replied, "I'll tell you when you're ready. Now let me get you to someplace safe. Do you want to go home with Isabelle and your uncle Mickey Blue?"

She shook her head, still fearful and worried for her uncle, and clung to him tightly, "Please don't die, don't die," she sobbed.

"Sweetie, I can't die, not anymore," said Michael and with that he hugged her and called Mickey Blue and Isabelle, asking them to pick Sally up and bring her with them into hiding.

When Mickey Blue and Isabelle arrived on scene, they were informed of all that had happened. Isabelle felt a hot rush of relief when she saw Sally and held on to her tightly, "Sally! Come baby, let's go." Isabelle and Mickey Blue took Sally to the car and the three of them drove off into the night.

49

THE TRUCE

On the other side of the hysteria that had taken over Las Vegas a man of darkness sat on the highest office floor of the Bolt building. "Has the virus been converted to the weapons?" asked the dark figure.

"My lord, all is well," said a young man, bowing with great respect for his superior. The dark figure turned around to face his servant, as the servant raised his head to look at his master.

"Well done, my son. You have brought to us new souls for our cause; the dark god Sagamu will be well pleased," said the dark figure.

"Lord Reynard Desbode, I have news of a strange breed of vampire that has tried to interfere with us. Shall we deal with him and his companions?" asked the man.

"No Alazar, we will deal with these fools later. Getting the shipment prepared is more important. We must have the Black Devils in our pocket, as we have our distribution established in Guatemala and Honduras for our followers," said Reynard Desbode.

"But father, have you thought about our enemies? Zoratus is gaining new allies, I can feel it," protested Alazar Desbode.

"That old fool is beaten. It does not matter, my son; we have superior allies and the knowledge that has been given to us from the dark god has helped us vastly," said Reynard Desbode.

"I think you underestimate them," disagreed Alazar Desbode.

"You dare question my judgment, son!" demanded Reynard Desbode. Reynard was an ancient and a force to be reckoned with; old as time itself. His face was filled with scars from battles and markings of rune symbols, his hair was pure white like the shimmering moon, and his eyes burned blazing hot green as if he was possessed by hell itself. He wore strange vestments and a cloaked suit.

"Not at all, father. I only desire to serve you and our empire better."

"Ahh, very well. I will put you in charge of this next mission. Gather your men and bring the dark warrior to locate these misfits you speak of. Kill them and seek the relic. It is hidden somewhere in this city; I can sense it," commanded Reynard Desbode, handing Alazar Desbode a parchment scroll that was engraved with the image of a jade dragon on it.

"At once father," responded Alazar Desbode.

"Do this and you will be greatly rewarded. The time of our destiny is upon us," intoned Reynard Desbode.

"Yes my lord," said Alazar Desbode as he rose and bowed, then disappeared into the shadows surrounded by an aura of darkness.

"Soon my son and I will rule this world and we will become gods!" laughed Reynard Desbode as he looked around his study, which contained a laboratory of ancient books and chemicals. A scroll hung on the wall was covered with writings and a picture of the relic. Reynard Desbode sought this relic's dark power. It was the key to unlock the doors of his vision. With his eyes glowing red, he looked out the window at the world he intended to mold into his image, which the entire world then would worship.

Jackie called Don Felice while Bobby Scarfo contacted Godfather Giorgio for a meeting. Both families agreed to meet at a hidden location to talk.

The bartender was signaled to close the place and bar the windows, and so he did.

"This had better be important, to bring us both here!" said Don Felice.

Godfather Giorgio gave a distrustful eye to the boss of his rival crime family. "Yes, what is this that you want us to talk about?" asked Godfather Giorgio, annoyed.

Jackie tossed the Dark Society's emblem that they had stolen off of Jubel on the table and looking at Michael and Serena, he said, "Show them."

"Show us what?" said Don Felice, and Serena and Michael transformed into their true forms, releasing their human disguise. Don Felice fell off his seat petrified with fear; Godfather Giorgio just opened his mouth, dropping the cigarette that he was puffing away on.

"What in hell," started Don Felice.

"Now listen well; what we have to tell you is a matter of survival for both of your families," said Serena. The two immortals told the godfathers everything about Franco's plots, the Dark Society, the Triads and the Russians, the encounter with Alazar Desbode and Serena's Coven. It all was unearthed and the two mob bosses were still shocked and dumbfounded.

"This can't be real!" said Don Felice.

"Does it not look real to you?" countered Jackie.

"Okay, okay, so what do we do about this dark organization and Franco?" asked Godfather Scarfo, fully convinced.

"We must seek out their arms facility and destroy it. Second, we must discover where Franco is hiding and get him to tell us what we need to know, by any means necessary," said Michael.

The two rival leaders agreed and shook hands to form a truce. "How can we help?" asked Godfather Scarfo.

"Send any men you have left that are loyal to search any research facilities in medical or biochemical companies, and collect any information they find. After all, you own portions of most of these types of businesses with these corporations," Michael directed.

"What about the rest of our own families?" inquired Don Felice.

"Send word to every contact we have to locate the Triad and Russian stockpiles of goods, be it drugs or weapons, and anything pertaining to this symbol," said Serena.

"Where are you all going?" Don Felice asked Michael and his crew. "To find those biological weapons, what else?" Michael answered.

50

BIO COLLECTION

Marianna sensed the danger as she sat in her room in Julius' mansion not too far from the outskirts of the city. Her sister Scarlet was playing the harp, a routine they enjoyed after feeding. "Sister, what is wrong?" Scarlet asked.

"Michael is in trouble. I can feel his emotions," said Marianna.

"What do you think he is doing right now? Has he completed his second trial for father?" asked Scarlet.

"No Scarlet; something has interfered, something dark," said Marianna. Suddenly she was caught in a deep trance. Her eyes became blue; she saw bits of memories from Michael's terrifying creatures of the shadow. Scarlet jumped from her seat and ran to her sister, who had by now fallen to the ground.

"Darius get in here now!" yelled Scarlet. Darius bolted through the door to help up his sister.

"What happened this time?" asked Darius.

"Marianna had another attack."

"She'll be all right," said Darius as he pulled out a small bottle of lucaliptiousberry juice.

"Here, drink this, it will revive you," said Darius as he poured the elixir into Marianna's mouth.

"These visions are getting too powerful for her. If she has any more it will weaken her until she dies," said Darius.

"That's impossible, she's an immortal," said Scarlet.

"No, he's right, every time I use this curse it drains my strength," replied Marianna.

"What did you see Marianna?" asked Darius.

"The dark force. I believe they have created a warrior unlike anything I have ever seen. I also saw beings around him," said Marianna.

"What exactly did you see?" asked Scarlet.

"Shadow spirits, demons, and a man draped in purple silk who has the power to control them," said Marianna.

"What should we do?" asked Scarlet. "We must tell father immediately. He may know something about this warrior you speak of," said Darius.

The three of them went to speak with Julius in his chamber where he was kneeing in deep meditation, chanting psalms in Latin. Jewish oil lamps burned along the side of the room and a crucifix hung on the wall. "Vene Sanctus Spiritus," chanted Julius.

Scarlet knocked on the doors of her father's chamber, "Come in, and bring in your sister and brother. What's wrong?" asked Julius.

"Father, I have seen the dark warrior. He is searching for the young fledgling and our cousin," said Marianna.

"Michael is heading into trouble, but I am confident he will handle this test. Do not help him. He must complete this task on his own if he is to be worthy of this Coven. After all, did you not each prove yourselves to be my bravest warriors besides being my children? It is the tradition of this Coven that has been held for seven centuries," replied Julius.

"The dark god has sent his warrior from Jinguko. The prophecy is finally being fulfilled," said Marianna.

"Do you think the fledgling could also be part of the prophecy?" asked Darius.

"I have pondered this too. It is said that Heaven will send a young, fallen warrior to lead the victory against the legions of the Dark God and restore our people and himself," said Scarlet.

"We will not know until it is shown to us," said Julius.

"In the meantime, wait until Damascus and his companions deliver the weapons to us. We will tap their power source and make it our own," said Darius.

"While we are waiting, my son, gather our best men and you and Marianna must lead two teams with through the city to search for the Dark Society's criminal affiliates. We must locate them and kill any enemy on sight," said Julius.

Darius beat his chest to salute his father and left the room with Marianna to fetch his men. Julius looked out his chamber window at the moon and spoke softly to his daughter Scarlet, who was still present. Julius then fell the ground in great pain.

"Father!" screamed Scarlet in fear, running to his side to help him up.

"I will be fine daughter," said Julius, limping to get up.

"Lie down father and rest yourself; let me see your wound," said Scarlet. Scarlet turned her father on his side, seeing that the wound that he received from Desbode years ago was swollen, it had never healed. "Scarlet there is nothing you can do, I am dying," said Julius.

"There must be a way to heal you," said Scarlet.

"No, if it is my time to die, then I will die. When my time comes to leave this world, you and your brother and sister will serve the Coven as my replacement. There are many of our kind needing our help. If we do not help them, they will turn to the Dark One. Promise me you will take care of each other," said Julius.

"But father," protested Scarlet.

"Promise me!" said Julius as he felt pain pierce his side.

"I promise."

"I love you all."

"Please father, sleep and rest."

"Play for me please." Julius turned over. Scarlet went into her room and brought out her harp to play into the night. Julius drank a cup of blood that was filled for him by a servant and he regained some of his strength.

Around the alleys of the dark and dismal parts of the city, where drug dealers and street crime was rampant, Marianna and Darius were searching with their teams for the whereabouts of the mafia. Michael and his crew searched the other side of town for the biological weapons.

Both units found each other in the red light district looking frustrated and flustered.

"What are you doing here?" said Serena.

Marianna did not look surprised. "Looking for spies and you," replied Marianna.

"We're looking for those weapons you guys wanted found," said Michael.

"This is just too weird," said Rocko to all the madness.

"Get used to it; welcome to the beyond," said Danny.

Suddenly, the prey they had been hunting came at them from the dark rooftops and hidden corners. They were dark shadow beings with red eyes and decayed flesh that was gray and thick. They stunk like rotten ash and looked like dead warriors, dressed in robes of tattered silk. They had taken the form of supernatural assassins. Among them was Jubel, emerging from a mist of darkness and fog. Alazar Desbode also appeared next to Jubel.

"It's him!" said Danny.

Jubel removed his hood to reveal his new power. His appearance was different than it had been during their first encounter. Jubel's skin was chalk white, his eyes were red and his face was covered in strange tattoo markings. His teeth were sharp fangs and his hands had become monstrous claws. He had become a devil from hell.

"The Dark Warrior, it's him," breathed Marianna. A silence crept over all, but it lasted for less than a second. Marianna unsheathed her sword in anticipation and Darius pulled the string back on his bow.

"Jubel, kill them!" ordered Alazar Desbode.

"Yes sire," responded Jubel as he gave the signal. A wanton flood of violence erupted as the shadow assassins fought against the vampires and their allies. Guns were useless against these beings; the zombies could not be killed. Jubel stood on the rooftop controlling the decayed warrior beings with his hands, as if he were a puppet master with an invisible line to each of these strange creatures. Alazar Desbode had conjured forth from the ground small portals that burned as rings of blinding white light and hot fire, calling for the demonic and supernatural beasts that served him.

"Children of the elder gods of darkness, come forth from the abyss, your master awaits," chanted Alazar Desbode in a strange language that was not human. Out of the hellish fire came forth three creatures of abomination, death, and discord. A being emerged from the ground with the wings of a giant eagle, the skin of a serpent, the torso and legs of a man, massive black claws that looked cretaceous, and the head of salamander. This creature was named Gerwraith.

Another creature rose from the fire, a bird-like beast with the head and neck of a crane and sharp rows of fangs that were jagged as blades. Its torso and arms were that of a white tiger, its wings and feathers were those of a black swan, and its legs and feet were those of a large peacock. It was called Iolcus. These first two beings were ugly and bestial.

Finally, a third creature came forth, but unlike the first two, this one was seductive and beautiful. It had a woman's shape and wore a pearl tunic. She had sultry black hair, eyes that were red as blood, the giant wings of a bat, white skin, and claw hands. Though she was beautiful and fair, she had the voice of a siren that was both seductive and deadly. She was the favorite of Alazar Desbode's warriors as well as his lover; her name was Tulina.

"Tulina, Icolcus, Gerwraith attack!" commanded Alazar Desbode. These three creatures unleashed unholy screams that sounded like a million souls of the dead trapped inside these evil creatures.

The creatures and the shadow puppets circled in twists and wisps of smoke, attacking their enemies. Darius and Marianna leaped high in the air, vaulting back and forth from the corners of the nearby walls of the buildings, slashing the reanimated corpses to pulp. Darius fired his bow and split open the skulls of the corpses, though nothing but ash and smoke poured out of the putrid creatures.

Michael engaged in hand-to-hand combat on the ground, smashing in the corpse's heads and dismembering his adversaries. Rocko and Danny fought the creature beasts while Serena fought against Tulina. In the madness Jubel jumped down from the building in front of Michael and drew his sword to attack.

"Now it ends!" Jubel declared as he drew the first strike. Michael back flipped to avoid Jubel's attack and fired back with his Mini Uzi, but the bullets just bounced off the force field of energy that Jubel had summoned up to protect himself. Jubel attacked Michael again by jumping in the air and zipping back and forth. One of the corpse beings below pulled out a strange energy pistol, a bio weapon, and fired. Michael swept past and dodged the shot, knocking down the creature and grabbing the weapon, but in the next instant Michael was struck down by Jubel's sword, which slashed his chest, wounding Michael deeply. His blood spilled and Michael fell weakly to the ground. Jubel stood over him ready to cut off his head.

"Hey buddy, heads up!" yelled Serena, who grabbed the gun that Michael had dropped and fired at Jubel. The energy blast sent Jubel through a brick wall.

Serena then teleported Michael and the others to a safe haven, retreating from the enemy. The escapees arrived in the catacombs beneath Julius' mansion. They all fell to the ground, each drained of strength from the battle. Darius and Marianna were the only ones who had suffered no injuries because as ancients they were strong and could regenerate quickly. Serena was injured from her fight with Tulina. Michael was in bad shape; the wound he had received from Jubel's blade was barely healing. He bled profusely on the floor. Darius picked up Michael, while Rocko and Danny helped up Serena.

"Yeah I'm fine thanks!" said Danny as rubbed his head from the blow he had taken.

"Terrific, just terrific!" said Rocko sarcastically.

"Come one you guys, it wasn't that bad," said Serena.

"Oh shut up!" everyone said in unison.

"Oh boy," said Rocko breathing heavy.

"Come into the main hall, we all need to talk," suggested Darius. They all limped upstairs. There was a large Victorian style sitting room off the main hall, with furniture and a large black marble fireplace. A warm fire was burning. The room was filled with assorted gothic gargoyle statues and sconces that had dragons sitting on giant demon claws. The place was decorated in rich purples, reds, and dark blues.

"Come in and rest," said Julius as he poked at the burning wood with a steel poker. They all plopped on the sofa, exhausted and beaten.

"Alazar Desbode beat us, the Dark Force and his minions were just too much. I hope you're happy. Though we did get the bio gun," panted Michael.

"Have a drink, sit, and tell me what happened," said Julius as he took out a bottle of red wine and poured glasses for everyone. He handed the glasses of wine for all to drink. Michael and Serena fed from a goblet that had an elixir given to him by Julius, and they were then healed.

After finishing the goblet Michael handed Julius the weapon to inspect, "Well done, Michael. You have passed the second trial. This bio weapon can be duplicated in our own weapons lab and we can harness its energy into new defense systems," said Julius proudly, handing the rifle to a servant who then left the room, closing the doors.

"No more trials please; we have bigger worries. The creep in the black robe called some strange beast-like creatures up out of fire," said Michael.

"Strange creatures?" questioned Julius.

"They were the most ugly son's a bitches I have ever seen. He called them Tulina, Icolcus, and Gerwraith," said Danny.

Disturbed, Julius dropped the bottle he held, shattering the glass on the floor. The telephone rang. Scarlet answer it. "Hello, yes. Father, it's for you." She handed her father the telephone.

"Yes, who is this? Takai? Why yes of course, I understand. Yes, immediately," said Julius seriously as he hung up the phone, turning around with a worried look on his old decrepit face.

"The time has come. All of you must come with me; the prophecy is being fulfilled," said Julius. They headed down the stairs into the cellar, where in the catacombs there was a shimmering pool of water that reflected the torches burning on the walls.

"What is this place?" asked Danny.

"Where the records of the Great Testament have been kept safe. The keepers have documented, over the centuries, the events of this war, including the scroll that speaks of the prophecy of its end. The end was foretold in a series of visions to an unknown monk who served the early church in Athens, after being visited by the Angel Gabriel who said "I have come from Jesus the Christ. Write down all that I tell you to prepare for a dark age that will come upon the earth. All of mankind will be persecuted. Now prepare." The writings were kept secret and the scrolls were locked away, hidden in an old cemetery. Pagans who hated the Church burned down many cathedrals at the time.

After being discovered by a band of thieves, the scrolls were sold to a notary. Then the Church bought them and the Pope transferred the keeping of the scrolls to the cardinals. From there, the scrolls were entrusted to me," Julius finished.

"And here are the scrolls encased in glass, well preserved," said Marianna.

"You mean, the story of you serving as a general for the church is true?" asked Michael.

"Where did you hear this?" asked Julius.

"Dominus," said Michael.

" I see," said Julius.

"But if this prophecy is true, why didn't the Church in Rome aid you?" said Michael.

"Fear can bring great confusion to men who are good. It was that fear and hatred that turned those we trusted against my legion and what I had become. The Sons of Judah believed I was cursed by God, so I was seen as a heretic and was driven out with my men by a private hired army, only to be captured by the Dark Society's legions," said Julius.

"What prophecy?" Michael pressed.

"The prophecy tells that through the ages a war between good and evil would be fought over the future of the world until heaven sends a fallen warrior to be redeemed and help defeat the Dark Society on earth. That is one aspect of the prophecy, but there is a second potential destiny. It is said that evil legions of men will seek a source of power, a book that if acquired will be used to resurrect the creatures of the damned to conquer the world of the living. The three creatures you spoke of are part of the prophecy also."

"I think you're hiding something else," said Michael as he saw on the scroll a woodcut of Julius and his men slaughtering people: men, women, and children, along with a man with red hair and green eyes dressed in red and silver armor that bore a strange seal.

"So you have figured it out then," said Julius noticing Michael's perception.

"Figured out what?" asked Darius.

"Your family is cursed because of what your father did while he was in Rome's service," said Michael carefully, looking closely at the mural on the wall. They had not recognized the figure in the picture until now. They all saw the true blood thirst of their lord, he who had played the innocent saint.

"Father you knew about this, and you never told us." Scarlet looked at her father with big sad eyes.

"Orders were orders. I was charged to wipe out the heathen influence at the Pope's command. If I hadn't, they would have brought destruction to everything we had accomplished in Rome. I had to do what was necessary to protect his Imminence from potential assassination," said Julius looking fierce, his eyes burning in anger.

"More like following your political loyalty. Now I understand the game you played; you killed a band of innocent people and now the big man upstairs is making you pay," said Michael.

"So that's your Great Test. You lied to us, Father!" Darius was enraged.

"Why should we listen to you anymore?" said Serena.

"Redemption can set you free if you seek it, this is true even for our kind. I want us all to be restored," said Julius.

"But that is what you want! Not me!" Darius was furious.

"Brother you shouldn't!" interjected Scarlet.

"Shut up Scarlet!" said Darius abruptly.

"He's right," said Serena.

Julius frowned in disgust at his eldest son and smacking Darius across the face. "Don't question my power Darius! If I could kill those pathetic humans – " Pointing his finger at the mural, he grabbed his son by the collar and lifted him off the ground. "I won't hesitate to kill you!" Julius threw Darius to the ground.

Darius sprang up with his eyes burning, then breathed in his anger and brushed himself off. "Our time has come father; vampires will eventually rule this world. You're a fool to believe becoming human again will make up for our family's past," Darius spat.

Julius was ready to draw his sword against his son's impertinence but Serena came between them, preventing the attack.

"Forget the past and focus on the present. What about the creatures? If we don't stop them there may not be a world left at all," said Danny.

"What are they?" asked Serena.

"The Shirakai Guardians. Each is a key to unlock the power of a source of darkness, a book called The Yomi Tengu, which is translated as, "The Book of Darkness," said Marko who had entered the room and overheard the conversation.

"What is this book, and what exactly are these guardians?" asked Danny.

"The Shirakai are a demonic race and dark spiritual beings, descendents of the tribes of Babalnite elders; the old ones, elder gods that were created by the legendary dark god Sagamu, the Japanese god of Jinguko, otherwise known as hell," said Julius.

"It's just a myth," said Rocko skeptically.

"No myth, I assure to you it's true," said Julius ominously.

"No offense, but I thought you believed in one God," said Michael.

"I do, but I've always been open to the idea of many things existing. Anyway, that is what we have learned from reading different records," said Julius. "Tulina, Icolcus, and Gerwraith are actually the keepers of the portals that the book can unlock. Each of them is not to be underestimated; they are very dangerous and powerful."

"I live for danger," said Michael boldly.

"You are brave but foolish. They would trigger your fear before you could land a clear shot at them. They feed off the essence of emotions, such as fear and anger," said Julius.

"What are their powers?" asked Serena.

"They share similar abilities. For instance, all Shirakais have the power to shape shift into forms of beautiful or grim beings. They can bring pestilence and death by screaming, and are workers of sorcery," said Julius.

"Anything else on the weirdo-meter we haven't heard yet dude?" asked Rocko.

"Each of them has a special gift. Tulina is a former witch of the cult of a demon goddess. She is able to control all forms of heat and fire. Icolcus has the power to create massive thunder and lightning storms, and Gerwraith is able to harness destructive winds and blizzards," said Julius.

"How do you know so much about them?" asked Serena.

"You were not born in the centuries when the rest of the ancients and elders clans were lords ruling over the world. During those times, the Shirakai race had formed armies to attack our vampire clans, as well as the other creatures of the supernatural realm we were allied with, so we did what any people would do," said Julius.

"Fight," nodded Danny. "Can they be killed?"

"Yes, but not all of them. Only Lao Takai knows all of their secrets. He has lived longer than I have," replied Julius.

"What exactly can this book do?" asked Danny. "We don't know actually; the records we did have from Takai were destroyed in a fire many years ago. After that, Takai disappeared. The Coven did not hear from him again until three months ago," Marianna spoke.

"Old fool should have stayed in the same place, makes our damn job a lot easier," replied Darius annoyed.

"I believe it; after seeing all that I've seen I'm ready to believe anything. But who is this warrior who was foretold?" Michael sighed.

"You," replied Julius.

"You have to be kidding me. I kill people for a living," said Michael.

It was then Michael saw an angel before him, shaped as a man and dressed in a white robe with a hood, holding a book in one hand. No one else could see the angel or hear the words he spoke to Michael. "I am Gabriel, sent from the Christ. You have been chosen Michael."

"You got the wrong guy," thought Michael.

"You must face your destiny; the order of light demands it."

Michael listened and Gabriel opened a book that he held in his hands; Michael's name appeared in it. Then the angel vanished.

Michael was astounded by the angelic visitation. He now believed that God was trying to reach him and his faith was restored.

But he still hated Phillips; he still could not let go of his desire for revenge.

Michael came out of it, and was asked by the others what had happened to him. He bypassed their questions, saying it was nothing but fatigue. "Who called on the phone earlier?" asked Michael.

"My old teacher Takai. He has been robbed. You and the others must help him to retrieve a special relic that was taken. It's a jade dragon statue. Please understand that this relic is a part of the puzzle. This is your final test. Now go to this address and help him," ordered Julius handing Michael a note with the written address on it.

"Real cute!" retorted Michael.

"Look at me. Go, now! Or this sword will cut your head off!" said Julius, annoyed and drawing his sword to Michael's neck. Feeling the sharp point at his neck, Michael knew that Julius meant business.

"When this is over my ass is out of here!" said Michael under his breath. The vampires and their comrades left quickly.

Alone again, Julius saw a woodcut of the relic on one of the scrolls he was reading through. He was nervous. "It's time."

PART EIGHT: THE JADE DRAGON

51

THE MAN CALLED LAO

Among the pagoda rooftops and decaying buildings perched majestic stone dragons layered in granite and marble. Below the mystical beauty of these guardians hung glowing lanterns that glistened brightly among the starry night, high above the masses of people celebrating in the streets. The center of the Oriental district was a wondrous place for festive spectacles.

It was the festival season and a grand parade was taking place at the heart of Chinatown. Fireworks lit up the night sky and firecrackers popped off in the distance. The Damascus crew and the Coven teleported to Chinatown, the group proceeded to the streets to locate Takai's shop. The streets were crowded with dancers in the center of the parade and Chinese dragons roamed up and down. Among the chaos came Darius's words, "How are we going to find Takai in this?"

"Be patient, we'll find him," replied Marianna.

Scarlet looked at her portable computer tracker, typing in the address 1620 Shimoto Street.

Serena looked at the computer tracker and asked, "How far are we?"

"Just a few blocks up, come on," replied Scarlet. The group continued to the upper part of the Oriental district, where the scene was quieter. Away from the crowds, they approached a very old Chinese temple. Its stone walls looked ancient and its pillars were darkened by dust. The sky had grown very dark and a windstorm was beginning to brew; black clouds formed and white-hot lighting alternated with blasts of thunder. Rocko began to feel a strange and evil presence, like they were being watched. "I don't like this guys, we shouldn't be here," he said.

"Quit being a pussy," said Michael casually as he puffed on the nub of his cigarette and tossed it the ground. A crack of thunder silenced them as it cut through the sky.

The doors of the temple opened and they saw an old Japanese man with a long white beard and black kimono standing before them. "Welcome, please enter. We have been expecting you," said the old man.

The large, embossed doors slammed shut behind them. The temple was lavished with Samurai armor. Katanas and blades of all kinds were mounted on the walls; Hachiman masks hung on the main wall of this dojo temple as the fragrant smell of jasmine in-cense burned at an altar in the center of the temple, in front of a large brass Buddha statue. On the shelves of this illustrious place were books of all kinds and small statues, the Japanese Capa and Oni creatures of legend."

Lao Takai, we were sent to you by Julius," said Michael.

"Yes, I know, he has told me much of you and your friends," said Takai.

"You want us to retrieve something for you that was stolen?" asked Danny.

"Yes, but understand, all of you: this item is very important. If the book is located through the map contained in the statue, and the power is unleashed, it could cause the world to be in grave danger," said Takai.

"Why did you even make the map in the first place if you knew this could happen?" asked Michael.

"To pass down to my generations of children should something happen to me. Old as I am, my time is growing short," replied Takai.

"How old are you?" asked Danny.

"Let me tell you why this book is so dangerous and the, you will understand. Long ago the god of darkness named Sagamu and his loyal followers, the Shirakais, created the Yomi Tengu Shira, The Book of Darkness. The Shirakais are devils, demons, immortal creatures and the children of Gikara, a sorceress queen who sacrificed and slained humans to Sagamu. In doing so, she and her children were granted the supernatural gifts and powers of hell. They became Sagamu's servants. For centuries they were believed to be reincarnations of elder gods. They became worshipped as deities by ancient cults who made blood oaths and sacrifices in fire. The offspring of the Shirakais were formed from mating female humans and Oni evil spirits. They are called Sepors.

My family hid the book for centuries to protect the world from its evil, for it was never meant for the living to see. The book had been created out of desperation to keep control over the disloyal Oni and Capa in the nether world and those on earth who plotted to destroy Sagamu. That was until a young shaman named Tovu, who was sent to Jinguko after being killed, took the book. This young man was a cunning shaman who was bold enough to deceive Sagamu in a wager; the wager was such that if the shaman could beat Sagamu in a duel of magic the shaman would be resurrected and returned to earth. The Shaman won. Sagamu was impressed with the young shaman's skill in deception and the Dark God believed he could use the boy to deceive mortals into worshipping Him; and so the young shaman was returned to earth. The price to return was the shaman's soul.

It was not until later that Sagamu realized that the book had been stolen. Enraged, Sagamu looked over the ages to locate the book and bloodthirsty human warlords who desired it to become immortal. These warlords had formed secret societies over time and later, before the Middle Ages, one sect became especially dear to Sagamu. Sagamu later took form as a man on earth, and had a son who he raised under the guise of a ruler of a small country in Europe. He taught the boy the art of warfare; he also taught him to hate, to kill, and that only the strong would be able to conquer the world. Soon the Dark Son of Sagamu became a great warrior. As a man, he married a woman as his dark bride. Later, he fathered a child. The Dark Son later went off to war with an unknown country and in battle the Dark Son was betrayed by Sagamu, who killed him to mock him for being human.

The descendent of Sagamu's Dark Son was a man who became a worshipper of evil and desired the power of evil itself. Impressed by the corruption of this wicked man, Sagamu gave this man the power of armies, the state of a fallen Oni, and charged him with a mission to destroy the Christian Church out of bitter revenge, as mortals had refused to worship Sagamu. This man was Reynard Desbode.

"But how did you get the book?" asked Serena.

"In 660 BC, I was the grand master warrior for the Jimmu-tenno dynasty. Jimmu-tenno was made the first emperor of Japan. I was cursed and charged as a traitor for an assassination attempt that I did not commit on the emperor. The people envied my family and my position, and so I was judged as a traitor for high treason. The emperor ripped out my heart, replacing it with an Oni demon's heart. I was cast out of the emperor's court, immortal, and destined to walk the earth in shame for disloyalty for all time. Though infected with evil from the Oni, the purity of my soul prevented me from becoming insane. However, the heart from the Oni has left me with an unnaturally long life. Now the curse is ending, my power is decreasing, and the prophecy of Sagamu is coming true.

"But what of the emperor?" asked Darius.

"The emperor was driven to madness by the dark power of the Shira book, which was given to him as a gift by his Shinto shamans, who had been given it as a dark spiritual guide. It was passed down from the old shaman Tovu," said Takai, "and the emperor planned to use the power of the book to conquer the world. Once I discovered his mad dream, my men and I stole the book and hid it, since it is impossible to destroy. I did this to thwart the mad emperor. I then put a map inside a jade dragon statue, which I gave to my youngest son to protect the hidden location. The book was hidden deep in Mount Fuji, in Japan. The book is so powerful that it can unleash evil powers from different dark realms of the nether world, and other worlds we know nothing of. These powers, if set free, are said to be vessels of great evil. This power has the ability to raise armies of the spirits of death, open portals to different dimensions beyond time and space, and the ability to reveal the secrets and innermost desires of a person's soul. It can prolong life.

It was not until the Dark Ages when the Dark Society's founder, Reynard Desbode, whom my clan later encountered, learned of the legend of the book and was attracted to its promise of power. So Desbode sent his followers to search all over the world for the book. Over the millennia, I had many sons and daughters who were half-human and half-Oni, giving my children an unnaturally long but mortal life, allowing them to follow and protect the secret of the Shira book. It has been kept a family secret for four thousand years.

"Four thousand years ago! Whoa!" said Rocko.

"As the centuries passed, I adapted well to the different periods of Japan's changing history and culture, becoming a man of many professions and skills. I was a scribe to a rich merchant for the Emperor Toba in 1140. After saving Toba's life I became a Samurai warrior for the Shogunate military Yorimoto clan and later for the Tokugawa Shogunate government during the beginning of the Samurai order, until its middle period. Later, I became a merchant and in the present day I am a teacher of Kenjitsu.

"But how did you meet my grandfather?" asked Serena.

"When my village in Japan was raided by the Dark Society's agents, Julius offered my clan an alliance to protect our village. In return we agreed to stand as allies to Julius and his legions to destroy the Dark Society's agents, and to protect the Shira from falling into the wrong hands."

"Why are you here now?" asked Scarlet.

"After a rebellion began in my homeland, the country was ravaged, so I took the statue that contained the map and fled to China and all over Asia until the early twenty-first century, when I came with my daughter Suki to America," finished Takai.

They were all in awe from what they had learned, and all knew what must be done.

"We have to get back that statue. Forget the test. If we don't, we'll be dead and so will the rest of the world," said Danny.

"I agree," said Michael.

"It will not be easy my friends; the Triads have many allies and a hundred hideouts in this city," said Takai.

"Then maybe I can help," interjected a young and beautifully seductive flower of the east. They saw a lovely Japanese woman come out from the red silk curtains of Takai's study. She was dressed in a wild sapphire kimono with a feather in her long black hair. Her eyes were as radiant as the morning sunrise and her lips were soft and red, like a rare cherry blossom. "Pardon me for not introducing you all, this is my daughter Suki," said Takai.

"What can she do for us?" asked Serena.

"I can do many things vampire, like read the ancient translations to the statue's secrets. I know people in Japan that have ties with our clan's organization," replied Suki. No one noticed a strange little creature scamper into the room. It was a red baby Chinese luck dragon, who began to beg from Suki like a little puppy.

"What the hell is that!" screamed Danny.

"It's impossible!" exclaimed Darius in awe.

"Oh him, it's just Pingu," said Suki smiling.

"There are more things in the heavens and on earth than your rational thinking, my friends." Lao chuckled.

"You have a pet baby dragon!" said Serena.

"Don't be afraid, he won't bite; he likes people," said Suki, laughing.

"Is he safe to pet? Said Rocko.

"Go ahead," said Suki as she picked up her pet in her arms like an infant. Rocko inched closer to it and the baby dragon gave him a slobbering kiss across the face.

"Oh yuck, that's worse than dog drool," said Rocko as he wiped his face.

They all couldn't help but laugh. Then, in a more serious tone, Michael said, "I think the real question is where do we start searching first? We must stop wasting our time talking here.

We should divide into teams to learn where the statue has been taken. Marianna and Darius, you will proceed to the west side of the Oriental district, Danny and Scarlet to the south, Serena and Rocko to the east."

"Where will you be?" asked Serena.

"I'm going to get in touch with Kat. She paged me a few minutes ago on my cell phone; she must have gotten out of the hospital. Let's see if she can help us," said Michael.

"You're not going anywhere vampire!" said Takai.

"Who says, old man," answered up Michael boldly.

"The Triads are masters of swordsmanship. The others are skilled in armed combat with the exception of your human friends. However, if all you can do is shoot a gun, well, then you will not be a match for the triads," said Takai firmly.

"Oh for crying out loud, I could take them on right now, snickered Michael feeling cocky.

"All right, young fool. If that's the way you feel about it, follow me. We shall put your words to the test, besides your temper," said Takai challenging Michael's thickheaded ego.

Takai led Michael and the others into a large dojo room, where training mats were already spread on the floor and two saber swords were already racked in place, waiting for duelists. Takai and Michael unsheathed their swords as they focused on who would make the first strike. Michael made the first attack as he clashed his sword with Takai's. The two battled in a series of twists and turns, until Michael was finally knocked to the ground with Takai's blade at his chest.

"Not too bad for an old man," said Takai as he helped Michael up.

"Fine, you're right; I'll stay and train," said Michael, rubbing his head.

"Good," said Takai.

Just then the skylight exploded as ninja assassins dropped to the ground from the temple roof.

"Who the hell are these freaks?" asked Danny.

"Triads," said Suki.

"Take them." Michael nodded coolly.

The room was caught up in a cutting spectacle of bloodshed as the crew unleashed their fury. Swords flew like the wind as Lao and Suki cut through their enemies and streams of blood splattered on the floor and walls of the dojo. Scarlet was knocked out to the ground cold. With Michael ducking the attacks and shooting back, Danny grabbed a shield off the wall, using it to defend himself as a black shadow ninja kicked Danny in the face, sending him head first to the floor. Thinking fast, Danny blocked the ninja's attempt to hit him with the shield, and then he flung himself to his feet, kicking the ninja in the balls. The ninja fell to his knees with his yellow eyes crossed in pain, as Danny kicked him to the ground and knocked him out.

Just as another ninja was preparing to shoot, Rocko pushed Danny out of the way and took a dart in the chest.

"Rocko!" screamed Danny, helping Rocko up and pulling out the dart. Flipping to attack behind them came a ninja, ready to cut off their heads; Serena zipped in behind him and slit his throat with her claws, ripping his head off as blood spouted onto Rocko and Danny, who were petrified by the violence. Darius and Marianna finished off the others, impaling them on with the decorative spikes that hung on the walls.

In an instant the fight was over and the whole place was soaked in blood.

"Well that was fun," panted Rocko.

"Quick Suki, go the herb room, he's been poisoned!" yelled Lao.

"Poisoned!" panicked Rocko.

Suki ran into another room, and grabbing a bottle named Dragon's Blood from a shelf, and raced back to Rocko.

"Drink this, it will help you sleep," instructed Suki. Rocko obeyed, downing the antidote; he then passed out.

"Will he live?" asked Michael.

"He's going to be fine; he just needs to absorb the antidote through his system. Bring him to my room. He can rest there," Lao ordered.

"Scarlet!" said Serena running to her cousin.

Darius came over to pick her up. "Just out, she can't fight in this condition," said Darius; he disappeared into the shadows then quickly reappeared. "Don't worry, I took the kid home," said he explained.

"What about the police?" said Serena.

"Don't worry this dojo is soundproof. We just need to get rid of the bodies," Lao said. As he said this, the bodies went up in black flames and smoke, dissolved to nothing.

"What the hell is going on here!" demanded Serena.

"Shadow agents, Triad shadow agents," said Darius.

"The Triads have joined with the Dark Society; only that creep Jubel and the black-robed guy on the rooftop could have done this!" said Michael.

"My son," said Lao sadly.

"What?" Michael exclaimed.

"It has already begun," said Lao.

"Their power is great," Suki agreed.

"I need to kill him!" said Michael.

"You'll get your chance," said Darius.

"Everyone all right?" asked Marianna.

"What do we do?" said Danny.

"Find the Triads and kill them, what else," Darius scoffed.

"Go and find any leads you can. Watch your backs, all of you; here, take these walkie-talkies and these pocket computers. Your target's picture is stored on it," said Lao, handing the others the devices.

"What about me?" asked Michael.

"You stay here and I will have you fully trained in four days."

"That's too long. The Triads will have found the book by then," Michael protested.

"Very well; two days," agreed Lao. "The rest of you will have my little friends to help you locate the statue."

"What friends?" asked Michael.

Lao turned his attention to the study. "Chow Ling! Kung Kung, come here!" he ordered. Out from the curtains flew a little creature no bigger than a man's hand, with the head and body of a woman, gray skin, and wings that were like a hawk's. It landed on Lao's arm like a well-trained bird.

"I don't believe this, it can't be!" said Serena.

"I don't see anything; it looks like an ordinary bird," said Danny.

"No, you can't see its true visage because you're human," said Suki as she tossed Danny a pendent.

"Put it on and you will see." Danny obeyed.

"Oh shit," said Danny, truly seeing the pint-sized beauty.

"What is it?" Michael asked, also seeing the creature for what it was.

"A Yosei, also known as a fairy. Its ears will be your ears, and its sight will become your sight," said Lao.

"Is he smart?" asked Darius.

"She, actually. Chow Ling is brilliant, not just intelligent," said Lao. Chow Ling gave a little cheep, folding her little arms, and then danced for joy in Lao's hand, like a ballerina.

"Cute," said Michael. Kung Kung then strutted into the room; a giant Siamese cat with the body of a young cougar, the claws of a lion, and nine tails of a leopard. The cat jumped on Michael in excitement, licking Michael's face. "Shit!"

"Easy Boy! Easy Boy," yelled Lao, grabbing the great cat. "He seems to like you Damascus," Lao chuckled.

"I can see that, now get this thing off me!" commanded Michael. Lao pulled the friendly feline off his so-called victim.

"Kung Kung has a superior sense of smell; he can track anything. He can also aid you with his unique ability to shape shift," said Suki picking up a piece of the shreds of a ninja's torn garment from the floor. Kung Kung inspected the torn cloth, sniffing it carefully. His eyes turned a hellish green and he let out an ominous scream, ready to pursue. "Now then; my friends will aid you. Command them to follow you and they will. They will look like normal animals to humans so do not worry; only the supernatural can see them. Split into teams in the city and seek out the Triads in lower downtown, mid town, and here in the Oriental district. If you find a Japanese vampire by the name of Mohachi Yung, who owns a few businesses in those areas, you will then find where they have taken the statue," instructed Lao.

"Who is he?" asked Serena.

"The Triad's boss," said Lao. They all left with the creatures to guide them, except for Michael and Rocko, who stayed behind.

52

STEWARDS OF SWORDS

After everyone had left the dojo, Michael and Lao remained alone in the tea room to talk. As they sat on comfortable pillows, they drank sake together. "Tell me everything, everything I need to know to kill this guy, this Jubel," said Michael.

"He's no man. He's a devil," Lao cautioned.

"You said he was your son."

"He was my adopted son at one time, yes," said Lao.

"Was?"

"Before I came to America, I trained the man you met. Jubel was my favorite student. He was the most deadly martial artist in all of Japan, an agent to the government. When shadow agents came one night to kill my daughter and I, Jubel prevented the assassination. I was proud to see a man with such honor. From that night on, he was made my son. For five years I trained him, taught him, and even loved him as my own," said Lao sadly.

"What happened later?"

"Late one night a man in a black robe came to our koryu school. He and Jubel talked. Jubel asked the man to leave, but the man attacked Jubel, and cursed him with a black orb. The poison of hatred consumed Jubel's mind. That was the man you spoke of earlier, Alazar Desbode, the son of my greatest enemy."

"So Alazar Desbode was the one who turned Jubel into a killing machine."

"Yes, and there has been no way to save him. He can't be killed as long as his soul is aligned with the dark forces that have merged with him."

"Maybe I can even the odds. Somehow I have to try," said Michael as Suki came into the room, pouring a fresh pot of green tea into cups for Michael and her father.

"I have prayed to Buddha that he will be set free, but my prayers have never been answered," said Lao, feeling guilt for Jubel.

"I believe in you Michael, I want you to know that," said Suki smiling.

We shall see, we shall see," said Lao firmly as he puffed on his Chinese pipe.

"I wonder what the future holds for us all," mused Michael.

"Your worst fear is your destiny. To destroy your fear you must face your destiny," said Lao firmly.

The clock struck twelve and Lao had gone to retire for the night; Michael stood on the rooftop with the moon shining high above him. Michael focused his mind on thinking of a way to kill Jubel and find the statue.

Suki came up not knowing he was there. "What are you doing up here?" she asked.

"Thinking how stupid I was to get myself mixed up in all of this mess," said Michael.

"Don't doubt yourself Michael. I see you have a warrior spirit," said Suki.

"Prophecies, vampires, mystical creatures; I've forgotten what normal life is like, just a normal, average life," said Michael.

"But they need you out there. Isn't that why you've now chosen to help innocent people?"

"You know, I used to believe that, the hero thing I mean, back in CIA; I used to believe in honor, justice and integrity. But when I got into the trade with the Family, all hell broke loose, and look at me now."

"Then change it. Use who you are now to make a difference. Just because you became what you are on the outside does not mean you have to be it within. You can be the hero you once were if you choose it. Look inside your heart. You can atone for your past mistakes you made by helping others."

Michael turned to Suki. "You're right; I can make a difference if I choose to."

"You can," said Suki.

All Michael could feel was grief for the terrible things he had done in his life, and for a moment he thought to himself, "Can I really be forgiven?"

Suki saw his sadness and kissed him on the cheek to say goodnight.

The next day Michael awoke to his training. The windows were shut tight; lanterns brought light to the dojo where he would train with Lao. Michael dressed himself in a traditional Japanese black robe and fastened sandals on his feet; he wrapped his ankles and hands with bands. Lao came into the room dressed in a red kimono holding a wooden practice katana in its sheath. Lao tossed Michael a practice sword, and the two both bowed to each other in respect and prepared to fight.

"Now then; Bushido is the way of the warrior. To defeat your foes you must become one with your sword, every breath you take, every step you make, every sound you hear, to become one in balance, discipline, spirit, heart. Your sword will become your reason for living. This is the essence and soul of a Samurai. Do this and you will be able to defeat any adversary."

"Let's just fight already," said Michael.

"Attack," commanded Lao. Michael lunged onward. Lao side stepped and knocked Michael down with his Kendo.

"Get up," ordered Lao.

"All right man, this is getting old," sassed Michael.

"Slow, attack slowly; feel the blade and let your opponent make the first move, then strike," said Lao. "Now again!"

Michael watched Lao's eyes move and his body turn, and then blocked the attack perfectly.

"Well done," said Lao. "Again, mimic the way I move, the motions I make, follow my eyes, and watch my hands."

Lao circled the room with the motions of a skilled dancer. Michael followed cautiously and exactly.

"Attack!" shouted Lao. The two began to match each other's movements and strokes of their blades. Michael grew more experienced in handling his sword, learning when to attack and when to keep his guard.

"Very good!" commended Lao after hours of intense training.

"So am I ready?" asked Michael.

"When the stars fall to the middle kingdom, so it will be," said Lao.

Michael grew impatient and lunged at Lao in frustration. Lao jumped kicked his opponent in the face, knocking him down. Michael spat up blood as a tooth fell out, a new one forming behind it.

"You have the will to fight and the resistance to pain, yet you miss the most important lesson of all," said Lao shaking his head in disappointment.

Wiping a drop blood from his face, Michael snapped, "What then!"

"Balance and control," replied Lao calmly, helping his pupil from off the ground.

"I'm in full control," argued Michael.

"You think you are, but your anger is your weakness. Conquer your anger and you will defeat your foe," said Lao.

"I'm tired of your proverbs," said Michael.

"Proverbs are a part of wisdom," said Lao.

"All right, I'll try," said Michael.

"Good. Now go and rest; we have trained enough for tonight," said Lao. Michael bowed good night to his sensei.

Then Suki took Michael into the bathhouse. "You did well today," said Suki as she undressed Michael and saw the deep scars on his body.

"What are you doing!" said Michael.

"Don't be afraid; I'm not going to hurt you. I'm just going to clean your cuts. You took a nasty fall earlier," said Suki as she led Michael to sit in a hot Japanese bath she had prepared for him. The water was filled with red rose petals. They filled the entire room with their scent of peace and sensuality.

"Aaah, damn it. Your father worked me over good," said Michael grunting in pain. His body was very sore and badly bruised.

"He has that effect on his students at times," said Suki, smiling as she lit lanterns in the dim room.

"So tell me, how does a pretty girl like you get caught up in all of this?" Michael asked as he sunk into the steamy water, relaxing.

"It's in my blood, that's all," said Suki as she changed into her evening kimono behind the screen in the room. "Now close your eyes," she said.

"What are you doing?" asked Michael with his eyes closed; he could hear Suki dipping her legs into the bath with him. Suki removed the bow that was clipped in her scented black hair. Michael opened his eyes to see a very beautiful creature before him; Suki was dressed in light violet lingerie covered by her see-through magenta kimono. Her breasts were round and full, her skin was soft, and her eyes shone radiantly like a rare jewel in the candlelight.

"Now then, let's take care of you," said Suki, bathing Michael with a warm cloth.

"Sorry, I just feel a little nervous," said Michael.

"In our culture men come first. Just enjoy this, relax, and let me work my magic on you tonight," said Suki. She cleaned his bleeding wounds with oils and herbs and her soft delicate hands caressed Michael's raw skin with a gentle touch.

"Suki thank you, that feels so good," sighed Michael.

"I knew you would like it. I used to do this for Yoshiro all the time," said Suki calmly as she massaged Michael's back.

"Who was he?" asked Michael.

"Just a man I loved, a long time ago," said Suki.

"Listen, tell me something Suki, why do you believe in me?" asked Michael.

"Because I can see that through all your tough exterior and your bravado, you're a caring person; you're not evil inside. You wish to redeem your mistakes by helping people you don't even know. These are the ways of honor."

"You're a sweet girl."

Suki turned to Michael and looked him in the eyes. She was about to kiss him, but Michael stopped her, shaking his head. "I can't," he said reluctantly.

Suki looked at him and smiled. "It's all right, I understand."

The two dried off and then went off to bed in different rooms for the night.

Across town, the other vampires searched through the ravaged tenements of the Oriental district, while their human companions searched in the lower district for the fat corrupted bastard known as Mohachi Yung, a snake and wolf all at the same time. Yung was infamous for his technique of killing his victims by ripping out their lungs and eating their eyes after they were dead, believing that it would give him great spiritual insight and power. Yung was also one of Vegas's largest suppliers of heroin and kroova, a synthetic blood hallucinogen for clubbing vampires.

"What the hell are we doing here? Michael gets to play Kabuki, and we're out searching for one of Vegas' most notorious drug king-pins," complained Serena.

"Our job, that's what. Lao wants us to find Yung, we'll find Yung," said Danny firmly.

"Team Nightmare to Team Vamp over!" called Danny over his walkie-talkie.

"Team Vamp here, over," replied Darius on his walkie-talkie.

"Have you sighted the target? Over," said Danny.

"That's a negative, Team Nightmare," replied Darius.

"Damn it," said Danny in disgust.

"Where are you located?" asked Danny.

"The south side of the Oriental District; we have Kung Kung sniffing out the area for Triads. Too bad we couldn't get trace on this guy. How about your end?" Darius asked. Darius wiped the sweat off his brow as he held his walkie-talkie.

"Chow Ling has been surveying the sky. Wait a minute; I see something through her vision," said Darius looking into the distance.

"What! What is it?" shouted Danny.

"Down below on Sing Way, there is a long black limousine driving up to the Raiko business building. The chauffer is opening up the door. I see a large bald Japanese man in a white tuxedo with dark glasses and a long black beard exiting the car, with several bodyguards in identical black suits," said Darius.

Danny transmitted the image of the target to Darius' pocket computer. "That's him," said Darius.

"Get him!" yelled Danny over his walkie-talkie. Darius whistled loudly to Chow-Ling to alert Kung Kung. Chow-Ling let out a terrifying scream, which Kung Kung heard instantly. The ghostly cat's eyes inflamed in burning orange as he shape shifted into a monstrous feline. Danny and Serena jumped on top of him, and with an ear-shattering scream Kung Kung ran at super sonic speed to intercept the target.

"Stupid cat, slow down! Slow down, you're going to get us killed!" screamed Serena as the beast leaped along the rooftops of the Oriental district at fantastic speeds.

Mohachi greeting his contact when they heard the clamor. "What the hell was that!" said the contact.

"Get Mr. Yung out of here!" yelled one man.

"Oh my God!" screamed another.

People on the street scrambled in panic. The massive cat shot forth from the shadows of the high rise rooftops, morphing into the form of a Byakokasha the hybrid flying demon cat, whose black and white stripes resembled those of a white tiger. Kung Kung swooped down straight toward Mochachi, who was frozen with terror.

"AYEYAHH!!!" wailed Mohachi as Danny grappled Mohachi. Mohachi's bodyguards fired shots into the sky trying to protect their boss, but Kung Kung dodged the bullets with ease. Taking off into the sky burdened with Danny, Serena and Mohachi, the hellish beast blasted up in a stream of white smoke, leaving the people on the ground motionless with terror.

"What! What! What do you want? I'll do anything; just don't let me die! Who are you people?" screamed Mohachi.

"That's good; now let's talk, you sleazy swine! Danny grinned with satisfaction as they flew higher into the clouds.

"Are you crazy?" screamed Mohachi.

"Maybe," exclaimed Danny.

Serena grabbed Mohachi, holding him up to her face, "Where is the Shira jade statue!" she ordered.

"My rooftop penthouse at the Tengu Pagoda Casino!" shrieked Mohachi.

"Anything else?" said Danny. "I've told you everything! Now let me down!" whined Mohachi.

Danny nodded to Kung Kung to set them down. The beast understood and descended to the rooftop of a nearby small building. "For your health, Mr. Yung, I suggest you leave Las Vegas." Danny let go of Mohachi and the spineless businessman fell into a large trash dumpster in the alley. Mohachi sprung from the dumpster, cussing out his attackers in Japanese as he pulled out his gun, shooting into the air at his assailants. Danny whipped out his trusty Cobra 76 and fired one shot, hitting the large lid of the trash container, which slammed down on top of Mohachi.

Back at the Raiko building the press were having a field day. Commissioner Hamilton made her statement to the public as the cameras rolled and bright lights flashed before her eyes.

"Commissioner, do you have any idea as to what is going on here?" asked one reporter.

"We are looking into this bizarre event to determine who was responsible for this attack," answered Commissioner Hamilton.

"Witnesses saw a large cat running off carrying the victim," stated one reporter.

"What about the reports of the victims of the Otis Way area who were drained of blood, the public wants to know, Commissioner," said another.

"We are still looking into that investigation," replied Commissioner Hamilton.

"What about the strange rumors that have been floating around the city of monsters living here?" asked another reporter.

"Ladies and gentlemen, our department has contacted a team of special experts to investigate these cases of unusual phenomena that have occurred; I assure you that when we have answers, the public will be notified. I have nothing further to say," stated Commissioner Hamilton as she left the podium.

"Well, you've heard it all: strange beasts, mythical monsters, or is this all just a case of an escaped animal from a casino? This is one reporter who will be here to keep you up to date on this story. Reporting for Channel 8 news. This is Mike Lee; back to you in the newsroom Todd."

"Imbeciles," said Julius in disapproval, as he switched off his TV monitor. Scarlet came into her father's bedroom carrying a cup of tea. Julius lay back as he rested on his bed.

"What happened? Was our little team discovered?" smirked Scarlet. Julius frowned at his daughter's remark.

"This is serious," he said sternly.

"You know it was bound to happen father, at one time or another," replied Scarlet.

"We are supposed to stay hidden, all of our kind; vampire, Oni, lycanthrope, etc. All of us are to remain unknown to the mortal world and now this has occurred," said Julius.

"The Council of the Nine will have something to say about this, I suppose," mused Scarlet.

"Naturally they will; you know well as I do that it is strictly forbidden for our kind to make themselves known to the public. We are to blend in with society, not stand out," said Julius.

"What do think they will do?" asked Scarlet.

"I don't know but I am now worried about Serena and Damascus. Things are getting very dangerous and you know the punishment is death to those that expose our kind. We might have to come up with a different plan of action to prevent any more sightings like this one," said Julius.

"Lucky for us that the crowd could only see with human sight what looked like a normal white tiger on the ground attacking Mohachi Yung," said Scarlet.

"It still doesn't matter; one mistake can bring ruin to us if our clans are not careful," said Julius.

The rest of Serena's team was on the Strip. Marianna called Michael's cell, assuming he was asleep. Michael awoke hastily, to the sounds of his cell phone. He answered drowsily. "Yeah, Marianna? What's up?"

"We found it," said Marianna.

"Where is it?" asked Michael, suddenly awake.

"Mohachi's Casino; security will be a problem."

"Maybe for humans but not for us," said Michael. "When do we move?"

"Tomorrow night," replied Marianna sharply.

"Understood," said Michael as he hung up his phone.

Michael woke in the early afternoon. The blinds were closed and the dojo was silent as death.

After Michael had completed his physical training with Lao, Suki escorted him into the meditation room where Lao was waiting for his pupil, already sitting with lanterns burning incense in the small room.

"Now then, Michael; you have taken great effort and have mastered the art of your sword with ease; I'm impressed by this. I have never had a student quite like you before," said Lao, proud of his pupil.

"Now am I ready?" asked Michael.

"You still must master mental and spiritual balance. This I can teach you, but you must be willing to participate," said Lao.

"What is it?" asked Michael eagerly.

"Simple. Gain contact with your soul in deep prayer and the gods or spirits you believe in will guide you," said Lao.

"Pardon me, but I don't follow these mystic beliefs." Michael spoke carefully; he did not want to offend Lao. "I understand. Focus then on what you will and the answers will come to you. I will leave you for a few hours, and then I shall return," said Lao respectfully as he bowed to his student and then left the room with his daughter.

Michael sat in deep thought for a time, and then he felt the compulsion to pray. Prayer was an act that he rarely performed, but he began to close his eyes and speak as he kneeled on the ground with his head hanging down, like a knight bowing before his king. He began to have faith again. "Jesus, my God in heaven, protect me, let me kill these bastards, and send their souls to hell. Without fear or regret, to save the ones I love and the innocent people in this city, be with me please."

A presence entered. The room was filled with tender warmth and a golden light shone; the presence of God himself appeared to the vampire. "I am Jesus Christ, God born in the flesh," said the Lord, wearing holy armor of silver lined with gold.

At this moment, Michael fell to the floor bowing to God, and then out of the blue he said, "I forgive the man that murdered my sister, forgive me Lord for my sins." Michael prostrated with grief.

"I have always been with you my son. I have forgiven you of all your sins because you confessed with your lips and have believed in Me with your heart. Go and protect the ones you love; I give you my Spirit to protect you and the means to defeat those who have sought to destroy my Church and all the people of this world, which the Father in Heaven created. But remember this: all people I forgive who come to Me believe and repent. I will never forsake you. Your power comes from the darkness and now I take it away, and give you a part of me. You now understand what your purpose is. I give you great power. My Spirit will guide you. However, because you have given yourself to crimes of revenge, and the murder of the innocent, you will suffer in chastisement for a time. When my enemies have all been destroyed, when not one of them has a last breath of life in them, then on that day I will release you from your curse and you will be free. Now go fulfill your destiny, my son." The Lord put a seal of heaven on Michael's neck, a mark to show that he was the chosen warrior. "Go now, my seraphim of light," said Christ.

As the Lord vanished, a great thunderclap could be heard around the entire building and flashes of steam and light emanated from Michael and he screamed as the evil spirits left his body. His faith was restored and he was free. The evil spirits left the room and descended into the ground.

Suki, Lao, and Rocko who recovered from the poisoning ran into the room to see what had happened to Michael. Michael began to glow brightly as his skin recovered its human color. His body became stronger. But he could tell he was not fully human; he still felt his fangs and sensed his eyes glowing like white neon.

"What has happened?" asked Suki.

"He has found his God and he is complete. No longer a vampire but now something else; he's a spirit warrior," said Lao.

"What does this mean?" asked Michael.

"It means that you can walk in the sunlight without it harming you. You will now be immune from many of your vampiric weaknesses, but be careful; it does not mean you are invincible. You are now ready. Time to fight." Lao placed his hand on his student's right shoulder, showing his congratulations.

At once Michael understood his transformation and knew the purpose of his life. Lao then went into his room and brought out two blades that were crafted from fine metal, a splendid saber and a perfectly balanced katana.

"These were Jubel's when I trained him. I want you to have these; you will need them," said Lao, bowing his head in respect. Destiny had called his student this night.

Just then Darius, Marianna, Danny, and Serena came to report to Lao what they had found; they were shocked to see Michael in his new form. Michael explained what had happened. Serena then noticed that her own body had changed just like Michael's, for her soul had been linked to his.

"What has happened to me," Serena shrieked.

"The two become one, redemption to walk in light. The children of darkness will become children of the light, for this is what is said in the prophecy," said Darius firmly.

"It is coming," said Marianna, as their beings were transformed as well.

"We might just be able to win this war," said Darius boldly.

A hellish wind blew the heavy doors of the dojo open and the group saw in the sky a massive storm of wind, snow, and red lighting descending upon the city.

"The Shirakai!" cried Marianna.

"Damn bastards, they must have followed us," said Darius.

"Oh shit!" Serena swore as they saw the three creatures shooting down from the sky to attack.

"Guys, I think we should get the fuck out of here now!" screamed Rocko with fear.

Lao looked at them all and said calmly "Leave it to me." This upset Suki.

"But father, you'll be killed!" said Suki with fear.

"Leave me all of you, go now!" ordered Lao.

Leaping into the sky he drew his katana. Using his sage's powers he turned his clothes into Hachiman armor in the royal colors of red and gold. Lao's eyes turned green, drawing on his mystical energy to begin battle with the three Shirakai beings. Beams of lightning and fire blazed through the sky like a vortex appearing from another world. Lao summoned forth a chi orb and chanted, "SHAMI KARI ZA!" catapulting the orb into the sky, which blasted hurricane winds and scattered the enemies. They fell to the ground, screaming unholy screams of defeat, silenced until the next battle began. Lao sheathed his blade and then plummeted down to the ground, crushing the pavement with his feet. Then he got up and brushed off the bits of rubble stuck on his armor like it was nothing, and the armor changed back into his regular clothing.

"Unbelievable!" said Danny.

"For an old guy he sure gets around," said Darius.

"Jealous," chuckled Lao.

"Maybe," said Darius boldly.

"You're safe now. Head to the Tengu Pagoda Casino and get the statue. Hurry! Before they have time to regroup," commanded Lao. Then he disappeared in a cloud of smoke and was gone.

"Wait everyone," said Suki, as she hurried back into the dojo, pulling a secret lever on one of the statues on the bookshelf.

"Damn!" said Darius as a multitude of combat firearms stocked with ammunition appeared in a secret compartment.

"I believe in modern warfare myself, come on!" said Suki as she tossed everyone a pistol or machine gun.

"Let me guess, you're into gun running too," said Michael.

"Everyone has to eat," said Suki. The group took off in Suki's old service van, speeding to the Tengu Pagoda Casino.

53

HEIST AT MOHACHI'S

C how Ling and Kung Kung slept in the back of the van as Marianna planned how they would sneak into the casino. "Listen, does anyone have a plan on how we're going to get up to the statue without being noticed?"

Rocko looked around the interior of the van, taking in the cardboard boxes that were stuffed into the back. "Hey what's in the boxes?" he asked.

"Old janitor uniforms, my father also runs a cleaning service, why?" replied Suki shortly, as she was driving. An idea came to Danny's mind and he hopped through to the back of the van, opening a box and pulling out a janitor's jumpsuit. They all looked at the outfits and had the same idea.

"Danny! You're a damn genius!" Serena exclaimed.

"Let's suit up," said Darius as he grabbed one of the uniforms. They parked the car in one of the casino's indoor parking lots and quickly changed into their disguises. Michael prepped his guns and pulled out his saber, cleaning the blade with a handkerchief.

"Let's go in for the kill," said Serena.

They all checked their weapons for priming. Kung Kung panted and with Chow Ling fluttered in the air; they wanted to join their companions in the heist, but Suki petted them and shook her head, telling them to hide nearby until they were needed. The two creatures obeyed and hid behind the massive stacks of wooden crates and boxes in the maintenance storage lot. The van crept into back service parking lot as Michael and his team infiltrated the area, proceeding to the penthouse floor via one of the service elevators.

"Remember, just be natural," said Michael, winking at his friends.

"Easy for you to say. This jumpsuit is hugging my nuts," complained Danny.

"Keep talking and you'll only have one," joked Serena as she lowered her pistol to Fredricks' crotch. "Just kidding."

Danny was relieved.

"Really mature, Serena," said Darius.

Swiping a couple of mops, access cards, and cleaning carts from the janitor supply room they pick locked, the crew walked through the casino floor as they heard the sounds of a busy casino. Flashing their IDs to a nearby security guard, the team was allowed access to Mohachi's office on the top floor.

The vast room seemed deserted, with no signs of life. It was dark and little light came into the room from the windows. Marianna pulled out a flashlight from her coat pocket to search for a main light switch. The rest of them looked around the room for the statue, finding it in a display case.

"This is too easy, something doesn't feel right," said Danny.

"Just your imagination," replied Serena as she found the light and turned it on. All around the room were Mohachi's guards, armed with Uzi's loaded and ready to shoot.

"Uh oh," said Rocko.

"Kill all of them. Mr. Yung's orders!" screamed one of the guards.

"We should have killed him," said Serena under her breath. Michael unsheathed his saber, and then warped behind one of the guards, poking his back. The guard turned and saw Michael just as his blade cut straight through the guard's head. Bullets flew around the room as Marianna and Darius avoided the shots, blasting away as the guard's flesh and gushes of blood splattered the walls and furniture in the room. Danny and Rocko jumped over a table for cover as a guard fired from the corner of the room; Danny pulled out his sawed off shotgun and fired, blowing chunks of the wall to bits. The guard fired back and Rocko grabbed a pistol that had belonged to one of the dead guards and fired, hitting another guard in the legs, taking him down.

When the smoke had cleared, the room was bathed in gore with dismembered body parts on the floor in pools of blood. The team could hear footsteps approaching the room.

"Time to go," said Michael, grabbing the Shira statue. Suddenly from out of the inner darkness a blast of wind and thick smoke enshrouded the room and time ceased. Everything was motionless, caught in a frozen block of time; the vampires saw every mortal freeze.

"What the hell!" exclaimed Darius. The shadows in the room spilt apart as a cloaked man in a silk black robe with long hair and a battle-scarred face came out of the shadows. With him was another man.

"Congratulations, Damascus, you have made yourself worthy of the game," said the man.

"Who are you!" shouted Michael.

"My name is Reynard Desbode."

"You mean it was a test?" asked Darius.

"Yes you fool, a test to see if the children and allies of my greatest enemy could stand up to the challenges I laid out for them. Mohachi was just a pawn in the game. I, on the other hand, am the king."

"Get on with it then," said Michael bitterly.

"I wish to offer you all a chance for power, power beyond all the glory that this defiled world has to offer. Abandon this futile crusade of yours; join me and become gods," Reynard Desbode offered.

"Forget it," said Michael.

"Oh come now, Damascus; surely you don't believe that I would let you leave here alive. If you're not for me then you're against me."

"Pity," said Alazar Desbode chuckled wickedly as he tossed a bomb into the middle of their group. The two men disappeared into a cloud of smoke. Time was then set back in motion.

"Oh shit!" screamed Serena.

Michael and Darius grabbed the others and they smashed through the door just as the bomb exploded, and they were swept through the hall by burning fires. SWAT teams ran through the hall to intercept the intruders.

"Halt, you're under arrest!" screamed the captain, enraged.

"Not tonight, buddy!" smiled Michael as he threw a tear gas bomb in front of the SWAT team. The exploding gas caused confusion that let Michael and the others escape; they ran to the elevator. But the SWAT team on the lower floor beat them to the punch, shutting off the main service switch and causing the elevator to shut down.

"Just great," said Michael as he tried to pry open the door that was jammed. Darius helped him open the sealed doors only to find armed guards waiting for them. Thinking fast, Suki sent a chi ball at the guards, blasting the SWAT team against the wall and disabling them. Michael and company raced down the lower flights of stairs and through the main casino floor with the statue in hand, as the guards fired their guns in pursuit.

"Everyone get down, get the fuck down!" screamed Michael to the casino-goers as they ran through the crowded casino, firing shots back. Danny was hit in the shoulder; the bullet went clean through.

"Mother Fucker!!" screamed Danny as he fell down in pain.

"Oh no you damn don't, come on!" screamed Michael as he hoisted Danny up and bolted for the main service door to the parking area. Suki whistled for her pets to come and help them, and Kung Kung and Chow Ling sprang to action.

"Decoy!" commanded Suki. Her pets understood and transformed into a likeness of Damascus and his friends leading the armed swat team on a wild goose chase through the streets, while Suki and the others hopped into the van and took off on the freeway back into the Oriental District. Danny was in poor shape, bleeding all over the upholstery of the van.

"Shit, hold on Danny man, come on buddy, you can make it!" screamed Rocko.

"Quick, find a cloth and apply pressure to the wound!" said Marianna.

Serena grabbed an old linen cleaning cloth from one of the boxes in the van and tightly wrapped it around Danny's wounded shoulder.

"Thanks," said Danny.

"That was too close back there," said Darius, unloading his Uzi.

"At least we got what we came for," said Suki.

"Quick let's get back to the dojo and inspect the map; then we'll be able to find the location off the map," said Michael. They all agreed and sped off to Lao's dojo.

"Damn it!" Michael slammed his fist on Lao's table upon learning that the statue had been switched with a fake; all that trouble for nothing. "What the hell are we going to do now? This was all a waste!" screamed Michael in frustration.

"Relax, Damascus; be cool as you say," said Darius.

"I would be more concerned with Reynard Desbode. He almost killed us; luckily, we all got out of the room before the bomb went off," said Serena.

"Incompetent. I could have done better than him," spouted off Darius.

"Shut up Darius, this isn't funny," yelled Michael in disgust.

"Screw you," fired back Darius in anger.

"Stop it, both of you," yelled Suki, pushing the two away from each other.

"Fine. He's not even a full-blood vampire anyway," smirked Darius.

"What makes you think I give a damn what you say?" smirked back Michael, brushing himself off.

Suddenly, the phone rang, catching the heated group off guard. Suki ran to answer in the commotion, frantically dropping the phone then picking up the receiver to her ear. "Hello! Hello!" she said nervously.

"Suki, this is your cousin, Shang Nishimora," said the Japanese man over the phone.

"It's your brother, Ken: he's dead," said Shang sadly.

"Dead!" Suki cried, distraught.

"Some witnesses saw men in black robes take him. I found his body dumped in the slums. Come to Tokyo at once with your friends. Your father is here with me now," ordered Shang.

"Yes, we will immediately!" said Suki as she hung up the phone.

"So," asked Michael.

"Dark agents. They are already in Tokyo," answered a shaken Suki.

"Then what are we standing here for? Let's grab a flight; we have to stop these bastards before they get to the book," said Michael.

Kung Kung and Chow Ling then flew in the door. Suki bowed to them and sent them back to her room to rest. Rocko then spoke up. "Listen you guys, I've had my fill of fighting monsters for one day. Danny is hurt pretty badly; perhaps the rest of you should go while I watch after him until he's healed up," said Rocko.

Danny shook his head in agreement. "You guys, he's right, I'm no good to you like this, that damn bullet went threw my shooting arm. I'll stay with Rocko, the rest of you go to Japan."

"Your call then; hold the fort until we get back," agreed Marianna, as did the others.

Back at the Tengu Pagoda Casino police barricades had secured the perimeter while detectives swept the area searching for clues on the shoot-out. Commissioner Hamilton shook her head in frustration as she saw the homicide body count rising yet again. "What do we have this time boys?"

"Six suspects broke into the upstairs penthouse of the Tengu Pagoda casino, owned by Mohachi Yung. We have the theft of a rare jade statue, fires burning upstairs in the building that we just had put out with water helicopters. There are 20 dead bodyguards, with casings left over from automatic machine guns, shot gun shells, and a casino filled of frightened guests," listed an officer on the scene.

"Any witnesses?" asked Commissioner Hamilton sternly.

"Yeah, we got 70 different ones, all who said they saw the attackers dressed in light blue janitorial uniforms come running out of the main hall, chased by the swat team. They appeared to be professional thieves, as they handled the swat team well; they were very dangerous and deadly," said the other officer. "And you guys couldn't catch these creeps," said Commissioner Hamilton. "We were in pursuit and it was if they just vanished into thin air," said the first officer.

"People just don't disappear into thin air officer. Find them or find new jobs, now!" barked Commissioner Hamilton.

She had a hunch about the identities of the criminals and muttered "Damascus, clever," under her breath.

54

DISCOVERY IN TOKYO

Grabbing a private jetliner from Zoratus Enterprises, the vampire allies took off in the black sky; they were worried as they traveled through the night about the duel of darkness they faced in Japan.

Seventeen hours later the jetliner landed at Tokyo's main international airport in the early evening just as the sun was setting in the west. Waiting on the airstrip was a Japanese gentleman dressed in a black traditional Japanese suit, his hair slicked back and a half-smile on his face. "Suki, welcome home."

"Shang," said Suki as she ran to hug her cousin.

"And these are your friends I have heard so much about," said Shang.

"Hello," the others returned the greeting. After getting in the limo Shang had waiting, they sped off into the city. The conversation switched to a serious tone. "Shang what can you tell me about what happened to my brother? How he was killed?" asked Suki.

"Our spies have also been looking for the Yomi Tengu Shira, just as your enemies have been. We needed to find Ken because he had in his possession a pendant that when worn translates the book's secrets. It was our best hope to find a way to destroy the book somehow. That was until your brother was kidnapped from his home and the pendant taken," said Shang sadly.

"Listen, do you know anyone we could find who can tell us the last known whereabouts of the Dark Agents in the area?" asked Marianna.

"Marianna, is it? Yes, we have a contact. He is a Shaolin monk at an old temple in the hills," said Shang while driving.

"Who is he?" asked Suki.

"An old acquaintance of yours, Yoshiro," said Shang.

"You have got to be kidding me," said Darius.

"No, it's him," said Shang.

"A monk is going to help us? What does he get out of it?" said Serena.

"Fulfilling a promise he made to Suki's father years ago, which was to help her in time of need," replied Shang.

"Well, at least we've got somebody to help us. It could be worse," said Michael as the car sped through the busy bright lights and streets of Tokyo.

"This city is fascinating." Serena took in the gigantic cityscape scaling high into nighttime clouds; it seemed like a lit stairway to the heavens.

"Tokyo is a city of wonders and many dreams," agreed Shang.

Two hours later the car arrived in front of an old temple in the hills, just west of outskirts of Tokyo. The temple was covered by an array of trees below the brightly shining stars and the symphonic sounds of the night. Birds, insects and fireflies fluttered around the temple.

There were large wooden doors in the middle of the temple and the columns had marble statues of samurai and shogun warriors that were partially covered by shrubbery. A large gong bell with a hammer stood by the side of the entrance. Michael and the others walked up the old limestone steps of the shrine, looking up at the massive structure, as pairs of glowing bird eyes could be seen in the trees. "You have arrived. Good luck. You will need it," said Shang as he bowed and then disappeared into a purple mist.

"Maybe we should knock?" said Marianna.

"How about this instead," said Darius, picking up the hammer and hitting the gong. The sound echoed through the temple. Two guards dressed in orange Buddhist monk robes opened the doors. "This way," said the guards as they led the group through the grand hallway where statues of emperors stood as a testament of Japan. Gold dragons and beasts were portrayed on wall scrolls by the hundreds and torches burned, emitting the smell of incense. In the center of the hallway the guards opened a set of doors to reveal a young-looking Buddhist monk in the midst of training other Shaolin warriors. Each one of them were different creatures; werewolves, angelic humanoids, kappa, gargoyles, feline cat beasts with the wings of giant birds, a bull man, banshee women, human monks, Slavic monsters, male and female Chinese sages, wraiths and strange creatures resembling ethereal monsters. Each one had a more hideous or majestic face than the other, gracefully moving in an elite poetry of skill and discipline to accomplish their individual destinies. The temple seemed so lively with such a force that it was a world of its own. The warriors clashed with weapons of every description, dodging arrows and gunfire with strange shields of energy, using charms, and different mystical weapons.

"Whoa," said the vampires as they watched this secret training compound.

"What is this place?" breathed Serena.

"Welcome to the Temple of the Seven Dragons," said the young monk, who flipped to land in front of Michael and the others.

"Yoshiro, right," said Darius.

"Lao sent you," said Yoshiro.

"Yes, he did," said Marianna.

"You're looking for the pendant, right?" asked Yoshiro.

"We need it to open a portal to locate the book," said Suki.

"I never thought I would see you again," replied Yoshiro.

"It's nice to see you, Yoshiro."

"Who are these entities with you?" asked Marianna.

"The Council of Eternal Light," answered Yoshiro. "Our allies have come from all over the world to fight the Dark Society."

"How many are there?" asked Michael.

"Here or all?"

"All," said Darius.

"Sixty thousand," said Yoshiro.

"Not enough," Michael shook his head.

"We don't know how many shadow agents we're up against," explained Suki.

"We can still even the odds if we get that pendant back. Then we can control the powers that our enemies wish to use against us to destroy them," said Yoshiro.

"Does anyone else know of this place?" asked Serena.

"No, just us and now you and your companions. Come, we have to get that pendant back," said Yoshiro.

"Do you know where my father is?" asked Suki.

"Right here," said Lao as he removed his cloak coming out of the shadows.

"Father, but I thought you were," stumbled Suki.

"Dead. I'm not, but we will be if we do not stop our enemy."

"Where do we go now?" asked Michael.

"I can finish training the warriors, but you must find the pendant before the translation of the gate opening spell can be completed. Once performed it can't be stopped," said Lao.

"Tokyo is a vast city; where do we begin to look?" asked Michael.

"That won't be a problem. We will let them find us," said Yoshiro.

"The one who we are looking for is a ninja named Jubel, he's extremely dangerous," said Darius.

"Jubel!" Startled, Yoshiro dropped his practice sword, looking terrified.

"What's wrong? Do you know him?" asked Marianna.

"He's my brother," said Yoshiro.

"What!" they all said in shock.

"It's true. We were both the martial arts students of Lao at one time.

The only difference is that we separated after an argument. Jubel wanted to train and fight all over the world, to be the world's strongest fighter. I chose to find the meaning of life. That is why I became a monk: to follow the teachings of the Buddha and continue to train in the Shaolin arts of combat. I worked mostly as a historian for the university in Tokyo. Then, after Lao told me about the current situation, I came here to continue to train, to aid my master and help you." Yoshiro bowed in respect.

"He's humble isn't he?" said Serena impressed.

"He may be humble, but can he fight," said Michael.

"Don't worry about me, I can take down a Shadow Agent anytime, I have had enough practice," said Yoshiro, relaxed as he grabbed a surprised Michael and flipped him over his back to the ground.

"Okay, you made your point," said Michael standing and dusting the dirt off his jacket.

"Let's go," said Darius.

"What about Shang?" Serena asked.

A man emerged from the room's shadows. "Sorry, I'm just the messenger, but I've got you a lead. Look for a vampire Yakusa gang member named Kengi Chang in the downtown district of Tokyo at Yamoto's Bar. He can help you," said Shang. He bowed and disappeared back into the shadows.

The group raced through the city in Shang's car to meet the Yakusa contact. Entering the bar, they saw a short Japanese vampire, his head shaven with a short goatee and black eyes. He was a young punk, about 25 in appearance, dressed in a bluish black blazer and black glasses, standing idle and smoking a cigarette.

"You Kengi?" asked Michael.

"Yeah, something is going down tonight. Mohachi Yung's thugs are meeting with someone important to exchange a precious stone of some kind." Kengi kept his guard up.

"Where can we find them?" asked Darius.

"The Midnight Haven Club. Take this card and they will know who sent you," said Kengi.

"Thanks," said Michael.

"No problem," said Kengi as he nodded and walked off.

Pulling the clutch back in the car, they sped off like pure heat burning nitro. The crew arrived at the club uptown; it was located off of a secluded alleyway and shrouded in darkness, though the moon shone above. Walking into the club was rough, as the place was not friendly to locals, much less outsiders.

"What's this joint about? It's so secretive," wondered Michael.

"It's not called a haven for nothing," said Suki.

As they approached the door two large bouncers were standing guard. Suki showed them the card, which was actually a magical charm. The guard's eyes glowed and their faces changed to look like boars. The bouncer on the left turned to the other and nodded; a snort as steam came out of his snout, and they were let in.

"Did you see that!" exclaimed Serena.

"This place is a haven for all of our kind. Humans can't see our true appearance," said Suki.

"You been here before?" asked Darius.

"Both of us have, in the past," said Yoshiro as his visage changed to the face of a handsome Oni demon. He had a light red muscular body, a small crown of black horns on his head, and was ready to attract breeding females all around.

"Oh, there's something I forgot to mention. I am an Oni demon too, half, at least," explained Yoshiro.

"What the fuck?" Michael asked.

"We used to be married; our union brought the transformation to him," said Suki, smiling a little.

The group entered the mammoth building to find a spectacle like no other in the world. Light devices lit the room, making it look like the set of a classic horror movie; fog machines blew eerie wisps across the multicolored nightclub floor and pulsing laser lights flashed over the supernatural party scene. Two spider-like humanoid DJs spun multiple turntables on both sides of the club, while a brutal sadistic horde of monster musicians rocked out on the main stage surrounded by ghoulish women dancers. There was a short goblin drummer, a she-alien bassist, a snake woman playing keyboard, and a werewolf dressed in black leather biker pants, metallic gauntlets with metal shoulder guards and leather straps as belts, playing a heavy metal guitar, singing wickedly cool lyrics about wild thrills. Harpy babes and goddess muses with beautiful humanoid bird faces and hot scantily clad bodies danced exposed their exotic breasts, feathered backs and lovely legs in colors of blue, red, green, and turquoise. One of them passed Michael, seductively smiling at him to get a drink. Serena nudged him in ribs for staring, while rocker and punker demons, along with a multitude of bizarre and deranged creatures, drank and ate merrily to the tunes. Frog- and centipede-like creatures with human faces sat at lounge tables smoking hookahs. Beautiful mermaids and sirens swam in colorful glass oval water tanks in colors of aquamarine, blue and jade. Some of them were talking to some of the males.

"What a place! I wish we had this back home," said Michael.

"Remember what we are here for," said Yoshiro firmly.

"Do you see Mohachi anywhere?" asked Darius.

"No," said Michael looking around the club, trying to spot him.

"There he is, in the back." Marianna pointed him out.

"I see him; let's play it slick and follow him," said Darius.

"Who's he with?" asked Serena.

Darius caught his eyes on a ninja. "It's Jubel," said Darius.

"Let's take this guy now," said Michael getting ready and sliding out his katana.

"No!" said Serena, locking his arm down and shaking her head in disapproval. "Not here, Michael," she said.

The crew moved to the end of the club while Mohachi and Jubel got up from making the exchange and left the room. The crew tried to follow them when a human guard stopped Michael at the door.

"Where you going?" spouted the guard, putting his hand on Michael's chest. Michael just gave an evil smile, and with his eyes glaring white and his fangs showing, he threw the guy across the room into a stack of boxes. Michael then opened the doors and continued to follow Jubel and Mohachi.

Suddenly Darius could hear a voice speaking to him in his head as he saw a strange green mist billow before him. "Become a Dark God Darius, forget the cause, be one of us," whispered the mist. No one else saw this but him. He remembered his own words from when he spoke to Julius at the manor, *We should be accepted for what we are, as vampires, not to bend to the laws and ways of humanity.*"

"No I can't," said Darius to himself in his mind. The phantom mist left him, but this idea grew stronger in Darius.

The vampire crew moved in pursuit of Jubel through an underground dwelling, the remains of an old Japanese mansion.

Jubel presented the pendant and the book to Alazar Desbode.

"How did you find both?"

"Where there is will, there is always a way, my friend. Now where is my money?" demanded Jubel.

"Thirty million in thousand dollar bills as promised," said Alazar Desbode as he opened a briefcase to show Jubel the money.

As the exchange was being made, Michael and Darius broke through the doorway, "Alazar Desbode! Let's dance, mother fucker!" yelled Michael.

"I thought you got rid of them!" said Alazar Desbode.

"What!" cried Jubel.

"Kill them!" commanded Alazar Desbode.

The crew whiplashed into the room and Alazar Desbode pulled out a high-powered assault weapon, spraying bullets; Darius and Michael fired back. Serena flipped, and Marianna took bullets through the chest as blood oozed from their bodies.

"Anna!" yelled Darius. Knocking over torn furniture to shield themselves, the vampires and oni's fired back with their guns as bullets flew, hitting the walls as they blew through Jubel. Alazar Desbode hid behind a rusted antique safe, returning fire and dodging bullets. Yoshiro and Jubel whirled around the room fighting, slamming each other against the walls and flying in short bursts.

"Sorry brother," cried out Yoshiro, slamming Jubel to the ground.

"No brother, die!" yelled Jubel as he flipped Yoshiro over on the floor pinning him down and getting ready to snap his neck like a toothpick.

Michael shot Jubel in the chest. Suki used her Oni powers to revive Serena, Marianna, and Yoshiro; their wounds closed up and were healed.

Alazar Desbode put on the pendant while skimming through the blood-inked pages of the book. He started summoning a spell. "Suca liah ittah marakai, rise, the god spirit Death of the nether world and become living flesh!" he chanted.

Suki dragged Marianna and Serena to the side. Green and red liquid flames erupted in the room and hot winds blew as the god formed from the fire. Jubel's chest pushed out the bullets that had not gone through as he lunged at Darius, picking him up and throwing him across the room. Michael shot a small katana out from his side, pinning Alazar Desbode to the wall.

"AAAH!!" screamed Alazar Desbode, dropping the book, but the portal continued to open.

"Grab the book!" yelled Suki. Darius grabbed the book and threw a knife into Alazar Desbode's chest. Blood poured out. "I have no soul, I can't die," laughed Alazar Desbode, pulling out the blade from his lungs as green blood poured out and the wound closed.

Suki slid across the bloody floor, pulling out her dagger and slitting open his chest. As his organs spilled out on the bloody floor, Alazar Desbode fell to his knees, choking on his own blood, struggling to reach to the god spirit who was forming. Suki ripped the pendant from Alazar Desbode's neck, grabbed the book and slit his throat as blood spread on the floor into green slimy pools that bubbled and churned like burning acid. Jubel disappeared into smoke. Then the vampires and oni's left the scene.

Alazar Desbode held his hands out to the darkness, wriggling and looking into the eyes of the spirit as it stared at him. Then the room faded into darkness and screams echoed in the background. The chambers began to rumble as the earth shook violently, "We have to get out of here!" yelled Serena.

"How! This place is going to come down," yelled Darius. The group all spotted a hatchway at the same time. They ran through the underground halls of decay, cobwebs and old Japanese lanterns. Suddenly, they noticed Jubel at the end of the hall. He smiled at them and then pulled a secret lever on a wall sconce, sealing them in the hall. The ground stopped shaking and a strange gas released from holes in the wall that no one had noticed before. The red mist caused Michael and the others to become delusional. They saw each other as enemies and began to attack each other.

The angel Gabriel appeared again to help them; he sent a flash of bright holy light that made the red mist disappear. The angel vanished and the hall grew silent as the group came to their senses and worked together to find a way out.

"How do we get out of here, I can't see a damn thing," said Marianna as she tried to find a light.

Michael hit his lighter trying to find anything to help them escape. He leaned back against a dragon statue head that unlocked the gate.

"It's open!" cried Yoshiro as they saw the gate go up. Running through it they found themselves in a large, circular, room. The room was pitch black, but something was wrong. Michael and others heard the sounds of slithering and hisses all around the room, and the floor seemed like it was moving.

"What's that noise?" said Michael.

"I hear it too," said Marianna.

Torches lit up one by one, revealing an arena of death and carnage. Rotten slimy corpses had been mangled and chewed to bits by something overwhelmingly evil. The ground was drenched in blood, snake venom, and bones, and the place reeked like shit in a backed-up sewer.

"What the fuck is going on!" said Michael, keeping his guard up.

"I don't know but I think we're going to find out!" yelled Darius.

"Look!" screamed Serena as a large, spiked gate open. They could hear chains clanking along with the sounds of something inhuman scream like the hordes of hell. A monstrous, drooling and disgusting worm came out with glaring red eyes; it was a giant centipede, a mutated beast with eight giant human limbs and three humanoid heads with monstrously oversized tusks and fangs.

"Kadee!" shouted Suki.

"What the hell is that!" shouted Serena.

"A giant monster that eats people."

"Fuck, how are we going to kill this thing?" shouted Michael. The creature came out of its dwelling, roaring and screaming and ready to devour them.

"Shit!" shouted Yoshiro.

"I'm thinking, I'm thinking!" shouted Suki.

"Well you better think fast!" shouted Darius. The creature lunged at them and they dodged its attack while avoiding the snakes on the ground. Suki noticed chains on the walls that decorated the arena. Signaling to the others, they understood and jumped to the walls, ripping off the chains and swinging them around the beast as it screamed with hate. They tried to tie the beast down as Darius and Michael leaped on top of the creature, trying to hold it like they were breaking a wild animal to ride. The beast threw them off to the ground, as the others held tight on the chains.

"Let's kill this fucker now!" yelled Michael. Darius shot out its eyes, blinding it with his bow, while Michael and Suki hacked at the beast, but they were unable to kill it. Serena pulled out a grenade she had in her jacket as the creature broke their hold.

"Eat this!" yelled Serena, pulling the pin and slugging it into the monster's mouth just as it was about to devour Darius. The blast blew up the creature and the snakes – gobs of blood and guts splattered all over everyone, the force of the explosion throwing them against the wall. When the smoke cleared all that was left was dead flesh and gore.

"Yuck! Slimy crap!" Suki threw off the bloody debris that covered her body.

"Everyone okay?" asked Darius.

"Fine here," said Michael wiping off bits of guts from his coat and pants.

"Serena, Marianna, Yoshiro," asked Suki turning to the others.

"We're good," they all said.

"Weird. It's a good thing your human friends didn't come with us," said Suki.

"Well that was fun! What's next?" asked Darius.

"We're going to find a way out of here, that's what," said Serena.

Suki picked up the book off the ground with the pendant and followed the others to find a way out, when suddenly the doors unlocked and the gates flew open. The group passed through and saw Alazar Desbode levitating in front of them. His face looked deformed and hideous, and tentacles and horns grew out of his head. His eyes glistened green with fire and his face looked like an alien's, gray and reptilian. "Die!" he screamed as he emitted a gas from the gills in his new body.

The gas made the group confused and sick; in the nick of time, Gabriel came again and looked at the devil. Alazar Desbode screamed and disappeared and everyone was all right.

The group escaped through a hatch that led to the street. As they emerged, the thumping sounds of a helicopter came from a rooftop above them. Running to the rooftop and up the fire escape they could hear the craft taking off. "Damn it! He's getting away!" yelled Darius.

"It's okay, I know where he's heading. Come on!" said Yoshiro.

"Umm, Yoshiro, excuse me but we have no 'copter to follow!" snapped Michael.

"Oh ye of little faith," replied Yoshiro as he removed a small whistle from his pocket.

"What's that?" asked Mariana.

"Our ride," said Yoshiro as he blew into the whistle. The stillness was interrupted by a flash of light in the sky as a great white flying beast descended from the heavens, rushing down at them.

"No way!" Suki yelled.

"Way!" Yoshiro answered.

"Koga! Come forth! You are needed!" commanded the monk. The great luck dragon landed on the ground for them to board.

"Climb on, he's harmless," said Yoshiro.

"I will never doubt storybooks again," swore Darius.

They all climbed on and set off in pursuit of the chopper. "Hang on!" yelled Yoshiro as they raced to catch up.

Jubel looked back at his opponents. "Damn them! Get us out of here!" he yelled at the pilot. Taking out a machine gun, he fired away. Koga dodged the shots and fought back with his fiery breath, scorching the craft and sending it to crash into the mountain, where it exploded on impact.

"That's the end of him," said Darius.

"No one could have lived through that," said Michael.

"I doubt that. Let's land and take a look around near the crash anyway," said Yoshiro. Koga set down near the forest brush of the mountain hillside.

"Wait here, old friend," said Yoshiro as he gently petted the great dragon. Koga nodded and allowed his passengers to dismount. Michael then caught a scent. It smelled like charred flesh and smoke, and it was on the move. Michael knelt down and sniffed the ground. "It's him! Come on!" he yelled as he took off running after Jubel, who was already running up ahead into a cavern.

The others quickly followed Michael into the cavern.

Back in Tokyo at his skyscraper compound, Reynard Desbode patiently waited to receive word on the deaths of his enemies. Looking at the sacred scrolls, he was studying the incantations to join the Shirakai to awaken the Dark God.

"Where is that fool, he should have been back by now," Reynard Desbode said to himself, intrigued with the scrolls. Suddenly Alazar Desbode burst through the door, falling to the ground.

"Father!" screamed Alazar Desbode.

"My son!" Reynard Desbode screamed, at his son's disfigurement.

"They escaped, it was Gabriel!" wailed Alazar Desbode.

"The warriors of light and Christ are helping them," snarled Reynard Desbode as he smashed the scrolls off his desk. "What about the book and the pendant?"

"They have it."

"Blundering idiot."

"What should we do, sire?"

"Mobilize your best men and find them, bring me back the book, now!" commanded Reynard Desbode.

In the cavern, the group lit a torch from some old wood and searched for Jubel, who was hiding somewhere in the cave. Spying from the stalactites, Jubel jumped down from above, scooping up the book and pendant from Suki's arms.

"Now you fools, it's my turn to play!" snickered Jubel.

"He's got the book," shouted Yoshiro.

A portal began to open, releasing a host of creatures as Jubel read through the book. Michael then noticed that Jubel was standing right near the cliff's edge, and he slowly pulled out his gun and shot at Jubel, causing him to lose balance and fall over the side. The book fell to ground, and Suki jumped and grabbed both the pendant and book, letting Jubel fall to his death. The portal closed and the cavern began to cave in from the disturbance.

"Let's get out of here!" Serena yelled, and they teleported back to Koga and mounted the beast.

Yoshiro looked back at the cave and spoke softly. "Sorry brother, but you did this to yourself."

Back at the temple, the group dismounted and everyone shook hands and said goodbyes.

"What will you do now?" asked Yoshiro.

"Take this book back to Takai and report to our lord," said Michael.

"Be safe, my friends," said Yoshiro.

"What about you?" asked Marianna.

"I will continue to train the men; this war is far from over," said Yoshiro.

"Where is Takai?" asked Darius.

"Back in the states," said Yoshiro.

"Come, let's go home," said Michael to the others, and the group took their plane back to Las Vegas.

55

BACK HOME

After landing in the Las Vegas Terminal, a limo came to collect the vampire team; in it were Danny Fredricks and Rocko. "So how did it go, or should we not be popping the champagne corks yet?" Danny asked.

"We got what we went for," said Michael.

"It was too close though," replied Serena, and the others agreed.

"So what's the plan now?" asked Danny as he drove. "I mean, do we sit back and chill or do we make a move on these secret society assholes?"

"I don't know about the rest of you, but aren't you all tired? We just got back from a long mission," said Marianna.

"Too true. I feel like my limbs are going to fall off," said Darius.

"Amen to that. I say we forget doing anything; let's get some damn sleep, and we can meet with Takai tomorrow night. Let's crash at the Coven headquarters," said Serena.

"No, we have to see my father first. He must have the book in his possession; we can't allow anything to happen to it," said Suki.

"Yeah, let's get it over with already," agreed Marianna reluctantly.

"Good," said Suki.

"How are you doing Rocko?" asked Michael.

"Good buddy, I feel great. Happy you crazies got back; if anything bad had happened I wouldn't have my drinking buddy to kick around with," said Rocko.

They all laughed as they drove to the Oriental district to meet with Lao; it was midnight when the car rolled in at the dojo. They pulled the doors open to see Takai sitting in the room reading a book. He was sitting Indian-style with a big pot of hot tea at his side, leisurely puffing at his pipe. "I thought you would be back here sooner," said Lao Takai without raising his face from the book.

"Lao cut us a break! We just got you back the damn book and you can't even say thank you!" yelled Michael.

Lao lowered his book and a smile slowly spread across his face. "I am proud of you all; you have proven to be great warriors." He rose and bowed in respect to them.

"So what do you think will happen now with the Dark Society?" asked Suki.

"What else? They will come looking for us. We must leave here and go to the Coven for safety. Julius would never turn us away," said Lao. "Too bad Yoshiro did not come with you, I wish I could have spent some time with him."

"But I did," said a strange figure who uncloaked himself from a portal out of the shadows.

"What the hell!" Danny exclaimed. "Sorry, I could not resist coming with you," said Yoshiro, looking human again.

PART NINE: THE MEETING

56

GETTING THE INFO

A call came in. It was from Kat, who had been released from the hospital and was back at work. "Thanks for having the doctors take care of me," said Kat gratefully. She was scanning the computer screens in her new apartment that Michael had paid for.

"No problem, kid, glad to hear you're better. Now how are we coming with the info on Frank Scarfo and his crew?"

"Not great. I'm hacking telephone data but I haven't been able to trace any important calls by the guy. I am doing everything I can. Why don't you talk to Danny and see if he has anything on his end?"

"Keep trying, and thanks kid, I appreciate it, I'll pay you back for this. It may take me some time though," replied Michael.

"No problem," said Kat as she continued to type away at her computer.

"Damn it," said Michael as he hung up his cell phone.

"What's wrong?" asked Serena, who was looking out the window as they stood in Julius' office waiting to speak with him.

"It's been too quiet out there. I know Franco Scarfo is up to something," said Michael.

"You think he and his crew are planning to make a move?"

"Positive, although there's no word on the street, no movement on the news, no nothing."

"You worry too much. We can handle anything," said Serena.

"I don't like it. I wish we could tell this prick to go fuck himself," said Michael.

"Relax," said Serena.

"Don't be overconfident Serena; we have the odds against us in this war. We can hold down the fort but we have to hit pay dirt soon. Otherwise it may become too late."

Julius came in the room to speak with them. "Congratulations on your mission, my son," said Julius proudly.

"It wasn't easy old man," replied Michael, still tired.

"Of course it wasn't; that was the point. I made it hard to see what you were made of and you passed the test with flying colors. It's official: you're now a member of this Coven. All who join us become one blood, one family," said Julius as he placed the ring of the Zoratus clan on Michael's finger.

"Thank you," said Michael solemnly.

"You earned it," smiled Julius.

"Grandfather, Michael's concerned," interrupted Serena.

"I know what is troubling you. We have sent our spies into the city to gather information on the current movements of the Dark Society's organization and on your Frank Scarfo," said Julius.

"How do you feel, grandfather?"

"Fine. I may be ancient but I'm not gone yet. I can still fight another day," said Julius confidently after drinking some rejuvenation elixir in small vile he kept.

"I'm going to call Danny; perhaps he has found something," said Michael.

"Good, you do that my boy," said Julius.

Michael punched up Danny's number, nervous as he waited for someone to pick up. "Yeah, it's me Danny. What do you got?" asked Michael impatiently.

"I got something. Rumors are that the crime bosses are having a gathering somewhere tonight at midnight, but I don't know where it is."

"At least we know something's going on now," said Michael. "Thanks Danny. I'll search the city."

"Are you forgetting that the cops have it in for us?"

"I'll be fine."

"Okay buddy, but be careful," cautioned Danny.

Michael set out to search all of Sin City, from the rundown alleys to the glitzy casinos, along with the warehouses and industrial areas, but he found nothing. Serena, Darius, Marianna and Scarlet also did their parts, but couldn't find anything either.

Then, in The Caligula Club on the strip, a local punk named Kage Rusoff, who ran the boxing rackets, caught Michaels' attention. Kage was a former con man, a recently turned vampire and a runner who worked for the Russian mob. He was tough and muscular with a few scars on his body and a shaved head; he looked like he was around thirty years old. He was dressed in black leather pants and a black muscle shirt. Michael knew he was always looking to help a person for the right price. "Kage! Well, well, it's been awhile," said Michael.

"Get lost Moschenniki," said Kage, looking angry as he tried to drink his cocktail in peace.

Michael moved closer. "I'm looking for information," said Michael.

"You know the deal, you pay me, or you don't play," said Kage.

"Fine, here's five yards," said Michael as he greased the prick. "Now we can do business, or as you Italians say, "make marriage."

"What or who are you looking for? I can tell you need something," said Kage.

"Word on the street is that there's a meeting somewhere going down tonight between the various crime bosses," said Michael.

"You want to know where?" asked Kage.

"Yeah," said Michael.

"At the old bottling plant down on Marigold Lane. It's been closed for years. Watch yourself; some of the city's most dangerous crews will be there. I'd carry a couple of pieces and taking some back up, if I were you," said Kage.

"Thanks," said Michael. "I'm surprised you don't care about this for your boss Cravenoff."

"Fuck him; he doesn't pay me good enough."

"I appreciate it."

"Yawl come back now, you hear, when you need something. I'll be waiting, comrade," said Kage as he finished his drink.

Michael took off on his motorcycle to the old bottling plant. It was midnight and the meeting had just begun. Against his better judgment, Michael went on alone, only intending to spy on his opponents, not attack them.

The bottling plant was about 20 miles out, on the rundown side of town. It was an old dump that had more rats and bugs than the crews that were meeting there. "I'd better watch myself," thought Michael as he made a pit stop at his weapons loft to pick up a couple of pistols and a grappling hook. He knew Serena was on the other side of town worried about him, but Michael had to be strong and hang in there.

After arriving at the abandoned bottling plant, Michael hooked himself up and crept onto the loft rooftop. As he snuck in the skylight, he stood silently in a dark corner and listened to what was being said.

"I don't care what's happening out there. The time has come, gentlemen, for us to make decisions on the current situation with the Santerinis," said Cravenoff as he sat among his fellow Russians.

"They have walked all over us for too long homies," said Sanchez from the Mexican crew.

"So it's time to snuff them out. Then we're all in agreement," said Tye from the Chinese crew.

"The Society wants them iced, so let's take them down; those fuckers have had this city in their hands for too long," said Sanchez.

"Cravenoff, how do you propose we do it?" asked Tye.

"You know how. Set them up," said Cravenoff.

"We'll make the call and say we're going to have a truce, make them feel nice and friendly. Then when we got them cold, boom, dead as dead," said Tye.

"I have a better solution," interjected Franco Scarfo.

"Oh now the mighty bastard of Sicily has advice for us," said Cravenoff.

"Shut the fuck up, Sov!" said Franco as he flashed his pistol, taking aim at Cravenoff's head. Guns were sighted everywhere and no one flinched.

"Hold it, let's hear what he has to say," said Tye, calling off the exchange of guns.

"I say fuck this truce shit. Let's just hit them hard in the wallet; nothing better to break a man than by taking his money," said Franco.

Putting down his gun, Tye agreed. "Make them look like fools and stamp them out, it's perfect, no one will ever want to do business with them again. That'll kill them."

"Now listen, you hot-headed fucks, I got two shipment trains coming in tonight from LA. We'll blow the train yard storehouse and the old airbase that the Santerinis own; a lot of their goods are stored there," said Franco.

"What about those bloodsucking bitches that have sided with them?" asked Sanchez.

"The Society has something extra special planned for them. Fuck them, don't worry, that's covered," said Franco.

Michael was furious. He wanted to kill them all, but he knew that there were fifty of them and only one of him. Instead, he crept out of the building and sped off on his bike to inform the Coven and the Santerinis. He was worried; a hit to the train shipping yard and abandoned airbase would mean big losses; most of the family's money came from mass illegal distribution of drugs and other goods. "This is real bad, how the hell did they he find out about the base and train yard! Mother sweet fucking rosemary!" thought Michael.

Making a stop in the red light district, Michael called Paulie at a pay phone to inform him.

"Hey Paulie it's me Mike. We got a big problem on our hands," said Michael.

"I'm listening," said Paulie.

"The chinks, cholos, and sovs are going to make a hit on us at the train yard and old airbase tonight."

"Fucking Oobatz, stop it!"

"I'm going to need some help on this one," said Michael feeling uneasy for what he was going up against.

"Call your crew and the people you hang out with. Do this and I'll pay you three million. We can't have anyone fucking with that train yard and airbase. I don't care how you do it, but stop it!" Paulie ordered. Paulie hung up and then called the Don to tell him what was happening.

On the other side of town, Phillips had enlisted a team of mercenary vampire slayers to hunt down the vampires and destroy them.

However, Julius' spies had traced Phillips and the other vampire slayers.

Julius contacted Michael telepathically. "Phillips has slayers coming for you."

"I know; we will be ready." Michael could sense the danger. "Where are they?"

"They are scattered throughout the city, but it's more than likely that they will be in your old neighborhood looking for you and Serena. Be careful," advised Julius.

Cutting off his telepathic connection, Michael found Serena in the hallway of Zoratus Enterprises and explained things to her. "Phillips has strike teams of slayers looking for us on the streets."

"How many?" Serena was ready to fight.

"Don't know but let's go." Heading to the weapons room, Michael, Serena, Darius, and Marianna loaded up with guns and ammunition for the attack. They also took swords and other hand-to-hand combat weapons. Scarlet stayed behind to watch over Julius.

The crew took off to Otis Way in Darius' black SUV, their blood pumping and malice ready to explode in their hearts ready. When they got there they saw a group of men already staking some local vampires on the streets.

"Bastards!" yelled Darius as they pulled a drive-by, unloading bullets with machine guns and killing three slayers, who were dressed in military gear. Jumping out of the SUV, they hustled into heated violence, swashbuckling swords and guns with the remaining five slayers. Darius and Marianna sliced off the limbs of one of them.

"How does it feel, jerk off!" screamed Darius with rage as he crushed the dead slayer's skull in with his boots.

Michael and Serena overpowered the other two, beating them to death and breaking their necks.

"They're weak like chickens," mocked Serena as she heard her victim's necks snap.

"Retreat!! Fallback!" The last two retreated into a blue van and took off.

The other vampires thanked Michael and company. Michael again telepathically contacted Julius to inform him. "Julius, we have dispatched the slayers in the area and are returning to base to report."

"Well done Michael, return to base for new plan of attack, meet me in the council room, the elders have arrived," replied Julius, cutting off his communication.

Michael and the others sped back to Zoratus Enterprises to meet with Julius.

Back at headquarters, Julius and the Council of Nine waited for Michael in the main council room. The creatures of different origin and monsters of secret races had revealed themselves from the shadow world.

Michael and the others approached the council chamber with uneasiness. A vampire guard opened the doors to let the group in as they entered into a meeting that was already in progress. Among the elders present were the leaders of different nocturnal clans and supernatural races such as werewolves, angels, fairies, sages, gargoyles, cat men, Oni, and ghouls. Also in attendance were Lao Takai, Yoshiro, and Suki.

"Ladies and gentlemen, thank you for attending these proceedings on such little notice. Now that you're all gathered here, I will get to the point." Zoratus removed a remote control device and pushed a button, bringing down a flat projection panel from the ceiling. Playing the feed, he again began to speak. "We have discovered in the past few weeks that the Dark Society has been moving to develop weapons using magical invocations."

They all paused to view the footage of the weapons. Takai rose to speak. "As Lord Julius has stated, the Society has sought to manipulate the powers of the mystic Shirakai."

"The Shirakai," murmured the elders, concerned upon hearing this. Drake, the leader of the Faye, spoke with caution. "The Shirakai have been imprisoned in the dark dimension for centuries. Impossible."

"No. They were released through an incantation; my team witnessed it," interrupted Michael.

"This is very unsettling news for the council," said Sokai from the Gargoyle clan.

"How have you taken care of this?" asked the werewolf.

"We recovered the Yomi Tengu from the Society's deadliest agent, who was killed in a fight with our newest agent," said Julius.

A beautiful red haired winged cherub stood up to speak. "Julius we are pleased to be here and proud of your organization's success, but we have other matters of concern. Our clans are facing financial extinction from certain members of the government who do not trust our kind enough to aid them in their business affairs."

"Luna, have you forgotten why the council was formed? Put aside thoughts of money at this moment," replied Julius, disappointed by the cherub's words.

"This is of great importance. We have gathered here to put our issues aside and adhere to the pact that was made," spoke up Argos the werewolf in agreement with Julius. The other supernaturals nodded in acknowledgement.

"The Society must not be taken lightly. I agree with Lord Zoratus; we must follow these gatherings by increasing the watchers in the city and also within other cities in the other states of the nation. It has been discovered by our own clan's agents that the Society's movements have been traced to Los Angeles, Miami, Chicago, and New York," replied the Cat Man named Zumar, who was dressed in a business coat and tie.

"Then we all agree about what has to be done," said Julius.

After adjourning the meeting, the other council members left the room.

"What was all that about?" asked Serena. She had been silent during the entire meeting.

"We've had other areas of movement of Reynard Desbode's agents in the states. This means the Society has grown," said Julius, concerned.

"What do you want us to do?" asked Michael. "Keep your noses to the streets in town, and keep alert. There is nothing else to discuss. You have my leave, now go," ordered Julius.

"Yoshiro and I wish to come too," said Suki. Lao gave Julius a look of assurance.

"Very well then, but watch your backs," said Julius.

The group left the room to discuss the matters that had been discussed. Serena and the others stayed behind but Michael got ready to leave, to meet up with Jackie and Anthony for the job they were going to pull.

"Where are you going?" asked Serena surprised.

"To keep a promise to Paulie. I'll be back soon. Try to stay out of trouble, however if I need you I will call you," Michael smiled to the others.

57

BOOM TIME

Michael, Jackie and Anthony hooked up in Anthony's old car for the job; they were aching for action. "Sons of bitches, I can't believe they were able to find out about the train yard," Anthony shook his head.

"Look, who gives a rat's ass how they found out; all we have to do is to take these pieces of shit down," said Michael.

"You gonna call Serena and her crew?" asked Anthony.

"Absolutely," said Michael, ready to rock.

Good thing, we need a back-up team. Listen, so what are we looking at here for targets?" asked Jackie.

"I say we got about fifty minimum," said Michael.

"Fifty! This isn't going to be easy Mike. You do know we're going to need some major fire power to do this job, right?" asked Jackie.

"I understand, and we'll have the heat. I'm giving my boy Rocko a call," replied Michael.

"What's he going to do for us?" asked Anthony.

"Supply us with the firepower, what else?" Dialing away on his cell phone he connected with Rocko, who was in the middle his nightly yoga session; Rocko's phone rang as he was twisting his right leg around his head. "Yo!"

"It's me Mike, listen Rock, we have a problem. I need you to do me a favor; I need some heavy weapons," said Michael.

Rocko untangled himself into a more comfortable position, and then spoke. "Sure, let me see."

Michael hung up his phone and ordered Anthony to head to Rocko's while calling Serena and the others.

"We getting paid on this job, by the way?" asked Anthony.

"Anthony how the fuck could you think of money at a time like this? We're in a Mafioso emergency here," snapped Jackie.

"Fucking stop yammering, I'm getting some good pay for this job, I'll give you each a hundred thousand. Does that sound good?" said Michael.

"That's fucking beautiful; old Paulie knows how to throw his money around," said Anthony, calmer with the knowledge of money in his mind.

"Serena it's me. I need you and the others; do you feel up to a bit of lovely violence?" asked Michael.

"Devilish," replied Serena on the other end.

"Meet me with the others at Rocko's pad. I'll explain the details later," instructed Michael.

They all met at the front entrance of Rocko's garage just as they saw the main door being pulled up. Rocko came out dressed in an old worn set of denim jeans and a gamer shirt with his work goggles on. The vampires and the Mafioso were gathered to hear the deal.

"Hey, where are Marianna and Scarlet, Suki, and Yoshiro?" asked Michael.

"They had to stay back at headquarters to repair some equipment, don't worry," replied Serena.

"Thank you all for volunteering on such short notice. Now let's screw the proper introductions and get down and dirty," said Michael confidently as they walked through the garage to the weapons room downstairs.

"What we got here is a hit that is going to be made on the Santerini's financial empire. I need all of you to help me destroy two trains that are coming in tonight from LA. Explosives have been rigged on these trains, I think. Our enemies plan on using it to destroy the distribution base of the Santerini goods," said Michael.

"Michael, please, you dragged us out here for this?" said Darius, exasperated.

"Just humor me for a minute, thanks Darius," Michael snapped back.

"Fine but it better be good man," said Darius.

"What do we get out of this Mike? I think we don't like being used as errand boys, it gets old after awhile, no offense I hope," said Serena feeling slightly annoyed. "None taken," said Michael coolly.

"Paulie is paying me three million dollars in cash for this job, you get a hundred grand each, including you too, Rock," said Michael.

"Done!" said Darius excited.

"Good. Now that that's settled, let's get to work. Rocko bring over the city grid for us," instructed Michael.

Rocko obeyed and punched in the visual map on his giant LCD computer screen.

"Okay, here's the train yard where the first Scarfo train is coming in. The second is going to be at an old airbase that is being used as a distribution storage center for drugs," said Michael as he pointed out the locations on the grid map. We need to hit the train before it pulls into the yard. We're going to have dispose of the train without causing structural damage to the storehouse, so forget using a bazooka or any rocket weapons. What we're going for is sneaky tactics using bombs. However, for cleaning the guards we're going to need some heavy guns," said Michael.

"How many guards?" Darius asked.

"Maybe fifty or more, I don't fully know," replied Michael.

"I got that department covered. Check this out, you guys," said Rocko as he opened a crate, pulling out a long chain gun. "It's a chain gun off an army helicopter, and I've modified it to act as a rifle by shortening the end of the nozzle."

"What's the max on this thing?" asked Serena.

"About a thousand rounds, and we have two of them. They got mad spraying power. This little sucka can wipe out a small unit. It's perfect for a job like this," said Rocko as he cocked back the sight and loaded it.

"How are we going in?" asked Darius.

"By helicopter of course," said Rocko, typing away at his keypad as a visual of the helicopter appeared on the screen.

"We're using a V22-Greenburg; it's a little old. It's been around since the late 2000s but it's still an amazing chopper. I managed to repair this one. I got it from my uncle, who's a colonel in the air force. He had it as a museum piece locked in his private hanger."

"Nice, but what about the second train?" asked Serena.

"We're going to drop scud bombs on the train from the chopper; they're simple artillery bombs but they should do the trick," said Rocko as he pried open another wooden crate with a crowbar.

"Darius can you fly a copter?" asked Rocko.

"Sure, we're always on top of aviation at headquarters," replied Darius.

"What about us?" Jackie asked.

"You guys get to shoot the chain gun," said Rocko.

"Cool!"

"Let's get to work," said Michael.

Loading the helicopter at a hanger in the desert, the adrenaline rush hit everyone. It was literally war. At midnight, just as Frank Scarfo had said, the first train started to come in to the train yard. The chopper flew over the area and Serena and Michael dropped down the first bombs, blowing up the train tracks and causing the train to derail and explode before it reached the train yard.

"Sweet midnight!" yelled Serena with ecstasy as she pulled the pin; she had a thing for demolition. A massive explosion of crimson fire came from the wreck. It burned so brightly that it looked as if the gates of hell had opened up. Chaos churned on the ground from the groups of different mob crews taking in the burning wreckage scattered over the area. Fires burned and engulfing clouds of black smoke that filled the air. Back on ground, clamoring gunmen fired up at the chopper in heated retaliation.

"Look at these pukes, it's party time mother fuckers! YEAAAAH!" yelled Jackie as he unleashed the chain gun. Anthony fired beside him, spraying bodies with bullets that pierced through flesh and organs of the horde below. The ground itself became bathed in blood.

"I live for rock and roll, babies, Yaaaooo!" screamed Rocko as he fired off a gas bomb that covered the ground, allowing the chopper to make its escape from the fire of the remaining stragglers below. The chopper then headed to the airbase. When they got there the train was just about to collide with the main building when Michael dropped the last set of bombs. They hit the train smack dab in the middle, blowing it to bits. With a thunderous blast the battle was over. Satisfied, the chopper flew away into the distance.

"What!" screamed Reynard Desbode as he heard the news of the failed sabotage attempt. "I want those interlopers dead, do you hear me! Dead! Now!" he screamed as he smashed his office window to pieces.

"But sir we're doing everything we can," protested one of the officers that had given Reynard Desbode the report. Reynard Desbode was so enraged with anger that he shot the man dead. The officer's brains splashed all over the floor. Just then Reynard Desbode's phone rang; he learned that the police had taken down Franco Scarfo's base of operations and there was no sign of Franco Scarfo or the other mobs that joined forces with him.

Infuriated that his dreams of power were collapsing, Reynard Desbode planned a desperate move that would be his last stand to claim ultimate power.

58

DOOMSDAY

Reynard Desbode and his son headed down to the main laboratory beneath his headquarters while his minions cleaned up the mess upstairs. The lab was a massive underground base of operations and full of so many strange and bizarre metallic instruments that it shone like pure silver.

"It's time to take the future of this world into my own hands," said Reynard Desbode.

"What are we going to do father? Our alliances in the city have fallen," asked a concerned Alazar Desbode.

"We have not the book to awaken the Dark God and we have not the manpower to help us exact revenge," replied Reynard Desbode.

"Then what do we have, father?" asked Alazar Desbode impatiently.

"We have this!" Reynard Desbode removed a glass canister filled with a strange chemical liquid from a storage unit.

"What is that?"

"EG 99, the virus we have been developing over the past two years."

"From our bio weapons division, but I heard that it was never tested, as it was too dangerous," replied Alazar Desbode.

"Now is the right time to use it. We will show these fools who has the power. Come my son," said Reynard Desbode as they made plans for their attack.

Suddenly on the Las Vegas Strip, every giant television screen flashed with the same transmission. "Attention all citizens of Las Vegas; unless the individual named Damascus brings to our organization the Yomi Tengu book, this city and everyone in it will be killed. Mark my words. This is not a threat. It is a promise. In exactly two hours my men will release a deadly virus that spreads rapidly in air. Its chemical effects will destroy everyone in the city within minutes." In the background of the video, men could be seen loading transport trucks with the virus. "Damascus, come to the old bottling plant and come alone! Rest assured Commissioner, do not interfere. Otherwise death will arrive, you have been warned!" cried Reynard Desbode, cutting the signal that had broadcast from a secret location.

The entire city had seen the broadcast.

"Jim! Get a trace on that signal, on the double!" shouted Commissioner Hamilton from her desk back at police headquarters.

The detective and the other men rushed into the computer room to trace the terrorist, but had no luck. The signal was stealthily covered and there was no time to evacuate the city.

Las Vegas had broken out into chaos as mobs of frightened people swarmed the streets. There was rioting and looting; hordes of police squads tried to contain the mobs. The entire city was in state of panic and rebellion; the balance of hundreds of thousands of lives was at stake.

"Damn it Damascus, you better be there," said the Commissioner to herself, worried. To trust an enemy or not to; that was the end-all question. All the commissioner could do was hope that Damascus would comply.

Michael and Serena caught the broadcast back at Zoratus Enterprises. "We can't give them the book Serena! But if we don't give it to them, Reynard Desbode will kill everyone in the city!" yelled Michael.

"We have no choice; we can't let this madman kill all these in-nocent people. We must go and meet with Reynard Desbode as he wishes," said Serena.

"You're right, it's time," said Michael as they armed up with some guns and the book. "We're going to need some help. Let's call Jackie, Anthony and your cousin Dominus. Maybe they'll back us up."

"I don't know, but let's give it a try," said Serena.

Destiny had arrived for the two immortals. Michael and Serena took off, super jumping over the rooftops to get the bottling plant to meet with Reynard Desbode.

On the other side of town Commissioner Hamilton stubbornly snuck down to the bottling plant, going undercover to get a trace on the target. Detective Maceson was at her side. "Commissioner, do you think this is a good idea?"

"We have no choice, Jim. I can't trust some punk who probably would rather run to save his own skin to do the job."

"Why not call for backup?"

"We'd be drawing attention then; we have to go in quietly," said Commissioner Hamilton, loading her pistol.

"Got ya partner," said Detective Maceson loading his 44 magnum.

"Let's do this thing." Commissioner Hamilton was ready as ever.

The two officers kicked in the main doors at the bottling plant. Darkness surrounded them.

"What's going on?" whispered the Commissioner. Suddenly a net dropped down from the ceiling and the two cops saw rope loops come over them, trapping them like rats. A figure covered hidden the shadows pulled the power switch, lighting the entire room.

"I expected to find one fool and instead I've captured two of them," said Reynard Desbode, smiling wickedly.

"What are you going to do with us!" hollered Hamilton.

"Nothing. You're not worth even killing, such easy prey; you walked right into a trap. You're perfect for bait. Alazar! Lock them up," roared Reynard Desbode.

"Yes father, but first how about an unwelcoming reception." Alazar snapped his fingers.

Guards pummeled and beat the captives to a pulp.

Meanwhile, Michael and Serena met up with Suki and Yoshiro near the cathedral. Dominus was inside making his rounds of the church for the evening in while Father Sullivan was in the vestment room. A pounding and tapping was heard on the front chamber door.

"Come in," said Dominus, smelling the vampiric scent through the cracks in the door. Serena opened the door and the four moved inside.

"What are you are doing back here?" asked Dominus, surprised to see them.

"We have come back in need of help. Reynard Desbode is about to launch an attack on the city. We need all the allies we can gather for this fight," Serena explained.

"You know I can't fight. I made a vow of peace with God not to ever kill again," protested Dominus.

"It isn't murder if you're going to protect the city from destruction. Or are you a coward, cousin?" said Serena.

"I'm not a coward. If it is going to save innocent lives, then I will help you. I am still good with a sword," said Dominus.

Father Sullivan came in after overhearing the situation. "Go ahead son, I will help you also," replied Father Sullivan.

"What are you going to do?" asked Michael.

"Look at this!" said Father Sullivan as he pulled up his sleeve, showing a coat of arms tattooed on his right forearm.

"It's the Judah seal. You were in the society of the Sons of Judah!" said Serena.

"Young girl, I wasn't just in the society; I was your grandfather's second-in-command!" replied Sullivan chuckling.

"But how, how could you have survived all these centuries, it's not possible!" exclaimed Suki.

Sullivan's face contorted as he revealed his true form beneath his human visage.

"You're a vampire!" Michael exclaimed.

"Yes, I am just as you are, fledgling. However, I developed the uncanny gift to be able to live in sunlight without illness or harm. I was in Julius' service in the war against Reynard Desbode's forces; we were captured and taken prisoner to work in the copper mines. My real name is Demetrius Meridian, and I am the son of a scholar and soldier for Rome. I escaped with the men before later separating from them. I found myself taken in at a monastery in Italy after I saved a young nun's life from a demon that was about to kill her. The monks knew what I was; I revealed it to them indirectly by killing the filthy beast. They chose to spare my life and took me in as one of their own. From then on I took a vow to serve God in devotion for letting me live. Years later I traveled to live in Ireland, changed my identity and later came to the states. So here I am. You see; all our destinies have been preordained. We have been waiting to meet and destroy the real enemy, the darkness that lives within each of us. By uniting we are completing the path that destiny has chosen for us. Dominus has never known any of this until now," said Meridian calmly.

"But how could you not have the devil at you?" asked Michael.

"You let your own hatred do that with evil spirits. I sense that they are now gone from you. Remember this though; you must still choose whom to serve, your Family or God, and make your choice. Now I know what you all did a little while ago," Meridian read Michael's thoughts.

"What does he mean?" asked the others.

"The train yard," replied Meridian.

Serena shut her mouth. Michael looked at the cross for a moment and then came to his senses.

"All right. When this is all over, I'm out of it, done," said Michael. Serena agreed too.

"Good; you're doing the right thing," replied Meridian.

"But Father, how could you," Dominus interrupted, still shocked by his mentor's secret.

"Son, I knew that I would have to tell you someday. I just did not believe that this day would come. Now you know I am sorry," said Meridian sadly.

"Look, we have no time for confessions now Father; we have an insane genocidal megalomaniac to deal with. Reynard Desbode is going to release a toxin in the city that will kill everyone unless we bring him the Book of Darkness, which we have here," said Michael seriously.

"The legendary Yomi Tengu. I have heard of the book but I never believed the legend to be true. How are you going to take down Desbode? As soon as you hand the book to him he will chant the proper incantation. He could open a portal to the dark universe, causing hell to invade earth," warned Meridian.

"We have no choice," replied Yoshiro, who had been silently listening the whole time.

"Where is he?" asked Meridian.

"The old bottling plant," said Suki.

"We need a plan," said Dominus.

Meridian changed into a long black coat and pants. He pulled out a chest from under his bed. Unlocking it, he pulled out two silver swords, giving one to Dominus and keeping one for himself.

"We have to find a way to stop the launch of the virus. I have to contact Kat. Perhaps she can dig something up for us on the virus. We have one hour and thirty minutes left before they unleash their attack on the city," Michael said. He called Kat on her cell phone.

"Mike, My God, where are you!" freaked out Kat.

"Calm down," instructed Michael.

"Haven't you seen the news? The city is in pandemonium," said Kat.

"We know who is responsible. I need you to hack into the city's main system to see if you can dig anything up on this symbol. It's of a secret society called The Order of the Stykains, also known as the Dark Society. I'm sending you the symbol from my phone. Find anything you can on any organizations that use this symbol," said Michael.

Kat hacked away at her laptop, cracking the city's main system. She managed to track the symbol to a corporate enterprise. "I got it! The place is called Detastone Corporation. They do military and systems research for the United States government. Among those sponsoring this organization are the Secretary of Defense and the Vice President," Kat spoke rapidly.

"Crack anything in defense development," instructed Michael as he listened intensely.

"Scanning," said Kat as she cracked into the system. "Gotcha!"

"So?"

"EG 99 antitoxin developments to ward off any biological attack."

"Damn bastards must have used it as a decoy when they were really developing chemical weapons."

"Damn," whistled Kat.

"Any way to counter the virus' effects?"

"Niccollizten coolant. The instant freezing effects should stabilize the toxin's chemical effects," Kat replied.

"Anywhere we can get some?" asked Michael.

"The Medical Warehouse, downtown."

"Shit; that's right where the riots are taking place!" said Michael.

"Sorry Mike." Kat sounded worried.

"It's cool, thanks," said Michael, hanging up. Michael turned to the others and told them what he had learned.

"How are we going to get to the warehouse with the mobs on the streets?" asked Meridian.

"Simple. Everyone hold hands together in a circle. I'm going to try something," said Suki.

Invoking a large chi orb around them all, they floated off encased in the orb to the Medical Warehouse. After breaking open the locks on the back door they snuck into the warehouse to look for the coolant. Yoshiro was overwhelmed by the size of the place. "You guys, this is going to be like looking for a needle in a haystack."

"A lot of boxes are here, but let's look for a cold storage unit; that's the place to store coolant," said Suki.

"That's a good idea," complimented Meridian.

After looking around for about ten minutes Meridian found the main freezers, where they found a case of coolant air tanks inside. This chemical compound was highly volatile. If anyone dropped the tank it could explode, freezing sections of the room.

"We got what we came for, now let's go," said Dominus as the others picked up the tanks. Suki used the orb again and to instantly transport them to the bottling plant.

"Okay, here's the plan. We bust in and take out Reynard Desbode and Alazar Desbode," said Michael.

"What about the virus?" Suki asked.

"Shoot the tanks, release the coolant," replied Michael.

"Hang on." Suki invoked the giant orb around them. Rotating the orb back and bolting forward, they smashed into the place like a pinball in a machine.

"Damn you!" screamed Reynard Desbode as they broke into the building, rolling around as guards shot the shield. The shells bounced off the orb, as Suki protected her friends from harm. The energy orb rolled around the plant, smashing the equipment and destroying everything.

"Now!" yelled Michael as he shifted out his pistol and fired at the coolant tank, tossing it in the air as the virus canisters were being loaded into a hovercraft. Dominus and Meridian also tossed up tanks, slicing off the coolant tank heads and releasing the freezing gas. The tanks exploded, causing the fast chemical chain reaction to freeze over the virus canisters. The canisters corroded and exploded, giving off steam as the virus evaporated into thin air; its lethal effects destroyed.

"NOOO! Hold it right there, fools!" screamed Reynard Desbode as he grabbed his hostages, the Commissioner and Maceson, pointing a machine gun at their heads.

"Shit! Hold your fire!" screamed Michael, knowing Reynard Desbode was about to kill them.

"This is not over fools," said Reynard Desbode, showing his hate as he dragged his prisoners into a shadowy portal and disappeared.

"Damn they got away!" yelled Yoshiro.

"At least the city is safe. Come on, we have to find where they took off to," said Serena.

"Hold it, let's do some investigation first. We don't know what traps they've set for us. I don't want us to run into any more surprises like this one," said Michael. They all agreed.

"Let's call Jackie and Anthony and inform them of the situation," said Serena. The others nodded.

Michael called Jackie on his cell.

"It's Mike, I need some backup on a rescue mission. Interested?" asked Michael.

"For you, anything. What's up?" Jackie was eager to help.

"Reynard Desbode has kidnapped the police commissioner and a detective. Did you see the news earlier about that chemical attack?" "Yeah, I saw it. Freaking scary shit," replied Jackie.

"We stopped it."

"Thank Christ!" said Jackie, relieved. "But what about my money?"

"When this problem is taken care of you'll get the money, as promised."

"Good."

"Inform Anthony and go see Rocko; he'll hook you up with gear. I'm going to call my hacker to see where these bastards took the hostages. Besides, if you guys help me you might get the cops to lay off," said Michael.

"Were breaking omerta, the mafia code of silence, you know that we are strictly forbidden to aid the police in anyway," said Jackie worried.

"Fuck omerta. The law of omerta can be bent for this, they don't know who you both are," said Michael.

"Okay," said Jackie as he hung up to contact Anthony.

59

SAVE THE HOSTAGES

Back in town the riots were being put down. Serena informed Julius that the chemical attack had been foiled. He sent a message to the government and a broadcast was sent out that returned order to the streets. However, police officers were still looking for the missing Commissioner and her partner, as they hadn't reported back in.

Michael and his friends met with Julius back at the Coven headquarters to regroup.

"You have done well, all of you," said Julius feeling relieved.

"My lord, it is good to see you again," said Meridian as he embraced his general.

"Good to see you again old friend, it's been too long," said Julius. "Michael how do you know Demetrius?"

"He was the chaplain when I was on active duty in the service."

"It's good to have you here again at my side. I thought they killed you in the mines, so many centuries ago," said Julius.

"I survived and your son Dominus is with me," said Meridian.

"My son!" said Julius, shocked. "Hello, father," said Dominus. Julius looked at his son as if he had seen a ghost come back from the dead. "Come here," said Julius as he held out his arms to Dominus.

They hugged tightly. "I thought you were gone forever, I can't believe it's really you."

"I came with the others and Meridian to help."

"I'm proud of you; you're finally becoming a warrior," said Julius smiling at his son.

A phone call came in on Michael's cell phone, interrupting them. Michael answered; it was someone he wasn't expecting.

"It's Reynard Desbode, you fool; come to the heliport on the top of the Monolith Tower. If you want to see the Commissioner alive bring the book, or you will hear this," said Reynard Desbode as he placed the phone next to Maceson and signaled Alazar Desbode. Michael heard the gun blast in the background. Maceson was dead.

"You fucking animal!" screamed Michael in rage. "Don't toy with me boy! Bring me the book or the next one to die will be the Commissioner!" Reynard Desbode hung up the phone.

"What happened?" asked the others.

"Reynard Desbode killed one of the hostages. He's going to kill the Commissioner unless we take him the book; he's not playing with us," said Michael.

"Damn it!" said Julius.

"What are we going to do?" asked Suki.

"We have to meet with Desbode," said Serena.

"We need some more time," argued Yoshiro.

"There is no more time," said Dominus.

"I have a hunch he won't be alone," said Julius.

"That's the chance were going to have to take," said Serena.

"It's too dangerous. I want to go on this one alone," said Michael.

"Don't be a fool," snapped Julius.

"Sorry, my mind is made up," said Michael, grabbing the Book of Darkness and shape shifting into the dark shadows.

"Damn fool, he's going to get himself killed! Quickly follow him, aid him!" ordered Julius. They left the room quickly to find him.

Michael teleported to the heliport at Monolith Tower, which was still in the early stages of construction. Nothing was there but red iron bars and a titanium landing pad a thousand stories up from the ground.

"Good, I knew you would come," said Reynard Desbode. Franco Scarfo was also present.

"Serve me slave and live," ordered Reynard Desbode.

"Yes Master!" said Franco as he fought with Michael. Michael easily knocked Franco to the the ground, unconscious.

"Are you afraid to face me yourself, demon!" yelled Michael.

"A demon am I; perhaps I can show you how demonic I can be!" said Reynard Desbode as dark clouds and purple lighting whirled in the air, filling the sky with chaos. Reynard Desbode transformed himself into a demonic abomination infested with unholy evil. He was a fallen angel and his satanic powers were unleashed.

"Now bow down and worship me or die," commanded Reynard Desbode.

"Never!" screamed Michael. Dark agents surrounded Michael, but Reynard Desbode had the agents encircle the two for a duel to the death.

"Then die!" screamed the large winged demon, drawing his demonic sword from his sheath. Michael took out his katana. Hellish winds blew around them as they battled, exchanging blows, slashing and clashing blades as sparks flew.

"You can't win boy, give up and worship your master!" gloated the demon.

"Burn in hell!" retorted Michael as he pulled out his pistol, shooting his enemy. The bullets penetrated their target and green blood spilled from the demon's body.

"Enough!" screamed the demon as he blasted Michael off the roof with an energy ball, grabbing the book as Michael fell. Michael teleported himself on to one of the rafters and started to super jump his way back up the tower.

"Now my lord of darkness the time has come! Alazar Desbode, merge with me! Become immortal forever!" roared the demon. Alazar Desbode pulled the glass orb out of his pocked and merged the trapped souls with his own body then merged in metamorphosis with the demon.

"Now we are one! The Dark God speaks through the blood that runs through our veins, and he says it's time. The demon opened the Yomi Tengu and began to recite the spell.

"Keepers of the Shirakai come forth and awaken your master trapped in the void between this world and the darkness," summoned Reynard Desbode as the Shirkai appeared from the shadows, merging their dark powers to open the portal. "Father of demons, of darkness, and death, Sagamu come to your son, who has served you well, take my essence with you and conquer this world!" screamed the demon.

A large portal was opened and the god Sagamu, the ruler of hell, was released. This hellish beast was a monstrous demonic dragon god with the face of a man and the body of dragon; he smiled in evil glee at his son and at being released into the world.

Michael arrived back on top of the heliport and saw the insanity. Suddenly, out of nowhere Julius, Darius, Scarlet, Yoshiro, Suki, Serena, and Marianna appeared on hovercrafts, blasting the demons in the air with their lasers and machine guns, killing the shadow agents that surrounded Michael. A military chopper flew above, circling around the heliport; Jackie, Rocko, and Anthony were inside. Jackie unleashed his mini gun, blowing pieces off the winged demon and shadows agents, weakening them.

"NOOOO!" screamed the winged demon as he broke Michael's sword. The heavens opened up and Michael saw a divine sword fall to the ground in front of where he stood. Picking up the blade, he heard a great voice as he was blocking the demon's attack. "Fulfill your destiny!" said the divine God of Heaven. Michael brought the divine sword down the middle of the winged demon, splitting the creature in half, as the devil screamed unholy cries. The blade slowly cut him down, blood overflowing and insides churning as his demonic body fell to the ground, dead, turning instantly into dust. Sagamu screamed with hate as he saw his son killed and attacked Michael with his fangs and giant teeth. Michael managed to cut off the beast's tongue. The beast screamed in pain and a powerful holy light shone from within the blade as Michael thrust the sword into the beast's heart, killing the Dark God. The creature exploded into fire and ash until only dust remained.

"I'll be back!" roared the demonic spirit. Then it disappeared.

More dark agents appeared from the shadows, fighting with Michael on the ground. Serena jumped off her hovercraft to aid Michael in the attack. Franco came to and attempted to kill Michael with his pistol but Jackie homed in on him, landing on the heliport roof and knocking Franco over the edge of the building. "Give up!" mocked Jackie.

Franco pulled out his pistol as he hung from the rafter for dear life. Jackie just smiled and stamped on Franco's hands; he shot Franco in the head, seeing his enemy's body fall listless to the ground far below. "For my family," said Jackie loyally.

Then the Shirakai, who were still present, knocked the book out of Michael's hands. Serena shot down Tulina, though the book fell away to the ground and was lost. Seeing they were outnumbered, the other Shirakai retreated into the darkness.

The battle was over; the shadow agents were dead, and the poor, terrorized Police Commissioner had seen too much to tell.

The others landed their crafts and the military chopper to speak with the Commissioner, who was shaking from the trauma.

"Commissioner, you are all right," said Serena, untying her.

"Who are you people? You saved my life and this city," shivered Commissioner Hamilton.

"Our names are not important. Just remember that you were saved by the Denizens of the Night," said Serena.

"Perhaps she should know, Serena, that my name is Damascus. You don't remember me, Commissioner but remember this; you owe us your life," said Michael before hopping climbing aboard the helicopter. The helicopter returned them back to a hidden airfield owned by Zoratus Enterprises. After landing, the Commissioner thanked Michael and his friends and promised to keep their secret.

The supernatural world would remain hidden from mortal men unless it wanted to make itself known.

However, yet another an unknown terror waited.

PART TEN:
THE FINAL CONFRONTATION

60

AN OLD SCORE

Across town in an old rat-infested hideout where the train tracks met, Phillips sat in his moldy and torn chair smoking a cigarette, worried about what was happening on the streets. Sergio Garcia was with him. The two were hiding out from the cops, as they knew that the police were closing in on their trail.

"I don't like it Garcia; the city has gone to hell, the boss is missing and we're caught in this roach coach hellhole," said Phillips.

"Shut up Rodney. The cops don't have us yet, fuck those pigs!" Sergio was shining up his hunting knife and spitting on the dirty carpet.

"Turn on the tube. Maybe the news will say something," said Phillips. Garcia turned on the TV that was on the old kitchen counter and they watched.

"This just in on our top story. Notorious mafia under boss Franco Scarfo was found dead at the bottom of the new Monolith Tower that has been under construction. For unknown reasons it appears that Scarfo was on the main floor of the building and may have jumped or fallen off by accident. Suicide is suspected. Police are underway with a full investigation. More information on this story as we bring you new developments. This is Mike Lee."

The reporter was cut off by the remote in Garcia's hand. "Seems like the boss had a fucking breakdown, or someone broke him," said Garcia.

"Those fucking monsters! It had to be," screamed Phillips.

"What do you want to do?" asked Garcia as he lit a cigar.

"We're going to snuff out those fucks for good and blow up the Don's main headquarters. Let's kill them all," said an insane Phillips.

"Send them all to hell. Then we'll have the power in the city." Garcia agreed and kicked over a crate that was filled with chemicals. Both of them began to create bombs and form a plan of attack.

Meanwhile, at the Terrace Tower, Damascus' crew and the supernaturals met with Don Felice to update him on the situation.

"So how did everything go with the train yard job?" asked Don Felice, looking out his window at the city ravaged from the rioting.

"Couldn't have gone better," replied Jackie.

"We managed to wipe out Franco Scarfo's thugs, save the train storehouses, and the merchandise within," said Serena.

"Good, very good. I am very pleased with you all, especially with you, Michael," said Don Felice lighting a cigarette.

"It's wasn't easy," said Anthony.

"And now that reminds me, Michael, your money for this job." Paulie brought over a briefcase that held the money.

"Oh, how I love the smell of fresh green in the air," said Michael.

"Your business is appreciated," said Don Felice.

"Always a pleasure, thank you both," said Michael, shaking both men's hands. He then turned around to his friends and crew and gathering some rubber bands from a little box on the Don's desk, bound up sets of 100,000 dollars to pay his crew.

"Michael, you're a man of your word," said Rocko.

"My word is my bond," said Michael.

"Now then, ladies and gentlemen, what about the news on the Society and Franco. Has that asshole been taken care of? I need to know," asked Don Felice.

"Yes, sir. The main members of the Dark Society have been killed," said Michael.

"Good. What about that bastard Franco?" asked the Don.

"I personally took care of his ass, Don Felice; we'll never see him again," said Jackie. "Very good, that's excellent news. Now that this chaos is over perhaps the city will return to somewhat normal. What about the other factions that were involved? Any other conspirators?" inquired the Don.

"The Mexicans, Russians, and Chinese wanted to stomp up us out," said Michael.

"I thought so; we'll take care of them soon enough. This war with the Scarfos has caused too much bloodshed already. It might be good for our families to try to rebuild our organizations instead of bickering, and especially rebuilding the district of the city that was destroyed. I'll rebuild your club Michael, since you and your friends help saved our organization from destruction," said Don Felice.

"Thanks," said Michael, shaking the Don's hand for such kindness.

"Now that the city is cooling down, I think I'll set up a party for you all. It's time to relax a little," said the Don smiling.

"That would be nice, Don Felice. It's going to be smooth sailing from here," said Michael stretching his arms behind his head and smiling.

A rumbling came from nowhere as the building began to shake violently. Phillips and Garcia sat in a car not far away, releasing the switches on the remote bombs they had hidden in different parts of the building.

The sound of thunder shook throughout the whole infrastructure.

"Earthquake!" yelled Suki.

"No it's a bomb," said Serena, sensing the danger and feeling heat from the fires that had begun to flow through building. They all ran.

"We're trapped!" screamed Don Felice.

"Not for long, hang on!" yelled Suki enclosing them in a force field of protection and levitating them out of the building, smashing through the glass and floating over the city.

"What the fuck!" the Don screamed, terrified.

"We're safe in here Don Felice. Everyone in the room is here," Michael reassured the Don as they floated farther away from the tower. They saw the place blow apart and start to collapse as explosion after explosion erupted. The building came crashing to the ground, completely destroyed. "You there honey, bring us to that rooftop, land this thing there," said Paulie, pointing. "Suki," she corrected as she landed the floating sphere on a nearby rooftop.

Everyone was shaken by what had happened. "I thought you took care of everything," said Don Felice, traumatized.

"I did; we left no one alive, I'm sure of it," said Michael.

"There's only one person who could have done this. Phillips, that's who!" exclaimed Serena.

"Find him and whoever may have helped him, and kill them. Chances are, they'll try again. We had many good people who worked in that building, and look, the media is already arriving," ordered the Don.

"You don't have to ask twice," said Michael.

On the ground, news crews were reporting on the devastation.

"Where are you going?" Jackie asked the Don.

"Paulie will inform Godfather Scarfo of the situation and I will be taken to his safe house," said Don Felice. "You all be careful."

61

RUNING FEVER

O n the ground below, Phillips and Garcia escaped from the destruction, laughing. "We fucking did it, hehaheehaha! This town is ours!" laughed Phillips wickedly.

"Now that the Santerinis are out of the way we can route their shipments of cocaine with ours from Spain. This city will become a great mecca for our distribution in the states," said Garcia confidently, lighting up a cigarette while driving.

"You think the other crime syndicates will be on us?" asked Phillips.

"Nah! Holy shit!" screamed Garcia as a large thump was heard on the car's roof.

"What the hell was that!" exclaimed Phillips as he slowly turned to look out his window. A large fist smashed in his teeth.

"Fuck!" screamed Garcia as he saw Serena and Michael on top of the car in the left side rearview mirror. Serena smashed in the back window, trying to get in to disable Garcia. Grabbing a knife he stabbed her in the leg, causing her to lose her footing and fly off onto the street; blood spurted on the windshield. Michael smiled an evil grin as he was upside down looking through the front windshield, punching it open with his fist and grabbing the wheel by force, trying to crash Phillips and Garcia.

"Fuck off vampire bitch!" cursed Phillips spitting up a shot of blood while shooting Michael in the chest with his pistol. Michael fired a tracer dart on the edge of the car before he fell off. The car escaped into the city.

"What the fuck! What the fucking hell was that!" screamed Garcia, still driving.

"Fucking Damascus! Jubel failed. That freak Reynard Desbode failed," spat Phillips.

"Look, I don't give a shit who it was. Let's just get the hell out of here!" yelled Garcia.

"Fine. There's a small plane at the airfield," said Phillips, trying to keep it together.

"You okay?" asked Michael back on the streets as he managed to catch up with the wounded Serena.

"I'm fine," she replied. Her wounds were rapidly healing, as were Michael's. "Damn bastards got away."

"Well, at least we spotted them on the rooftops," said Michael pulling out a tracking device that Rocko had given to him.

"They're heading to the airfield, probably to escape," said Serena.

"Contact the others through telepathy," said Michael, catching his breath.

Serena contacted the other supernaturals and told them to meet them at the airfield to close in on the attack. "Julius, we need air support at once," said Serena via telepathy.

"I know. Rocko, prepare the mini bombers," ordered Julius to Rocko where they were in the main underground hanger checking over equipment.

"Roger, chief," said Rocko, setting up the bombers as he and the other supernaturals took off, flying to the airfield to rendezvous with Michael and Serena.

"Ready to rock baby!" said Michael as he loaded his machine gun with a fresh clip, smelling the lead.

"Ready as I'll ever be." Serena reloaded her gun; they were looking for a car to steal to catch up with Phillips.

Without warning they were spotted by Rocko and the others, who set down the mini bomber jet cycles. "You two need a lift?" Rocko asked.

"What took you so long?" said Michael as he and Serena hopped on.

"We had to fuel up," explained Rocko.

"Where's Phillips?" asked Darius who was with Marianna and Suki who were silent.

"At the old airfield. It's been closed for years," said Michael.

"What are we waiting for let's go!" said Suki.

"Copy that," said Marianna. They took off to engage the prey. The supernaturals closed in just as Garcia and Phillips made their way to the plane.

"Fuck! They're here!" screamed Garcia.

"Just don't stand there, shoot them!" yelled Phillips as the two unloaded bullets at the incoming bombers that were ready to strike.

" Black Devils come in! Get your asses here! We got company!" yelled Garcia on his communicator.

Black Devil Society terrorists in rows arrived on the scene from the hangar, firing away at the jets as they closed in.

"Evasive action! Evasive action!" yelled Michael as he and the others led evasive maneuvers away from the incoming projectiles.

"Destroy the plane!" ordered Serena as she fired a missile that blew the plane to scrap metal.

"No!" screamed Phillips.

"Kill them!" screamed Garcia as they shot back, evading the explosion.

"Retreat! Retreat!" yelled Garcia as he and Phillips got in a back-up getaway car.

"Drive!" screamed Phillips as Garcia sped off. Phillips pulled out a M60 machine gun from underneath the floorboard and blasted the gun back at the supernaturals that were still firing away.

"Black Devils! Get your asses here and follow our lead!" yelled Garcia over his intercom in the car.

"Yes sir," reported the terrorist in one of the jeeps.

"Draw their fire and send them to hell!" ordered Garcia as he sped off into the city's abandoned rock quarry that was just around the bend.

"Fire!" ordered Darius as he and the others blasted the jeeps, destroying them and killing the terrorist goons.

"Let's get out of here! Now!" screamed Phillips as Garcia hit the gas to evade the attack. They escaped, releasing bombs that blew up and exploded with light that blinded the supernaturals, causing them to crash.

"Jump all of you!" screamed Michael as they ejected from the bombers as exploded. All landed safely on the ground. They were in good shape except for Rocko, who had broken many bones.

"I can't get up!" said Rocko trying to move. Serena helped him up but Rocko screamed in pain. "Sweet Jesus!"

"Come on Rock, hang in there, get it together!" ordered Michael.

"Michael, go after Phillips. Marianna and I will take him back to headquarters," said Darius as he and Marianna picked up Rocko.

"Okay," said Michael as Marianna and Darius teleported back to Julius. Phillips and Garcia escaped into the night, speeding off like a streak of burning fire.

62

THE A BOMB

"How could those fools have found us? How did they know where we were?" said Garcia.

"What different does it make now? Those creatures discovered our attack on the Terrace Tower," said Phillips.

"What are we going to do? Wait until they come and get us?" asked Garcia.

"No," said Phillips uncovering a bomb that was hidden on the lower level of a maze of stairways of the old hydro electrical plant. Phillips brought the small bomb out of a metal box and placed it on the main power generator.

They were hiding out in the dingy dive. It had been abandoned for years. The place was filled with grime and rust and smelled like old lead paint and turpentine. Long sheets of metal covered the windows in the massive plant, protecting the hideout from the peering eyes of meddlers.

"This place is a dump. What the hell are you doing Phillips?" asked Garcia as he reloaded his pistols.

"What should have been done before," said Phillips, lifting the bomb out of the case.

"What is it?" asked Garcia curiously.

"A miniature subatomic device. I'm going to activate it. The city will burn to a cinder and we shall have our revenge!" yelled Phillips.

"Are you mad Phillips? You'll kill us all," screamed Garcia. "Who cares!" said Phillips, setting the timer.

"I am a God!" raved Phillips.

"In hell you'll be, but my men are not going to die for you!" yelled Garcia, lunging at Phillips and knocking him over as he and Phillips exchanged blows.

"Can't you see you fool, we win this way!" said Phillips idiotically.

"Die!" screamed Garcia, shooting Phillips in the chest. But Phillips got up, shooting back as bullets pierced through Garcia's flesh and skull, killing him instantly. Phillips took off his bullet-proof vest.

"Damn fool, he never was too smart. Now to destroy this city and have my revenge. I may burn in hell, but I'm taking this town with me. HEHAHEHAHHHAAAHAHAH," laughed Phillips madly.

He linked the atomic bomb to the power core and activated the device to the plant's main computer board. "Within in one hour this city will be sent up in a blazing inferno!" screamed Phillips.

Back at Zoratus Enterprises Julius, Michael, Serena, Suki, Marianna, Darius, Dominus and Meridian scanned the computer tracker systems, searching for Phillips' car.

"Damn tracking system is terrible," said Meridian scanning.

"Zero in on Phillips' frequency," said Dominus, tracing the signal.

"Damn!" yelled Meridian slamming his fist on the control module.

"What's wrong?" asked Darius.

"We can't find anything; the damn signal must be blocked. The only thing that could do that is a radioactive device," said Julius scanning the system.

"You don't think Phillips would use a bomb? Holy shit!" guessed Michael.

"I can feel it," said Serena.

"We have to stop him," said Yoshiro.

"First we have to find out where this asshole's hiding out. Then we can stop whatever he's up to," said Michael.

Kat contacted Michael on his cell phone. "Kat what's up?" asked Michael, looking at the data on his screen.

"Just want to check on you," said Kat typing away on her computer.

"I need some help looking for all known associations with the name Rodney Clarence Phillips. And can you find out if any radioactive or electrical disturbance signals are anywhere in the city?"

"I got you; it may take me a while but I'll see what I can do," said Kat.

"Try to hurry. We may not have any time to spare," said Michael.

"Why what's wrong?" asked Kat.

"A bad feeling just hit me in the gut and Phillips is part of it. This guy is dangerous. He's bad news. Find him quick," said Michael.

"You got it."

"Thanks," said Michael as he hung up.

"So what do we got?" asked Suki.

"Kat's hacking the different systems in the city. Hopefully she can find why the signal isn't registering with headquarters' systems," said Michael.

"That's not going to be good enough; we have to contact the other covens to do a citywide manhunt for this maniac," said Julius.

"I agree," said Serena.

Julius set about contacting the other vampire covens that were loyal to his. He sent Michael, Serena, Suki, and Darius split into separate pairs to search the Scarfo hideouts to find Phillips.

But Phillips was well hidden in the silent shadows of the electrical plant. No one could find him and the clock was ticking. With thirty minutes to go it looked like the city was going out with a bang.

Just then Michael and Serena were contacted on the strip. "Who is it?" said Michael picking up his cell phone.

"It's me, partner! Come to the hydro electrical plant; you'll meet me there unless you want me to blow this city to Hades. If you beat me I'll give you a password that will deactivate my surprise. Come now," said Phillips hanging up his phone.

Michael didn't understand this sick game that Phillips was playing, but he knew how to end it with his final move.

"What's up?" asked Serena.

"It's Phillips; he's at the old hydro electrical plant," said Michael.

"Were your suspicions correct?"

"Yes. Let's go."

Michael as he hopped on his motorcycle with Serena, taking off with wheels smoking to the plant. Speeding to the plant, Serena's mind was filled with curiosity.

"Michael, why do you think Phillips called us?" asked Serena as the wind blew her beautiful hair back.

"I don't know; maybe he's looking for payback. Watch your ass out there baby," said Michael.

"Watch your own," said Serena, giggling as the duo arrived at the back of the plant. "Punch it!"

Michael sped onto an amalgamation of boards that acted as a ramp, crashing through a large glass window that was dirty and smeared with paint. They landed in a 360-degree motion, stopping the bike with them in one piece.

Phillips looked down from a rafter and saw them. He swung down on a chain rope, pulling a switch from the wall.

"What the hell?" said Michael as he and Serena saw vents from the floor emitting a green gas that immediately knocked them out. It seemed like time stopped completely.

"Wake up asshole," yelled Phillips, kicking Michael in the stomach.

Michael and Serena woke to find themselves covered in chains. Their arms and legs were bound and they could see the timer moving; the bomb was about to go off.

"I must say, congratulations for that marvelous entrance," chuckled Phillips wickedly.

"What's your catch, Rodney?" shouted Michael.

"No catch at all, old friend. I just wanted a perfect excuse to get you down here. That and a chance for you to do what you always wanted to do to the man who killed your beloved sister. Well here I am, what are you going to do about it?" mocked Phillips. "This is going to be fun." Phillips reset the timer for the bomb.

Turning to Michael, he said "Did you really think it would be that easy to take me down, you and your prissy girlfriend, just walking in here and winning? No Michael, it doesn't work that way."

"What do you really want?" Michael asked.

"Nothing but the pleasure of seeing you beg for mercy before I kill you. It's payback for abandoning me back on the mission back in Spain, so fuck you!" said Phillips.

"You fucking spineless coward," roared Michael.

"Let me tell you why I took the pleasure of killing your sister before you die. I did it because I was always jealous of you. Your charisma, your kindness, your love for life. All your sister saw me for were dollar signs; she never really loved me. But she cared for and loved you as her brother," said Phillips.

"Regrets?" asked Michael, looking Phillips in the eyes dead center.

"None," replied Phillips calmly.

"Bastard!" raged Michael, infuriated. "Are you man enough to face me, or are you a pussy who can't fight for shit!" he challenged.

"Come on then; if you can get out of this," challenged back Phillips.

In a superhuman rage Michael picked the lock off his chains; a surprised Phillips began to back off. Serena watched the standoff. "We'll do this the old fashion way with guns," snickered Phillips.

Phillips whipped out his pistol as he tossed Michael his M9 pistol that he earlier confiscated from his enemy and the duel began.

The two squared off, shooting and dodging between corners of metal pillars. Michael hid behind a batch of steel barrels to reload; Phillips was hot on his trail, firing back.

Running head to head with Phillips, Michael dodged his enemy's shots with vampiric leaps through the air, frightening Phillips as he turned behind him, and knocked him out with a head butt and upper cut to the jaw.

Serena freed herself from the chains and scrambled to get to the computer. She ripped open the system with her vampiric strength and she managed to cut the red wire linked to the atomic bomb, deactivating it.

"Pleasant dreams big boy, your ass is headed to jail," said Michael, dragging the unconscious Phillips to a large pipe, tying his body up with the chains and sealing the lock with his telekinetic powers to prevent escape.

Michael called Commissioner Hamilton. "Hey Commissioner, It's Damascus. Come pick up your terrorist, the one who blew up the Terrace Tower. He's tied up at the old hydro electrical plant. His name is ex-Special Forces CIA agent Rodney Clarence Phillips," said Michael.

"What the hell," said the Commissioner as she hung up her phone and ordered police and SWAT teams to the scene. Busting in the door of the plant, they handcuffed Phillips and dragged him off in a police car to be taken to the state mental hospital.

After it was over, the Commissioner met with Michael and Serena who had been spying from the shadows. "Listen, I owe you two a big debt for what you have done."

"Consider us even now, Commissioner, a life for a life and an eye for an eye," said Michael. His debt for Watson's murder had been paid.

"Where are you two heading?" asked Commissioner Hamilton.

"Wherever life leads us, that's where," said Serena. Michael smiled, his arms around her waist.

"Will I see you two and your friends again?" asked Commissioner Hamilton.

"Yes, but keep that a secret. See you around," said Michael as the two vampires sped off on their bike deep into the dark shadows of the night.

EPILOGUE: "A NEW REASON TO LIVE"

Months had passed and a time for living had come again, with the chill of autumn in the air. The holidays were about to begin. Las Vegas had begun rebuilding and things had gotten back to normal. The Santerinis and Scarfos had made an alliance to help each other rebuild the communities that were destroyed. Undead and the living had begun to migrate back into the city. Las Vegas opened new casinos and clubs and people went on with their business as usual.

On one very special night Michael sent out invitations for his wedding with Serena. A party was being held at the Black Spider, with the Scarfos, Santerinis, and his Coven present. The place was jumping; Isabelle sang on stage with little Sally joining in. Old Mickey Blue blew his saxophone loud and clear. Drinks were poured and nothing but good times hung in the air. No one had a worry in the world; it was pretty as a picture.

"Honey, I never thought this day would come," said Serena affectionately, straightening at her black bridal gown.

"Neither did I. Can you believe all that has happened since we have known each other?" Michael smiled.

"Pretty wild isn't it," replied Serena, kissing him on the lips.

"Have you chosen a best man?" asked Serena.

"Jackie, of course. I love that kid," said Michael.

"Suki is going to be my bridesmaid," said Serena.

"Happy Halloween baby," said Michael.

He held Serena tenderly in his arms as she looked at him sweetly in his eyes, then glancing at the silver engagement ring on her finger. They walked out on to the balcony and looked at the rising moon from their new penthouse above the Black Spider Club, courtesy of Don Felice.

"You ready for Paris, love?" asked Michael.

"Sure," said Serena.

"Tomorrow night is our wedding night. I'll love you for eternity," said Serena.

"Now and for all time," answered Michael kissing Serena deeply.

Suddenly a little burst of laughter came from behind their door as Sally popped her head in giggling. "Hey come on downstairs you two, the party is about to get started," she said, feeling happy for her uncle and soon to be aunt.

"We'll be down in a minute, sweetie," said Serena kissing Sally on the cheek. Sally left the room happy. All Michael and Serena could do was gaze into each other's eyes and smile. After all, it was just another night at the Black Spider.

To Be Continued

ABOUT THE AUTHOR

Born Dominic Rocky Daniels, in the city of Anaheim, California in 1984, he was raised in San Gabriel, CA. At a young age his passion has always been in films, animation, and storytelling. Trained in fine art at the age of 10, he decided to go into the entertainment business and become a writer. He is a self-taught author and electronic dance music arranger under his Nega Blast X production brand. He has a Bachelor Degree of Science in Media Arts and Animation from The Art Institute of California-Los Angeles. He has lived in Burbank, for six years and often visits his grandparents, in his spare time he reads graphic novels; his favorite music is heavy metal.

www.ingramcontent.com/pod-product-compliance
Lightning Source LLC
Chambersburg PA
CBHW062006170626
46813CB00001B/54